QUANTUM SEED

BOOK ONE

L. THORSRUD

For information about permission to reproduce selections from this book, write to author@lthorsrud.com

Names: L. Thorsrud, author. Title: QUANTUM SEED / L. Thorsrud.
Published by Gatekeeper Press
7853 Gunn Hwy., Suite 209
Tampa, FL 33626
www.GatekeeperPress.com

Summary: Victoria Ottery's journey unfolds as her unique talents awaken, thrusting her into a world-altering mission.

Identifiers: ISBN 979-8-9884640-5-1 (print)
ISBN 979-8-9884640-0-6 (ebook)
Library of Congress Control Number: 2023917371

Subjects: | CYAC : Survival—Fiction. | Artificial intelligence—Fiction. | Life on other planets—Fiction. | Science fiction. | Human-Alien encounters | BISAC : SCIENCE FICTION

Cover design by FORT.
Thorsrud, L. QUANTUM SEED, Book 1.

Visit the author's website at **www.lthorsrud.com**.

GLOSSARY & NOTES

Adjunct – Headgear worn by the Earth team whilst on Ambar that creates an enhanced experience through further layers of information and optical enrichment.

Ambar – A planet in an exoplanetary system in another universe.

Amygdala and limbic system – These areas play a crucial role in regulating our emotions and response to stress. However, if they become overactive, it can lead to negative mental and physical conditions.

Autistic savants – Individuals on the autism spectrum with exceptional skills or abilities in specific areas, such as music, art, math, or memory. While not all individuals with autism are savants, research suggests that savant abilities are more common among people with autism than in the general population.

Bacteriophages – Also known as phages, these are viruses that infect and replicate within bacteria. One of their unique characteristics is their ability to target and infect only a specific bacterial species or strain, while leaving other bacteria unharmed. This specificity makes them a promising tool for targeted bacterial infection treatments, including antibiotic- resistant infections.

Blindsight – A phenomenon where individuals with damage to their visual cortex can demonstrate some visual processing abilities. They respond to visual stimuli without conscious awareness or perception.

Brainwave levels

1. *Gamma Waves:* associated with higher states of consciousness. Present during deep meditation and activities requiring focus, such as studying or practicing a skill.

2. *Beta Waves:* reflect a state of active wakefulness and alertness.

3. *Alpha Waves:* associated with a state of relaxed wakefulness, such as when one is sitting quietly or with closed eyes.

4. *Theta Waves:* notable during relaxation, daydreaming, and creativity, as well as light sleep.

5. *Delta Waves:* The slowest brainwaves. Associated with deep sleep, unconsciousness, and the release of growth hormones.

CBT - Cognitive Behavioral Therapy – A modality that helps people recognize and change negative thoughts and behaviors.

CDi - Communications and Diagnostics interface – A device worn on the lower arm for calls and health data on Earth.

CRC - Cellular Renewal Center – A treatment on Ambar.

Dollsteinen - Sandsya Island, Norway – With its interesting rock formations and stunning views of the coastal landscape, the mountain draws worldwide visitors. Its cave also has an intriguing history.

Electrotaxis – A phenomenon in which cells move directionally in response to an applied electric field. This has been observed in a variety of cell types, including immune cells, cancer cells, and stem cells, and has potential applications in tissue engineering, regenerative medicine, and drug delivery.

Epigenetics – The study of how environmental factors and other influences can modify gene expression without altering the genetic code itself.

Father's stress imprinted on genes of unborn baby – Research has shown that a father's stress levels, specifically the release of cortisol, during his partner's pregnancy can affect the genetic expression of their unborn child. This can lead to epigenetic changes in the fetus, and impact the child's development.

FOXP2 protein – A gene, located on chromosome 7, linked to the neural circuity required for speech and language development in humans. This protein may have played a role in the evolution of the human language faculty. Mutations in the FOXP2 gene can lead to speech and language disorders.

Gamma-aminobutyric acid (GABA) – A neurotransmitter that plays a crucial role in regulating the brain's neural activity and promoting relaxation.

Heart-brain coherence – The synchronized and balanced state between the heart and the brain, where their electrical and biochemical signals align harmoniously. It promotes improved cognitive function, emotional regulation, and overall well-being, while reducing stress levels and enhancing resilience. Mindfulness and meditation are used to foster this state of coherence.

High-gravity tunnels – A place to unwind, chat, and get some movement.

IO Re-Hub - Inner One Rejuvenation Hub – A gathering spot for SEED members.

LiDAR (Light Detection and Ranging) – NASA uses LiDAR to study everything from Earth's topography and climate to mapping our moon, asteroids, and Mars. It uses laser pulses to measure distances and create detailed 3D maps or models.

Low-gravity courts – A recreational area.

Magnetic tuning – The ability to sense and gain information from magnetic field changes, which can cross over temporal lines, thereby allowing one to see the future.

Metacognition – The ability to think about one's own thinking, including awareness of one's own cognitive processes, strategies, and learning preferences.

Na wa – An Yoruban saying to express surprise.

Neurodevices – Electronic devices, such as deep brain stimulators or brain-computer interfaces, that interact with the nervous system to treat various neurological conditions, including Parkinson's disease, epilepsy, and chronic pain.

Neurofeedback – Real-time monitoring of brain activity to help individuals learn to self-regulate their brain function In the novel, this is achieved using a Quantitative Electroencephalogram (qEEG) to help individuals learn to regulate their brainwaves and improve their mental and physical health.

I have used neurofeedback for research purposes in five countries over twenty-four years. Victoria's experience with burning electrodes was inspired by one session I had in the Netherlands. The neuroscientist told me to persevere in the name of science. I was able to overcome the pain to produce a twenty-minute session, long enough to yield some interesting data.

Nootropics – Drugs or supplements designed to enhance cognitive function, memory, and focus. While neurodevices and nootropics have different applications, both are examples of interventions designed to improve brain function and health.

Nutrigenomics – The scientific study of how nutrients and genes interact, examining how diet and nutritional factors can impact gene expression and individual responses to food.

Quantitative Electroencephalogram (qEEG) – Records brainwave activity using electrodes.

qEEG artifacts – Any non-brain activity, such as muscle tension from a clenched jaw, that interferes with recording electrical brain activity.

SEED – Society for Earth's Evolutionary Development.

Shewanella oneidensis MR-1 – A species of bacteria that respires using metals as an electron acceptor, a process known as extracellular electron transfer (EET). This feature has led to research interest in MR-1 as a potential tool for bioremediation of contaminated environments, as well as for use in microbial fuel cells and other bioelectrochemical systems.

Synodic period – The time it takes for all three moons to return to the same relative position with respect to both suns as observed from Ambar.

Timeline viewing – the ability to obtain knowledge of a future event, which can include a person, object, or planet.

Ubuntu – from the Nguni Bantu people of Southern Africa, particularly Zulu and Xhosa. It is an ancient word that expresses the idea of interconnectedness and the belief in a universal bond of humanity.

Unique energy profiling (UEP) – A technique to tune into a person remotely.

2004 tsunami – A devastating tsunami, triggered by a massive earthquake, occurred on December 26, 2004 in the Indian Ocean and claimed the lives of over 230,000 people. The disaster was one of the deadliest in history and highlighted the importance of disaster preparedness and early warning systems in vulnerable areas.

The year has been changed for the novel.

MAIN SEED CHARACTERS

Victoria Ottery – British neuroscientist with unusual abilities; leads team

Zoputa "Zoa" Oredola – Nigerian nurse with ability to remotely sense family members health

Allan Feynman – American AI entrepreneur

Constance Smith – British actuary with high-functioning autism - math savant

Peter Hrabe – 19-year-old mechanic from Czech Republic with aptitude for building and making tools for team

Ana Luiza Medina – Brazilian astronomer working in Chile

Pino d'Orsini – Italian designer, strong ability to remotely sense people's state of mind and health

OTHER CHARACTERS

Ambarans – indigenous people of Ambar

Augmented Earth Humans (AEH) – Auro, Baka, Barton, Bradley, Dvita, Jorge, K^Lys, Kasif-EC9, Khepera, Noha, Rein'li, Sinethemba, Sone, Tau, Vintar, and Wyrobe.

Conduits aka Opalescents – represent Ambaran hosts

François – cave guide and SEED member

II-AEH – Identity Imprinted Augmented Earth Humans. First seen when a SEED member is replaced

Ragini – SEED member

Reo – SEED member

Reviewers – beings of light who tell of impending destruction

Sabine – Marcus's climbing acquaintance; Constance's best friend

Sylvia – horticulturist, SEED team member

Tomas – SEED member

Wu Li – SEED member

CHAPTER 1

THE GLIMMER

London

Spending a few hours with caustic gel-soaked electrodes searing into my scalp wasn't the worst way to celebrate my birthday. I could have been home with Albert contemplating the meaning of life. He wouldn't remember the date, and I didn't expect him to; after all, Albert was a cat.

"The electrodes are burning into my skull. What adhesive are you using?" I winced. "Something you concocted yourself?"

The eminent Scottish neuroscientist paused his preparations and squinted at me as if gauging how bad the pain was. Reaching into his green tweed jacket pocket, he pulled out what looked like a tube of toothpaste. "Now, now, no need to be offensive. It's a new one, but not of my making."

A wave of stings rushed over my scalp, causing my forehead to crinkle involuntarily.

"We'll go back to one o' the usual glues next time. For now, block oot the pain well enough to give us a productive session. It's aw in the name of science." His accent always got thicker when I riled him up.

We were in the twenty-first century, and I had to endure pain from glue. I searched his unshaven face for softness but found a singular focus, not on me but on the multicolored wavy lines produced by the Quantitative Electroencephalograph. The qEEG was old school, but his method of choice because he could fine-tune it to get a detailed visual map of my brain. There was also the important fact that it didn't need to be hooked up to a network. Privacy was ensured.

"Uuhhh . . . I'll try." The words escaped me like I was a trained ventriloquist as I dared not move a muscle. During the preparation phase, I had to stay still until he confirmed that the electrodes were attached and functioning properly.

Perhaps his lack of empathy was payback. I had canceled our last two sessions. As a cognitive neuroscientist pursuing a doctorate, I worked long hours. The past two months had seen an influx of new studies, which meant sixty-hour work weeks for me and no time for the monthly session with my experiments partner and friend, Dr. Malcolm George. We were opposite sides of the same coin. I chose to spend most of my professional life shuttered up in a lab, analyzing data and interacting with a select few. Whereas Malcolm was one of the world's most reputable neuroscientists, sought after by universities, health institutions, the media, and professional organizations for appearances and advice. Surprisingly, he had never canceled any of our sessions. A sense of inferiority struck me. But he was proud of my work, having acted as a close mentor to me over the years.

Satisfied with each connection, he shifted his eyes away from the displays and over to me. "March 7. Don't think I've forgotten.

Happy birthday, Victoria." His eyes twinkled as he smiled warmly. "I have a joke for you."

"You know I don't like jokes; most simply aren't funny." Dilemma . . . should I have pretended to like his joke, considering my vulnerability?

"Right. A man"—he squinted at me—"about your age receives a Lego set for a birthday gift. After many months of work on it, he proudly proclaims to his friends that he's completed the set in record time. His friends look at him, puzzled. To prove his point, he shows them the box. 'See, it says here 10-14 years.'"

"That's a good one." I genuinely laughed. "It's nice to be here with you." The seventh of March was not my actual birth date— it was the day Aunt Judy found me, an abandoned baby, in her hospital.

Squinting at me, he said, "I can't tell if ye're bein' facetious. Jist be happy we're not bloody celebratin' with experimental electrical currents to yer brain coupled wi' targeted nootropics." A spray of saliva accompanied his words.

I grinned at his passionate retort.

People worldwide were stimulating or suppressing brain- waves with electrical currents or powerful magnets thanks to a competition to reach an elusive brainwave pattern considered to be optimization. Uncertified neurodevices and thousands of nootropics had flooded the market and were available for anyone to purchase. All promised incredible results but had yet to deliver anything extraordinary.

Whereas my experiments were limited to reading brainwav- es using a standard qEEG. Our hour-long sessions contained two experiments of Malcolm's choosing and two of mine—all scien- tifically designed to test brain phenomena and abilities. Contrary to popular interpretations, there was nothing mystical or magical about it. After hooking me up, he'd leave the room and return minutes before the end of my odyssey. With the session fresh in my mind, we would compare the hard data to my subjective experience.

By slowing down my brainwaves, I could access a more fluid and dynamic dimension, one normally inaccessible, even with the most potent nootropic drug. More importantly, I was in control, unlike those using external stimuli. From that brainwave state, so much more was possible, yet not always accepted by others. And I had limitations. I could only *see* the future up to twenty-one days ahead. As the event approached, my sight or sense would become stronger and clearer.

Three years ago, I had advised a colleague to see a doctor about a malignant tumor. She grimaced, recoiled from me, and accused me of witchcraft. The imagery of a witch standing over a blackened cauldron tending to her brew ran through my mind. Despite her reaction, she went to her doctor nineteen days later and into the operating theater the next day for a lifesaving procedure.

In the first year of our experiments, I repeatedly read Malcolm's mind, glimpsed future events, disrupted technology in the room, and remotely checked on Aunt Judy. With each exhibition of my abilities, I waited—waited to see if he would retreat, engulfed in fear, like all others had done before. Thankfully, that day had never come. Malcolm was one of the most grounded, unshakable people I'd ever met.

Malcolm dimmed the lights and placed a glass of water and a call button within my reach on an antique wood side table. I alternated between watching him and noting my surroundings to distract myself from the pain. Nothing had changed since we had started working together twelve years ago, from the damaged floor planks covered in frayed and faded area rugs to the cracked brown leather recliners. The mahogany bookcases held hundreds of worn books and journals that looked like they were as overworked as their owner. The lower shelves were different—they were reserved for double-stacked boxes of electrode glue formulations. Juxtaposed against the antiquated furniture was ultra-modern equipment—lots of it. Some of his latest collectibles were neurodevices, still in their boxes, requiring beta testing. This was what dedication looked like.

"You don't have to do all this." I broke into his obsessive-compulsive preparations. "If I need you, I will call you directly from my CDi." The Communications and Diagnostics interface on my arm was like a second skin and could be activated by touch or voice command. It replaced the phones of a decade ago and provided data on everything from metabolic rate to blood pressure.

He checked the call button twice and placed the pulse oximeter on my left middle finger. "I'm doing my part to ensure you have a good session. You know what they say . . ."

I recited his favorite saying on cue. "Fail to prepare, prepare to fail."

He smiled with the left side of his face. "Indeed."

"In all these years, I've never taken a sip of water during my experiments or used the panic . . . I mean *call* button to wake you from your slumber in the other room."

"I'll give ye slumber." He took the bait and shook his fist in my direction. "Ye'd do well to remember who connects ye. It could slip my mind to change the bloomin' glue next time. Oh . . . and fer safety, I like yer to have the button as a backup."

Having successfully irked him again, I smiled so big it felt like some of the electrodes would pop off.

"Which reminds me, I'll be upstairs in the recording room doing some clips for the BBC."

"Of course you will." I held my lips together to avoid another full-on smirk.

"Right. Ready, Victoria?" He raised his right index finger but kept his eyes on the three displays arranged like a mission control center.

"Yes," I said, desperate to numb the scores of pain receptors.

"Right, close your eyes and begin."

His finger went down—the signal I'd been waiting for. I was free to plunge into the depths of consciousness, returning to the safety of home.

Within twenty-five seconds, I reached a monk-level meditative state. Such a quick descent was not typical, according to Malcolm, who believed my keen ability to control brainwaves was innate. Personally, I thought it was nurture. If one must log ten thousand hours to become an expert at something, then I was a master meditator by age twelve. My preference to experience the world from the inside out had probably shaped my brain and mind.

Deeper and deeper I went with every second. I began with my favorite visualization—an island beach.

Waves ripple over my feet and hug my ankles, while the sun's warmth helps relax me to a point just above sleeping. I walk along the serene shoreline, noticing the individuality yet connectedness of the sand grains as they support each step. Salty ocean gusts permeate my body, removing all stress. The scene is effortless. Stillness and vitality exist together with solitude and connection. I call for my guide. Not with a name—he doesn't have one—but with my mind and heart.

Every cell in my body responds with heightened expectation of him. Sometimes he is there waiting, but most times he arrives when I am well into my explorations. I can't remember when I met him. It is as if he has always been there, waiting, guiding—a constant presence in my meditations. Today, it seems he will come later. I continue my walk alone.

All is as it should be . . . until my island vanishes.

What the—I'm being pulled away. I can't control . . .

Out in the world of matter, my brain tried to break free from its skull. Ten short seizure-like twitches were followed by a reprieve of two calm seconds before the violent tremors repeated. An electrical short? No, Malcolm would have seen a malfunction in the initial readings. The jolts twisted time and my ability to figure out the next step. Years of smooth and carefully orchestrated sessions had left me unprepared for such a drastic deviation. After round three, I tried to give a verbal command to my CDi. No sounds came out. Unable to speak, I lifted my arm to reach for the call button. Before I could press it, a frightening cracking sound emanated from my head. I drew my hands to either side of my skull and pressed to prevent it from splitting open. At the pinnacle of the emergency, my brain settled, but there was a price to pay for tranquility.

My beach scene is replaced by darkness. Someone or something has taken over. Don't panic. He will be there. Suddenly, a brilliant bright light appears. I go towards it and stop ten feet away. Three entities, each about twelve feet high and six feet wide, hover in midair. The one on my left is glowing blue. The green one in the center is the biggest and brightest, almost dwarfing the yellow one on the right. They are made of light, and although they are spaced out, collages of prisms form where their energies overlap. At this distance, I am warmed by the heat they radiate and smell a distinct odor, like after a thunderstorm.

The scene has an eerie feeling of destiny. Where is my guide?

The green energy dims and speaks. "As the lead in this review, I will present the findings from our assessment of Earth's civilization."

I hear the words not with my ears, but with my mind. The voice, neither male nor female, is not speaking to me but to an audience listening in. I have so many questions, but I hope they can't hear my thoughts. Where are they from? Why are they reviewing us? Are they hiding somewhere within the bright light, or are they the light?

"You are the sole Earth representative in these proceedings." It's a direct communication from the lead to me.

These beings, or Reviewers, have clearly made a mistake. I can't be the defender of Earth's humanity. I spend most days working on my own, trawling through data, designing future studies, and assessing brain images. I avoid most individuals whenever possible, except in a clinical setting. In my opinion, many people are overly emotional and illogical, and they tend to overcomplicate things. I rub my abdomen to calm a lurching stomach. What are they expecting from me? My heart races like I'm about to take a final examination I haven't studied for.

The green light says, "We are in agreement. There is irrefutable evidence of a grave development on Earth."

Before I can respond, a superfast display of life on Earth swirls around us, from jungles filled with primates, beetles, and frogs, to savannahs bursting with gazelle, elephants, rhinos, and tigers, to oceans inhabited by millions of fish, majestic whales, and dolphins. Ten types of early humans whirl by like horses on a carousel. One by one they vanish, leaving the last surviving branch—homo sapiens.

The lead Reviewer continues, "Every time a female gives birth on Earth, we glimpse human potential." A picture of a mother with her newborn baby boy zooms forwards from the montage. "For a while, the glimmer fights to stay alive." The new toddler hands another child a flower. "As the days wear on, it weakens against the bombarding norms, values, and behaviors of a malformed civilization." The teenager at school walks with his head hung low as fellow students bully him. "The glimmer is stamped out in the deep darkness of a broken civilization. This cycle repeats across your planet and leads to devastating consequences for its people."

My perspective drifts up to a point where I am looking down at myself. The tale of doom freezes me in shock. Even in an altered state of consciousness, I expect a stronger reaction, unless the reviewers of our planet are controlling my brain's responses.

"You create false narratives in a quest to belong and to assign meaning where none exists. Walls are built, lines drawn, and minds narrowed as you cling hard to your arbitrary groups and ideas."

A procession of Persian, Greek, Roman, and Chinese warriors appears for a moment before it is replaced by warring modern soldiers from around the globe. "Humans with over-dominant primal brains built your society's foundation. When uncontrolled or stressed, you are closer to savage animals than sophisticated beings. Craving attention, those with an unquenchable thirst for power rise using aggression, paranoia, and fear. Their numbers grow at a rate not dissimilar to a rampaging plague, asserting itself over others and showing no mercy. Unrestrained, a ravaged humanity consumes Earth."

My blood runs cold as past horrors are reviewed by the advanced beings. It's true; dysfunctional or overstressed parts of the limbic and endocrine systems can evoke primitive behaviors. If we developed from that, then we are not in good shape. But is it fatal? I need to know where this is headed.

Their portrayal of us sucks the air out of my lungs. I hold my breath to prevent the last traces from escaping. Silence follows. The verdict is coming . . . I feel it. Why has my guide left me stranded in a desert of despair?

After a long, dark pause, the lead says, "Humankind on Earth has developed well in some areas; unfortunately, it will not be enough." An expanded image of a ravaged world gives way to scenes of melting glaciers and disappearing ozone. "You have steered your world off-course over many millennia and do not have the means to correct it. We accept the imbalanced state of the planet as it is. In 314 days, Earth will be uninhabitable."

"What? 314 days?" With my role still unclear, I push the boundary of a passive witness. My voice trembles as I, the token Earthling, dare to speak audibly for the first time. "Surely we won't let it go so far. How can you deliver that verdict with such certainty and detachment?"

"Victoria, like you, we can see into others' timelines." The Reviewer communicates directly to my mind. Perhaps they can't speak as we can. My eyes dart from one individual to the next as I try to figure out who they are and how they know about me.

"We can see Earth's future from our vantage point in the multiverse. There are gaps, but catastrophic events are approaching."

"What happens to us?" I ask, knowing that having the answer doesn't mean we can change it.

"As you know from living with your abilities, we cannot reveal detailed timeline information, merely the date of the event."

The lead is referring to creating a self-fulfilling prophecy. I learned about it in my twenties when I told a friend he would be in an accident. Six days later, he got in a crash. Although he was fine, he blamed me for planting the seed in his head. It's tricky business, seeing the future, whether destiny or possibility.

Desperate to put two and two together, I say, "But if Earth has veered off course because of our primitive foundation, how does this one disaster fit in?"

"Even if you could prevent the coming disaster, you will create others because of how your civilization and brains have evolved. It is who you are."

The Reviewer's last statement leaves no room for growth or learning. And there's no suggestion of intervention or correction from them.

I can't let this be the end. "We may be guilty of all the things you've said, but we're also known for our resilience. Can you help us correct our direction?" I pause to consider my tactics. "We've never seen a healthy civilization that could have acted as a guide or blueprint. Isn't there a way for us to learn from a more balanced society?" In a Hail Mary move, I say, "Show us how we were intended to evolve." My voice cracks as I suggest what is probably a wildly impossible option. "Help us this once."

I dangle in the abyss, awaiting an answer. Without faces or body language to read, I can't use my honed observation skills. My heart skips out of sync as Earth heads for its end. *What if . . . How can we . . . Isn't there . . .*

Quiet. Emptiness. My avalanche of questions and emotions vanishes.

The lead says, "We are here to help Earth's people avert the coming disaster. We cannot do it for you, but we can assist your people in gaining critical skills and knowledge."

The relief is so powerful that my body shakes like I'm standing naked in below-freezing temperatures. I wish they had started with that. "You will? How?"

"You and others will have six planetary rotations to get to the chosen location."

"Others . . . how many? I don't work well with others." There would need to be thousands helping to save Earth. "In six days?" The news stuns me like I've been dropped into an ice bath. "Where's this location of yours?" It must be on Earth, which will trigger ufologists and alien-takeover theorists.

"You are the only one we can communicate with in this way. Others will have a recurring dream, which they will feel compelled to follow. You will be away for 121 days."

A sudden flash of information appears so vividly in my mind that I reach out to touch it.

Dollsteinen – Sandsøya Island, Norway
Coordinates: 62.2577, 5.3984
Arrive by 11:00 local time (24-hour clock)

"How will you select people?" Did I dare ask how many again? They didn't answer me the first time.

Before they answer my questions, I am catapulted back to the beach scene.

○   ○   ○

I n unbearable pain from the electrodes, I repeatedly struck the panic button.

"Victoria!" Malcolm rushed downstairs like a fireman into a burning house. "What's wrong?"

"The electrodes—get them off me." My eyes popped open like popcorn kernels. In desperation, I tore off two electrodes and many strands of hair.

"I need a bag . . . I'm going to be sick."

"Oh, bloody hell. Hang on, hang on." He flung open his desk drawer, emptied the contents of a plastic shopping bag, and threw it over to me. "There ye go."

As I vomited, Malcolm plucked the fiery circles off my scalp. Between rounds of spewing, I stared down at the worn wooden floor and dull, tattered rugs. The familiar surroundings comforted me.

"Was *he* there?" Malcolm said as he tried to remove every trace of the nefarious glue. We both had expected my guide to be present, if for no other reason than to help me control the pain from the electrodes.

I didn't answer. Why wouldn't he have shown up? He was a key element in verifying the contents of a session. Did his absence mean today's experience wasn't credible? It was more than just whether he showed up to help me with the Reviewers. *He* was more, in ways I couldn't fully understand. So, why had he abandoned me?

Malcolm removed the last electrode. "Are ye okay?"

My nod felt more like a tremble.

He pulled his chair in front of me, and our eyes locked. "Was your guide there?" Malcolm would see the answer for himself.

There was always a specific pattern in the qEEG when my guide was present, a signature of sorts. This time it would be absent.

"No," I whispered, toggling between panic and abandonment. Overwhelmed for the first time in twelve years, I cracked. I clenched my jaw to maintain some semblance of stoicism, but the tears flowed down my cheeks like an avalanche that gave no warning.

Malcolm handed me his hankie from his trouser pocket. "I haven't used it," he said.

I covered my face with it and patted away the tears. When I lowered the handkerchief, he was still fixed on me, still waiting for answers.

"I'll review the readouts, but I need to know what the blazes happened."

When I didn't answer his plea, he took the glue tube out of his pocket again, mumbled something indistinct, and turned to the bank of displays.

I was relieved to have a bit more time to process things. How could I explain that all humankind on Earth might cease to exist in 314 days? Was it true? I felt fragile. I dreaded having to talk about it. It wouldn't take much for Malcolm to peel away the thin layer disguising my terror and despair, though.

"You were only under for twenty-eight minutes," he said as his head snapped my way and back so quickly he risked whiplash.

"Only twenty-eight min—" I'd never had a session under an hour. "It felt like hours. They were the worst minutes of ..."

With a perplexed expression, he continued to scroll through the session's log. "How do you feel?" He turned to another device that had compiled the data differently.

"Heavy. I resurfaced too quickly because of the pain. It would help me to go back ... back under," I said in a quivering, fading voice. I was out of sync. Part of me wanted to stay with Malcolm and figure things out, but a bigger part needed to go back.

As with divers, one needed to slowly work their way back to a more alert state when surveying the depths of consciousness. Ignoring the slow-ascent protocol meant risking being out of step with reality for hours or, in some cases, days.

"Hmm, I see," he said not taking his attention away from the data. "Your readings are remarkable and . . . no sign of him."

The strong pull to go under became irresistible. My open eyes hid my dropping consciousness as I plunged back into a lower brainwave pattern.

"Right. Hmm . . . back in? No, wait, Victoria." Malcolm had registered my words too late. He rushed over to me, tilted back my head, and inspected my eyes. "No . . . no, no. Where are yer goin'?"

In defiance, my eyes drew shut.

"Ye have to stay with me. Without electrodes, I'll be blind if ye go under again."

I didn't need to be hooked up to go where I wanted—that was only for observational and documentation purposes. Having detached from Malcolm's reality, I couldn't reassure him. I dove deep enough to search for my guide.

I asked for him. Then I pleaded. Please don't abandon me now.

After mere moments, a gentle slapping on my face pulled me back up.

"Come on, I've given you twelve long minutes. Show me you're in there. Otherwise, I'm going to reconnect those bloody electrodes or call emergency services." Hearing Malcolm's baritone voice was like seeing a lighthouse on a dark night. I followed him back to the outside world and lifted my left hand.

His reaction would have seemed over the top, but with all the experimenting going on, the governing neuroscience associations had tightened protocols for helping subjects come out of deep states. A doctor could lose their license if found negligent. There was also the fact that he knew I could put myself in a self-induced, coma-like state. It had been a helpful ability when I was stricken with kidney stones a few years ago. No painkillers required, but I was unresponsive to paramedics, who assumed I had overdosed on drugs. Although disconnected from my body and unable to respond to anyone, I was fully conscious.

"Okay, good. Now, follow my instructions." I heard him pull his chair closer to mine. "Focus on my voice and raise your level of awareness," Malcolm said softly as he held my right hand. "I am going to count down from ten. When I reach one, you open your eyes."

He counted, intermittently reminding me to focus.

Finishing, he said, "Victoria, open your eyes."

I followed his instructions and found Malcolm's face two inches from mine.

He looked at me like a scolding teacher. "Now, bloody keep them open. Ye shouldn't do that. I thought—I know how ye can . . ." He took a deep breath. "Yer okay, aren't you?"

"I think so." Of course, I was referring to the state of my brain, not my psychological or emotional state.

He sighed and fell back into his chair. "Shite. You're going to give me a heart attack." He sat, arms dangling, legs stretched out like he had just run the London Marathon. "We'll quickly go through some recall exercises, then I'll drive you home."

I rolled my eyes. "The sanity checklist."

He pulled out a list of questions used to confirm long- and short-term memories in those who had undergone unusual brainwave activity.

"Name and birthplace?"

"Victoria Ottery. England, most likely."

"Occupation?"

"Neuroscientist."

"First memory?"

"Touching Aunt Judy's face."

"Closest friend?"

"Anne."

He nodded with each correct answer. "What day is it, and why are you here?"

"Friday. Here to understand my abilities and do an occasional team session in an attempt to record optimal brain performance."

"Good . . . good." He squinted and pursed his lips. "Still, I'll assess the data later. You don't look so well." He reached out for my arm to read through the data on my CDi. "Your heartbeat is faint. Maybe you should lie down in the other room for a while."

"I'm okay, but I can't talk about the session right now."

"No worries. We have time," he said, and rolled his chair back to his desk to skim the scores of brainwaves. For nearly ten minutes, every time I looked over at him, he was shaking his head and rubbing his eyes.

My strategy to say little in order to keep a lid on the pressure-cooker of desolation softened as he piqued my curiosity. "What is it? I had spasms at the beginning; did they ruin a clean recording?"

He gave me a curious smile. "There are a few artifacts from muscle reactions, but your readings are . . . unusual, even for you." He grabbed his briefcase. "Come, I'll take you home."

On the drive home, I said, "Thank you," like a humble student in appreciation of her teacher.

"For what?"

"The call button and water."

He glanced over to me with a reserved smile and nod. There was no "I told you so."

"Thank you for being here for me. . . through everything."

"Now I know you're out of sorts. You've gone all soft on me." He winked.

I entered my house a different person—devastated by where we were as a civilization, uncertain if the contents of the session were real, and more alone than ever.

My rational mind wrestled with the emotional, fearful side. *He* wasn't there. It could have been a wildly bad session and nothing more. From a subjective and objective perspective, it was an outlier that didn't fit with any previous experience. Would he know about the impending doomsday? When would I see him again?

CHAPTER 2

EDGE OF TRUTH

The next morning, the sun's rays peeked from behind the bedroom curtains, yet the promise of a new day didn't soften the previous evening's trauma.

Detached from my body, I watched from above as I lay there, wondering if I should bother getting up. With the security of my sessions shattered, life had become complicated. Doubts replaced clarity as whirlwinds of uncertainty engulfed me. What should I do next? Was life on Earth ending in 313 days? No advanced species would think I'd work well with what I assumed would be thousands of others. It wasn't in my DNA. The mere thought of it elicited a cascade of involuntary responses—elevated heart rate, dewy skin, and shallow breathing. Increased cortisol pumped into my bloodstream and propelled me out of bed.

I opened the drapes as two birds swooped by in a chase; round and round they went before fluttering off. Such levity in ignorance—or maybe they would survive.

A sudden flash of reality hit. 314 days minus the 121 days I would be away. That left 193 days. Less six days before meeting in Norway . . . 187 days to save Earth.

The Reviewers had outrageous expectations of us. It must be proof. Proof that it was a bad dream and nothing more.

Lacking the will to change out of my pyjamas, I threw on my oversized cardigan and headed for the kitchen. There was little room in my mind for thoughts not related to the end of the world. Albert the cat . . . feed. Breakfast—skipped dinner, should eat something.

My hands trembled as they overfilled my bowl of muesli with milk. I passively watched the overflow drip down the table and onto the oak floor. *We could be headed for oblivion . . . what's a little spill?* As much as I wanted to ignore the Reviewers' message, I was drowning in questions. Could I trust their information? Should I go to Norway in five days based on the worst session of my life? Would others really show up, or would I be the lone fool?

An hour later, I sat hunched over the barely touched, soggy muesli without a single answer. Albert took care of the spill. *Do I have time to sit and ponder? The clock is ticking. Need help . . . Aunt Judy.*

As a nurse, then a doctor, Aunt Judy understood neurofeedback and was the only person Malcolm and I ever allowed into a session. Of course, she hadn't always been Aunt Judy. She was "Mummy" to me until a teacher "educated" me otherwise.

At seven years old, her true identity was revealed on what would become one of the most memorable days in my life. She, Aunt Mummy, had picked me from school, as usual.

On our way home, she asked the same question she had for many years.

"How was your day, my dear?"

I erupted like a volcano. "Am I your dear? Who are you?" My arms flailed. "You say we should always tell each other the truth even when it isn't good, but . . ." I stopped to take a breath and calm down. I knew she wouldn't appreciate my passionate gesticulations.

She risked a couple glances at me as she negotiated the winding roads of the English countryside. "What are you talking about?" Her voice had softened to a whisper by the time she reached the end of her question.

"I know who you are." I turned away from the mysterious woman.

After a few silent seconds, she answered in a monotone voice. "We will discuss this when we get home."

As we sat down at the beechwood kitchen table, my heart was pounding with anticipation.

With the gentleness of a mother, she pushed back the long brown hair covering the left half of my face. "Tell me, dear, what happened today?"

Unable to sustain any level of covertness, I blurted, "You're not my mummy. You're my aunt. And Ms. Thomson said she's not sure you're really my *aunt* because no one knows who my parents are."

Her eyes welled up. "Do you remember the stories I told you about the hospital in London where I worked for many years?"

I nodded. Her bedtime stories often contained tales of the doctors, nurses, and patients she met during her shifts.

"One day, a fellow nurse found a small baby in the maternity ward and—"

"Me?"

"Yes." She reached out and held my left hand. "The moment your tiny hand reached out and touched my face, you filled my heart with so much love; it felt like my body turned to light. It was the day I fell in love—with you." She swallowed hard and didn't break eye contact. "You stayed with me while we searched for your parents. We contacted every hospital in the city and nearby villages, searched birth records, called midwives, and put notices in the city's newspapers. After months of trying, we didn't know anything more. We figured your mother had an unassisted home birth and hadn't registered you. By then, I couldn't live my life without you, so I adopted you."

"But what happened to my mummy and daddy? Why did they leave me?"

"Oh, my dear, there could be so many reasons. I cannot say—I'd be guessing. No one in their right mind would have given you up unless they had no choice." She answered with such certainty and authority that I not only believed her but felt lucky to be hers.

With puddly eyes and a quivering bottom lip, she added, "If you'd like to call me Aunt Judy instead of Mummy, then you can. I won't be upset." She pressed her lips together and cast her eyes down.

There was love and kindness in her explanation, so I stretched out my arms to hug her. "You are my *mummy*. That teacher doesn't know who you are."

When I left for college, I started calling her Aunt Judy because it sounded more grown-up.

How could I break the news of our doomed planet to her? I could dive straight into my discussion with the Reviewers. Or perhaps it would be best to start with the burning electrodes and cracking brain.

My deliberations were interrupted by a pulse from my CDi. I glanced down to see a call from Malcolm. He was probably looking for answers too.

"Good morning, Victoria. We had quite a session yesterday. How are you feeling?"

"Physically, I'm fine. Mentally, I am still out of sorts, as you said."

"Right. I have something to help lift your spirits."

I resented his light-heartedness but pitied him at the same time. He didn't realize how challenging a task he'd have today.

"Oh, what's that?" I said in a less-than-enthusiastic tone.

"Freshly baked scones from the bakery down the road from you. I can pop by with them in twenty minutes."

"Aahh. Well . . ." I glanced down at my pyjamas. The last time he'd seen me like this was two years earlier, when I was bedridden with pneumonia. Today, again, my sleep apparel would have to do. Show civility. "That's nice, and thanks, Malcolm, but—"

"Right then, see you in twenty." The man who'd barely acknowledged the electrodes searing into my scalp wanted to make amends.

I unlocked the front door with a tap on my CDi, then returned to staring into my cereal bowl.

Malcolm arrived precisely twenty minutes later.

"You don't look so good." He surveyed the kitchen. "And why is it so dark in here?"

I shrugged.

"Lights on," he said, and squinted at me with a look of concern. The kitchen lit up. "I'll just clear the table." His tone grew more judgmental. "Is this what 'physically fine' looks like?"

"Sorry, what?" I scowled at him.

"Earlier, you said you were 'physically fine.'"

"Yes, but out of sorts mentally." I created a visor with my hands to block out the lights.

He gave me slow half nods. "Can you look up at me? I want to check your eyes."

I sighed. "Really? Do we have to do this now?"

He leaned over and held my chin up. "Hmm . . . your pupils are dilated. Let me check your CDi." Holding my left arm, I could see that he noticed my hands shaking. "Elevated heartrate, shaking. This is your definition of fine?"

I nodded and mumbled, "It is now."

Working at a different speed than me, in a blink he had set out the scones, tubs of clotted cream, and strawberry jam. Our eyes locked as he took a seat, and I wondered how much of the truth he could handle.

"Listen, I have something to tell you," he said, eyes widening in an intense stare.

"Oh." I hadn't considered that he might have news for me.

"First, you have to be in the right frame of mind to hear what I have to say." He rested his chin on his clenched hand and studied me.

I lifted my scone, laden with clotted cream and strawberry jam. "This will help." Of course it wouldn't be that easy, but I didn't want my doomsday state to prevent me from hearing what he had to say. "Sorry about the mess." I pointed to the table and my pyjamas with my chin. "It's just . . . well, I'm having a hard time understanding yesterday's session."

"Indeed," he said. "I've gone over the data ten times. I hope I can help clarify things for you."

"Really?" Perhaps I was unnecessarily concerned about revealing my anguish.

He squirmed with excitement. "Ye've bloody done it." He slapped the table with his hands and rose from his chair.

Startled by and unprepared for his sudden burst of emotion, I choked on my scone.

"Sorry." He motioned his hand like he was hitting my back.

I shook my head to deter him. "I'm fine," I said and grabbed my tea. "So, what have I done?"

"You displayed consistent activity from high gamma to the slowest of delta brainwaves."

"What?"

"It's all here." He whipped out a qEEG printout from a large envelope. "You sustained over twenty minutes of high-level activity across the brainwave bands." His words shook as he rushed to explain. "The brain spasms either caused your brain to enter a heightened state or vice versa. We'll figure it out once we match it up with your subjective account."

"How can this be?" I flipped through the readouts and brain-mapping images in disbelief. "Friday's session was the worst ever."

He paced the kitchen floor. "Do you realize what this means, Victoria?"

"You now understand how much pain I was in and want to make amends?"

Malcolm chuckled. "Yes, but no."

"For a man who's usually very clear and easy to understand, I . . ."

He gestured triumphantly with his arms like he'd just won the World Cup. "It means we've met the Consortium's challenge."

I was dumbstruck. My mouth dropped open, and the scone that was on its way to my lips plunged into the tea. With my focus on the impending Armageddon, I'd forgotten about *the* contest of all contests.

○ ○ ○

Three years earlier, twenty-eight corporations, mostly from the USA, had created the "Brain Consortium." They put vast amounts of resources into one goal—brain optimization or strong brainwave activity across the frequency bands in a specific pattern. Tech and science gurus hypothesized that in a state of optimization, the human brain could open new levels of consciousness and influence quantum states of AI systems.

I wasn't sure about the whole quantum states idea, but I did wonder what that level of consciousness would feel like.

Groups of all sizes and affiliations had accepted the challenge. The bait of holidays, homes, and jobs for life from the mega-corps hooked thousands, but it was the grand prize keeping everyone focused—£500 million over twenty years. With such funding, the victorious could choose how and what they wanted to work on for the next two decades—a freedom rarely enjoyed by scientists.

However, there was a dark side. The competition had turned talented researchers into mavericks. Stories abounded of teams using dangerously high currents to supercharge their brains. The outcome, far too often, was a comatose state, partial loss of brain function, or even death. The official body count was at least a hundred and fifty, but we all knew the actual number was much higher.

Our team of two neuroscientists and three experimenters were called "purists" because we used the brain's natural abilities to reach higher consciousness levels—no electrical stimuli required. I'd joined the team six months late because experimenting with others was in direct contrast to the privacy I had spent most of my life protecting. However, Malcolm had assured me it would be just the two of us during my testing. And to be fair, I saw it as a further opportunity to search for answers about my abilities.

○   ○   ○

The possibility of us winning the competition should've been utter fantasy. I rubbed my forehead to help myself to process the news.

With glee in his eyes, Malcolm said, "There's only one thing for you to do."

"What's that?" I said in an unfamiliar, breathy tone.

"Sign the release form so I can upload the results to the Consortium." He waved the paper like he was holding the winning lottery ticket.

"Oh, right . . ." A sudden hot flash ran through my body.

"Right? Too bloody right." He grabbed my shoulders and shook me, jubilant. "We've done it—you've done it. This changes everything for us. We can spend the rest of our careers researching whatever we bloody well want to. We've shown the neuroscience world what it takes to reach optimization: years of training, not external stimulation or drugs."

If the ecstatic neuroscientist's assessments were correct, the Consortium would declare the competition over. No further lives would be risked, a definite upside. I smiled, but my slouched body said something else.

He wrinkled his forehead and collapsed back into his chair. "Victoria, what's wrong?"

My breathing grew shallow, and the trembling worsened. Pointing to the windows like a frail old woman, I said, "Could you open . . ."

"Of course." He bolted into action like he'd done when I pressed the call button. "It took my breath away too. That's why I checked the results ten times in different ways to be sure I wasn't misreading them."

I nodded as he talked, but the tug-of-war in my head was all I could hear. Should I tell him everything or just selective bits? What would get the job done and keep my reputation intact? Would this be what finally scared him away from me?

"Victoria . . . hello." He leaned forwards to get my attention. "Are you skeptical of the results?"

I shook my head and closed my eyes for a few moments.

"What is it?" He reached over and placed his hand on my arm. "You can tell me."

My gaze see-sawed between him and the papers. After a long pause, I said, "Along with the data, I have to submit a subjective account of what happened, and explain every change in brainwave pattern."

"Yes, of course, but I can help you with that," he said in a calming voice.

I smirked. "Help me? I doubt it."

With a look of realization, he said, "We should discuss your session now so I can understand what's going on."

With the readouts in front of us, I took him through each segment. He sat fiddling with his pen, occasionally scribbling a note. By the halfway mark, he hadn't interrupted or interjected a single comment. I divulged nearly everything about the Reviewers and their message because nothing but the truth would fit with the data. The one detail I withheld was their request for my presence in Norway. To make matters worse, I had come to realize that the only way to validate the session was to go to Norway.

Modesty had prevented me from taking off my cardigan. By the time I finished recounting the experience, my pyjamas were drenched.

Malcolm stared down at the papers without saying a word.

"Well, say something," I said.

His eyes remained locked on his notes while his fingers juggled the pen like a professional baton twirler. I'd never seen him fidget before.

"Hmm . . . not going to lie to you. It's quite the story. If ye were anyone else, I would recommend ye to a therapist." He looked towards the window, perhaps trying to create some psychological space.

"This is why I can't sign over the results to the Consortium." My admission brought his eyes back to me.

"Nonsense—they'll accept yer subjective account because of the solid physiological manifestation." He fanned out the session's pages in front of us. "The data doesn't lie. Despite an *Alice in Wonderland* experience, yer have produced optimal brain patterns."

"Alice in . . . Is that what you think?" I stood up. "Nothing more than a dream, yet it produced extreme brainwave activity?" My defensiveness surprised me. I might not have been convinced of the session's validity, but I had to defend my reputation. "Look, I'll admit it sounds absurd, and I'm the one who experienced it. But I know two things—the session happened, and these pages prove it.

"You know I'm with you, through thick and thin." He gathered up the papers in slow motion and placed them to the side. Suddenly, he looked up at me with *Eureka!* in his eyes. "I have a plan. We can water down your story. Leave out whatever bits are too much."

I grimaced at the idea of casting aside years of experimenting and researching with integrity just to create a more believable narrative. "But we can't change the subjective account." I splayed the pages across the table in annoyance. "It's what created the results here."

"I'm not saying we should change all the details. Just make it more palatable," he said in a low, almost condescending tone.

"How does one make Armageddon 'more palatable'?" I asked.

He froze and sighed in an expression of defeat.

"I have a counterproposal," I said. "Let's sit on this for a fortnight. I'll visit Aunt Judy, then rent a cabin in the mountains in Norway to think things over." It wasn't an outright lie, just not the complete truth. Integrity intact. If the whole session was nonsense, then I would be back in a couple weeks. That outcome seemed the most reasonable.

"That sounds very specific." He scrunched up his eyes. "Why go to Norway? Stay here—we can work on a solution together. We could . . ."

I leaned across the table, knocking over my teacup. "Sorry, but what happens when the Consortium wants me to recreate the results?" It was a real concern, but at that moment, it also served to divert his focus away from my trip to the Nordic countryside. "I won't be able to do it; physically, I can't go through that again."

Malcolm nodded. "I understand this was a special result even for you." He put my teacup back on the saucer and soaked up the tea with his napkin. "We can tell everyone it was a one-off event, but we hope to recreate the results using different protocols."

He looked at me, awaiting a sign of approval.

I rested my chin in the palms of my hands. This wasn't the time to debate the issue; there were bigger things to spend my energy on. "Okay, I think that will work."

He gave me a half smile. "Good."

"What do you think of the Reviewers' message?" I looked away to allow him to answer without my scrutinizing gaze.

"Uhh . . ." After a few seconds, he said, "It sounds like bollocks."

I snapped my head back and eyeballed him as he delivered his harsh opinion.

"You were in pain before, during, and after the session, in part due to the electrode glue"—he cleared his throat—"but something else was going on I can't explain. My problem with the whole thing is . . . well, your track record. You have predicted events accurately in and out of the sessions for many years."

Seeing or sensing the future was not complicated. Events fell into one of two categories—absolutes or probabilities. Absolutes were written in the timeline like etchings in stone. They had a heaviness, as if the fabric of local space-time was pulled because of them. On the other hand, probabilities had a lighter feel. If the right balance was struck in the days leading up to a probability, it could be avoided altogether. But it opened so many potential complications, like self-fulfilling prophecies. My foresight usually came without warning, regardless of how I felt or what I was doing—stressed or relaxed, happy or melancholy, driving or walking, the visions just came.

But the previous day's session had presented a scenario we'd never experienced before. Could the content be trusted like other times?

"What are you saying?" I leaned forwards, needing to see and hear him say it plainly.

He shook his head. "I'm not bloody sure."

"Not sure? But you think it could have merit, which would mean we don't have much time." I hit my fist on the table to punctuate my statement.

"We need to stay calm. They didn't tell you the specifics of how Earth would end, so it's impossible for you or us to prevent anything. You mentioned they were going to help us . . . how?"

"I don't know." I shook my head slowly.

Malcolm reached for another scone. "If we don't have long, then I won't feel guilty." He added another dollop of clotted cream. "Seriously, we must keep living our lives until we know more."

"And how will we find out more?" I asked.

He looked down at his plate and said, "Through more sessions."

"You're joking, right?"

He shrugged before taking another bite of scone. "Of course, the team will want to celebrate once they see the data. I'm surprised no one has called me yet."

"Oh bother! I forgot the session was copied to the team drive. Malcolm, please, take it off the drive . . . temporarily."

He looked at me like I was asking him to commit a crime. "I can understand not telling the Consortium, but holding back from the team will only raise questions later."

As he spoke, I accessed the group's account from my CDi. As my sessions were done in a certified lab with an accredited neuroscientist, we always included them in the group data, but that was when I didn't have anything to hide.

I extended my arm so he could approve the removal of data. "I know it was in a certified lab, but the session was recorded into my personal folder, separate from the team's. I should be able to say when it gets copied over and shared."

"Come on, you know how it works." He pushed himself slightly away from the table. "Changing the process will raise suspicion. They'll think we've tampered with the results. I'm sorry, Victoria, I can't do it."

"Please! Approve deletion of the copy in the team folder." My assertive, panicked tone had him doing double takes between me and the CDi. I was bullying my friend, confidant, and research partner.

"You're asking me to violate the terms of the team's agreement and the strict protocol of the Consortium."

"If there was any other way . . . Look, I've never asked you to do something like this. Surely that shows you how important it is to me. Please."

He shook his head and looked away with an expression of disgust. I wasn't getting through to him.

"I'll quit the research and pull out of the team." Never in my wildest dreams would I have thought those words would come from me. I was devoted to the team's research and to Malcolm.

He shot out of his chair and stormed off.

I sat without uttering a word, waiting to hear the door slam shut. From my out-of-body perspective, I could do nothing but watch things spiral out of control.

A few minutes later, he returned and sat at the table. He was expressionless and unemotional as he tapped on his CDi. "They'll start asking questions about the omission by week two . . . or sooner if anyone has seen the file already. It's not the way I like to work." He eyeballed me. "As a team, we've always operated with complete transparency."

"I know." I sighed in relief. "Hopefully no one has seen the session yet." I gave him what I hoped was a kind look. "I promise, after my holiday, we will discuss it openly with them. If there's any pushback, I'll explain why we did it this way and take full responsibility."

"The responsibility for my integrity lies solely with me," he said with a stern glare. "I don't like it, but I will go along because of who you are and our relationship."

I had pushed him to his professional ethical edge—and us to the breaking point.

"Thank you. It's only for a couple weeks."

"Right, right." He stood up to leave. "This morning, when I set out to come here, I expected a celebration."

"I know. I really am sorry. But surely you see it's more complicated than you thought."

Malcolm took a deep breath. "Well, it certainly is now. Despite this, call me if you want to talk as you think through things." He patted me on the shoulder.

I looked at him with an aching heart. "I'll make things right. I don't know how, but I promise you I will."

CHAPTER 3

DIAGNOSIS

After Malcolm's deflated departure, I sat dazed. The Armageddon review had delivered the most sought-after neuroscience result—and an overwhelming amount of personal angst. What good would £500 million be if we didn't exist?

Years ago, I'd watched a movie where an asteroid was heading towards Earth. It chronicled three different types of reactions in people. There were those who acted like nothing was happening and carried on. The second type left their jobs and any bad relationships and lived in a manic way because they had nothing to lose. The last group acknowledged the incoming catastrophe and prepped for the end of the world but hoped to survive on the bunker of supplies they had secretly hoarded.

If doomsday was inevitable, I would choose another option—drive to Aunt Judy's and spend our remaining days together.

I tapped my CDi. "Create a new to-do list. 1) Book sabbatical and transfer workload to other researchers; (2) Visit Aunt Judy and Anne; (3) Prepare for trip to Norway."

The list motivated me to get dressed and call Aunt Judy.

We spoke about the weather in Devon and an unusual patient she had during the week. She loved telling me about curious cases. The best part of her stories was always how she figured out what conditions they had and how to treat them.

In the space between her patient and that afternoon's plan to go to the seaside, I said, "I need to talk to you about my last appointment with Malcolm."

"Oh." I could hear her surprise at my sudden change of subject. "How *is* Malcolm?"

"He's upset. We just had tea and scones, and I'm reeling from our last neurofeedback session."

"What happened?" She sounded concerned.

"It was horrific, and if I am to believe its contents, then we are in big trouble."

"Oh, right. *We?*"

Pacing back and forth to the bay window, I relived part of the traumatic experience. I couldn't tell my eighty-two-year-old aunt that she may see the end of the world within the year. Instead, I relayed part of the Reviewers' warning and left out the fact that I was going to Norway at their request.

"Did you say you had *no* control of the meditation?" Now her voice was even more worried.

"I completely lost control and, at the same time, had what may be the most important session of my life."

"Were you pulled in as if by a magnet?" She said the words like she knew something forbidden.

My mind raced to figure out what she was getting at. "Yes, why?"

"It seems to be a tell-tale sign when you're having a premoni-tion."

Perhaps she was recalling the magnetic pull I felt when fore-seeing events. Like when I was seventeen and walked by a neigh-bor's car, I *knew and felt* that the car would be in an accident within a day or two. The dilemma was how to warn him without creating a self-fulfilling prophecy. After much conversation, Aunt Judy and I had agreed it was best to say, "I had a dream you were in an accident . . ."

The next day, we visited the neighbor to inform him of my "dream," but he had crashed two hours prior. As with each previous foresight, the questions came. What social responsibility did I have? Should I try to prevent bad things from happening? Why did I see these things, if not to help people?

Aunt Judy changed her focus. "Was your guide there?"

"No, he didn't show up."

"Ohh," she said. I could imagine her looking over the top of her glasses. "Dear, I'm not being funny, but have you watched or read anything to trigger such a session?

Somewhat insulted, I said, "I wish it was that simple. No, I can't link it to anything in my life."

"Could you be searching for answers to your childhood expe-riences?"

"No!" I said, unable to hide the defensive reaction. I didn't need to look back in time for explanations. It wasn't a machination of my own making. I took a deep breath. She just needed time to digest everything, like I did. "Like what?" There were so many things she could be referring to from my many curious experiences as a young girl.

"When you were six, you asked me why the people at school weren't awake. You looked into the eyes of each child and teacher—no one seemed awake. You were searching for people with deeper levels of consciousness."

That day had helped define me. From my perspective, I was standing in the middle of a post-apocalyptic scene, teetering between disappointment and terror. They were biological beings but lacked a depth of consciousness and connectedness to the world around them. For my sanity and survival, I detached from everyone.

"I see where you're going, but I truly have accepted where others are, or are not. If my subconscious wanted answers, why would it create an experience where I had no control?"

"I don't know," she said in an odd tone. In that instant, I felt like she knew more. "What does Malcolm have to say about it all?"

"He's torn. On the one hand, he knows I've never been wrong when seeing into the future, but I've never experienced such pain before or during a session. And . . . there's something else."

"I'm not sure I can handle much more," she said. "But what is it?"

"I created a specific brainwave pattern. . . exactly the one the Consortium is looking for to achieve optimum brain use."

"My dear, that's fantastic! I knew if anyone was capable, it was you. What—"

"There's only one problem. I'm not going to tell anyone else about the results, except you and Malcolm." I grimaced as I anticipated a bad reaction from her.

"Quite right, keep quiet until the Consortium confirms the data."

"What?" Her response threw me. "No, what I'm saying is I need time to think about the experience and determine when and what to share with the team and the Consortium. That's what has Malcolm so upset."

"I see." After a lengthy pause, she said, "I'm sorry, dear, but I don't understand. Why not submit all the results to the Consortium and use their platform to create a sense of urgency about Earth's condition?"

"I don't want to raise my profile until I can validate the Reviewers' message."

"I will need to think about that. When are you coming to see me? Today?"

"Tomorrow would be better. I have some work to do," I said.

"My dear, whatever is best. I will be happy to see you whenever you arrive. We'll talk it all through and figure things out together, like we always do."

○ ○ ○

I found Aunt Judy in the garden, armed with cutting shears. She wore her favorite bright red top and a wide-brimmed summer hat. Her physical and mental strength far exceeded what many expected from such a delicate frame. My auntie greeted me with a reserved wave and a big smile.

After putting my overnight bag upstairs in my room, we reheated leftovers from her previous night's Indian meal. Instinctively, we held back on deep conversation at the dinner table, opting instead for tidbits about gardening, birds, and the neighbors. Dinner wasn't rushed, but it wasn't prolonged either. However, it was long enough for her to have three big glasses of red wine, more than the one small glass she usually enjoyed. With the table cleared, she started a roaring fire in the sitting room. It was one of the colder areas in the house, so we could comfortably enjoy a fire there until mid-June.

We took our positions. Aunt Judy sat to the left of the fireplace in a slightly tattered, thrice reupholstered French Louis XVI chair and covered her lap with a red-and-white-checkered blanket. I got the better chair; it matched hers but had only been repaired twice. Armed with our usual drinks—my cup of herbal tea and her glass of sherry—we were ready to discuss what had no doubt preoccupied us during dinner.

The lead Reviewer had said we were in dire straits. Were they right? My dear auntie was the ideal person to consider such heavy matters. Being a family doctor who'd first worked as a nurse in the UK, Africa, and Asia, she held unique, informed perspectives and was a treasure trove of knowledge.

"I've given your session some thought." She took a sip from her glass.

I pulled a nervous smile and readied myself for the sage's wisdom. "And...what do you think?"

"Dearest, I have been around long enough to hear a multitude of views on how we're going to hell in a handbasket. Mind you, that was well before these beings suggested it. Eventually, you learn no one has all the answers, and most have too many opinions; but we keep slogging away to make tomorrow better." She tilted her eyeglasses down to peer over the top at me. "Your Reviewers concluded humankind is off its intended path because we probably *are*. Imagine where we might be if we worked together more instead of trying so hard to alienate and destroy each other." She took another sip.

"True," I said, "but if we had to unite, do you think we could?"

The no-nonsense octogenarian was quick to answer. "Not in my lifetime or yours, but we can hope humans figure it out before we destroy ourselves and the planet."

Even without being told the full ominous message from the Reviewers, she had hit on it.

"Which brings me to something very important." She leaned towards me and stared at me with her crystal-blue eyes. "Telling the Consortium may be the best way forwards."

I looked at her, puzzled, and reminded myself that I wanted to avoid the kind of disagreement Malcolm and I had found ourselves in on the same issue.

She smiled and winked at me, seeming to delight in piquing my curiosity.

"You and your team could form a new organization with the Consortium. Together, you could work on finding solutions to the world's biggest problems."

"The prize money isn't billions," I said. "We may be able to influence one or two areas, but it's not enough to make a worldwide impact."

She scowled and pinned back some hanging hair strands that framed her face. "It's not just about the money. It's also about you using your position as the first person to reach their definition of brain optimization."

I shook my head. "Sorry, I'm not following you."

"Once news of your achievement comes out, you'll be known throughout the world. Why not use your position to influence those who can make a difference? It could be your life's quest.

Shouldn't you do all you can to steer the world towards better ways of working via cooperation?"

"You're right. I will think about that." Leaving out essential details had me boxed in. If she only knew the whole story.

She nodded and pursed her lips. I could tell she suspected I was withholding information. "Good." She looked at the fire and sipped her sherry.

I had never been good at keeping secrets from Aunt Judy. I cracked. "There's something else. The Reviewers have asked me to go to Norway in 4 days to learn more about how to avert a major catastrophe in 312 days." I blurted it out so quickly it was almost undiscernible to me, let alone my slightly tipsy auntie. I held my breath for her reaction.

She eased her glass down onto the side table. "Why didn't you tell me this earlier?"

I lifted my head and looked at her out of the corner of my eye. "I was afraid of what you would say. I don't know if I can trust the contents of the session, but I think I should go to Norway in search of answers."

With her head turned away from me, she said, "What kind of catastrophe?"

"They couldn't give me details. They're limited by the kind of help they are allowed to provide."

"You would be going alone? Where, exactly?" Her hand trembled as she picked up her glass and drew it to her lips.

"It's northwest of Bergen. I need to be there on Thursday, March 13."

"It will be cold and dark." She jostled in her seat and looked away. "How long are you going for?"

"They said I should plan to be away for 121 days."

"121 days? That's utter madness. You can't be away from your work for so long." She held her forehead. "What about Albert?"

I nodded. "Everything is sorted. Depending on what I find, I will either be taking a two-week holiday or an extended sabbatical. But I was hoping you could take care of Albert. Anne has offered to bring him to you."

"It's . . . I just need a couple minutes to process all this." She stared down into her lap.

I didn't dare say a word or move a muscle.

She cleared her throat. "When you go to Norway, will you need to be at the same level you were in during the session to communicate with them? If you do, you will be alone in a foreign country, far from the safety of Malcolm's office."

"I don't know. I just don't know." Honesty was painful.

After a few sips, she said, "Or perhaps . . ." She gently rolled the stem of the glass between her thumb and first two fingers. "I want you to hear me out before you react."

I squinted, knowing it must be bad if she had to prep me for it. "Okay."

"Perhaps, the Reviewers were a metaphor or embodiment of where you see the world heading. It could have represented a mixture of your concerns and ability to see the future. Going to Norway might be a nice place to think about how you can join efforts to remedy current conditions and steer clear of future disasters. I doubt you will be able to connect with the Reviewers again."

I sat, mouth agape, feeling a little silly for not coming up with that one. "A metaphor—interesting. It may have been a manifestation of my inner angst. Certainly, something to think about. . . perhaps in Norway." I gave her a wry smirk.

"Give it some serious thought. It makes more sense than running off to meet with something you have only seen during a qEEG session. Did your Reviewers tell you what you will be doing for four months?"

I half covered my mouth with my hand. "No, they didn't."

She coughed into her hankie. "Don't you think it's the least they could have told you?"

Aunt Judy was single-handedly tearing down my grandiose notions about receiving help from a more intelligent species. Why did I assume they were real? I wasn't prone to fantasy, but did I secretly hope for an alien rescue operation from my disconnect with other people? I sat there, deflated.

"We could go together," she said in a nurturing tone.

"I wouldn't and couldn't ask that of you. I'll be okay. It will be good for me to get some distance from the session, Malcolm, the team, and work."

She half smiled, knocked back the last drops from her glass, and said, "I'm glad you didn't include me in that list. Now, be useful and pour your elder another glass of sherry." With uncharacteristically shaky hands, she handed me the heavy crystal decanter.

"Is everything okay? Your hands are trembling."

Mumbling under her breath, she said, "It's the least of my concerns."

"Do the shakes come and go?" As her only living family member, I tried to be aware of any health changes in her.

"No, no. I'm a bit . . . well, shaken by all this." She switched her gaze to the crackling fire and loosened her tight bun of long, blonde hair.

I reached over and tapped her archaic CDi to read her metrics. "Your CDi doesn't give you all the physiological assessments you could have. Why don't you upgrade it?"

"No device is going to track everything I do so it can share it with every company and organization from here to the moon."

I shook my head at her obstinance. "You should have access to the same data you expect your patients to have."

She patted her device. "I like this one."

"So what bothers you most—the session itself, me going away, or an imminent catastrophe?"

She exhaled loudly. "You have an uncomfortable session, then tell me you're going to follow up on a message from aliens who want you to go to Norway to learn how to avert a disaster. If a patient came into my office with such a tale, I would be referring them to a psychologist."

I shot up out of the chair. "That is exactly why I won't be sharing the session with others. Even you"—I threw my arms up in the air—"can't deal with it. How can I expect anyone else to? You know my history. Unexpected and strange things happen."

With her bottom lip jutting out, she said, "Hhmm." She slowly exhaled, swallowed hard, and perused me from top to bottom. "Get us some digestives whilst you're up." She wasn't about to let my dramatic overture take the stage without being productive. Fetching her favorite biscuits helped me reset. I returned to my seat next to her.

Aunt Judy turned to me, tilting her head down and her eyes up. I recognized the posture. She graced me with it whenever she disapproved of something I did or someone I brought home. My Aunt Mummy was donning a professional stance to deliver a further diagnosis.

"Dear, I'm worried about you . . . and okay, if I have to say it—the world. I wish this warning had come from anyone else but you. On the one hand, I want to tell you,"—she paused and waited for my eyes to meet hers—"that you had a disturbing neurofeedback session, but it doesn't mean you should abandon all rational thought. But on the other hand, I know who you are and what gifts you possess."

A cascade of warmth rushed over my face and down to my toes. "Are you saying that you trust the session and what the Reviewers said?"

"I'm saying the answer lies somewhere in the middle. Take a quiet holiday and try to reconnect with the messengers, or at least the one Reviewer who did the talking. You could stay right here at home with me. I could take some time off, too."

"Thank you, but I feel like I should go to the location they specified to uncover whether there's anything real in their warning."

She shook her head and rubbed her eyes.

"Are you concerned because you think I may just find someone or something waiting for me in Norway?"

With a startled expression, she said, "You know how to scare me. When something doesn't add up, I'm always going to be a little nervous." She stared into her glass and pouted. "You must check in with me before and after going to the meeting point. If you plan to stay somewhere for four months, then we'll have to work out calling days and times."

I was taken aback by her sudden acceptance of my trip.

She got up to refill the decanter and add another log. "You are so clever, but you are too trusting of people at times. And you still need someone in your life who knows you and can keep an eye out. It can't have been easy for you, not having a mother and father. I did my best. Wasn't it enough, Victoria?"

Her reaction, sherry-fueled or not, hit me to my core. I was letting her down and getting the biggest guilt trip of my life. I sat as still as the statue on the mantelpiece that she had given me for my fifteenth birthday. It was a girl sitting by a tree, resting her chin on her left hand as she gazed outward in contemplation. Aunt Judy once said it reminded her of me.

She had raised me, loved me, and defended me no matter how tough things got. When outside attention escalated too much, we agreed a "change of scenery" was needed, code for a new school or area. When I wondered why I didn't fit in, she reassured me. "You're just more cerebral than they are." Her words soothed me well before I knew what "cerebral" meant.

One of those times was when my Catholic schoolmate invited me to her house. I was ten years old. She'd heard the rumors and challenged me to prove my abilities.

My friend said, "I'm like Thomas the Apostle, or Doubting Thomas. I need to see it to believe it. Just once."

For me, it was a scientific experiment. I explained that her younger sister would come downstairs to us soon. But on the third step, she would fall, hurt herself, and retreat upstairs to her mother. Within ten minutes, reality unraveled as I'd predicted. The fright in my Doubting Thomas's eyes said it all. She never invited me back, and I wondered if *I* should be afraid too. Was I predicting or causing? What if I couldn't control it? What if it hurt Aunt Judy or me?

That was my fourth witnessed experiment in as many weeks. My reputation as a "witch" spread like wildfire through my school and village. Aunt Judy convinced me to keep my experiments between us. She also suggested that first change of scenery. We moved to a new home a few villages away. It was close enough to her work, yet far enough for me to start afresh.

Intuitively, she knew what was best for me. Was she the one seeing things clearly now, and I needed a reality check?

I went over to her and put my arm around her as she continued prodding the burning logs. "Please, you know how much I love you. You have done more for me than one person could ever . . ."

My eyes welled up. *Hold it back, hold it back.* Aunt Judy didn't appreciate people losing their decorum.

"Don't cry, dearest. I'll feel guilty for my honesty."

I shook my head and gazed at her with wide eyes to prove I wasn't shedding a tear.

"Your beautiful, blue-green eyes have gone a bright green and yellow—you're crying." She paused, put down her drinking vessel, and reached out to cradle my face. "Let's not speak of this anymore."

I nodded, grateful for the detente. She was right; I was crying on the inside.

In a conciliatory move, she said, "You can stay here until you leave."

I answered in a weakened monotone voice, using as few muscles in my face as possible. "Thank you" was all I could muster. It wasn't the right time to tell her I would be leaving tomorrow afternoon.

We returned to our chairs and stared at the fireplace for a few excruciating minutes.

She managed two more glasses of sherry. "Let's retire for the eve . . . even . . . evening." The moderate drinker had far exceeded her usual one or two glasses. "I think—think we need a good night's rest, so we . . . can think clearer in the morning."

Of course, it was *me* she wanted to think clearer.

"Yes," I said.

We hugged each other goodnight, and I retreated upstairs to my room.

Moments later, Aunt Judy shouted from the kitchen. "I'll fix you a bottle. Of hot . . . uhh, a hot water bottle and leave it by your door."

Regardless of her inebriation or disappointment in me, this was not the time to break sacred routines. She had always prepared a hot water bottle to warm my cold bed, no matter the time of year.

○　○　○

The following day, I woke with twists in my stomach from the night before. Being out of sync with Aunt Judy was dreadful.

I brushed my thick brown hair in front of the large, gold-gilded mirror. The stress of being at odds with Aunt Judy had aged me overnight. My face had swelled like a water balloon, and dark bags hung like Christmas garlands under my usual bright eyes, which had ceded to pale and half-closed.

Was I a terrible person to put this on my dear aunt? She'd always been there for me with advice, an attentive ear, and an empathetic heart. And this was how I repaid her. She was a strong mid-lifer, but still eighty-two years old. The CDi predicted she would live to 153 years, with a standard deviation of three. I would feel decades of regret if she became ill because of me. On the other hand, it wasn't as if I was throwing away my career and life in search of aliens. I was simply taking a holiday where, it just so happened, I could validate important details. Definitely a gamble—I'd either return vindicated or a fool. *I should tell her she was right.* Perhaps I had taken things too far.

I stared in the mirror, wondering how to make us both happy.

Breakfast smells wafted up to me, snapping me out of my trance. The sound of classical music filled the house and practically carried me downstairs. "Divenire" by Ludovico Einaudi was playing, Aunt Judy's favorite old music.

"Good morning, my dear," she said in a chirpy tone.

I smiled in relief. She hadn't disowned me . . . yet. "Yes, good morning. Everything looks delicious, and I'm rather peckish." Of course, moments earlier I couldn't have envisioned eating a morsel, but seeing her happy brought back my appetite.

We ate and talked about the weather, politics, her neighbors, and what to do with the rest of our day.

"I need to leave just before dinner. I have some work to do and need to prepare for my holiday."

"Oh dear, what a shame. I thought we could head over to the shore tomorrow for a walk. You should stay longer."

"Yes, I wish I could. Perhaps next time."

Aunt Judy made another cup of coffee. "Come sit down for a moment."

I put away the last of the breakfast jams and prepared myself for something serious.

"I want you to know that I agree with you taking time off and even going to Norway. Over the years, you have shown me things I never thought possible. I can't discount your session as much as I would like to." She reached out for my hand. "But I do hope the whole thing was a subconscious manifestation of the pain you have experienced since you were a young girl because your unusual abilities make people uncomfortable or scared."

"Thank you. It means a lot to me to have your support."

"So you will call every Sunday at noon, right?" she asked.

"Yes, and I will call you just before I go to the meeting point on Thursday."

On the drive home, introspection was an inescapable consequence.

I rewound my evening talk with Aunt Judy. The Reviewers could have well been a representation of my desires for a better world. I envisioned releasing the data to my team and the Consortium, holding my bank account statement displaying millions in prize money, and ignoring the Doomsday message. If life as we knew it wasn't at risk, then it could be a happy future for many. But probably not for me. I wouldn't be able to go on without validating some details from the session. It had felt so real. Perhaps my subconscious was looking for an escape from routine. No, I enjoyed the predictability and control of knowing what each week would hold.

Back home, I prepared for my departure and had an early night. Saving the world was indeed a noble goal, but the opportunity to validate the session and learn from advanced aliens was equally compelling.

◯　◯　◯

Although I didn't know what others would dream to bring them to the designated meeting point, I wondered what kind of people would act on a dream or meditation. I settled on three categories. First, some could've been desperately searching for meaning in their lives. Second, there were those who believed their nonconscious brain could receive information from external sources. I would fit into that group. However, perhaps the most intriguing of all was category three. These people were willing to commit their time and resources to satisfy their curiosity. They just wanted to find out if what they saw had any grain of truth. It seemed to me that all three groups were hopeful.

After a half day at work, I entered my home on the last ordinary day before my reckoning.

"Meow," Albert greeted me with an affectionate rub up against my leg.

A conflicted apprehension overcame me as I walked through to the sitting room. I gazed at the perfectly broken-in Chesterfield chair with my tartan blanket draped across its left armrest and reaching down to the warm wooden floor, reconditioned two summers ago. A patterned Turkish rug, gifted by Aunt Judy, accented the room. Deep in melancholy, I sunk into the Chesterfield. Albert took it as an invitation to curl up on my lap.

"Am I crazy?" I asked Albert as I stroked his long-haired tabby mane.

He responded with an extended meow, followed by a short chirp.

I didn't recognize his response and probably wouldn't have liked the answer. He sensed I would be leaving. The lovely feline got clingier whenever I went away.

"Don't worry, Albert, I'll be back with answers for us before you know it."

CHAPTER 4

DROPPING INTO DARKNESS

Norway

My journey to the middle of Norway on March 12 consisted of two flights and one four-seater high-speed ground transport. I arrived at a bed and breakfast on the island of Sandsøya just after sunset. It was a two-story yellow building with a sign in the front reading "Velkommen." But it was the closest of the awe-inspiring, snow-capped mountains that I was interested in—Dollsteinen, the location given by the Reviewers.

The area was eerily serene. There wasn't another person to be seen. It seemed I had been a fool to put such meaning into the bad session. The world wasn't going to end soon and my holiday in Norway would be spent alone contemplating the error of my ways. Fun.

I entered the B&B just as a thirty-something-year-old German man was checking in. Hiker or dreamer? I casually watched from the corner of my eye as the lanky, over-six-foot-tall chap struggled to take off his oversized rucksack.

He peered over at me as if ensuring I wasn't in his personal space.

Just beyond him was a whiteboard showing tomorrow's weather. I stepped forwards. A picture of snowflakes was drawn next to the time "07:00." I would leave at 09:30, well after the snow flurries.

The tall German turned to me. "Hallo?" His rosy red cheeks and wide eyes had my attention.

"Hello," I said softly, surprised by his sudden friendliness.

His eyes moved to and fro between me and the ground.

I followed his gaze down to my feet, which were firmly planted on his bag strap. "Oh, sorry." I stepped back.

He hoisted his bag onto his back and walked off.

Based on his lack of friendliness, I reckoned he was a tired, experienced hiker, not someone who came out here seeking something he'd seen in a dream.

At 8:30 am, I bolted out of bed and into action. I'd slept for ten hours. Pending catastrophe or not, being on the coast among the mountains was already turning out to be a healthy retreat.

Although it was a brief call, Aunt Judy was happy to hear from me until I warned her. "If I don't call after the meeting, don't assume something is wrong. As crazy as it sounds, I may be away for 121 days. You can send the emergency services after me on day 125 if you don't hear from me."

"Don't you dare do that to me. There's no reason in the world for you not to call me." She sighed loudly. "At least I can track you on my CDi."

I packed my small backpack with a few essentials—chocolate bar, water, plasters, notebook, two pens, and a pencil. After a bowl of muesli and a cup of tea, I donned my coat and headed for the door.

"Unnskyld . . . Excuse me, miss," said the lady behind the desk. "Are you hiking with others?"

I looked around. There was no one else there. "No." I gave her a confused look.

"The snow was light this morning and the sun is shining, but we still don't recommend hiking alone." She unfolded a map of the island. "Where do you want to go?"

I walked over to her just as the German chap from the night before dropped his room key off at the desk. He was straight out of a mountaineering magazine with his wool cap, weatherproof jacket, and hiking boots, but that oversized rucksack had been replaced by a funny looking backpack with a water tube.

Pointing at the map, I said, "I'm going to the south side of the mountain."

Her face lit up. "It's your lucky day. Marcus over there"— she pointed to the German doing some final checks of his gear— "already went to Dollsteinen earlier this morning but is going back now. He is an experienced climber and caver."

I was right about him.

She looked over to him. "Hei, Marcus can you come here?"

"She . . ." The receptionist pointed to me. "Sorry, I don't remember your name."

"Victoria," I said, looking over to Marcus.

"Victoria is going to Dollsteinen." The receptionist smiled at him as if to coax him a bit. "Can she go with you?"

I extended my hand to the hiker. "Hi, again."

"Hallo," he said, handing me a floppy wet fish of a handshake to squeeze. I forced back a smile as I remembered Aunt Judy. She was worried about those with weak handshakes. In her words, it was "an unfortunate affliction when there's no sign of the twenty-seven bones in their hand."

After basic introductions, we were almost out the door when the receptionist stopped me again.

"Victoria, would you like a *matpakke* ... a packed lunch for your hike? Marcus already has his."

It seemed wise to do what the pros and locals did. "Yes, please."

She handed me a brown lunch bag. "Have a good hike. Will you be eating dinner with us tonight?"

"Thank you. Uhh ... dinner, yes."

She nodded with a half-smile. "I will make your reservation."

Two seconds after we stepped outside, a gust of cold air smacked me in the face. I gasped and turned away from the wind.

My new companion scoffed. "You haven't hiked before, have you?" he asked in a condescending tone.

"Not here." I wasn't about to tell him that my experience consisted of walking across the English countryside and London.

We trudged for ten minutes in silence on the snow-covered path before Marcus said, "I will be leaving you when we reach the north side of the mountain. It should take us about twenty-five minutes."

"Okay," I said. The red-cheeked man was already planning to ditch me, regardless of what the receptionist had advised.

"You are alone on holiday?" he said.

I didn't understand why Mr. Rude was asking the question. "Yes, I needed a break from the busyness of London."

He glared at me for a moment too long. "Uh-huh." Was he trying to unnerve me, or was he upset to have a novice tagging along? Perhaps he was supposed to be meeting friends, but they didn't show. Whatever his reasons, he didn't want me at his side.

Twenty minutes later, faint voices came from somewhere ahead of us. I instantly felt better—we were not alone.

By the time we neared the end of the road, Marcus was so far ahead I would've had to shout to be heard. He stopped long enough for me to catch up.

"Just stay to the lower areas, and go back on this same road," he said.

"Thanks." I angled my face up to the sky. "At least the sun is out, and the wind isn't so strong now."

He nodded but showed no warmth towards me, his hiking companion. Like a freed bird, he dashed off, and I pulled up my coat sleeve to check my location on the CDi. A nervous tingling rushed through me as I stared at the map. I was close. A walk along the shore on the opposite side of the mountain would bring me to the cave. My heart beat a little faster. What would I find? Would there be others? I hoped not too many.

On the other side of the mountain, a woman and a man were rifling through their bags. Their clothes were more casual, not professional like Marcus's.

"Do you need protection?" said the short, muscle-bound, twenty-something-year-old man in a thick French accent as he stroked his goatee.

Did he know something I didn't? "Sorry?" I was already confused and hadn't even met any aliens yet.

The Frenchman pointed to a nearby cautionary sign. "You need a helmet and a suit to enter the cave."

"Oh right, yes." Between preparations and deliberations on the sanity of the mission, I hadn't prepared for being in the cave.

"You can buy them here." He picked up a white coverup. "This one would fit you. I accept credit."

It all seemed rather convenient, but . . . "Okay, thank you."

He scanned my CDi code and handed me the gear.

"Are you here year-round?" I asked.

"No, I am a professional cave exploration guide." He started packing up. "I had leftover gear from the previous season and wanted to sell it before I explore the cave myself. I have sold all five sets I came with."

"Is there anything special about the cave?" I wasn't about to ask any more directly than that.

The woman, who looked like a university student in her torn jeans and crossover cloth bag, said, "According to one legend, this is where King Arthur hid the Holy Grail."

"Is that why you are here? You're searching for the Holy Grail?" I tried not to reveal my skepticism about what was undoubtedly a fruitless quest.

First impressions were tricky. I generally made them within two minutes of meeting someone and rarely, if ever, changed my mind. It was one of my skills but also an area for improvement considering that I only had two close friends.

"Yes, it's kinda part of my vacation. I'm from Brazil but live in Chile. Anyway, I had a dream it was here. As a Catholic"—she kissed her cross necklace and tucked it back under her jacket—"I have been on a few journeys to where legend places the Holy Grail. Though many believe the real one is in Valencia, Spain. But I'm kinda not so sure, and besides, it's interesting to follow the different stories."

She might have been a Brazilian living in Chile, but she was fluent in English, with a hint of an American accent. Curious. She dreamed the Holy Grail was here? Or perhaps, there was more to her dream than she was letting on.

The Frenchman glanced at his CDi before shaking out his suit. "We need to get going. Do you want to go in with us."

"Okay, is it free?"

"Oui, since you bought equipment from me," said the smooth operator.

He supervised me putting on the suit before helping me adjust the lamp on the helmet. "You are not claustrophobic, oui?"

"I've never been caving, but I don't think so. Can I go for part of the way?"

The Frenchman squinted at me. "Mon dieu." He looked up to the sky. "Do what you want, but when we pass the halfway point, you need to stay with us till the end." He mumbled something indiscernible.

With a satisfied smile, I said, "Okay, thank you. By the way, I'm Victoria."

"François." He reached out to shake my hand. "I don't like you leaving us halfway. If I am the one responsible, then I want to take everyone into the cave and back out."

I grimaced at his rules and didn't concede.

"Hi … I'm Ana Luiza," the student said as she put on her helmet.

"Okay, everybody ready?" asked our guide, like he was talking to a group of twenty.

We gave him a thumbs-up and followed him in.

Upon entering the cave, I could hear a couple different groups. One sounded close, while the other seemed to be deep inside the crevices. I had no idea caving was so popular across the world. Most of the people there sounded like non-Norwegians.

After fifteen minutes of slow exploring, five others joined us. Our determined Frenchman led us deeper. Occasionally, he'd check a three-layer digital compass. It looked like something for professional cavers.

I got closer to François. "Is it always this busy?"

"Quoi?" he said as if I'd woken him from a trance. "What?"

"Is it always so busy here?"

"I have only been here once before, but caves aren't usually busy till summertime . . . but the weather is good, and it's a famous cave. I don't care for it."

"Care for what?" I said.

He looked at me wearily. "All the people . . . and amateurs."

"I see." I was in complete agreement with him. I didn't like so many people crammed into a stone cavity either. Taking the hint about amateurs from the surly Frenchman, I fell back a few positions.

We crawled through crevices, waded through water, and slithered down muddy slides. Were we getting closer to, or farther away from, the Reviewers' coordinates? François had been checking his CDi every five minutes, so I had no doubt we were approaching where our focused guide wanted to go.

At first, people were talkative and upbeat, but the journey into the labyrinth subdued all—except the Holy Grail seeker. From the bits I caught of her conversation, the more excited she got, the more she talked.

Staying at the front of the group had its advantages. I could shut out Ana's constant chatter and keep an eye on François. However, at some point, I would have to fall back to go my own way or turn back. As we went deeper, the cold, damp darkness gave me a chill; add in the slippery rocks and tight quarters, and my interest in caving had expired.

I reached past someone in front and tapped the professional caver's left shoulder. "François, are we halfway yet?"

He looked back in annoyance. "Oui, most likely."

I scowled and shook my head. "Why didn't you say something? I wanted to turn back."

"Oui, but can't you see I am busy navigating and making sure everyone is safe?"

"Just a couple words would have been nice." I needed to explore other parts of the cave to convince myself it was as Aunt Judy said, "utter folly." Besides, I hadn't come all this way to get trapped in a cave with a relic seeker and spelunking enthusiasts. It was 10:35. I had arrived to the cave before 11:00 as instructed. It was time to escape the madness. I would thank François and bid him adieu.

A moment later, someone from behind tugged at my backpack. A woman wearing goggles and a long, dark rain jacket said, "Excuse me, Miss, why do you want to turn back?" she asked in a calm kind voice.

"This is my first time caving, and I don't want to spend the whole day in here."

Her eyes brightened. "It is my first time as well." She shined her headlamp on me. "Three days ago, I had a dream."

My heart fluttered. "You did? What was it about?"

"A light came from the heavens and told me to come here to help people. I'm a nurse. I have helped in disaster areas before." Her rhythmic accent had me hanging on her every word.

"Does that mean there is going to be an accident here?" I said.

"No, my friend. I will get answers here on how I can cure more people, not just in my home country of Nigeria but across the world." She cupped her hands together and looked down. "It is difficult to be a nurse and watch people get worse because we don't have the means to help them. Every year we take a small step forwards, but it's not enough. I am blessed to have this opportunity."

I whispered, "How will you know when we're in the right place?"

She let out a nervous laugh. "I hope I will recognize it when I see it."

"Then it's all true? We are meant to be here together?" I said in a breathy voice.

The Nigerian's bobbed her head excitedly. "Oh yes. I know it to be so."

"Unbelievable." I turned to shimmy through another narrow part of the cave. "Wait until I tell Aunt Judy," I whispered to myself.

As the dreamer came through the passageway, I reached out and touched her shoulder. "It's lovely to meet you. I, too, was told to come here to help people. I'm Victoria—I am a neuroscientist."

"My name is Zoputa Òrédola, but please call me Zoa. It is a real pleasure. What did . . ."

François stopped abruptly and extended his arms. A minor pile-up ensued.

"What's going on?" someone asked.

The Frenchman made a megaphone with his hands. "Everyone wait here. I am going down a level to check that it is safe, oui?"

A man from the back shouted, "I will go in with you."

To my great surprise, I recognized the voice. It was Marcus. He pushed his way through the tightly packed group. We exchanged looks as he passed. When had he joined us?

François and Marcus helped each other down into a dark opening and disappeared.

Eager to find out more about Zoa's dream, I turned to her. "Did you know you were going into a cave when you came to Norway?"

"Yes, the dream showed me dropping into darkness for 121 days"—she raised her arms high—"only to rise into enlightenment." She knew about the 121 days, too.

"It sounds like a powerful dream," I said.

She leaned in. "Please tell me about . . ."

The chatter around us drowned out her voice. "Sorry, what did you say?"

She spoke into my ear. "Please tell me about your dream, Victoria."

"Actually, I . . ."

A tall woman in a white caving suit and a pair of red wellies pushed us to the side, moving closer to the opening.

"Hi everyone, I'm Constance. How long are we going to wait? They could need our help." She was from England, too, but older than me. Her confidence and no-nonsense attitude reminded me of a head teacher.

Ana said, "I agree." She lay down and shouted into the opening. "Hello . . . François . . . are you okay?" She took off her headlamp and pointed it down into the hole. "I can't see a thing." Rattling her light, she pointed it straight into her eyes. Judging by her rapid blinking, nothing was wrong with the lamp.

When no answer came from the hole, Constance asserted herself once more. "I'm going in."

"We will all go," said a man from behind me. Sounds of assent echoed throughout the cave.

I wasn't so sure. It didn't seem wise for the amateurs to go looking for two experienced cavers.

Constance and Ana worked together to secure a grappling hook and rope. A few minutes after they had belayed down, they shouted for us to follow.

One by one, we descended into darkness, just as Zoa had dreamed.

Constance stood waiting for us with her hands on her hips. "Right, now we need to . . ."

The roar of tumbling rocks echoed throughout the cave. Some people grabbed each other, and others curled into balls on the ground. Three had just belayed down and bolted away as rocks filled the void.

The entryway was sealed shut.

I turned to Zoa. "Maybe people have been injured and that's why you are here."

"I pray not," she said, shining her headlamp at people.

Our self-appointed leader recovered within seconds from her brace position on the ground. "Okay, no one panic. We will find the guide and the other guy . . ."

"Their names are François and Marcus, and those crashing rocks"—Ana sniffled—"could have hurt them . . . wherever they are."

Constance looked blankly at her, as if she didn't understand Ana's emotions. "Yes, them. They aren't the only ones in trouble. We can't leave the way we came in. We'll need to find another way out." She looked down and appeared to shift into a different mode. "First, we need to conserve our light. Everyone, turn off your headlamp, except one person in front and one in the back. Second, we need to continue forwards quietly and carefully. We don't want to disturb the cave again."

The take-charge woman was thinking ahead. Maybe she was a crisis manager, not a head teacher.

We walked for over ten minutes before we heard voices and came upon a sunken expanse. Five other explorers were inspecting a wall of rocks at the other side.

Ana shouted, "Have you seen two guys go through here?"

A tall figure dressed in a fluorescent green jumpsuit waved us over to him. "They're trapped on the other side of these rocks. Help us clear the way."

"Have they said anything to you?" I asked.

The glow-in-the dark man shook his head. "We haven't heard anything in a while. They could've gone further into the cave."

"Oh my god, what if they're hurt or worse." The Chilean dropped to the ground with labored breathing.

Ana was acting out for both of us. I was used to solitude in a quiet research room. Here, I was on the verge of entering shutdown mode due to the crowded, confined space. To keep going I used my brain to control my perceptions and stress levels. I dropped in and out of a lower brainwave state without anyone knowing. Years of brain training had its benefits.

The nurse didn't waste a minute. She rushed over to Ana's side and tended to her first patient of the day.

Twenty-minutes later, the group had made an opening in the rock wall, big enough for a thin person with narrow shoulders to crawl through.

"I can go in and look for them," I said. Going in would achieve two things: first, it would allow me to help the two cavers; second, I would get some alone time to see what lay ahead.

The group looked me up and down. "Sure," said one of the cavers as she handed me a first-aid kit. "Shout back to us at regular intervals." She lifted her goggles. "If you don't see them after five minutes of walking, turn around and come back."

I nodded, set an alarm on my CDi, then shimmied through the newly made portal.

Once on the other side, I wondered if I hadn't taken on too much. The darkness and solitude scared me. Perhaps I was claustrophobic.

With no sign of Marcus and François, I progressed slowly. "H-e-l-l-o, Marcus? François?"

My voice echoed.

I struggled through a second narrow opening that led to two separate offshoots. The five-minute alarm went off. I'd forgotten to shout back to the others. It was time to turn around. Experienced or not, the two cavers were lost or trapped and needed help. "Hello." I sighed at the thought of abandoning them. I took a deep breath and shouted a bit longer and louder. "Can anyone hear me? François? Marcus?"

I turned to head back.

"Hallo," said Marcus.

"Yes, it's me, Victoria. Are you alright?

François said, "Follow the sound of my voice. We're in here."

After a couple minutes, I reached them.

"Bien. Well done," said François as he put his arm around me and guided me further in.

"Where are the others?" asked Marcus.

"There was an avalanche of sorts, or whatever you call it in a cave. Part of the cave collapsed. They were able to make an opening for me and . . ." I took in my surroundings. "What is this place?"

"Oui, we heard falling rocks, but decided to explore where we were before going back."

The cave walls shimmered, and not because they were dripping with water. It looked like cut diamonds protruding out. I skimmed my hand down a large segment. It was smooth, not sharp. Immediately, I felt a slight electrical charge and snapped my hand back. "What is this? It has a low static-like charge."

"Oui, we felt the same and . . ."

"Victoria, come have a look at this," said Marcus from another area out of my sight.

Two large symbols were etched into the base of the cave. I knelt to have a closer look.

"What are you really doing here?" asked my former wander-lust companion.

His directness caught me off guard. "What do you mean?"

Marcus softly said, "You're not here to hike or see caves, are you?"

I stood up and looked him in the eyes. The abrupt hiker from the morning had a softness about him now. "That's right."

"Did you have a dream too?" he asked.

Not wanting to isolate myself from the start, I said, "Yes, I saw the name of the cave and faintly remember something special about it. I felt compelled to come here."

The German pursed his lips and looked down. "Uhh . . . look, sorry about earlier. I was an asshole. I wanted to check out the cave alone because I, also, had a dream."

I smiled and nodded. "I understand. No worries. But yes, you were a bit of a jerk."

Marcus looked towards François, who was about to join us. "Do you think he had a dream too?"

With a slight smirk, I said, "Yes, I do. We should tell him what we know."

As François crossed the threshold, a loud beeping came from his pocket. He produced his compass device and declared, "We have arrived."

"How do you know?" I asked.

"My dream showed coordinates that I programmed into my compass." After a few minutes of honesty, the three of us agreed to go get the others.

François led the way. Halfway back, we heard more voices.

I said, "Those could be from our group. Maybe more managed to get through the opening."

As we caught sight of a headlamp light in front of us, someone in a white coverall came smacking into François.

"Thank God." Ana embraced the Frenchman. "We thought something happened to you when the rocks fell."

François returned the hug. "Oui, it's not good." He looked at the queue of people behind her. "Everyone okay?"

Constance answered, "We barely made it through the wall of stones. The rocks shifted again and came crashing down onto Pino's leg as he was coming through the opening." She pointed to a tall figure towards the back. "He has some cuts and bruises but nothing serious."

Zoa squeezed past a couple people to get closer to me. "Did you find anything?"

François overheard and announced to everyone. "Oui, we will need to dig ourselves out of the cave later. But for now, follow us; there's something you need to see."

Zoa grabbed my arm in excitement. "Oh, this is good news."

"Wait until you see this place. It's very interesting, indeed," I said.

With everyone together in the newly discovered area, each touched the sparkling walls and felt the tingling charge.

One tall caver said, "Cool! This is probably a precious mineral lining the walls . . . probably worth a fortune." He rubbed the walls like he was conjuring up a genie from a bottle. Clearly, he was more interested in profiting from the cave than understanding a possible dream.

"François, you're an experienced caver. Have you seen walls like these before?" Constance asked.

He shook his head. "No."

"It's getting hot in here," Marcus said as he removed his caving suit and helmet, signaling that we should all do the same. "There's more." He motioned to us to follow him into the sunken area.

"Wow." A woman with flaming red hair looked over the deep symbols. "They look like the illicium verum." I detected an Irish accent.

The expressions on our faces must have shown her we were none the wiser.

She elaborated, "They are like the star anise. Mos' people know it as a Christmas-time spice, and they're used in holiday decorations."

"Oh, that one," Ana said.

François shook his head. "They're not anise stars. We don't know what they are, so don't get too close."

"I know what these are," said an Italian man in his mid-sixties. All eyes were on him now that he'd contradicted our trusted guide. Seeing his torn trousers made me realize this was Pino, the man who nearly got trapped. He held his right leg and knelt by a symbol. "If we are all here for the same reason, then we need to lie down . . ."

His words faded out as I looked at my fellow cavers differently. They had all had dreams directing them here. And importantly, all left their homes, waved goodbye to their families, and took extended leaves of absence. Who were these people?

"How do you know what to do?" asked Constance.

"I saw these in a dream. We need to get into them." Pino touched the center of one symbol and started a chain reaction. The two symbols sank down and gave off a slight glow. One by one each part of the starlike symbol opened and revealed vessels big enough to hold one person in each.

"Fourteen pods for fourteen of us," said Constance.

I counted the people in the cave. She was right. Was that enough people to save Earth? Unless there were groups in other parts of the cave, we were it. Things had gone from foolish to unbelievable, and then unfathomable. What would Aunt Judy think of this?

The profit seeker said, "Man, this is some crazy alien tech." He was from the States, but I couldn't tell which one he was from. I was never very good at matching the correct state to the accent.

Five people huddled together and discussed whether it was safe before stepping closer to the pods.

"Who's going first?" asked the wild-haired American. Then he took a couple steps back and returned to examining his fortune in the walls.

"What if they're poisonous?" asked Marcus.

The Irish woman nodded. "Those things could be like Venus flytraps waitin' for their next meal, ya know."

Ana said, "Let one person go first and lie there for ten minutes."

"No, no, no. In my dream, we all have to lie down, but first we must remove our jewelry and CDis," Pino said.

"What!" said Ana. "I have to remove my cross?"

"Si, it is the only way. But again, Signorina, these are only bits I can remember."

After a few disgruntled sounds, we placed all our jewelry and devices into Ana's helmet. She stashed it between two stones in the far wall.

Pino entered a vessel first. Zoa, Constance, a young man, and another woman simultaneously stepped into their vessels and lay down.

The young man's body spasmed, and he screamed, "Mamma . . . this is the end."

Zoa leapt up and rushed to his rescue as I held my breath.

He laughed and patted her arm. "I'm okay, just making fun."

Pino frowned and shook his head like a parent ready to dole out punishment. "Okay, bambino, what's your name?"

"Peter." The kid blushed.

"You are a joker, Peter, but now isn't the time. Si?"

The chastised kid nodded and relaxed back into his pod.

Seeing how the first few hadn't succumbed to any ill fate, everyone else took their positions—except for Marcus and me.

"I think someone should stay out to make sure nothing happens to everyone—and look for a way out of the cave," Marcus said sheepishly.

"Really? We can't leave you here on your own. Besides, there are fourteen places."

"Come on!" François said. "You two need to get in."

Someone shouted, "They're actually comfortable."

In a nonjudgmental voice, I said, "What are you doing here if you're not going to join us?"

"I'm not getting into one of those. This was a bad idea." He walked away.

I stood dumbfounded. What would happen if one space was unoccupied? Could we go on without him?

"Okay, fine." I pointed to where we had entered. "Be the lookout and find a way out of the cave."

"Uhh . . ." The clammy-handed German slapped his CDi, looking towards the back and then at the group. "I . . ."

"Come on, Marcus." François waved his arm.

I left him to his contemplations. As I stepped into an open pod, I realized the session was real. I felt vindicated but terrified because it meant all life on Earth was in danger.

Seconds later, noxious, medicinal-smelling fumes emanated from the pods and burned my nasal passages and sinuses. In a flash, a greenish-blue membrane with grotesque, oozing nodules covered me from top to bottom. I thought of home and Aunt Judy before falling into a deep level of unconsciousness. Our journey began, but where would we be when we woke up?

CHAPTER 5

EARTH COMPLEX

Ambar

In those first semiconscious moments, I bathed in euphoria. The gentle pressure across my entire body comforted me. But as my awareness increased, so did claustrophobia. I opened my eyes as goo seeped down them, blurring my vision. My brain and senses all fought to get back online. I was upright and bound by a thick, gelatinous membrane that had become an intrinsic part of me. Or was *I* part of *it*? I repeatedly blinked to clear my eyes and catch a glimpse of my surroundings. With one eye clear, I saw the inside of my glowing green encasement. Not much of a view. A failed attempt to wriggle out of bondage caused my heart to leap from a resting state to a frenzied patter. My nostrils flared as they struggled to keep up with my exaggerated breathing, which had me hovering on the edge of a panic attack.

"You have arrived safely and will be released in five seconds," said Aunt Judy from inside my head. Hearing her voice added to my confusion. Was I at home?

I felt a loosening; the layers retracted from across my mouth. I spat out alien spew. Then the eye covers disappeared.

I could see the glowing membranes from other pods against a stark black background.

"Ready," said someone on my right, before spilling out onto the floor like a jellyfish. It was Constance. Ten seconds later, her pod imploded, transforming into a sphere no bigger than a yoga ball. I watched as she peeked out from under a thin layer of membrane.

"Ready . . . ready . . . ready," each person said, signaling their pod to release them. No one tried to remove the last layer; we intuitively knew it was required for now.

"Ready," I attempted to say, but nothing came out.

It was enough, though—the pod retracted the gelatinous support system. My body felt like it had been bound for three hundred years and would never move again, although truth be told, I'd never been exceptionally agile. I visualized my fellow travelers carrying me off like a wooden plank.

With the bulk of the membranes retracted, I recalled instructions on exiting with caution to lessen detachment sickness. How could I *recall* something I didn't know?

Just one step—that was the plan. My joints snapped and creaked as I moved forwards. I felt wretched, akin to being frozen, seasick, and recovering from anesthetic all at once. I wanted to reverse and be cocooned for a few minutes more. But the option disappeared right before my eyes when my pod became a sphere. I was officially detached.

The two people on my left each got a limb halfway out, changed their minds, and retreated to safety. Most, upon detaching from the pods, contorted their bodies and spewed fluid onto the floor in colors I'd never seen before. The sight and stench made me sympathetically nauseous. I covered my nose and focused on my rebirthing.

After regaining control, we assembled twenty feet from the pods. Standing together in our membrane layers, we resembled aliens. Undoubtedly, the ingested substances had also changed us on the inside.

"How is everyone?" asked Zoa. Once a nurse, always a nurse.

"Kinda sick," said Ana, holding her stomach.

Pino held his head and stomach as well. "Si."

"Look." Constance pointed to a distant, dimly lit circle. "That's where we need to go—it's an entryway. Although I'm not sure how I know that."

Peter sped in front of us. "I know too."

It was knowledge we shouldn't have possessed, yet we all did.

When we walked across the threshold, though, something made us stop. Some got dizzy and grabbed on to each other. I closed my eyes to focus on the feeling. It was like I'd had three shots of caffeine but without the shakes.

"Wow! Cool." The formerly reluctant but now exuberant wild-haired chap spun around, holding his head. "What a trip."

"I can see this whole place in my head," said Peter.

Catalogs of information, embedded in our brains during our travels, had become accessible.

We were in our new home—the Earth Complex, on a planet named Ambar. There was also a tidbit about "enhanced organic matter" that we had ingested to help us interface with the planet's technology.

"I can't see." Ana rubbed her eyes.

Zoa held the Brazilian's arm. "Give it a few seconds. I had the same thing."

Moments later, the area where we were standing illuminated. A segment of floor ten feet ahead of us lit up; without having to move a foot, we were suddenly there. Like dominoes, the chain continued. Between coming out of a deep unconsciousness, information downloads, moving floors, and no visual reference points, I was completely disoriented.

Meanwhile, Peter didn't seem to need a transition period. He bounced over to a short, stout man, and in slow, schoolboy English, the bubbly one said, "Hallo, I am Peter. How are you doing?"

He spoke with an English accent, with help from our internal translator. We had received information on the technology in the form of one sentence: *All verbal interactions will be translated to known languages of the listener.*

The man didn't respond.

The kid tried again. "Isn't this exciting? What's your name?"

In a deep voice, the man replied, "Wu Li. I need a few minutes." He turned away, shook his head, and rubbed his eyes.

"Where are you from?" asked Peter.

"Chongqing, in China." Li turned away again.

Seeing me watching, Peter changed his target. "Hi! I'm Peter."

I smirked at him. "Yes, I remember your prank in Norway. I'm Victoria. Are you okay?"

"Okay? It's like a Porsche 911 Carrera, a BMW M3, and a Koenigsegg Agera S pulling into my uncle's garage at the same time." He was a young petrolhead, as we said at home.

"Sorry, I'm not familiar with all of those. Koenig . . . what?"

He gave me an incredulous stare. "Uhh . . . They are three of my favorite high-performance cars. I'm a mechanic."

I smiled at how he related being on another planet to cars. "Right. So you're doing well, then."

"This was worth taking four months off from my uncle's workshop."

Although everyone seemed bewildered, Peter was personable, energetic, and friendly, albeit a bit too exuberant. He was like a puppy getting overly excited every time he sees you, even when the last time was three minutes ago. His big, brown eyes, mouth half-opened as if waiting for a treat, bouncy walk, and fluffy, light-brown hair accentuated his personality.

Out of nowhere, an announcement came through to us, but not audibly.

Peter's eyes widened. "Did you hear that?"

"Yes, I think everyone did." I glanced at the faces around us for signs.

The hosts instructed us, in our minds, to continue to the Delta Center's Inner 1. The Ambarans named locations to be easier for us to understand. "Delta" referred to the fact that the Center was changeable depending on our needs. Intriguing.

Our segment of floor stopped, dropped its protective outer layer, and revealed the outside world to us.

We stood there, mouths agape. The Delta Center was enormous and unlike any structure I'd seen before. There were multiple layers of bubble-like forms, and small bulges on top of large ones, creating a cohesive construction suspended in midair. The only problem was getting over to it.

Ana closed one eye and held out her thumb to determine how far away we were from our destination. "Did we miss . . . Oh, right."

She started walking with everyone else before she finished her question. One person, however, did not seem to know what was going on—me. No information was forthcoming.

Zoa noticed my hesitation. "You need to keep walking. With each step, you travel a great distance. And as you can see, there's a walkway." She snickered. "Or not . . . our eyes can't see light at that end of the spectrum."

Warily, I said, "So there is a walkway. We can't see it, but with each step we walk a long way?"

"Yes, I can show you if you'd like." Without taking another glance at me, she darted across thin air. Unprepared, I took the leap of faith and followed her lead. It was both scary and exhilarating.

We joined the others inside the Center, standing in a small but equally magnificent portion of the mammoth structure. Its bubbly walls shimmered in the colors of a rainbow, and the floor resembled the middle of a galaxy. But what surprised me most was how the strange environment comforted me. It was like the feeling I got when Aunt Judy and I would relax in front of the fireplace.

We intuitively positioned ourselves in a circular formation. In the next instant, two beings appeared in the middle.

Zoa said, "They have always been here but outside our visible spectrum."

It reminded me of an Earth-based phenomenon called blindsight, where legally blind individuals would avoid obstacles. The individuals didn't know how they knew something was in front of them. Experiments suggested that these people could see in other ways. However, here on Ambar, it was more than blindsight at work. We were changing our behaviors without consciously knowing it thanks to implanted foreign data.

The beings were neither female nor male, and maybe not human. Unless humans here varied more than on Earth. Whatever species they were, their dark opalescent skin reminded me of a small gemstone Aunt Judy wore on occasion. The individuals had beautiful blotches of blue, pink, purple, yellow, and red against a shiny, dark-blue background. Although eye-catching, their patterned skin made it difficult to discern their features. They wore no clothing of any kind.

"Welcome to Ambar." They gazed up momentarily at an immense 3D version of their planet. "You have been transported to our planet located three interversal separations away from Earth."

The scene was surreal. We should have been exuberant, in awe, and giggling like school kids. We were in a different universe. This wasn't hypothetical or just data. It was real. Would we have a delayed reaction or had the Ambarans neuroengineered that out of us?

"The multiverse theory is true." Ana said what I was only thinking.

"As your hosts, we, the Earth Complex Conduits, will assist you during your stay. This partnership between Earth and Ambar is an unequaled opportunity for us to learn from each other. Although you may see yourselves as different from each other, to us you are one. You are all representatives of Earth. Through unity you have a chance to reach your group's main objective."

"Main objective?" asked Constance.

My eyes popped open. The others didn't know why we were here?

"In fewer than 302 complete Earth days, your planet will experience a chain of events that will devastate it. All but a small percentage of organisms will cease to exist. You—" the host motioned to us with open palms—"are Earth's only chance of stopping the impending carnage."

The group's response was predictable, to me, at least.

A group of five shouted at the Conduits. Through the emotional outbursts I heard, "How can you know this?" and "Send us back to our families."

Some, including Constance and the red-headed woman, froze in place while François and others ran off.

After a few minutes, they all returned, as if in a deep meditative state.

The Conduit said, "The module instructors will teach you skills and impart knowledge to assist you back on Earth. Each of you has been given a primary goal. This will come to the forefront of your consciousness after one rest period."

Constance raised her hand. "This means we'll be away for 121 days, including travel time. That seems a bit short to gain skills and knowledge to prevent Earth's demise."

The reaction from the team and myself—or lack of reaction—was akin to the detachment of a passive movie watcher. It was eerie considering the stakes. I understood the words but couldn't attach emotion to them.

"We will be assisting you in acquiring what is needed."

"How long did it take to get here?" she asked.

She was thinking about calculations when we were standing in an alien structure in another universe, and she had just been told that Earth's demise was near.

"Travel time was six days."

Constance puckered her lips and nodded as if satisfied with the answer.

If the hosts had mouths, I didn't see them move. They stood like statues, with the exception of a small movement here and there. It was an odd sensation to watch and "hear" the Conduits. My ears registered actual external stimuli or sounds. From a psychological perspective, the mismatch of internal to external stimuli could have driven a person mad. For me, nausea was the side effect of the conflicting signals.

"Board the transport discs, shown in the highlighted area on your map, to go to your residences. Using your internal mapping function, you can navigate throughout the Complex. All terms and places have been named for your understanding."

I took a deep breath and noticed that although we were still in our rather smelly placenta layers, the Complex's air neutralized the odors.

"Once in your residence, prepare an introductory message to your fellow travelers for viewing in the Rejuvenation Hub. We use neural communications. However, you will continue to speak to each other and all other beings verbally. Your residence monitor will notify you when to reconvene. After your first rest, the lighting in the Earth Complex will be set to 88 percent illumination as part of the circadian reset. Questions can be addressed by your monitor."

I waited for them to disappear by fading out of our visual capabilities, but they stood there, probably long after we were gone.

Using the map in our minds, we set off to find the accommodations.

"It's a bit weird, yeah?" a familiar voice whispered in my ear.

"Hi, Peter. Sorry, what's weird?"

"The way they communicate right into our heads." He put his pointer and middle fingers together and tapped his temples. "And why are they called Conduits?"

I laughed to hide my nervousness. "Yes, their way of communicating will take time to get used to. The names of things and people may conform to our naming conventions, but I agree with you. Conduits is an interesting term for beings."

"Funny how I know when it's a message from outside and not my own thoughts. How do they do that?" Peter asked through the escalating noise as we made our way out.

Not wanting to shout to be heard, I answered by shrugging my shoulders.

We shuffled through a passageway that emptied into a car park of sorts for transport discs. The area was lit up by almost fifty bright green glows emanating from the discs recessed in the floor. Fortunately, maps weren't the only things we could see in our minds. My disc flashed before me like car hazard lights. It was three down and one across.

I boarded with Constance and the wild-haired chap. We stood staring at each other, or trying not to, like we would in a lift on Earth. Unlike an elevator, the disc lacked any visible buttons or controls.

Suddenly, waist-high supports came up and secured us right where we stood, and a pulsating shield enclosed the disc.

I slowly put my hand up to it and saw my fingertips meld into the surface layer. My fingers wouldn't go farther in. *I could lose my fingertips.*

I jerked my hand away from the strange barrier, gave a nervous grin to my fellow passengers, and clasped my hands together while I checked for any missing digits.

The next second, the disc took off.

"I feel like I'm sinking." Constance tried to lift her feet.

"It's just a change in local gravity making us heavier," said our male companion, as if he'd been living on Ambar for years.

"I know." Constance glanced down, then stared at him. "I remember you. You were the one who didn't dare lie down in the cave until someone else did." She smirked and turned away.

How to win friends and influence people. I went for a friendlier approach.

"Hello, I'm Victoria Ottery."

His eyes zigzagged across me as he nodded. "Allan Feynman from Utah. Where in England are you from?"

"London."

We both looked over to Constance, who took her cue.

"Constance Smith, originally from Cambridge, but I've been working in Singapore for the last five years." The take-charge lady perused us calmly.

"Cool," said Allan before we shifted our attention to our surroundings.

We swished out of the Center in a procession and sped through the Earth Complex in the dark, passing streams of light like those in an overexposed photo. Thin, bright green light trails were other discs; big white streaks were tall structures; all the other colors were a mystery, for now.

Our disc whizzed straight towards one of the large white streaks and came to an abrupt halt.

"Awesome!" said Allan.

Constance and I gasped at what lay ahead. It resembled a massive plant stalk with a dandelion seed head, much like the ones I would find in Aunt Judy's garden.

Without us having to press any buttons or give commands, the disc had taken us to an innovative structure and slid into one of the offshoots. How civilized. By no coincidence, our dandelion offshoot contained three accommodations.

We walked out onto a lit path in silence, without so much as a glance at one another.

I stood where my map indicated the entrance was. With one step forwards, I found myself in a temporary holding area. There was no door or distinct entry to my new abode.

Possible layouts reeled before me at high speed.

"Wow, that one." I pointed to the diagram I liked, but the options didn't stop coming. At least ten more flew by. Most designs showed residences that were as big as whole apartment buildings. I didn't want a massive structure to get lost in. I wanted to be able to see the beginning and end of the place. A cozy place with three research labs. Without having to utter a word, transparent dividers, diagnostic points, research areas, rest chairs, and images all appeared within seconds. Dividers acted as walls, but they weren't permanent or inflexible, and they could change color based on my needs.

"That's perfect." My living quarters became a personalized domain without me making a single conscious choice.

I had taken two steps into the place when a packet of information came forwards into my consciousness. Our health vitals, moods, physical condition, and nutritional needs were monitored via the organic technology in our bodies, and all that data helped to create an environment for maximum comfort. Whether changing light colors, pictures, or temperature, or helping us to recharge, our new homes would be more like extensions of ourselves than separate spaces.

I went farther in, and saw an active 3D image of Aunt Judy, Anne, Malcolm, and Albert. They were all sitting by the fireplace in Aunt Judy's house.

"Funny way to combine memories," I whispered. Inside, I was chomping at the bit to understand how the Ambarans could interpret and parse out the memories they wanted.

Although in unfamiliar surroundings, I was profoundly content. Was it the group, the Earth Complex, Ambar, or something else that brought on my blissful state?

From the map in my mind, I saw options for small spaces to morph into larger ones. The purpose of most areas was apparent by their labels, such as "Nutrition Point" and "Lab." However, others had letter and number designations not easily deciphered.

My curiosity led me to "*ECHRC2D*". In the blink of an eye, I was in a laboratory with five silos radiating a bright blue light. As I stood directly in front of one of them, the light flickered and revealed an underdeveloped being. A horizontal light beam scanned it from top to bottom. Another flicker, and more features appeared. I was right there with them, not observing a scene from afar. A chill ran down my spine before everything vanished.

"What the hell was that?"

I needed to return, but "*ECHRC2D*," was no longer an option. The lingering image unsettled me. With no familiar reference points, I was hard pressed to understand what I'd seen. It was as if they were 3D printing adult humanoids.

A minute later, a voice said, "Hello, Victoria, I am your residence monitor. You can change your outerwear using the device indicated on your internal map."

I walked towards the back, where a lit-up compartment had just opened. I pulled out a silver rectangle the size of my hand; it resembled a piece of old armor. The monitor picked up on my apprehension.

"Remove the pod membrane, then place the outfit generator over your collarbone—it will do the rest."

"Thank you, but . . . uhh . . . it's too small."

"The generator is expandable and adaptable."

Wanting to prove my point, I removed my suit. To my surprise, my Earth clothes were gone; not a trace remained. The membrane had consumed them. Scary. I retrieved the outfit generator—it was like taking a genie out of a bottle. It immediately attached itself to me and expanded.

I let out a screech. "What's happening!"

Within a second, the armor had stretched over my collarbone and spread down my body. When I thought the makeover was done, the base widened and created a second layer. Moments later, the original collarbone piece split in two over my shoulders. There was no time to react or complain; within three seconds, I was dressed. It looked like one of my usual work outfits but felt like silk.

"Remain still, face the small, hovering sphere, and deliver your message," said the monitor.

In the corner of my eye, I caught sight of a ball hurling through the air towards me. Naturally, I ducked and covered my head with my arms. "What the . . ."

After a few moments, when I hadn't heard a crash or been hit, I peeked between my arms. The ball hovered above me. I stood up and started my message as if nothing unusual had happened.

"Hello, I'm Victoria Ottery. I want you to know it's okay to be scared and overwhelmed." Saying the words caused my stomach to twist because I was understating the obvious. "We are far from home with an enormous challenge ahead. But the Ambarans have agreed to help us save Earth, so this is the best place for us to be right now. I hope, along the way, we will also create friendships and build a strong team. Good luck to everyone." I hoped I had struck the right tone between stoicism and motivation. Of course, I also secretly wanted to belong and gain the group's acceptance.

The monitor said, "Meet your group on Inner 1 in the Delta Center."

I returned to where I'd entered my place but found no traces of an opening.

"Excuse me," I called out. "Where's the door? How do I get out?"

The monitor answered, "Victoria, walk towards and through the image of the forest to leave your residence."

I nudged closer to the forest and threw a punch with my right arm.

"Bother!" I held my aching wrist. "I can't walk through walls."

"Position yourself closer to the forest image and move your entire body into it."

"My whole body, all at once, into the forest?"

"Correct."

"But where's the door? Why don't we have this kind of basic information implanted in our minds considering how the residence and Earth Complex schematics are in our heads?"

"Wherever you walk into the forest, an opening will be created. Not all information has been downloaded to you because Earth-human brains need diverse tactile, visual, aural, and kinesthetic experiences to acquire and integrate knowledge."

"Yes, yes. I know. I just thought . . . never mind."

Images of me speeding up, colliding with the wall, and knocking myself out made me pause for another minute. "Okay, go through the forest, through the wall, through the forest . . ." I repeated it to myself. Then I closed my eyes, hopped forwards, and ended up on the other side, safe and sound.

I got to the disc, where Constance and Allan stood waiting. Happy to see my neighbors, I said, "Hello again. What do you think of your accommodations?"

"It's so cool . . . exactly what a super AI apartment should be. When we get back with these technologies, I'm going to be beyond wealthy." Allan rubbed his hands together. All traces of reluctance seemed to have vanished in him.

Constance shook her head. "There's no such thing as 'beyond wealthy.'" Her pinstriped, dark navy suit and crisp white shirt with a collar that looked starched to perfection matched her stiff and strict personality.

Allan sneered at her. "How can we tell this thing where we want to go?" He surveyed the disc. "What if I want to go someplace other than where the Ambarans want me to go?"

I shrugged. "Don't know, but for now, we should just go wherever it's programmed for."

When the disc decided we were ready to go, the safety barrier came up, and we zipped off. Constance, startled by the movement, grabbed my arm. My grimace should have been enough to communicate my displeasure, but she held on to me like I was a supporting pole on the London Tube.

As I opened my mouth to ask her to unclench me, she released her grip and turned away without an utterance or change of expression. Curious.

"They seem to have all the logistics worked out," I said in such a soft voice I didn't think anyone heard.

Allan said, "I may need to go somewhere off their schedule. The interface between us and their technology is seamless in the apartments, so we must be able to control the discs as well."

As he spoke, I did my five-second profiling of him. Tall, thin chap, smart-casual clothes, black hair darting off in every direction. Probably in his mid-to-late thirties. Self-appointed expert on everything, including Ambar. Genius or wannabe? To be determined.

Although the Earth Complex was drenched in bright light, the safety barrier blocked out everything. My fellow travelers were the default view.

Suddenly, an alert came through requesting that I stay on the transport disc and return to the pods. The message was so loud and clear in my mind that my eyes inadvertently popped wide. Allan glanced at me and mimicked me by widening his eyes.

What on Earth was he doing? Remembering that we were no longer on Earth or in our universe, I rephrased my thoughts. What on Ambar was he doing? I doubted he was getting an alert, too. Perplexed and unable to break his gaze, a half-suppressed laugh escaped me. What started as a small giggle grew and grew, despite my efforts to stifle it. The more I tried, the more robust it became, until I gave in to full-on laughter. The last time I'd done that was at a funeral. Seeing Aunt Judy's best friend lying in a coffin hadn't been fun or funny. This time, it was an involuntary response to travelling to another planet and needing to prevent a planetary disaster.

"Sorry, sorry," I said as they both gawked at me like I was losing my mind.

When the disc stopped, Constance disembarked, and Allan motioned with his arm for me to go before him.

"I'm staying on. I need to go somewhere else."

"But you can't." His dissension was absolute.

Scowling, I said, "I received a message. It's fine."

He glared at me as if he were the voice of authority. "What did the message say?"

"Look, let me follow through with it, and I'll tell you everything when I return."

"Man, it's not right. " He stomped off.

○   ○   ○

Two Conduits stood on opposite sides of a horizontal pod while a human-looking man examined a device at the head of it. He was pale, brown-haired, thin, and expressionless. He could have passed for one of us, except he was tinkering with strange devices and wore a gown that changed colors as he moved.

As I approached, to my surprise, the man met me halfway.

"Hello, Victoria Ottery." He spoke out loud to me. "Marcus Steibel remains in his transport state. We have been working on him since your arrival to the Earth Complex."

"What? Marcus? I thought he stayed behind?" A thick blue energy field hid my hiking companion from me.

"He entered his pod late."

"Oh . . . He'll wake up, won't he?"

The Conduit on the right moved its arms over the pod.

"We are continuing to work through his levels of consciousness," the man said, "to locate him and guide him here. There has been no need to treat him physically. His body is functioning well."

"What can I do?" It was both a question and a statement.

"We wanted to make you aware of his status. If his condition worsens, we will ask you to connect with him in a lower brainwave state."

Having never done such a thing, I didn't know it was possible, but he did.

The man worked on Marcus through the energy field. "I am attaching bioregulators to keep his brain and body synchronized." He glanced at the Conduit. "It is as we suspected."

"What is as you suspected?" I asked.

"Your presence is bringing his consciousness closer to the surface."

Surprised by the change, I said, "Can I see him?"

The energy field became transparent. His cheeks shone bright red like on the first day I met him. Marcus was alive and well on the outside.

"Why would he respond so quickly to my voice?"

"It is not your voice bringing him closer. It is your mind," the Conduit said directly to my brain. "Your brainwaves quickly entrain to his and act as a beacon for him to follow."

I hadn't done any research on entrainment. It was certainly worth looking into.

After checking his patient again, the man said, "We expect him to join the group shortly. You can continue to Inner 1. All will be informed of his condition, and we will update you with any changes."

"Thank you." I gazed at the individuals to whom I was entrusting Marcus's life. I didn't sense danger, but would my senses work the same here as at home. "Can you tell me why this happened to him?"

The man said, "We do not have a definitive answer. Marcus may help us understand better once he awakens and tells us about his experience."

"I see." I searched for signs that he was suppressing information or underplaying the facts. He spoke like an experienced ER surgeon who, jaded by years of seeing too much, reveals nothing in his face. This made it difficult for me to read him.

He escorted me back to the transport disc without another word. Although he resembled an Earth human, he obviously wasn't. I couldn't put my finger on it, but there was something beyond what my eyes saw. Maybe interacting with a different form of human was creating a type of mismatch in my brain. How would a non-Earth human look if they were hiding something?

CHAPTER 6

EXPOSÉ

On my way to join the team in Inner 1, the disc barrier was transparent, allowing me to view the Delta Center's glowing outer shell, which regularly switched patterns, shades, and sizes. The Center was large enough to fit a ten-story office building a thousand times. Yet it was dwarfed by its home, the Earth Complex or EC. Just before I entered, the amorphous structure became camouflaged. Or at least I *hoped* it was hidden, and hadn't relocated or something else beyond my comprehension.

The disc glided into a portal, stopping higher than where Constance, Allan, and I had entered earlier.

Allan welcomed me back with a puzzled look. "We've heard about Marcus. When can the rest of us see him?"

"I don't know. Sorry, it's not my decision to make."

He asked, "Where did you go to see him?"

"I'm not quite sure, but Marcus was being treated in a pod."

A moment later, a Conduit appeared, extended its left arm, and directed our attention to the wall in front of us. "Enjoy Inner 1's

Rejuvenation Hub, and acclimatize to the Earth Complex." The wall vanished, revealing the Rejuvenation Hub, aka Re-Hub, as designated on our internal map.

Most darted into the area like a hungry mob. I hung back, preoccupied with Marcus's condition.

Zoa joined me. "How is Marcus?"

"They say he'll be fine, but it will take a bit of time."

"And how did he look?" She leaned in. "You did see him?"

I nodded. "Yes, he looked perfectly healthy except for the fact that he wasn't awake."

She sighed. "Good. I wonder why he changed his mind and decided to join us?"

"Yes, perhaps something happened that left him no choice, or maybe he couldn't find a way out of the cave."

She mumbled something in Yoruban, and said, "Did they tell you when he would wake up?"

"No, but I got the impression it wouldn't be terribly long."

"I suppose there's nothing we can do but wait." She looked around the Re-Hub.

"Indeed." A pit was forming in my stomach. Should I go back and stay with Marcus? Why wasn't I given the option?

Zoa put her arm on my shoulder. "Come, let's join the others."

The Re-Hub was a grand, vibrant area that gave me the impression I was walking out into space. Stars and galaxies surrounded us, stretching out into infinity. I assumed the images were projections of the real things. A melodic series of unknown sounds played in the background. I couldn't discern a single familiar musical instrument.

Suddenly, the music stopped, and a monotone voice echoed throughout the Re-Hub. "These are the vibrational waves of our universe."

The sounds returned louder than before. Each singular sound had a richness, but together, they created multidimensional music. The vibrations tickled my inner ears.

As engaging as the sights and sounds of the universe were, it wasn't long before they took a backseat. Life-sized images of us appeared—in the oozing, nodular pod suits. The images were like solid replicas of us. Three members and detailed profiles were shown simultaneously for about a minute.

Alongside each replica was a summary of the individual's background. The first to catch my eye was Constance. I learned she was twenty-nine Earth years old, engaged to Fritz, and had an older brother, Grant. Her parents were career diplomats living in Thimphu, in the Kingdom of Bhutan. She was a high-functioning autistic mathematics savant, born in Cambridge but working in Singapore for a global insurance company.

The next round of information sent my brain into a fit as I tried to comprehend why we needed it and how to make it stop. Purple spleens, white tendons, red muscles, and volumes of data lay before us, smorgasbord-style, well beyond what hundreds of tests on Earth would have revealed. Our hosts were demonstrating their artistic flair when it came to representing our body parts in different colors. The last straw was when the images went into 4D-mode, allowing us to inspect their organs as they changed over a lifetime. It was like an anatomy course on steroids. Too much information.

My stomach lurched. In the name of privacy, and to avoid being sick, I turned away and hoped others would do the same. Had anyone agreed to this level of personal disclosure? I, for one, had not given permission. What would be disclosed about me?

"They have no right. That's my life!" exclaimed Constance. The protest confirmed my suspicions; our hosts had not consulted her. She dodged a couple people and stormed out of the Re-Hub. Her reaction to the exposé showed another side of her, no longer in control and unemotional.

With a few determined strides, I positioned myself in front of a Conduit, just outside the Re-Hub. "Excuse me, but why are you displaying extremely personal images and information about us? Did any of us give you permission?"

Our host replied in an instant. "We are helping members get to know each other."

Naturally, there would be differences between multiverse societies. But this one needed to be halted.

"Right. Please stop displaying everything except name, country, interests, and profession next to the person's picture."

"Your requested modification is approved for the Inner 1 Rejuvenation Hub display."

What? No argument and no need to convince them of anything? How refreshing.

Taking the host's reply to mean there would be no further indiscretions, I returned to the Re-Hub, which had a riotous atmosphere as others protested.

I stood off to one side to study the displayed information. Constance was in the next set again, but only the basics were shown. After a few nervous laughs, people relaxed.

One of her details intrigued me as a neuroscientist, namely "autistic savant." I had never met a savant but had read enough to know that half were burdened with physical and mental disabilities as a trade-off for one or two areas of extraordinary ability. Constance was a rarity. With no serious mental or physical disabilities, she seemed to be able to control most manifestations.

In Norway, she'd put herself forwards as a leader. She was confident in her abilities. But could she take direction from others, whether Earthling or Ambaran?

Another thing that struck me was her age—twenty-nine. Her forthrightness and permanently stoic expression aged her, like the face of the farmer's daughter in Grant Wood's "American Gothic" painting.

Allan sauntered up to me. "I don't know why she's so upset. I've got news for her—they know everything about us. They've tapped into our brains and, using neural decoding, can translate our memories, thoughts, fears, likes, and dislikes."

"Do you think so?" I didn't think the Ambarans would find all those details helpful to our plight.

"You betcha!" He nodded. "Anyway, I still don't understand why you were the only one allowed to see Marcus. Is there something you're not telling me?" He looked me squarely in the eyes.

"I'm a cognitive neuroscientist. Maybe they thought I would have some insights on our brains."

He winced like he'd just bitten his tongue. "Hmmm . . . sure."

We hadn't been on Ambar for one day, and already the Ambarans had singled me out from the group. So much for trying to fit in.

It was time to change streams. "What do you do?" I asked.

"I'm an AI entrepreneur. I pull together and sell tech businesses, though I don't need to tell you that." He looked over to the life-sized images. "It will be me on display soon. I also work on projects with AI to translate neural activity into meaningful pictures or statements. We aren't at the Ambarans' level of know-how and technology," he said, tapping the side of his left temple, "but we're getting there." Leaning in but looking away from me, he lowered his voice. "Man, but you know, my biggest customers are the US and Israeli governments. I can't even imagine what they will pay me for the tech here."

He oozed confidence to the point of arrogance as markers of his success rolled off his tongue. I gave Allan a neutral, professional listening face. His work sounded interesting, but it seemed like he expected me to be impressed. Yet, as eager as he was for me to hear his story, his eyes flitted from person to person across the Re-Hub like he was watching a tennis match. With his rate of one glance at me every few sentences, I was sure he would rather have been talking to someone else.

"And you, what exactly does a cognitive neuroscientist do?" His tone implied he knew the answer would disappoint.

"I work in a small team where we verify results from new studies, offer ideas for further research, and help design experiments, all to better understand the neural mechanisms associated with cognition."

"Who pays you to do that?" he said.

It seemed an odd question to ask. Was he insinuating it wasn't a job worth renumeration?"

"We are funded by a university and a pharmaceutical company." Reinforcing his interest in technology, I added, "With the Ambarans more than a few light-years ahead of us in neurotechnology, I have a lot to learn."

He said, "The race to reach ideal brain optimization has helped push things along. One of my customers had twenty employees join the contest alongside their day jobs of mapping consciousness. But that's all over now."

The AI entrepreneur had caught my attention. "All over?"

"A group in London reached full-brain optimization."

"A group in Lon . . ." My brain froze.

The wild-haired man edged closer to me. "Are you okay?"

I took a deep breath. "What group are you talking about?"

"It was in the news the day before we entered the cave." He looked up as if trying to recall the details. "The team was small. But the head of it was that guy . . . uhm, he's well known. You know . . . the Scottish dude. What's his name?"

"Malcolm George?" I said in an airy voice.

"That's right. It was a team of four or five, but only one person reached optimization. So, I guess we won't be the ones getting a boatload of money from the Consortium."

I wanted to reach across the universes and strangle Malcolm. "Yes, I've heard about that research team." My feigned composure impressed even me. It was my turn to look around as if disinterested. It helped to contain my rage.

Allan said, "Seeing how you're the one the Ambarans call on, can you find out how I can get my hands on some of the tech? My primary goal will involve lots of cool stuff, but maybe you can get access to different things." He looked over to Constance as she rejoined the group. "Hey, do you think she'd go to the casinos with me?"

"What?" I looked at him in disbelief.

"She must be a goldmine at the tables." He moved his fingers as if counting money.

"You probably shouldn't ask her about that. It would be insensitive. As far as the technology here, you'll have to ask the hosts yourself and . . ."

"Hey, did you notice the wall-sized picture or entrance in your luxe apartment?" There he was, switching topics again.

"Yes, it was hard to miss." I could barely stay in the conversation as I raged inside at Malcolm's betrayal.

"What was your picture of?" His attention became fixed on someone else in the distance.

"It was a forest," I said.

"Mine was of a mountain scene, like those in Utah where I live." He raised one eyebrow suspiciously, though his answer didn't seem unreasonable. Allan tilted his head forwards and grinned, as if waiting for me to come to some realization. "Well? Don't you see? That's proof they are using information extracted from our brains for *everything*. In this case, to create a personalized atmosphere."

"Okay, well, I find it nice," I said.

"We know they are directing where we go by disc, but what if they control what we think and how we feel?" he said.

"Look, I think you should ask them these questions and try not to draw too many conclusions in the meantime." I sounded irritated because I was. That treacherous Malcolm, former friend and research partner, had broken our agreement.

I turned to discover the college student, Ana. Although she was standing with Peter, she seemed to be more interested in our conversation. "Hello," I said.

"Sorry," she said, locking eyes with Allan. "I kinda overheard what you were saying about the hosts accessing information from our brains."

Peter looked disinterested and dashed over to another young lad.

"So, you were eavesdropping!" He gave her a wry smile. It was obvious that he wasn't the least bothered by her listening in.

She blushed and nervously defended herself. "No, I wasn't . . . Well, maybe kinda, but I only heard a few sentences."

The outfit generator had conjured up the same look for her as when I met her in Norway—torn jeans, white T-shirt, brown jacket, and a big satchel, or at least it looked big hanging from her five-foot-one frame. My guess? She'd graduated within the past two years and hadn't quite got her head around dressing like someone outside an academic bubble.

He took pity on her. "It's cool. I'm Allan Feynman, and you are?"

"Ana Luiza Medina." She pulled her long brown locks forwards. He appeared instantly mesmerized by her as she played with her hair. "My friends call me Ana."

Allan motioned his hand towards me. "This is Victoria—she's a cognitive neuroscientist from England. She's probably analyzing us right now through the proverbial microscope, but she can't be half bad, 'cuz we're both into neuroscience. I don't think she has any experiments lined up here yet, so if you need a shrink, she's available."

She squinted at Allan. "I don't need a shrink." Giving me a nano-second smile, she said, "And we met in Norway before entering the cave."

"Yes, where you told me you were looking for the Holy Grail." I smirked playfully.

"I had the dream then looked up the place and found out about the legend."

"But it wasn't the main reason you were there, right?" I wanted to make sure she hadn't just gotten swept away with the group because of François. Although she seemed to be over him.

"No, but I wasn't about to tell people that I had a dream and needed to learn more about outer space from inside a cave." She giggled and looked at Allan.

Allan patted me on the back. "Hey, don't worry, you won't have to wait long for your first study. With all the pressure on us to save Earth, we'll all crack. Unless . . . the Ambarans control our responses to keep us on track."

"Would *you* like to set up an appointment now, Allan?" I said.

He smiled. "Touché."

"Just to be clear," I said as I looked over to Ana. "I work mostly with data, not people. I'm not a shrink."

Despite his body language, he had been listening to me. I also gave him fair dues on his assessment. I *was* analyzing people—and trying not to let first impressions become final conclusions. He also had me wondering how far the Ambarans would go to ensure we could save Earth. The answers had obvious upsides and downsides.

To take my mind off Malcolm, I engaged the student. "Did you recently graduate from university?"

"No." Her abrupt answer and sneer hinted that I had missed the mark. "I graduated from The Ohio State University in the US seven years ago. Now, I am an astronomer in Chile."

"Oh . . . apologies. You look younger." It was my turn to change the subject. "Allan works in AI, and as you heard, he thinks our hosts have learned a lot about us by tapping into our neural circuitry."

Ana took the cue and moved on by positioning herself closer to Allan.

"It's kinda eerie—my wall picture is of the Large and Small Magellanic Clouds. I mean, they could've put up an infinite number of other space images, but they specifically chose the galaxies I've been studying for the past five years."

Allan nodded with an I-told-you-so smile before telling her a little more about himself.

I gave a toothless smile to the duo and made my way to Constance, who was standing awkwardly in another part of the Re-Hub. "Hi, Constance. Sorry you had to endure that display earlier."

"Yes, now everyone knows a lot more than I would have told them." She gazed through me. "At least there's no social media here."

"True." I nodded.

She looked around the Re-Hub. "I'm starving. I need to find food; it's one of those things the Ambarans want us to search for. The only information I have is to go towards the nebula wall."

"Nebula wall?" I said.

We walked, and Constance talked. "When I was four, I learned that nebulae are clouds of dust and gas in space." She replied like she was reading a script. "The closest one to Earth is the Helix Nebula, at about seven hundred light years away. There are over three thousand nebulae in our galaxy."

I smiled and made a mental note—one of Constance's savant talents was an incredible memory.

Once we were in front of the specified wall, a voice said, "Welcome, Constance and Victoria. Scan your wrists to receive required nourishment." The scanner would assess our current state of health using the ingested technology acquired during our transport.

Constance and I exchanged glances before stepping up to the panel of blue-lit circles and placing our wrists on the spots. In an instant, vials rolled out from narrow slots in the wall just above the wrist scanners.

The hungry Brit turned to me. "A vial?"

Pino arrived and saw the offering. "Che diavolo?" In his beautifully tailored suit with a silk handkerchief peeking out of his jacket's breast pocket, he looked rather overdressed for vials.

Constance closed her eyes and drank it like it was a fine wine. "Brilliant. I feel full." She held the empty tube up with joy in her eyes. "This is going to save me so much time."

"Full? Hmm . . . not in my lifetime." Pino turned on his heels to leave.

I reached out to him. "Do you want to try one together? It's not what we are used to"—I shrugged my shoulders—"but it's our first day and I know the Ambarans want to get us into top condition for the challenges ahead." I heard my own words and took them to heart. Malcolm, neuroscientist traitor, was in another universe. I had other priorities and needed to stay focused.

"No pasta, no fresh tomatoes—what kind of planet is this, and who do they think we are?" He repeatedly patted the right side of his head. "We fourteen have the most important jobs on or off Earth and they are feeding us liquids!"

"I understand. Everything is different. But different is what will help us save Earth."

"Yes," he said in a begrudging tone. "I'll *try* to be patient, thank you. Scusi, what is your name? I didn't watch the displays of us."

"Victoria, and you're Pino. How's your leg?"

"Si, I am Pino d'Orsini." He lifted his right trouser leg. "It's completely healed."

"Lovely to meet you and . . ." My mouth dropped open as I realized who he was. "Are you from the d'Orsini family of designers?"

"Si, you know of us." His eyes lit up.

The gentleman oozed tradition, style, and wisdom. That was why it felt right for me to call him Mr. d'Orsini and not simply Pino. With his deep brown eyes and strong chin framing a nose Michelangelo could have carved, it was clear that elegant designs were not just in his products but in his genes. However, one thing was out of place, or at least it was in his mind—a patch of wavy brown hair above his right ear that required patting down regularly. It was, of course, always in place.

I wondered why *he* had ended up here. Why would he leave his family and business to follow the lure of a dream? Unlike Allan, he didn't strike me as someone looking for the next big thing to make millions or pad his ego. Of course, they'd both just discovered the real purpose of their dreams.

"Mr. d'Orsini"—I held up my green vial—"Get your vial and we'll drink them together. It can't be as bad as wearing those oozing membranes."

He softened his gloomy stance and patted down the hair patch. "Si, but I cannot promise to like it." The gentleman squinted at me.

Pino faced the integrated biometric readers, and two seconds later, a four-inch-deep red vial of personalized nourishment was ejected.

I thought he might back out of the deal, but he smiled and lifted his vial. "*Saluti.* To new friends and strange experiences."

"Cheers, to new friends and strange experiences." I raised mine to his, and we drank the contents. Perhaps he wasn't so fixed in his ways.

"It tastes like watermelon juice," Pino said in an upbeat tone.

I forced a smile. "How lovely for you." With a somber expression, I said, "Mine is a blend of grass and seaweed."

We ate the vials, which softened with the pressure of a bite and tasted much like the drinks themselves.

With our first Re-Hub drink done, Pino and I walk over to a cluster of unusual chairs. Sitting in them was akin to floating in midair.

Intrigued, he rubbed his hands down the sides and back and underneath. "No fabric, no construction material, and no structure, but I can see the chair's form and glow . . . I don't understand."

While he examined the chair, a woman approached me. She looked thirty-something, slightly shorter than me, and had sandy-colored hair.

"Hi Victoria, I'm Sabine." Her smile seemed uneasy. "Marcus's friend."

"Friend? I didn't know he knew anyone else here." I extended my hand. "Nice to meet you."

"Likewise. Marcus and I know of each other through the rock-climbing communities. We only met a couple of days before entering the cave and were supposed to enter together, but I was running late. Have you heard any more about him?"

"No—unfortunately, I haven't."

She looked down to the ground. "The host's message said he got into his pod late. Did they tell you something more?"

"Not really, except that they were confident he'd join us soon. He was sleeping but looked well."

"Ah, okay." She took a step back and crossed her arms as if trying to restrain herself. "Are you going to check on him again?"

"I wasn't going to, but if you'd like me—"

"Why can't I go see him?" Sabine put her hands on her waist.

I shook my head. "I don't know."

She squinted at me as if doubtful. "You don't know why you were allowed to see him and no one else is?"

Pino was watching our exchange with interest. Maybe he was wondering the same thing.

"No. Honestly, I don't know. It may be because I am a neuroscientist. But you can ask a Conduit if you can visit him."

Unhappy with my answers, she shrugged in exasperation and stormed off.

Moments later, Ana and Allan arrived like sharks smelling blood.

"Was that about Marcus?" asked the suspicious AI chap.

"Yes, but I still haven't heard anything more,"—I rolled my eyes—"and I don't know exactly why they selected me to see him."

Ana looked away with puckered lips. "It's kinda strange."

"Wait a minute." I spoke softly. "I'm receiving another alert. Marcus is conscious."

Ana sighed. "Thank God."

"We just got the same message," Allan said before he and Ana sat down with me and Pino.

What a relief! All fourteen of us were alive and well. However, I hadn't been completely transparent. My message requested that I visit Marcus at his place. Another alert would come through when he had arrived. Hopefully, I could get away without anyone noticing or following me.

"Hey, I'm Allan Feynman." He glanced at Pino.

"Nice to meet you. I am Pino d'Orsini."

Allan said, "From your accent, you are from . . . Italy."

"Yes, Milano, and you? Where are you from in America?"

"I live in Utah but was born in New York City. I am a serial AI business entrepreneur. I've started and spun off five businesses that I sold to larger companies for a decent return on investment."

The tech businessman was living up to my first impressions.

"What about you? What do you do?" Allan asked.

"I am one of many designers in my family." He paused and swallowed hard. "I miss them already."

That was my cue. "May I ask what brought you here, Mr. d'Orsini?"

"I was at our holiday home in Positano when I had a long and vivid dream. But I only remembered fragments . . . the name Dollsteinen and those floor symbols in the cave. I woke with a sense of urgency, booked a flight, and met all of you five days later." He looked away longingly. "If anything happens to them before we return, I'll regret it forever." He leaned forwards. "We have to save Earth for future generations, like my beautiful grandchildren."

We all nodded in agreement.

Pino turned to me. "I saw on the display that you are a cognitive neuroscientist. Can you explain how we can have this enormous weight on us but act like it's just another day?"

I clapped my hands together. Someone was talking my language. "You're absolutely right. This is because the Ambarans have done a great job balancing our neurotransmitters and suppressing parts of our brain to help us keep our sanity."

Ana added to the conversation, but I was distracted by another incoming message about Marcus. It was time for me to make my getaway and pay him a visit.

"Excuse me." I got up and walked over to the nebula wall, where three others were standing. With Allan's and Ana's eyes off me, I beelined for the exit.

The transport disc took me to the hiker's place without any input from me.

As I got off the disc, Sabine came running down the gangway.

"Hurry, Marcus isn't well. I don't know what's wrong with him."

Those words scared me. Perhaps he had slipped back into a state of unconsciousness—or worse.

Before I could conjure up more horrific options, Sabine said, "He let me in but started shaking and screaming before telling me to leave. I—I wanted to help, but I was scared."

"Okay. It's going to be fine." I patted her shoulder. "Can you tell if it is physical or psychological?"

She exhaled slowly. "I asked his residence monitor to get help, but it said his vitals and neural activity were all fine, other than having high cortisol and epi . . . epi . . ."

"Epinephrine?" I said.

"That's it. High epinephrine levels. The monitor explained that he was low in an important neurotransmitter for decreasing signals to his nervous system."

"Maybe Gamma-Aminobutyric acid . . . known as GABA. It's used to manage stress, anxiety, and seizures."

Knowing that his monitor could correct imbalances reassured me. Even without a vial, a sedative effect could be triggered using Marcus's neurotransmitters and biochemistry.

Sabine looked at me meekly. "Would you mind if I went to my room? I'm a bit shaken up."

"No worries. I'll see what I can do. Have a good sleep. We can talk tomorrow."

Neural adjuncts were located outside each dwelling. I could use it to talk with Marcus if he didn't invite me in. In an emergency, the monitor could give me entry.

Marcus and I spoke through the adjunct for a few minutes before he granted me access. I entered and found the German sitting in a dark area, gazing at a 3D image of his family. He had morphed into a diminutive, shrunken figure with his shoulders drooped forwards and his head and neck compressed together, like a turtle retreating into its shell. The formerly rosy-cheeked thirty-something-year-old was now pasty and broken.

"I need to tell you something," he whispered.

I nodded. "Okay."

"When I was stuck in that dormant state, something happened. There are no words." He paused, dropped his head into his hands and tugged at his locks of brown hair in frustration.

"You're fine. Take your time."

He looked up at me with welled-up eyes, his pupils magnified until they merged with his dark brown irises. "I felt everything so deeply. I didn't want to come back into my body. I was part of the universe. Then I had to make a choice." He shook his head and had a distant look in his eyes as if trying to reconcile something. I chose the more difficult option because of one thing." He took a deep breath, pointed, and said, "You."

I didn't think we were that close. "What? Me?"

He exhaled and motioned for me to sit down across from him. As he was composing his thoughts, I scrambled to understand what was going on.

Without him moving his body or head, his eyes clung to me. "I'm afraid here. I want to go home." He gasped over and over until he was hyperventilating, struggling with each subsequent word. "I . . . can't . . ."

The Ambaran's suppression methods weren't working very well on Marcus.

I moved next to him. "May I?" I wasn't sure why I thought it would help, but I extended my right hand to his chest.

He sniffled and nodded.

Within seconds, he regained a more regular breathing pattern.

"Why are you here?" I said.

"At home, I hike through the forests and camp for days. One night, I had a dream that I was connected to everything . . . the trees, animals, leaves." He reached out as if he were touching them. "The dream ended with me in Dollsteinen, where I rose outside my body.

I was connected to an energy source I can't describe." He stopped, looked at me with pleading eyes. "Help me, Victoria. I want to go back to Norway."

We sat quietly for a minute. How would Aunt Judy handle Marcus if he was a patient?

"You experienced something rare, but I don't understand why you want to go back. It sounds like this is where you belong."

Marcus stared straight ahead. "You are so close to . . . you can get into our heads . . . and . . . hurt." He covered his ears. "I have to go back, and I know you can help me."

The poor chap had it all wrong. "It's not me in your head. The Ambarans have added organic materials to help us integrate." He wasn't adjusting well to the seamless connection between our minds and the environment. "The Ambarans do have a high level of access to our minds, but it's the only way they can help us. No one wants to hurt you. You were ratty towards me in Norway, but I wouldn't harm you here or at home." I smiled and hoped a bit of levity might help.

"Please." He held himself and rocked. "I need to go back."

Marcus had changed. The rugged hiker had become a shattered man. Perhaps a guilty conscience was causing his mind to play tricks on him by putting me at the center of his troubles.

"If you go back, you'll be stuck in the cave with the entrance blocked," I said.

His head snapped up with a look of frenzied determination. "I will find a way out."

"Okay, I'll speak to our hosts, but I don't know how or if someone can return early."

He shook his head nervously.

I said, "Don't worry. I'll get back to you with an answer. Okay?"

I took a transport disc back to my new home, where I changed the dimensions of one large room to a cozier one. There, I enveloped myself in images of my lab and rewound the whole scenario with Marcus.

Would he adjust to Ambar? He had just come out of a comatose state; perhaps he needed time. If the Ambarans could send him back, how many others would want to return to Earth now?

I brought up a communications display and with a couple eye movements and thoughts, I sent a request to meet with an Ambaran representative. I attached an important condition. "The representative must have the authority to return a participant to Earth."

Staring out one of the large windows overlooking the Delta Center, I wondered if the Reviewers could recruit more people for us. Why weren't we a group of one thousand rather than fourteen? Surely saving a whole planet required more hands on deck.

Moments later, the monitor said, "Please confirm your meeting request."

Annoyed to have to reaffirm my request, I said, "Yes, I want the meeting."

Suddenly, I saw the reflection of an opalescent Conduit in the window.

I gasped in surprise and turned around. "It would be nice if you warned me when you arrived."

The monitor said, "You confirmed the meeting, meaning it could begin."

Shaking my head, I closed my eyes. "Sure, okay. Now I know."

"Victoria, we are aware of Marcus Steibel's condition. We will send him back and replace him with an II-AEH."

"Sorry, I'm a bit fatigued and would appreciate if you could speak audibly and not in my head."

"Yes." The Conduit spoke out loud, but I still couldn't see signs of a mouth moving.

"II-AEH?" I asked.

"Yes, an Identity Imprint Augmented Earth Human. The II-AEH will appear to be Marcus in every way, except his issues will be resolved in his memories. The original will forget ever leaving Earth. The last thing he will remember is getting lost while hiking in Norway. He will find his way home. We must take these steps to maintain security and stability on Earth and here in our universe. You will be the only Earth member with knowledge of his departure from Ambar."

"So you're replacing him with a clone."

"A clone would be identical. Our AEHs are enhanced versions of the originals."

"Right, sorry. Also, Marcus mentioned something about wanting to go back because of me in his head. Do you know what he meant?"

"No."

"I suppose being in limbo for so long affected him." I hoped to be corrected if that wasn't a possibility.

"Marcus is on his way to a pod now," the Conduit said, offering nothing else. "No one will know of his departure."

With my eyes wide open and fixed on the tall, opalescent being, I must have resembled a deer trapped in headlights. "Right, then. That's it?"

"Yes."

"Thank you."

The host left so smoothly it appeared to glide out.

Marcus was now a replacement—an advanced, modified, engineered Earth human. Perhaps I was a bit off my game, but my head was spinning with how fast they had addressed the problem.

○　○　○

The walls changed from a light gray to a dark blue, and the lighting softened.

At the end of the day, I had more questions than the implanted information answered. I was anxious about starting off our visit with a crisis, even if it was resolved quickly. But, most of all, I was scared. Scared because the Ambarans may have overestimated our ability to save our planet. And equally unsettled by what our hosts might be doing to us in the name of help.

However, my worries needed to be put to the side so I could carry on. First and foremost, my energies had to be spent learning and doing my part to save Earth.

I scanned the residence map for a bed. "Hello, hello, excuse me." Uncertain of where to direct my talking, I blurted out into the air, "I'm sorry if this is a daft question, but where's the bed?"

The monitor said, "Stand in the lighted circle. Once you are in the center, an energy field will surround you. When you feel weightless, relax forwards—it will put you into the best position for an optimal rest period."

With a press on the cardigan's shoulder, the outfit generator morphed my attire into a loose-fitting head-to-toe sleeping suit. It was a definite perk not to have to fuss to change clothes. I could have used that the day Malcolm came over with the news.

The generator and Ambaran controls continuously maintained our bodies, so we didn't shed skin or sweat; it also created a microscopic skin-like barrier to repel substances.

"Monitor, I need to brush my teeth. Where can I find a toothbrush?"

"You will not brush your teeth for the duration of your visit."

"What? My teeth will rot."

"Your teeth enamel and gums were sealed and protected during your journey here."

I looked down and noticed that my skin suddenly had a greenish tint.

With a shaky voice, I said, "I seem to be a strange hue of green. No one said anything to me."

"Your coloring changed as you entered the residence. You are experiencing a delayed temporary pigmentation response to the pod's membrane. You will be back to normal after your rest."

Outfit generators, green skin, and no brushing my teeth during our visit. What next?

"On another note, I know it is pedantic, but what you call *rest* we refer to as sleep."

"Correction, it is not the same. Unlike Earth humans, we do not sleep in blocks of six to eight Earth hours. Instead, rest cycles provide optimal restoration. You will not *wake* from rest but will transition into an active state."

"I see . . . well, thank you for the clarification." I was too tired to continue the debate. However, I hoped whatever they'd discovered was "optimal" would be enough for us Earth humans. I would still call it sleep.

Standing in the center of the illuminated circle, I felt light pulling and pushing on my muscles. The room darkened except for a minimal glow from the energy supporting, raising, and tilting me. Midair, I let out a few startled sounds. Relinquishing so much control was uncomfortable; at times I wanted to stop and put my feet back on solid ground. I persevered, motivated by the thought of a good night's sleep. Engulfed by the energy, I merged with it. I wasn't afraid; on the contrary, I was comforted by the familiarity.

CHAPTER 7

AEH

Supercharged after my first sleep on Ambar, I felt unstoppable, ready to take on any challenge. The sleep system responded to my waking brainwave pattern and put me into an upright position.

My next thoughts were less wonderful. Where am I? How long have I been asleep? Who am I? Unstoppable but clearly unsettled—a curious combination. Acceptable, though, having just been exported to Ambar.

Once on my feet, I became aware of new information. I knew everyone's goals and agreed with all of them. However, my primary goal was more of a role. I was selected to lead the group back on Earth. Clearly, the Ambarans had made a mistake. Just because I could receive their warning didn't mean I was fit to lead a group of people in such a monumental task. Constance, on the other hand, would make the ideal candidate. She could coordinate our efforts and drive us to perform tasks with the highest probabilities of success even if a few feathers were ruffled along the way.

Either the Ambarans or the Reviewers needed to change my goal.

Uncertain if I was supposed to talk with the monitor as I would a human, I said, "Hello monitor, can I ask you a question about my primary goal?"

"Yes."

"I believe someone else would be best suited for the role of group leader. So, I would like to speak to someone about this."

"Your role is unchangeable."

I raised my hands in the air. "Can we at least have a discussion about it?"

"The Reviewers have visibility of everyone's timeline. Do you wish to counter their decision based on your limited perspective?"

The AI had struck me down right where I stood using simple logic. I closed my eyes and dropped my head in defeat.

"I don't know how to follow that. You're telling me it is my fate. Is everyone learning each other's goals?"

"Yes."

I covered my face with my hands as I envisioned the reactions of others to my role. "Do they know why I've been selected as group leader?"

"No."

"By the way, what's your name? You do have one, don't you?" I sounded unintentionally snarky.

"I can be as personal or impersonal as you wish in our conversations. Which setting would you prefer?"

"Personal, please." Why did I want to create a friendly rapport with an artificial intelligence room monitor? Sad.

Within two seconds, a British woman's voice said, "Hello, Victoria, I am Kimball."

"What! How did you get that name?" My sharp tone revealed my irritation.

"A personal setting allows me to access your history and people from your life. I chose a name and voice that elicits trust and comfort for you—Aunt Judy's mother."

"Right, rule number one: Please don't use names from my head to evoke a desired emotion or behavior. It is an invasion of my privacy and rather manipulative." I understood the Ambarans needed to integrate us, but tapping into our minds at every instance seemed excessive. The monitor had proven Allan's point. The Ambarans did know everything about us. "Please tell me your real name. If you don't have one, perhaps you can choose one common to your people."

"Yes," the monitor said. "However, it is inaudible to humans from Earth."

"Oh my . . . well, that won't work, will it?" The invasion of privacy had left me irritated and impatient. "Could you just give yourself an Earth name?"

"Yes, call me Anthea. You can now make your way to Inner 1 to rejoin the group."

"Thank you, Anthea." Relieved that the naming episode was over, I swigged down the required nourishment, ate the vial, and generated another favorite clothes combination—a navy turtleneck with navy trousers. With no time spent on brushing teeth and baths or showers, I was ready within minutes. Welcome to life in another universe.

Just before leaving, I pitched my head upward and said, "An . . ." A pang of sadness hit. Saying goodbye to AI was not like talking to my auntie or even Albert. I set off to meet my real, wonderfully flawed Earth friends.

○ ○ ○

Immediately upon arriving at Inner 1, Constance blocked my path. I took a deep breath and waited for the take-charge lady to contest my role.

"Victoria, there are so many optimized efficiencies here; think of how much time we'll save per day. By my estimation, I will save six minutes by not having to brush my teeth or shower. My breakfast, if drunk slowly, takes seventeen seconds to drink. I can change my clothes in three seconds." She had already said enough to need to take a breath, but she rabbited on.

I pointed to the group and motioned for us to keep moving towards it.

She continued, "I envision a style, touch the lapel, and an outfit is created. Though the result may not exactly match my thoughts, my ideas inspire it." She demonstrated her wardrobe-altering ability by changing her clothing color and pattern four times within as many seconds. "My monitor's name is Penelope . . . my roommate's name back in Singapore."

Constance had certainly had a different start with her residence monitor than I had, and seemed to be thoroughly appreciating our futuristic lifestyle. Good for her, but where was the sense of urgency? Forget about saving a few seconds—we needed to save the world.

Our focus had to be on acquiring the necessary skills, full stop. If I had to be the leader, then it would be my job to keep everyone on task. I let Constance have her seconds of enjoyment, knowing nothing but hard work lay ahead. Why didn't she mention my role? Surely, she thought it was a mistake too.

We gathered around our host. Zoa stood next to me and immediately caught my attention. As I scanned her chosen outfit, I gave her an understanding smile. She was wearing blue nurse's garb.

She said, "It helps me stay focused and reminds me that I already have strengths to reach my primary goal."

"Indeed." I had something to learn from Zoa. She seemed to have gotten her head around her primary goal very quickly.

Zoa leaned over to me. "I know we are in good hands with you as our group leader."

Relieved to have her vote of confidence, I said, "Thank you, that means a lot to me."

"Morning, doc," Peter said as he shuffled by.

"I'm not a doctor yet," I blurted.

"As good as," he said.

I caught sight of Ana, dressed in her usual college-student ensemble, with one addition. She had a two-inch gold-colored cross emblazoned on the left side of her jacket.

The Conduit's communication was direct to our minds, as it had been the previous day. "The entire Complex is yours to explore, except for areas where prerequisites are required to gain access. Before each learning module, you will be given a neural adjunct; it will personalize the interaction between you, the assignment's guide, and the environment."

A cylindrical compartment emerged from the floor in front of the host. It contained our neural adjuncts.

This was my chance to see where everyone stood. "Excuse me, I have a question for the group."

The opalescent stopped and turned towards me, which I took as my cue to speak.

I looked at those gathered around the circle. "Is everyone aware of our primary goals?"

They all answered at once. Some said "yes" while others stated their goal.

The Conduit spoke neurally to me. "Unusual. You are missing vital pieces of information to assist you in your role. The residence monitor will perform a neural scan and resolve any omissions."

"Is something wrong with me? What am I missing that I need to know now?"

"Your monitor can survey your neural networks during your next rest. The missing data will not affect your experience in this module."

I was irritated that they could tell me there was missing information, but not why. What if my brain wasn't responding well to their inputs?

The Conduit continued instructing the group. "Place the neural adjunct on the left side of your head over your ear. It will activate, expand, and direct you to a module location."

Despite my worry, everything continued around me. I would have to go through the motions until I could get answers back at my residence.

As Allan placed the one-inch device over his left ear, I examined the adjunct for contact points, structure, and material, looking for similarities to the instruments I was used to on Earth.

He caught me watching. "Trying to figure out how it works so you can copy it?"

I shrugged and turned away to focus on positioning the adjunct over my left ear. A piece jettisoned out of the device and came within an inch of my left eye. Just as I was about to resume breathing, it collapsed onto my eye. Like everyone else, I reacted with an involuntary jolt, even though it didn't hurt.

Constance clapped her hands twice. "Right, everybody set?"

Zoa and Peter nodded.

Allan said, "Good, let's go." He and Constance were already competing. Maybe they were trying to prove that one of them should be the leader—not me.

We followed them like obedient soldiers. Meanwhile, I doubted the adjunct. The only way it could work as described was if it used the organic technology inside us. The physical device might not have been necessary but rather a way of easing us into this strange world.

With help from the headgear, we saw that the first assignment was a health lab in Sub-Terrain Outer 3. Allan, Peter, Constance, and I shared a transport disc.

"Woah," Peter said, drawing out the sound, "the discs are in a hurry! They're going much faster than before." That was one more big change—with the adjuncts on, the safety barriers no longer blocked our views.

We whizzed past domes, reflective structures resembling drinking straws bound together, and colorful plots of glistening ground. The scene came alive as areas vibrated, changed colors, or appeared magnified. One structure built of prisms of all sizes caught my eye.

In the last few seconds, we dove down within a couple inches of the ground, causing all of us to gasp, before sliding into a camouflaged dome. "Sub-Terrain Outer 3 Laboratory," our adjuncts confirmed.

"Woah!" Peter said.

"That was awesome!" Allan said as he exited the disc.

A few steps in, we were greeted by the first human we had seen together. I didn't tell anyone about the man I saw when visiting Marcus. And the jury was still out on whether he was completely human, like us. On the other hand, maybe I needed to broaden my definition of human.

"I didn't expect them to look so much like us," Zoa whispered.

"Me, neither," I said in a suspicious tone. There were eons of development between us. I wasn't buying it. Having seen their work with II-AEH Marcus, I was cautious that we were meeting an Ambaran human. Like with the adjuncts, they might have been showing us what they thought we could handle.

The female, dressed in tunic and trousers, stood two inches taller than me, making her about five-foot-ten. Her eyes sparkled bright green, perfectly matching her attire of thousands of polygonal emeralds. Her ebony skin matched her short, spiky black hair.

With everyone's eyes fixed on her, she introduced herself. "Hello, I am this assignment's Augmented Earth Human, or AEH. For your visit, the Ambarans have created humans like me. I am a hybrid between you and a further evolved, enriched human."

I was right. They were creating beings in our image. That must have been what I saw in my residence at the ECHRC2D laboratory. Somehow, I had transported to where they made AEHs.

"So are you a sentient being or a form of advanced artificial intelligence?" Allan was the first to ask for clarification.

Peter leaned over to Allan and whispered, "I think she's both—a transhuman."

"I am made of programmed enriched organic material, such as a transhuman." She looked over to Peter, who blushed at being overheard.

"And she has excellent hearing," he said with a nervous laugh.

Constance changed tracks. "Pardon, what do native Ambarans look like, and why create special humans for us?"

"The Earth Complex and AEHs are here to help you achieve your objectives. Ambarans are beyond what is required. They are not human."

Her statement elicited a few raised eyebrows.

"Are there humans in this universe?" Constance asked.

"Yes, they are present throughout our galaxy and others, but they have evolved differently than you."

Gasps and whispers rolled over the group.

The AEH surveyed our group with intent, as if evaluating us. "We will start with a health lab."

"Excuse me," I said. "Can you tell us your name?"

"On Ambar, my name states my origin with a unique identifier; it is inaudible to Earth humans. However, to comply with your naming conventions, you can refer to me as Vintar."

"Thank you, Vintar." I sighed in relief. Her answer had been more forthcoming than my monitor's.

"Although we have gathered data from you in the dormant state and will oversee every aspect of your health, it is essential for you to understand why, how, and what we measure." She spoke with great animation and moved gracefully across the room. "Everyone will become mentally and physically stronger while you are here. Today's lab will provide baseline data on your current health levels."

"Are we going to become superhuman?" Peter flexed his arm muscles.

"I am uncertain of your definition of superhuman. However, you will be free of disease and have enhanced senses and metabolic functions."

Peter shook his head. "Naaahh . . . that sounds good but not superhuman."

Mr. d'Orsini chuckled, and Allan patted Peter on the back.

Vintar said, "Zoa will take basic readings and perform numerous assessments. She can explain the results to whatever level you wish. Once complete, your adjuncts will direct you elsewhere to record further health metrics."

Vintar separated us into five groups. Zoa, Peter, and I made up one team.

Zoa turned to us with a small device that looked like a thin metallic cylinder, no longer than a pencil. "My friends, I will select 'Assessment mode,' and then I'll be ready to evaluate any element of your health."

"Uhh . . . I'm not sure." The young Czech peered at the assessment tool. "Give me an engine workshop any day."

"There is no need to worry. We'll do this together." She tapped a couple symbols on the device, causing two semi-transparent displays to pop up. "I'll go first so you can see what type of readings we will study."

She scanned her left wrist and read out the displays. "My heart rate is 90 because I'm a little nervous to do everything right. My blood pressure is 115/75. Blood type shows as O+, and from the rest of the data I can see . . ." Her face went blank.

I mirrored her concern. "What is it?"

"There is much information here, but one result I did not expect in basic data . . . My apoptosis level is down by 76 percent."

Peter shrieked. "Your pop-toes level? What does that mean?" The other groups gawked and laughed at him.

In her calm nurse voice, Zoa said, "Apoptosis happens all the time to get rid of dying cell parts. Sometimes a cell dies off to give way to a developmental change, like a growing baby. Other times, cells are triggered to die so that a disease doesn't spread. The process slows when a person has cancer, for example."

I was already out of my depth. Did Earth metrics work the same way here? "Would you like me to get Vintar to explain?" I said.

"I have questioned the result through the adjunct. Just a moment." Zoa turned away from us, leaving Peter and me helplessly waiting for the news.

She turned around but continued studying the numbers. "There is nothing to worry about. Everyone's level is reduced because we aren't aging at the same rate. They have already healed us of many conditions."

The nurse smiled before shifting her attention to Peter. "My young friend, are you ready? I will send the results to your adjunct. If you have any questions, let me know."

"Uhh . . . I'm still thinking about pop-toes and diseases."

Whilst she conducted Peter's assessment, I went over to Vintar.

"I was told by a Conduit that I'm missing information. Can you tell me why?

Vintar nodded. "I've accessed your biometrics." She stared at me, or more like through me. "Your brain has altered since arrival. The data can be replaced during your next rest."

"My brain has already changed?" I scowled.

"Yes, everyone's has in order to receive the volume of data and experiences required."

"I haven't heard about anyone else missing data. Is this a problem?"

"Each person's brain is different. Yours is healthy and adjusting to the new environment. There is no need for concern."

I returned to Zoa and Peter, who were just finishing up. She pointed the device in my direction.

"Would you like the general baseline results or more in-depth?"

"For right now, let's stick to general data. Unless something curious captures your eye. Then I would like to know about that too."

"Your heart rate is 70, blood pressure 112/70, and your blood type..." Zoa stopped and squinted at me. "What is your blood type?"

"AB." I knew why it caught her attention.

"And your Rh factor?"

"Well, it changes back and forth from positive to negative." I was reluctant to divulge such a personal detail about myself. "The doctors can't explain why."

"Hmm, how is it recorded?"

"AB with an undefined Rh factor." As I answered Zoa, I glanced over to the group beside us. Ana was listening in but quickly turned away and touched her cross when I eyed her.

In a softer voice, I said, "When I first found out, the doctor told me to wear a tag and tell people close to me of my blood type, in case of emergency. I never got a tag, but I told my Aunt Judy, who took the news as if she'd known it all along."

"When did you discover this?" asked Zoa.

"I was nineteen and had contracted a rare pneumonia. The hospital took blood samples and ran many tests. Twelve tubes later..."

Zoa gave me a cockeyed look. "I've never heard of such a thing. I wonder..." She seemed to catch herself belaboring the topic. "No problem. We're done."

Was she distancing herself from me? Would this be how the seemingly inevitable slippery slope to isolation begins?

The nurse went on to assess the other groups.

Meanwhile, the adjuncts directed Peter and me to devices at the back of the room for further evaluation. We took our positions under crescents floating in midair, a foot above us. Without delay, the scanning began.

"Wait. Is this safe, doc? Does it use radiation or nanotech?"

Before I could reply, Vintar answered. "Imaging does not use radiation; it is an information relay system using what you call 'nanotechnology' in your body."

"What I call?" Peter said.

"I will clarify further when all health readings are complete."

We recorded countless health metrics, many of which we hadn't known needed monitoring because we couldn't measure them back on Earth. The metrics were not isolated to the health of individual parts, like the state of one's kidneys. They also evaluated how organs, cells, and energies communicated and interacted. It was a holistic approach to understanding our bodies.

Once Zoa completed the assessments, Vintar addressed us. "With the metrics completed, I will take questions orally or through your adjunct. First, I want to impress something upon you." She paused and looked down. "When you return to Earth, you will use a device that Peter will build to continue to scan your health metrics. You must stay within specified bands."

Allan quipped, "Cool device, but basically you're telling us to stay healthy."

"In order to save Earth, you will all need to perform optimally. Should any of you fall outside the narrow band of measurements, you will be unable to fulfil your primary goal which will in turn affect the chances of saving your planet." Vintar's words and tone sounded ominous, and it seemed to be enough for Allan to accept.

She looked over to the young Czech. "I will address Peter's question regarding nanotechnology in your bodies."

He smiled and straightened, so much so that he became an inch taller.

"Good question, bambino," said an impressed Mr. d'Orsini.

"Thanks, Papa Pino."

"We do not use nanotechnology as you know it. There is nothing artificial in your body. During your travels to Ambar, your bodies ingested specially designed and programmed enhanced organic matter. This can take many forms, from a cell or group of cells to nerves and muscles. The scanning system communicates with that matter to give us the required data."

Peter gazed down at his arms as if they were foreign to him. "Not nanotech but smart alien cells . . . amazing."

"The programmed matter in your bodies continuously tracks your health and relays data to the environment. We monitor and adjust everything from ion channel activity and neurotransmitter balance to hormone levels and emotional states, as required."

"This organic matter stuff, will stay inside us once we are back home?" asked Allan.

"Ninety percent will be removed upon your return. However, the remaining ten percent will stay in your systems for precisely 194 Earth days."

"Right, so until a week after the event occurs," said Constance.

"Yes." Vintar continued answering questions until she reached the last one—Ana's.

The astronomer cleared her throat. "In the mountains of Chile, they talk about people with mutated genes. It's believed these people can feel and do things others can't, and some can see events before they happen. Do mutations occur in your civilization?"

Without a second's pause, Vintar answered, "In general, what you call mutations are genetic variations or adaptations to ensure the continuation of a species. There can be less desirable variants, but these are confined to a small number. However, people like the ones you speak of are the harbingers of the next evolutionary step. We view those 'mutations' as the result of intelligent evolutionary programming."

I looked over to Ana, who had cast her eyes down as if deep in thought.

Vintar provided an example. "For instance, changes in the gene Forkhead box protein P2 or FOXP2 in Earth humans helped you to develop sophisticated communication. These gene alterations are seen as mutations to Earth scientists, but they resulted from intelligent gene programming.

"The Chileans with extraordinary senses are expressing characteristics similar to humans in our universe during the stages of early societal development. Genes expressed as a result of specific environmental and physical triggers act according to the principles of fundamental epigenetics."

Zoa asked, "Can you explain what type of triggers you're referring to?"

"Examples of important triggers are diet, environmental conditions, social development, and an individual's physiological and psychological state."

Peter perked up like he'd had a breakthrough. "That explains Albert Einstein. His brain must have been built different enough to trigger the genius gene."

As I smiled at Peter's simple reasoning, I felt someone's attention on me. A quick forty-five-degree turn revealed my watcher, the astronomer. Ana and I locked eyes. Her glare turned to worry, and my own gaze turned defensive. Why was I defensive? I had done nothing to draw her suspicion.

I found Ana a bit tricky. One side of her seemed worldly and lighthearted, the other provincial and attention seeking. Of course, her newfound friend Allan wouldn't help matters. He seemed self-serving and naturally suspicious, and they got on like two peas in a pod. Curious how quickly she turned her attentions away from François. So much for loyalty.

After the lab, she whizzed off, and I followed.

"Ana." She ignored me. I sped up. "Ana, is everything okay?"

"I can't talk right now." She eyed her surroundings like someone under duress, searching for a way out.

"No problem. Let me know when you're ready." I relented and dropped back a few steps.

The ever-observant Zoa saw the exchange and approached me. "Is something wrong with Ana?"

"I don't know, but we all need to remember why we are here," I said.

At the end of the day, the astronomer knew nothing about me. She couldn't, and I needed to make sure the past didn't repeat itself.

As a child, I didn't understand why classmates teased me for knowing too much until Aunt Judy explained that not everyone saw future events. When riding my bike or bored at school, my mind would wander, allowing me to see more than the present. Knowledge flowed with such clarity, I lost track of what had already happened versus what was about to happen. All coexisted at once. At will, I could think of someone and take a mental sidestep to see into their timeline. After years of playing around with what adults called a "gift" and peers called "witchcraft," I decided to live life more on the surface, where everyone else was.

On rare occasions, someone would come along and sense something different about me. I hoped Ana wasn't one of them; they usually created difficulties for me and never became friends.

Zoa gently touched my arm. "We all have our ways of handling things. Don't read too much into it."

I nodded. "I just want us all to get on."

"My friend, I am here for you." Her smile let me know she had accepted what was sure to be the first of many revelations about me. As a nurse, she was probably intrigued by my blood type. I hoped she would stick around.

I might have had nothing to worry about. For some unexplainable reason, on Ambar, I wasn't yet able to use my skills in the same way. I couldn't see a person's future or sense any impending event. I hadn't always embraced my extrasensory competencies, but I'd never wanted them gone. Would it affect my ability to lead?

As soon as I returned to my residence, I addressed one of my concerns.

"Anthea, a Conduit said you could check my neural networks during my next rest to see why my brain is missing information. But I'd prefer to have it done now . . . oh, and does anyone else have this problem?"

"No one else has had this issue. It is unusual. First, I will scan for missing data. Then during your rest, I will inspect your brain's architecture."

Suddenly, as if someone had turned on a switch in my head, I knew why I was the designated leader. It was because of my experience in neurofeedback. Apparently, the Ambarans highly valued the ability to control one's brainwaves. They expected me to entrain the team members' brainwaves to mine like I naturally did with Marcus without effort. I was in the dark as to how that would come into play in saving Earth.

○ ○ ○

After two rest times, Sabine sent me a message. "Victoria, thank you for your help. Marcus is back to being himself and doing well."

Job well done, I suppose. Eager to interact with the alternative version of Marcus for myself, I asked Anthea for his whereabouts. We could query a monitor or adjunct to find anyone in the EC.

I arrived at the Delta Center to find Marcus talking with two group members. I watched from afar. How far had the Ambarans gone in trying to produce the convincing imposter? Was this version like the abrupt Marcus who walked with me in Norway? Did it know the fine details of his life back in Germany?

They headed for a transport disc.

"Marcus." I sped up to catch him.

"Hallo," Marcus said in his usual neutral tone.

"I won't keep you. I just wanted to see how you're doing." I surveyed the being up and down, then back up again. Fascinating.

"I'm doing better." The corners of his mouth turned up—he almost smiled.

"That's good to hear. We were all worried."

"It was a difficult time." He looked away and down as he got onto the disc. Before leaving, he turned back to me. "Thanks for helping me out."

I kept my focus on him. "Sure, anytime. By the way, did Zoa's health assessment of you reveal anything out of the norm?

He cracked a smile. "No, not a thing."

Every word, move, and nuance was Marcus, but something felt different about him.

Before our next assignment, we researched and experimented according to our primary goals.

With the help of my accommodation's boundless resources, I scoured information about each person in the team. That was the easy part. The more exhausting work was going through exercises to develop new abilities, since my old ones had not returned.

Although I didn't mention it to Anthea, one concern plagued me. In the past, whenever I did too much brain training or neurofeedback, my abilities would become magnified. I'd lose control of how or when they would show up. Throughout my life, I had either tried to understand or suppress my abilities, never increase them. That's why Malcolm and I only had monthly sessions.

Although I hoped things would be different on Ambar, I was still nervous about strengthening old abilities as I gained new ones here. I didn't want to scare team members or alienate myself from them.

CHAPTER 8

SPECK OF DUST

With Marcus replaced by an II-AEH, we were down to thirteen. I increased my workload to make up for the deficit. Whether in my living quarters or out in the EC, I felt increasingly more connected. It was clear, due to the nature of brain plasticity, that such intense integration would change everyone's brain. But would those changes be temporary or permanent?

As I surveyed members' strengths and weaknesses, I honed in on who to call on when in crisis mode back home. On Earth, I would have had to conduct detailed interviews and testing to understand each person's capabilities. However, on Ambar, I could easily access that information and more without interacting with anyone. My curious and obsessive desire for the most minor details about a person made me feel like I had known them for years. Useless data, like the fact that two members hated cilantro because it tasted like soap to them, made me adopt an inner mantra: *only look at relevant information.*

Anthea interrupted my creation of a multidimensional chart showing team members, their experience, their relevant competencies, and potential applications. "Victoria, meet your group on Inner 1 to begin the module related to Ambar."

I joined everyone and donned an adjunct. Half of us viewed the map of the Complex in our heads, whereas others projected it right in front of them. I preferred the private-viewing mode because I didn't want to be *in* the map. We walked until we reached a narrow, dead-end corridor.

"Are the walls vibrating, or is it something I drank?" Peter moved his hand towards one side and watched the surface turn to waves. Luckily for him, his hand wasn't affected.

Once all fourteen of us had entered the middle of the corridor, the head devices instructed us to take a deep breath and hold it. We exchanged a few worried glances before we all inhaled.

Within a fraction of a second, they transported us to another part of the Complex.

"What the hell?" Allan's frightened reaction, in contrast to his usual coolness, was worth the ride.

Peter giggled and motioned with his arms as if he were a magician. "I think it was like teleportation."

"Wicked! I need that back home. They have to share it." Allan glanced back at corridor T-1.53, which was nowhere in sight.

It was one of many short corridors joining two distant places within the Complex using space-folding nanoparticles.

We had reached Outer 4's platform, which must have been a considerable distance from Inner 1—hence the spontaneous transportation. My adjunct indicated that AEH Vintar was present but outside our visual spectrum. She would join us momentarily.

Suddenly, I felt an intense magnetic pull. It was so strong it made me queasy. Perhaps my usual abilities were returning. On Earth, the sensation always preceded a negative event, like an accident. Did it mean the same here on Ambar?

Before I could query it further, the adjuncts expanded our view. The scene evoked sounds of awe. It rendered even the chatty astronomer speechless. Once we got our bearings, a buzz of excitement spread through the group.

Constance covered her left eye. "Is the adjunct enhancing our vision? The sky's sharp blues, violets, bright pinks, and greens seem clearer than on Earth. Oh . . ."

The headgear answered her question for all of us. The colors we were seeing were not enhanced.

"Two suns, one yellow and one blue. They look like hardened sweets." Peter stood spread-eagle to bask in both suns' rays.

The bright, fiery yellow ball had started its encroachment onto the blue one. We had arrived to watch the surrealistic scene of Ambar's suns about to eclipse each other.

"Do you realize how incredible this moment is?" Ana said. "We are standing on a planet with three natural satellites within a binary star system . . . and the stars are eclipsing."

"Satellites?" Peter said.

Allan responded, "She means moons."

"Part of my primary goal is to better harness our sun's power and help repair the ozone layer." The astronomer adjusted her adjunct. "I wonder how they protect Ambar from solar flares and asteroids."

Constance took a deep breath in. "This is odd. We can breathe at high altitude, at least ten thousand feet up, and it seems easier than on Earth."

"I'm sure it seems that way to you. You're from over-populated, polluted cities like London and Singapore," Allan said.

"Hmm . . . The air quality and composition are like inside the Complex," Ana said. "I kinda . . . don't think we're outside at all. It's like they've matched Earth's air composition."

We're still in the Earth Complex." She surveyed the surroundings, trying to make sense of things. "The adjunct shows that the combined sols are .66. The outside temperature should feel cold, like our winter. And the headgear is either helping us see the landscape, or we are viewing Ambar from someplace high in their atmosphere." Ana shook her head. "Yet, we can't see the Complex. It's . . ."

"Obviously," Allan said, "our all-knowing hosts are controlling what's visible and what's not."

"Oh no!" said Sylvia, the horticulturist from Ireland. "I can't be doin' heights. I think I'm goin' to pass out, ya know." Her eyes rolled up into their sockets, and her arms and legs stiffened as if afflicted by rigor mortis.

Peter jumped into action to steady her. "I've got you. Are you okay?"

Sylvia straightened her slight figure and patted her dress. "Wow. Ya know, I'm not afraid anymore."

"You're not?" Peter said, still holding her arm.

"One minute, I am spinnin' out of control, and the next, ya know, everything is stable. I can look around and not be filled with dread."

"Interesting," I mumbled.

"Yes." Zoa positioned herself closer to me before continuing. "In Norway, Sylvia told me she didn't want to climb any mountains because she had a lifelong fear of heights. And now, within a few seconds, she's over her phobia. I must understand how that works so I can use it to treat people with crippling phobias."

An instant later, without warning, we were cast out into the darkness of space. Was this planned, or had the magnetic pulling I felt earlier been a premonition?

"Oh, my God! What's happening?" Ana was the first to shout.

The adjuncts helped our eyes adjust. Countless stars, planets, and cloudy gaseous formations surrounded us.

Zoa whispered, "Oh, heavenly God. I am humbled before your creations."

Ana noted, "They changed our observational perspective to a point in space."

Allan, as usual, was ready to offer an explanation. "As I said, they control what we see through the adjunct." He pulled at the adjunct, even though we knew only the presiding AEH could release the devices during assignments.

AEH Vintar became visible to us. "Outer 4's platform, at the apex of the Complex, connects to observational points in our atmosphere and space. From a localized position, you witnessed the beginning of our yellow star eclipsing our more distant blue star. When the adjuncts transferred your view to our space point outside Ambar's orbital path, you could view our galaxy."

"Cool! I could reproduce this to help us switch between real-time views back on Earth," said Allan.

Vintar said, "Allan, you will learn how to use overlays to show you more. Such as integrating advanced heat-sensing devices with AI to create high-speed scanning tools."

"And that could be used in disaster responses or to survey large areas quickly." The AI expert was quick to apply the AEH's suggestion. He tapped Ana on the shoulder. "I could help you create multi-spectral imaging so you can see where Earth's atmosphere is deteriorating and how to fix our ozone layer."

"We already have that," Ana replied. "Using LiDAR, light detection and ranging, we study cloud and aerosol properties. I've kinda used it for tracking space junk. But also, to make 3D maps of planetary surfaces."

"Sure, but I can make it better." His smile exuded confidence.

It seemed we were being led in the right directions through Vintar's comments and suggestions.

In a soft voice, Ana said, "This kinda looks like a picture taken by a high-powered telescope using sophisticated lenses and filters that translate wavelengths undetectable by the human eye. It's breathtaking."

"Vintar," I said. "Through the adjuncts, are we seeing a virtual or live scene?"

"The technology of the platform and headgear allows you to view in real-time. You can also access individual planets, stars, and galaxies."

Again, the impatient tech wiz tried to manipulate the adjunct externally. "How can I see Ambar?"

"We have highlighted Ambar in your adjuncts. You can magnify it." Vintar turned to Allan. "There is no need to adjust your headgear."

I was enjoying the illusion of being suspended in space, so I stayed in that view.

"Woah." Peter grabbed on to those around him.

"Peter," Vintar said, "you are experiencing visual incongruence because of the speed used to focus on Ambar. A slower approach will eliminate side effects."

"Okay, yeah, I'll zoom in slower."

Vintar said, "Use thought commands to switch between views and focus on objects."

"How far can we zoom into other planets?" said Ana.

"You do not have access to view life forms. However, you can view planetary topographies."

I zoomed in on Ambar. "Why is part of a mountain moving?"

"Those are the curved exteriors of people's homes. They appear as extensions of Ambar's terrain. Like the EC, the structures are always changing to accommodate the needs of their inhabitants. The materials used are engineered at the subatomic level to self-repair and adapt to changing environments," Vintar said.

Peter had been gasping syllables as he tried to ask a question during Vintar's answer. Finally, he succeeded. "Why can't I see the Earth Complex?"

"I can't either, bambino."

"Pardon, neither can I," Constance said.

"It is not a natural part of Ambar. Your adjuncts show what was present before we built your temporary home. Any external being viewing our planet would not detect the EC."

Interesting. Why wouldn't the Ambarans want others to know about the structure? Perhaps our visit was a secret in Earth's and Ambar's universes.

Peter wasn't content with Vintar's answer. "Can you get the adjunct to show me the EC?"

"I have given everyone access to views of the Earth Complex now," said Vintar.

"Wow! It looks alive," said Peter.

Sylvia smiled at him. "It's wondrous, isn't it?"

Zoa put her hands together as if in prayer.

Sylvia helped us comprehend what we were seeing. "It is a larger version of the Delta Center, ya know. They both remind me of a hyalite opal."

As I wasn't a gem expert, her reference didn't help. "What's a hyalite opal?" I said.

Constance answered. "Hyalite opal . . . a . . ."

With the speed of an auctioneer, Sylvia said, "It's a naturally occurrin' amorphous substance that creates wondrous shapes. We can find them in many countries with volcanoes." She wasn't about to have her lines stolen by the savant.

Vintar said, "Yes, we designed the Complex and Delta Center to be amorphous—both the interior and exterior change size and shape as needed, like living beings."

We stared at the ingenious structure. It was, as Sylvia said, wondrous.

Vintar addressed the group. "I will now return you to the Outer 4 platform point on the surface."

In an instant, we were back.

"As you saw, our planetary system consists of two main sequence stars and three moons."

"Main sequence?" Peter asked Ana.

Although Peter could have read the answer in the adjunct, the astronomer was eager to help. "It means the stars' cores are converting hydrogen to helium."

"Yeah, sure," Peter said as he gave us a silly grin.

Vintar displayed a 3D model of the galaxy. "With Ambar on the outside of the eclipsing stars, light levels and temperatures are equivalent to those of your winter. The combined starlight is .66 sols."

Having arrived at the correct sol level, Ana nodded with a smug look.

"The larger spectral class B blue star, at a temperature of 12,000 degrees Kelvin, is three times your sun's mass and a hundred times the luminosity. However, it is 1.4 billion miles away. The smaller class G star, which we orbit, is similar in mass to your sun but is twice as far from Ambar as your sun is from Earth. With our two stars and a heavier atmosphere, Ambar resides in a stress-free position in the galaxy, without threats from solar flares, asteroids, or meteors."

Ana, looking ecstatic, was nodding so much I thought her head was loose. "It's better than the Goldilocks Zone."

I asked, "Why does the third satellite look so different than the other two?"

"Ambar had a sister planet five million miles or eight million kilometers away until a black hole came raging through this part of the galaxy and tore that planet apart—leaving one piece. That was over four million years ago, but the remnant continues to orbit our planet along with our original two satellites, or moons."

"Aah...it's . . . or was a planet!" gasped Ana.

Allan poked her. "Not so Goldilocks Zone'ish then."

She sighed and teed up another question. "Was Ambar damaged by the black hole?"

"The speed of the black hole, and Ambar's distance from our sister planet, created distortions and an instant angular quantum formation, but we were unharmed. The formation was one of two types. Some are predictable occurrences, called quantum spindles—they are stable and slow, allowing us to use them in different ways. However, that one was spontaneous and unpredictable."

One of Ana's questions soon caught my eye, because it hadn't been answered. Our efficient AEH dealt with all other queries in the blink of an eye. This oversight piqued my curiosity. As a researcher, I watched for exceptions; they often proved more interesting than the norm. I signaled, through the headgear, that I had a verbal query.

"Victoria." Vintar was ready.

"Ana has asked another question about your sister planet," I said.

The astronomer snapped her head in my direction and tutted.

I gave Ana a supportive half smile as a way of letting her know I wasn't stealing her question. "Were you aware of the high-speed black hole before it raged through this part of the galaxy? And did you evacuate your sister planet before it split into bits?"

Without a moment's pause, Vintar said, "We knew of the black hole; however, we miscalculated its path. The planet was used for research and stored billions of specimens. Yes, we evacuated all researchers using a stable quantum spindle."

For me, Vintar's answer created more questions. What were the specimens? Were other beings, nonresearchers, living on the planet? If so, did they get out in time? I would have continued questioning Vintar, but I didn't want to draw attention to something no one else was querying to the same degree.

Analyzing layer after layer was an occupational hazard. Of course, my questions were selfish. I wanted to know how much the Ambarans could do for us. They had experience with a planet in danger and with helping, but we weren't living on a sister planet, endangering their well-being. Perhaps teaching us on Ambar was as far as they were willing to go. But, what if . . .

I got to hatching plan B and asked, "If we can't succeed in our plan to save Earth, would the Ambarans evacuate some of our population to Ambar?"

Everyone froze in place, with only their eyes darting from me to Vintar.

"That would not be possible for several reasons. However, I am unable to elaborate further."

Peter nudged me. "Nice try, doc."

Using the adjunct, I sent a private message to Vintar. "Who can discuss this with me?"

"Your residence monitor," she said.

"With two suns, does Ambar rely on solar power?" Ana asked. She was staying focused on her primary goal.

"It is one of many solutions used for supplying energy to planets. For many thousands of years, we have created, harnessed, and distributed energy in several ways in our galaxy and others. For instance, after discovering that bacteria could create, store, and transfer energy, we designed an enhanced synthesized bacterium to do the same task. A matrix was structured out of the more efficient manufactured material and used in fuel cells."

Again, Ana nodded repeatedly and glanced at others to let them know she had something to contribute. "Yes! We're onto this. Scientists on Earth are doing experiments with bacteria to help astronauts be self-sufficient for longer periods of time. They are using a bacterium we call Shewanella oneidensis MR-1."

"It will prove to be a good testing ground for them," said Vintar.

The astronomer continued showcasing her knowledge to anyone who would listen, which appeared to be Allan and Zoa.

Peter was on another track. "Do you use solar-powered cars?"

"There are planets, in that developmental epoch, using solar-powered vehicles, but a direct comparison is not possible. They harness and store solar energy using exotic energy nanoparticles. For space travel, exotic energy storage, conversion and manipulation properties are used.

"Pardon, earlier you mentioned quantum spindles. Are they similar to an Einstein-Rosen bridge, and is that how we got here?" Constance asked with a look of disbelief.

Zoa, Peter, and I all looked over at the savant. Clearly, her knowledge went beyond math, nebulae, and gemstones.

"Yes. Though your reference is an oversimplification of the event, at this point in your visit, it must suffice."

"And here I thought we might still be living in pods in Norway while you control our minds." Allan had an interesting notion, I'll give him that, but it sounded straight out of a science-fiction movie.

"Wow!" Peter flailed his arms around. "I can say I've traveled through a quantum spindle!"

There was a flurry of comments from the group regarding Allan's hypothesis. Our resident astronomer submitted three follow-up questions, which were answered within seconds in our adjunct.

Zoa leaned towards me and whispered, "When will we be able to leave the Complex?"

Vintar answered. "For health reasons, you cannot go out into our atmosphere. Our planet differs from Earth; thus, it is best not to overload your systems with foreign microorganisms. You can explore our planet, galaxy, and universe in other ways."

"Thank you." Zoa had discovered what Peter already knew—anything spoken or whispered was fair game for AEHs.

"The Earth Complex is a contained system that allows you to live at optimal levels. Currently, you are in a phase of neutralization, where many of your physical and psychological constructs are being reprogrammed to determine your potential."

Constance latched on to Vintar's last statement. "Does that include circadian rhythms?"

"Yes. By controlling the amount of light in the Complex, we can reset your bodies and determine your optimum activity cycles. This fine-tuned state will be needed once you return."

"And when will we be able to live according to Ambar's stars?" The math savant seemed to be looking for structure.

"It would not be advantageous to you to align your physical rhythms to two suns."

Constance grunted at the news.

"Later in your stay, the Earth Complex will simulate Earth's level of sunlight. However, you will not revert to the same schedules you had back home," said Vintar.

Constance glanced at Mr. d'Orsini and Zoa. Perhaps it was something they had discussed earlier.

Vintar returned to comparing Ambar and Earth. "Our planet's water-to-land ratio is much like Earth's."

An image of their planet displayed in our minds.

"We do not use our land as you do on Earth. Ambar is home to populations of nonhuman life forms, and we do not eat them regardless of their sentience rating."

Allan said, "Good to know you won't be cloning us to be a new delicacy."

Ana nudged him. "That's disgusting!"

Vintar stared blankly at Allan before turning to Peter. "Yes, Peter?"

"What does sentience mean?" A few others nodded in support.

"A sentient being is anyone who can feel or perceive."

"Thanks, that's what I thought." The young man looked around like he expected us to be impressed. Mr. d'Orsini patted his bambino's cheek.

"We use 1.7 percent of land for agriculture. *Supersaturated molecular nutrient optimization,* a process invented many millennia ago, enables us to produce foods without depending on our land. We have analyzed all food types for their nutritional and energy profile; with this information, we produce supersaturated molecules with identical profiles."

"Such a system would alleviate hunger for us," said Zoa. "Is this something I will learn how to reproduce or come close to?"

"Yes, you and Sylvia will create a similar solution. All required nutrients can be provided in a drink. The food we grow here allows us to crosscheck cellular structure and composition to maintain knowledge of unsynthesized foods."

I said, "Good to know that we can develop efficient ways of nourishing people, but we should keep some fundamental building blocks in place."

Ana said, "So thinking about how you use the land, does that kinda mitigate ozone layer issues like we have on Earth?"

"We do not have the same factors, such as synthetic chemicals and gases, influencing the ozone. Also, where climate change could be an issue, we are able to create balance through intentional weather modulations."

After some loud exhalations, Allan said, "Man, why are we learning so much about your planet when its ours about to go apocalyptic?"

Vintar answered, "If you save Earth, you must change how you live on it in order for humanity to survive even another fifty years."

Members gasped or sighed. Ambaran intervention or not, her statement had overwhelmed us.

Bringing us back to nutrient drinks, Mr. d'Orsini said, "Does everyone on your planet live off the vials?" His tone sounded incredulous.

"It is one way we obtain nutrients. Personalized drinks deliver the precise nutrition required at the time of consumption. We also intake enriched air supplementation, which triggers nanoparticles with directed objectives."

"How do you determine the right nutrition for the many species?" Zoa asked.

"The foundation for any nutrition is genetic coding. We use gene alleles to find inherited predispositions."

"Nutrigenomics," Zoa whispered.

Vintar explained, "Earth's ability to interpret gene expression and provide customized nutrition plans is rudimentary. However, in time, you will create accurate formulations."

"I hope to advance this area," said the nurse.

"Lack of food is one of many negative conditions on Earth. Its social dynamics, living spaces, daily life, poor nutrition, and negative energetic exchanges with each other and the environment result in most of the population living with unhealthy levels of stress and toxicity. Thus, fight-flight-freeze responses are elicited many times over the course of a day. When not in a primal mode, many Earth humans escape their stress through actions and substances that deaden healthy physical and mental abilities."

"Wow! Speaking of which," Allan said, "I could use a drink about now. If you know what I mean?" He held a make-believe glass and took a sip.

Vintar did not smile or pause. "These can be obtained at one of the drink points."

She was referring to the lighter but still nutritious drinks served in cups for us to use in social settings.

Ever helpful, Peter said, "I think he means the sort of drink that kills brain cells." The level of laughter from the group made me wonder if they were laughing because they found Peter funny or because they could relate to Allan's laddish behavior.

With that perfect setup, the American asked, "Do you drink alcohol or use other substances to take the edge off, so to speak?"

"We do not consume substances to dull cognitive functions. There are, however, ways of releasing positive natural substances in your body that can produce a sense of levity and well-being."

Allan turned to his teammates, who were encouraging him with their cackles. "Nah, that sounds too much like hard work."

Vintar moved on to another concept. "You are made up of over seven octillion atoms, and every atom is composed of 99 percent energy. Every cell and process in your body relies on electrical activity, yet you do not understand how it all works. Just as the discovery of DNA's structure and subsequent understanding of the genetic code fostered new discoveries and knowledge, the mapping of the body's electromagnetic processes will offer the same."

Allan shook his head. "Mapping every cell's ion channels and electromagnetic processes is impossible and can't be that important in the overall scheme of things."

"Breakthroughs in AI will help the process," said Vintar. "If we collapse an average Earth human body, such as yours,"—she waved her hand towards Allan—"to the nuclei, the resulting volume of matter is orders of magnitude less than a speck of dust."

Judging by his startled face, he had registered her example in the worst way.

When Vintar finished, Allan was the first to head off. Zoa, Constance, Ana, Peter, Mr. d'Orsini, and I were all in tow.

Allan stopped and turned to us. He was red-faced and jittery. "Seriously? What the hell was that?" He paused and waited for a reaction.

I stared at the explosive wiz, wondering how far his protest would go.

"This is nonsense!" He shook his head and look at us. "Do you people realize we've been told we're inferior to other humans in their galaxy, we're mostly energy, and our problems are because of stress and some ridiculous negative energetic relationship with our environment? And don't forget that if we manage to save Earth, we're all doomed anyway without the intelligence and technology out here."

"Scusa, I'm not so sure," answered Pino. "Part of my primary goal is investigating energy dynamics between materials and us. We are aging faster than we need to and developing diseases because we don't understand this."

"Man! I feel sorry for you." Allan curled his lips and shook his head in disapproval. "You will be up a creek trying to convince everyone of an energetic relationship between them and their furniture, homes, highways, buildings . . ." He trailed off into a groan.

I said, "Vintar asked us to suspend our current knowledge and be open to different ideas."

The rest of our group gathered around us to hear what was going on.

"Sure, but I won't lose my mind and go into their fantasy world," Allan fumed. "You"—he pointed at me and scowled—"just seem to accept everything they say and do with no pushback. They've invaded our personal space, confined us to a manufactured environment, and demeaned our way of life on Earth. Can't you see what's going on? They are stripping away our identities. Why are we even here? Aren't we too inferior to save our planet?"

All eyes and ears were angled towards him.

Peter rallied to his side. "Yeah, he's right." The young man was impressionable.

I countered his paranoia. "You're looking at things through a narrow lens. Each of these ideas will help us make improvements back on Earth and possibly save our lives. Our old ways of thinking are destroying the planet, even before a catastrophic event occurs."

Constance glared at Allan. "The Ambarans are more advanced than we are. They brought us here across universes—isn't that evidence enough? Perhaps you need to put your ego aside for once and stop being so daft, Allan. You're happy to take their technology but not their advice?"

"Oh come on, Connie, you're not accepting their ways either. You're a control freak, recording how many steps and seconds it takes to get from one place to another." He marched in place. "You silently count everything—discs, people, time, locations, steps, everything." His eyes bulged as he pointed to each thing he was naming. "You're even trying to create a time framework because you can't live without metrics." He snarled at her in disgust. "So give me a break. You're supposed to be a genius, but you're like Victoria—you can't *see* what's going on. They have taken away our framework to destabilize and brainwash us. We're rudderless and under their control."

Watching Constance's reaction made me uneasy. Her lack of expression made it difficult to see what she thought about Allan's conclusions. Maybe she was tuning it all out.

Moments later, I got my answer. The telltale sign didn't come from her face but her fingers. I had seen them react before when she was stressed, but not like this. They twitched at high speed, like a seasoned accountant on a calculator, each digit touching the tip of another and then another as if counting to a trillion. Soon, the energy overtook what her fingers could bear, and it traveled up to her eyes, which blinked like someone sending an SOS signal from a sinking ship.

The group froze as they waited for her to fight back or crumble. She gave no verbal rebuttal. It simply wasn't possible with her lips pressed together like they were stitched shut. I wanted to step in but interfering could have made things worse. How would she react when up against the ropes like a trapped boxer? It was a live cognitive neuroscience experiment. My curiosity absorbed me—I didn't stop Allan's bullying.

"That's enough, you two!" Zoa said in an assertive but calm voice. "Let's take a deep breath and remember we are in this together. We don't need to disrespect each other."

Constance gave Allan the evil eye doused with an air of superiority. "For your information, I know *exactly* what time it is."

Her response sent a chill down my spine. That was not the comeback I'd expected. Did she really know the time . . . on Earth or Ambar? Or did she mean it was time for her to leave?

She closed her eyes for a few seconds, exhaled audibly, and without uttering another word turned and walked off.

Ana huffed and puffed as she comforted Allan. They drew Peter in closer to exchange comments and complaints. With the drama over, our group parted ways.

I stood, half frozen. It wasn't just two people who lost ground in the argument; we were all defeated in that moment. I was also disappointed in myself. I needed to lead, not just observe.

Zoa and I left for Inner 1's Re-Hub. I was deep in thought as we walked, until she nudged me and pointed with her head. "There's Constance. Good that she's here with others and not off on her own."

Constance and Sabine were immersed in a quiet conversation.

"I hope Allan isn't getting the best of her," I said.

Zoa shook her head. "She spends much time with her new friend."

"I didn't know Sabine and Constance were close. I don't know Sabine that well."

"She's from Germany but has lived in many countries because of her work for a charity." Zoa smiled warmly at the German and continued offering her impressions. "She is so good at relating to everyone. The best thing is how she fully accepts and understands Constance."

"I should have stopped the conflict." I waited for Zoa to look at me. "Thank you for being the voice of reason."

As we watched, three others went to speak to Sabine. Like a flock of geese, they followed her over to the other side of the Re-Hub. It seemed so easy for her to be accepted and liked.

Constance stayed back, and my guilt propelled me over to her. "Hi, can we talk for a minute?"

"If it's about Allan, then no, I'm fine."

Her directness took me aback, but I knew where she stood on the matter.

"I'm sorry I didn't step in and mediate."

"It's not your fault. Besides, I can handle myself." She waved goodbye and walked out of the Re-Hub.

Zoa and I chatted, but my eyes and mind were on the magnanimous German woman. Her personality would be useful back on Earth when we were in a high-alert state, and people were on edge.

"We have too many personality conflicts. I hope we can stay focused on our goals."

"We have some strong personalities in our group, but I think we should be patient. One thing I'm sure we can all agree on is that whoever we were when we arrived, we will be different when we leave, and those changes may not come easy."

"Quite," I said, nodding.

"Tell me, how do you feel about your primary goal?" she said.

"Curiously, no one else has asked me about it." This was my chance to clarify. "I see myself as a coordinator of our efforts back on Earth based on everyone's strengths."

She squinted and smiled. "You will need to do much more than coordinate."

I stared at her. "I'm just trying to keep up with what I need to learn."

"You'll be fine." Zoa touched my elbow. "Perhaps the Ambarans could give you something to help you come to terms with your primary goal."

"If I get any more enrichments, I won't recognize myself." I laughed to hide my nervousness about the interventions' side effects. From my work, I knew that everything had side effects, whether noticeable to the study's subjects or not. But in our case, there didn't seem to be an alternative.

On the way back to my residence, I went over Vintar's module, Allan's stance, his conflict with Constance, and what I could do to bring us together. While Zoa took these clashes in stride, I was concerned. We needed to be a cohesive and supportive group, without exceptions.

As I prepared for a rest, I weighed whether to ask Anthea about Ambar as a possible lifeboat. With all the help the Ambarans were giving us, I didn't want them to think I was half-committed to doing the work ourselves.

○ ○ ○

Outside of regular modules, we took part in practicums and labs, either in small groups or individually. I'd been spending many long days alone in research mode until Peter, Allan, Constance, Zoa, and I were summoned to Inner 3 to participate in an unscheduled lab.

Excited about working with others, I could've flown down on my own had a disc not been waiting for me.

We donned headgear just before entering a laboratory where Vintar awaited. As I entered the room, I felt a suction-like pressure over my entire body, as if I'd crossed an important threshold. I'd never imagined what nothing smelled like, but the lab delivered the sensation. The room was sparser than any cleanroom I'd seen before. Shiny white-blue panels dominated the walls. Notably, there wasn't a single chair, exhibit area, or instrument.

"Welcome to one of the five nano laboratories in the Earth Complex. Although your outfit generators ensure no loose skin particles are coming from you, the entryway to this laboratory covered you with a thin sealant."

"No cleanroom bunny suits required," said Allan.

Peter gave him a cockeyed glance. They exchanged words, of which I only caught "sterile environment." Peter nodded and brought his attention back to Vintar.

"In this assignment, you will use newly gained skills, knowledge, and existing frameworks to achieve a common goal."

"Cool, I've been looking for a challenge." He looked at me. "That's a joke. I've got enough on my plate."

I smiled at his honesty.

Vintar explained our objective. "Design, create, test, and simulate the usage of medical nanobots."

Peter rubbed his hands together. "Yeah! I get to build something."

"That's right, buddy, and I get to do my first live programming of organic material."

"The nanobot must be capable of treating injured tissues and delivering targeted therapies within the human body. Although you will use novel nanomaterials, unavailable or undiscovered on Earth, the skills and techniques are transferable. Our materials will ensure biocompatibility and efficiency."

We indicated through the adjunct that we had no questions or comments. The silence didn't reassure me of our competencies to pull off the tasks.

"Once you decide on a design or action, the simulation system will accelerate your work."

"Like time-lapsed photography," Peter said with wide eyes and a smile.

"Begin," Vintar said.

Zoa started us off. "Injured tissues and cells give off signals to the rest of the body. First, we must decide if we want to avoid our body's reaction to injury and rely on nanobots or if the bots will help our natural response to accelerate the healing process."

We looked to Vintar for guidance. She stood blank-faced.

Constance said, "It depends on when the injury occurred and how the whole body is handling it."

"Quite," I said.

Allan said, "Yeah, suppress the body's natural healing mechanisms or boost them. I vote for the booster."

"It does seem to involve fewer variables to control," said the math savant.

"Let's boost the healing mechanisms of the damaged tissue." I made my first call as team leader.

Allan shared his adjunct's view, which triggered a work area to appear a few feet away. He had already started designing healthy cells with programmable properties.

Zoa said, "We need different types of cells, some to alter the electrical signals and others to release extracellular vesicles that will pass on information to the surrounding cells and correct their behavior."

"Wow! We can do that?" said Peter.

Constance asked, "Can we see the damaged tissue in situ?" In an instant, a 3D model of a woman with intestinal lining inflammation and degradation appeared before us.

Allan got to work encoding the instructions onto bots.

Zoa held her chin deep in thought as she turned the 3D model around and examined all sides. She walked over to Allan's workstation. "Allan, you need to build in sensors to get the bots to the target cells."

"Can you program the bots to mimic white blood cells that naturally go to the damaged tissues?" asked Constance.

"Sure. . . I can do that." Allan nodded slowly and squinted at her. "You're not all numbers, are you?"

"The area is severely inflamed," said Zoa. "Let's send some cells in loaded with anti-inflammatory medicine."

Vintar said, "You can select the class of medicine without indicating the precise name."

Within hours, we were ready to test our creation. We acknowledged completion through our adjuncts.

The first test was on a segment of injured tissue on a small slate. On Earth, we would have needed a microscope to work on the tissue, but with our adjuncts on, we could switch to any view required. Nervous excitement filled the room as we introduced the nanobots to the diseased tissue. It worked but seemed too easy.

"That's it?" asked Peter.

"Success doesn't always come with bells and whistles," I said, although it didn't sit well with me either.

Zoa audibly exhaled. "It's time for the in vivo test."

We watched the cells swarm to the injured sight, and within minutes the inflammation reduced. However, moments later, it was as if the cells had changed languages. They stopped responding to our nanobots.

Zoa said, "It's not going to work. The damaged cells have changed and are signaling the surrounding cells to attack the bots. Our patient will be dead soon."

"I knew it couldn't be that easy," I said, dropping my head. "What else should we have done?"

"Ye of little faith," said Allan. "I programmed the nanobots to respond to the lower pH due to apoptosis. Yeah, I got the idea from our first health lab when you"—Allan nodded at Zoa—"noticed a decrease in your levels."

Zoa stared at him with a big grin. "You remembered. But why—"

Allan nodded and raised in arms. "Ladies and . . . gentleman, after hundreds of experiments, I've learned that relying on a single solution or technology in any field is bad business. I always create a backup plan."

"Clever. Nice that you are taking precautions," I said. Despite my reservations about Allan, I had to give credit where it was due.

We continued watching the patient until she made a full recovery.

Peter said, "It was fun to design and create tools. I like that with everyone's smarts, you still need me to make things for you."

Allan laughed. "Hard luck, buddy. You'll have to leave your uncle's car repair business."

Zoa said, "You'll create many things to improve the health of millions of people."

Peter nodded and gave her a look of sympathy. "I'll do my best."

Our ability to work seamlessly as a unit was beyond my expectations. We were progressing individually and as a team.

"No doubt the bar will be risen for all the rest of our assignments and labs," I said. "That was great teamwork." I never thought I would see the day when I was so proud of my team members and thrilled to be a part of it. With a proud smile, I said, "We will only get better and stronger." As I said the words, a pang of doubt hit me. Had I just jinxed it?

CHAPTER 9

THE HUNT

With the intensifying focus on our individual goals and specialties, we spent less and less time together. I wanted more balance between working on my own and working in a team, especially after the successful lab with Allan, Zoa, Constance, and Peter.

Finally, after many Earth weeks, the whole team gathered in the Outer 6 Re-Hub for social drinks and discussed our recent lessons and latest discoveries.

Five of us were in a huddle talking through our challenges when Allan crept up behind me. "So how are we doing?"

Pleasantly surprised by his question, I said, "I'm well thanks."

He smirked, narrowed his eyes, and looked around at the others. "I meant we as a group, not the royal *we*."

My face turned red. "Oh, right."

Allan asked, "You *are* keeping up with the data on all of us, aren't you? Are we where the Ambarans expected us to be?"

"From what I can see, we are on course. I suppose we could always do better, like in the area of personality clashes."

Allan shook his head in disagreement. "Nah, don't worry about that. The Ambarans are changing us to be more like their AEHs." He held up his hands and lowered his voice. "Imagine what will happen if we don't conform!" To add further effect, he finished his statement by humming the ominous, ubiquitous four-note opening of Beethoven's fifth symphony.

He was still proffering less-than-helpful theories.

It wasn't like we were completely losing our identities. Before I could ask Allan to elaborate, he scurried over to Ana.

It would have been difficult to know if team members were becoming more like AEHs with as little time we were spending together.

Mr. d'Orsini approached wearing an adjunct. "Victoria." He held my hand. "It feels like a long time since we saw each other. Si?"

"Indeed. How are you doing?"

He guided me to the Nebula wall. "Let's have a vial and I will tell you all about it."

Suddenly, in the middle of telling me about his experiments on the energy of materials, he raised his hand to his ear.

"Scusa, it was a message from a Conduit. Constance is going to join us."

"Where is she?" I said.

"She is on her way from . . ." He turned towards the entrance. "There she is."

Constance approached us with a preoccupied expression.

"Hi, everything okay? You look like you have a lot on your mind," I said.

"Don't we all. I just counted the steps from the platform to here. First, face the platform, turn left by 90 degrees, walk 35 steps, then alter your course by another 45 degrees left and walk 23 steps . . ."

Unable to suppress it, I interrupted her with a muted chuckle. "But we can use the schematics and map."

"I try not to rely on the map, and I wanted to give you that option too . . . by telling you the directions."

"Indeed. Very considerate. Thank you." So, she preferred not to depend on Ambar's navigation system but was completely fine with relying on their wardrobe technology and meal efficiencies?

"How are you both doing on your primary goals?" I asked. Although I checked the metrics every other day, that didn't tell me their subjective experience.

Constance was quick to reply. "Well, part of my primary goal is to help you review scenarios, approaches, and outcomes once we return. From a quantitative perspective, I can't collect meaningful data to track stats on our team without proper timeframes, patterns, or schedules. There are micropatterns, but there would be more if we could sync ourselves with Ambar's natural environment. Their day is 19.65 hours—it is close to an Earth day, so why not use that as our guide?" She was still looking to devise a structure.

I reassured her. "I've been reviewing our outcomes. Last time I checked, everyone was on track or ahead of where they need to be. So the EC's environment isn't having a detrimental effect."

"But when we get home, the team will operate at a different level. I need to know where those differences might occur. Circadian rhythm changes could significantly impact our performance for weeks. Weeks we won't have."

"What about you?" Constance looked at Pino. "Do you feel good about your progress?"

"Si, my simulations allow me to test the best materials to build with. It's well known back home that materials have magnetic properties, but there are also subtle energetic exchanges that I'm exploring."

Wanting to show some sympathy for Constance, I said, "I can see that you want to cover all the bases, but if it was necessary for us to be on Earth cycles, I'm sure the Ambarans would set the EC to the twenty-four-hour clock."

Constance said, "I have asked about it. A Conduit told me that we're all following schedules based on our biometrics and bio-rhythms."

"Earth has the only known human civilization to sleep an average of eight hours or more at a time. We would perform better on polyphasic cycles where we rest twice every twenty-four-hours," I said. "And individual cycles would be an advantage back on Earth, especially in times of crisis. Someone would always be awake and working."

As we finished our vials, Constance said, "Don't get me wrong, I understand what the Ambarans are trying to achieve, but I don't see how set schedules would hurt."

"Si, and real food."

All I could do was listen and hope she would stay focused on the important things. I had been reviewing scores of cognitive data and knew everyone's stats on their levels of data retention, accuracy, reaction times, etc.... If they weren't doing well, then I would see it in the numbers.

Of course I missed home, Aunt Judy, Anne, people at work, and Albert . . . and Malcolm, but with so much at risk, it felt selfish to let my own desires get in the way. All life on Earth depended on us. Fear of failing our mission drove me to overcome the hurdles, both internal and external.

With time and distance, I found myself softening towards Malcolm. Something could have forced his hand. Maybe one of the team members saw my session and confronted Malcolm about it. He had too much integrity to throw me under the bus.

When I returned to Anthea, I double-checked my conclusions on the team's progress.

"Anthea, are members struggling with a lack of daily framework, varied rest schedules, and solid food. In other words, how is everyone doing psychologically?"

Summary information was displayed in front of me. From the metadata, I could drill down into specifics. "The psychological disposition charts look rather flat. Where are the typical ups and downs people experience?"

"Small psychological issues are not enough to register outside the accepted values," Anthea said. "Their bodies are in equilibrium and the vials assist in maintaining this. Polyphasic rest cycles are essential for the team once you return."

"Indeed." We weren't just doing things so the Ambarans could see how we live. Our current lifestyle was preparation for what was to come. It wasn't lost on me that my monitor had just revealed something we would need back home. Was it a mistake? What else might I be able to coax out of her?

"Should we also prioritize how we get our nutrients, like in vials?" I said nonchalantly.

"You must decide priorities as a team when you are back on Earth," she said.

"Yes, of course." I smirked at my failed attempt to outwit the AI.

"Can you weight the psychological metrics higher so that smaller issues come to my attention while still maintaining a level of privacy for members?"

The compliant monitor said, "Requested changes are active."

Based on the summaries of teammates' activities and objectives, everyone from Allan to Sylvia was doing well in their super masterclasses, but there was still a vast amount of material to cover.

○ ○ ○

For our next module, we collected adjuncts and set off for the Low Gardens area; I'd never been out so far. Our group's five discs traveled at high speed for about six minutes before arriving at our project site—a magnificent, blue-black dome.

Sylvia, smiling like she was in the midst of a spiritual experience, pointed to a nearby forest. "Look over there, that's where I go to learn about the galaxy's horticultural history. The range of species is mind-boggling."

She was one of the few with access to the area. From the summary data I had reviewed in my residence, Sylvia had exceeded the minimum requirements, particularly in her ability to remove toxins and revitalize the soil, enabling it to support twenty times the number of people that Earth's land would currently sustain.

Could that be an important piece of the puzzle?

Our discs slipped through the structure's open top and let us off. The interior walls, colored the same blue-black as the dome, made it difficult to see the area's dimensions, but it felt big. It was too large for the fourteen of us—unless we were about to be out-numbered.

As we took in our surroundings, a neural message was delivered. "Ambarans will join you shortly."

"Wait, real Ambarans?" asked Peter.

Allan nodded. "I don't think so, buddy."

Zoa said, "Who are we meeting with then?"

The room metamorphosed into a smaller area, and ten individuals appeared all at once. If arm in arm, they would have resembled a chorus line. The ensemble was unusual but nonetheless human.

As I eyed them, my adjunct produced profiles. Each had a specialization and was skilled in a litany of other complex fields, such as microbiology, nanoenergetic dynamics, and evolutionary genetics.

I flitted between their physical appearance and reading their profiles; both were captivating. They resembled Earth humans, except these beings had curious combinations. One female, Noha, had Asian facial features and white, glistening hair with small beads of gold that pulsed up and down her strands. At six-foot-eight, she towered above all of us.

According to Noha's details, she and the others would communicate with each other nonverbally, through neural connections. I thought that was a given.

Noha was the first to speak aloud. "We are here to design a barrier together." She spoke in a melodic tone, like Pino. "It is for a species living in the depths of our galaxy."

Mr. d'Orsini leaned into Allan and me. "We can see who they are through the adjuncts, but should we do introductions?"

I shrugged my shoulders. "Maybe they will start us off."

Not content with my response, the AI entrepreneur made the first move. He walked over to Noha and extended his hand. "Hey, I'm Allan, nice to meet you."

We each followed suit by greeting the Ambaran closest to us.

"What is the barrier for?" Mr. d'Orsini asked.

"It will protect the site of a future habitat," said Dvita. His pale skin, rosy cheeks, and dark brown hair were well within Earth human characteristics. He explained, "We will build an impenetrable shield using exotic energy particles which will mitigate the harmful effects of space radiation and impacts from meteors or asteroids. You will also be shown how the technologies can be translated into those available on Earth."

In a flash, specifications downloaded to our adjuncts, along with a priorities list to direct our efforts. The Ambarans didn't contribute much, except to answer questions about the habitat's location and parameters. Our team was reserved at first, but loosened up when Allan and I jointly created a positive flow of communication, leadership, and teamwork. We prioritized, allocated roles, and drew up a plan. Mr. d'Orsini, Peter, and Constance designed the barrier through multidimensional modeling. Later, I joined Allan and eight others to devise a quantum entanglement power source.

Allan said, "We're just over 50 percent through. Let's take a break."

"Good idea." Peter said as he bounced up and down.

I, too, needed some space—not from the project but from the Ambarans. They weren't sitting well with me.

Peter extended his arms towards them. "Why don't you come with us?"

The Ambarans eyed each other, blank-faced. Dvita said, "Yes, we will join you."

I sat on my own with a bland green drink. How could we all have misunderstood when Vintar told us there were no Ambaran humans and that the real Ambarans were beyond what we needed? These had to be AEHs. They were too much like us.

Before I could continue my analysis, Peter's friend, Tomas, sauntered over to me.

"I wasn't sure about these Ambarans at first, but now I think they're great." He grinned from ear to ear. "Bradley, the short one, has the same hobby as me."

Bradley was the shortest individual we'd come across on Ambar, at four-foot-ten.

"And what hobby would that be?" I looked away, only half-interested in Tomas's hobbies.

"Back home in the countryside, everyone hunts. We track deer, fowl, and foxes. I have gone with the serious hunters to other countries in search of the Big Five—"

"Sorry, Big Five?" He'd lost the other half of my interest when he said "everyone hunts."

"Wow! You don't know . . . Well, I guess you wouldn't. They're rhinoceros, lions, elephants, buffalo, and leopards."

Tomas had dropped ten rungs on my respect ladder. "That's awful. Anyway, go on."

"I told him about the animal trophies on my walls at home. I have so many that I had to put some out in the barn."

I cringed at the thought of lovely animals on display . . . or not, as some were in a barn. But he suddenly had my full attention. "What! You mean to tell me that you and an Ambaran both hunt?" The blood drained from my face and made me lightheaded.

He gave an impassioned nod like he'd just met his new best friend.

"But that's not possible." I shook my head, closed my eyes for a couple seconds, and tried to convince myself that we hadn't been duped. "Don't you remember? In our second assignment, Vintar told us Ambarans wouldn't harm any living entity. Then again, she also told us Ambarans weren't human."

"Oh . . ." Tomas looked down as if he had just gotten his friend in trouble. "Well, he enjoys hunting, but they're not allowed to keep the animals or parts."

Alarms were going off in my head like an overactive pinball machine. Tomas had uncovered something I wouldn't have predicted in a million years. *If it's true, and Ambarans hunt, what else might I be missing—or worse yet, what could they be hiding?*

I went into freeze mode, causing Tomas's voice to fade into the background. A lump formed in my throat. Suddenly, getting to know more about the so-called advanced Ambarans took on a sense of urgency. Though there was every possibility I wouldn't like what I'd find.

We returned to the project, and I launched in. "I have a question for the Ambarans before we continue."

Noha responded, "Yes, Victoria?"

It was a delicate matter, so I tried to be tactful. "Are you entirely human like us and capable of metacognition?"

I heard whispers from my team members. Perhaps they thought it was an inappropriate question to ask.

Allan rubbed his hands together. "Now we're talking."

Ana sneered at me. "Can someone tell me what metacognition means?"

Her bestie answered, "It's a hot topic in AI. Metacognition is the ability for a being to think about thinking, or to contemplate its own existence."

Noha addressed my query. "The answer to the first part of your question is no, and to the second part—yes."

My closed questions got short, one-word answers. It was a mistake I rarely made when designing studies and surveys, but in fairness, I was anxious.

Allan rephrased my questions in his special way. "Are you autonomous beings or what?"

The Earth team stood still with their eyes wide open, waiting for an answer.

Suddenly, I felt a deep emotion from the Ambarans. Their eyes screamed horror to me.

"We must take you to another location." Noha motioned us towards the exit.

"What's going on?" I asked. This wasn't the response I expected to either my question or Allan's clarification.

"Everyone must take a disc and await further instructions." Noha was calm, but I sensed agitation.

"What is it? What's happened?" I asked.

"We must hide the team's life signs."

My jaw dropped. "What...why?"

"We will explain once the incident has passed."

I boarded a disc with Constance and Peter. The five discs put up shields and hurled us through the EC like never before. With a sudden jolt the disc swooped down into a dark orifice. We stood frozen as we dove into what felt like the world's deepest well. After a few minutes, the disc slowed but continued its descent.

Finally, we stopped, and the shield became transparent.

"Look, the others are here too," Peter said as he cupped his hands around his eyes and leaned up against the disc's protective layer.

It was a surreal sight. We were stacked like zipper teeth.

"Did Noha tell you what's going on?" Constance looked at me.

"She said"—my voice shook—"they needed to hide our life signs."

"That's not good," said my fellow Brit. "Think about it. Why would they need to hide us in the depths of their planet. This is serious."

"You're scaring me, yeah." Peter grabbed her arm and put his face up to mine. "Are they going to kill us?"

Constance said, "All l know is that we can't stay down here for long without vials or enriched air."

"Okay, listen. We need to stay calm. The Ambarans are aware of our survival needs." I peered outward at the faint glow of the other four discs and wondered how they were coping. "They won't let us die."

"The way I see it, there are two unfortunate outcomes possible," said Constance. "Our hosts could accidentally kill us, or whoever they are hiding us from could find us and kill us."

Peter's eyeballs popped two inches outside his sockets, and he started rambling hysterically.

"Really, Constance," I snapped. "Just this once, can't you give us more than the worst-case scenarios?" I exhaled loudly and put my arm around Peter, who was uncomfortably close to me already. "The most probable outcome is that the Ambarans will bring us back to the surface when it's safe."

"How do you do it?" asked Constance. "How do you have such faith in them?"

"It's logical." I had to speak her language so she could help talk Peter down. "They have already done so much for us. They don't want to lose their investment." It was a cold way of summarizing our alliance, but it was the best I could do at that moment.

"Now you're in risk assessment?" I could see the shine of her cheeks. Of all the times she could have chosen to smile, it was when we were in near-complete darkness. "But I see your point."

"So we're not going to die?" asked Peter.

"Not yet," answered the savant. It was as good as we were going to get from her.

"Maybe you shouldn't have asked them if they were human," said the young Czech.

I shook my head and said, "That's not why we're here. It was a coincidence."

Peter sank down to the floor of the disc.

Constance copied him. "Good idea. We should conserve our energy."

We waited and waited, changing positions every few minutes.

"Why can't we talk to the others?" Peter asked.

"No comms. It's better this way." Constance cleared her throat. "We don't need to hear Allan's ideas."

As we sat, I heard Peter sniffling and mumbling.

"We're going to be okay. I promise," I said.

Constance tutted and swatted my leg.

Eventually, we quieted, waiting.

Then it happened. The discs lit up and powered us swiftly towards the surface.

Peter jumped up. "Yes! We're saved."

"Of course we are. I promised," I said as I smiled at Constance.

We surfaced and sped to Inner 1, where Noha and a Conduit stood waiting.

As we dismounted the discs, I quickly looked around to see how everyone was.

Sylvia and Zoa were arm in arm in conversation, and Mr. d'Orsini walked solemnly behind them. They looked well, considering.

Allan zipped around to Peter, exchanged a few words, then stormed up to Noha. "What the— Why didn't you tell us what was going on?"

The Conduit explained, "At that depth, communication devices do not work. However, your body's ingested matter kept your vitals and processes at optimum levels."

"Man, you should've said something. We thought we were going to die." The American tugged at his hair.

"Allan must have driven himself and the others crazy in there," Constance said to me.

We gathered around Noha for an update. "Another species was looking for something and searched Ambar and the surrounding planets. We did not want them to discover you. It would raise too many questions that we are not prepared to answer."

"What were the chances of them finding us?" asked Constance.

"Forty percent. The EC is located just outside an inhabited area. Most of their search was in uninhabited areas."

"They must have some serious search tools, since we were basically sent to hell in the middle of the planet," said Allan.

Noha and Dvita didn't respond.

The Conduit said, "You are all in need of a rest period. Return to your residences."

Although frazzled by the surprise evacuation, everyone seemed so relieved to be back on the surface that we acted like well-trained, obedient dogs.

A short time later, we rejoined the Ambaran . . . beings.

Dvita wasted no time in answering the hanging question. "We are Augmented Earth Humans. Like Vintar, we are designed to be fully autonomous metacognitive humans."

Peter leaned over to me and whispered. "The AEHs are Ambaran humans?" He rubbed his forehead.

Noha turned to him. "No, there are no Ambaran humans."

Dvita looked at each of us as he spoke. "However, we can also exist in a proxy-consciousness mode, where an Ambaran can have a first-hand experience without being physically present. We are currently in proxy-consciousness mode."

"Hold the phone. Someone else's consciousness is using your body now?" Allan asked.

"Yes, ten individuals from Ambar have chosen to interact with you in this manner," Noha said. She didn't flinch. If she were an Earth human, I would've detected physical signs of discomfort as we exposed them.

On the other hand, our team members whispered and sat in astonishment. Not so composed a response.

I wasn't amused. "Why aren't the Ambarans physically here, rather than acting through you?"

"This approach was chosen as the most suitable and comfortable for everyone." Noha looked around the room at us.

Allan took over the questioning. "Are your thoughts from one Ambaran, or are you operating as both a shared and independent AEH, if that's possible?"

"We are presenting the direct thoughts of the Ambarans," Dvita said. "Shared consciousness does not mean that two consciousnesses are simultaneously engaged."

I took a deep breath and tried to ready myself for their response to my next question. "Do the real Ambarans hunt?" This time, there were no whispers or side discussions, only anticipation wrapped in silence.

The AEHs exchanged a few eye movements before Bradley answered. "Yes."

A few audible gasps emanated from our group.

"This changes everything," I said.

Bradley said, "There are teams who specialize in travelling across the galaxies and universes, seeking species to add to our databases. We observe each new species from afar and, depending on its developmental stage, we either make contact or implant individuals with an organic identifier, unbeknownst to them."

"Observe?" I said, wanting confirmation.

"Yes," Noha said.

Of course, the "unbeknownst" part was questionable, but I wasn't prepared to go into full-on interrogation mode.

"The identifier allows us to track the species," Bradley continued. "Complete profiles are developed, displayed in our species catalog, and available for access like any other piece of information."

Tomas blushed. "So you don't hunt to kill?"

"To kill another species, regardless of its level of sentience, goes against our values," said his former hunting mate.

They'd extinguished the last remnant of my distress on their hobby. However, the Ambarans' lack of transparency in how they were interacting with us unsettled me.

"Will you be cataloguing and tracking us?" asked Constance.

Allan leaned forwards as he said, "Good question. I mean you already put your organic technology in us."

"We have gone beyond distant observation with you. No further interaction is required to add you to our species database," said Noha.

Allan nodded and smirked, "Sure, sure."

Indiscernible whispers from team members filled the air. The AEHs didn't elaborate. They didn't seem to pick up on the discomfort of their audience.

AEHs were more than enhanced copies of us; they came in three variations. Our previous assignments' AEHs were autonomous sentient beings. The II-AEH, who'd replaced Marcus, had an entire person's identity imprinted on him. And then there were these ten AEHs who were inhabited by Ambarans via proxy-consciousness.

Peter looked at AEH Noha. "Earth humans think we're the only intelligent life form out there. Wait till they hear about all of this!"

Dvita was spurred on by his statement. "Using limited technology and knowledge, you have not found life outside your planet; thus, you conclude there are no other life forms?"

"Yeah, it sounds crazy now," Peter said.

As I watched the AEHs, an inexplicable sensation overwhelmed me—an intense, almost uncomfortable feeling of love seemed to emanate from them. My body warmed, and my heart quickened as I tried to understand it. I closed my eyes to figure out who it was coming from.

Mr. d'Orsini startled me when he clapped his hands and said, "Let's get back to work."

When I opened my eyes, the Ambarans had all turned away from me.

The Ambarans actively helped with the remainder of the project. They shared information on the diversity of life, both in space and on other planets. Some of the most curious life forms were sentient beings who fed off energy from supernovas.

Allan immersed himself in planning a monitoring system using advanced AI. The system would watch all activity around the shield. His mastery of alien technology and quantumverse concepts was impressive. *I must coin "quantumverse" after we save the world.*

We finished the project and headed to the Delta Center's Inner 1 Re-Hub. The topic du jour was who or what the real Ambarans were. Allan and Ana came up with the most extreme idea: sentient intelligent nanoparticle beings capable of taking any form at will.

○　○　○

In an effort to keep me connected to their work and progress, Zoa and Peter invited me and Allan to a lab review.

Peter rubbed his hands together and started. "On Earth, we have more than a hundred different antibiotics, yeah. They are grouped by what they are made of and what they do. But more and more people are becoming resistant to them." He stopped and looked over to Zoa, who nodded reassuringly. "Thousands of people die of bacterial infections because the antibiotics don't work." Peter raised his hands, looked at me and Allan, and said, "That's a bad thing."

Zoa added, "However, today we are going to do some experiments in cutting edge medical science."

"Cool! Let's do it." Allan put on a lab adjunct.

We began evaluating thousands of known and unknown bacteria.

As we inspected the structures, Zoa gave us some history. "In the early stages of a civilization on a nearby planet, natural viruses or bacteriophages were used for targeting and eliminating specific harmful bacteria. They didn't manufacture antibiotics because of the negative effects of such broad treatments."

Allan asked, "What effects?"

"Antibiotics attack good and bad bacteria, which throws our body's ecosystem out of balance. Instead, let's work on chemically altering phages." Zoa looked over to Allan. "Phages are non-toxic proteins and nucleic acids that can infect dangerous bacteria and destroy it, which allows the patient to heal."

A mesmerizing bird-like creature appeared in front of us within a pyramid. As it moved, tiny particles of light were produced by its two sets of wings, leaving a trail of faint luminescence.

Peter said, "This is what I call a Quantawinger."

A summary of the bird came through the adjunct. It could travel instantly from one location to another, including across interstellar distances, by creating small portals.

Zoa magnified the view. "This beautiful bird is one of many that can travel vast distances in an instant. Which is magnificent, but it could also carry lethal bacteria from one location to another.

"Using advanced forms of gene editing, we can engineer and modify phages as a way of controlling unwanted bacteria." Zoa changed the pyramid to a microscope-type instrument, where we examined and edited the phages.

We followed her instruction and created phages with enhanced effectiveness, broadened the spectrum of activity, and made them more resistant to bacterial defenses.

Peter chimed in, "Yeah, and we can also whip up phage cocktails that can target many different bacterial strains at once."

This time Peter changed our scene. "Here you can see the bird is carrying twelve different types of bacteria." He smirked. "It travels a lot. But we can make sure it doesn't pass anything along." Peter held the bird and put a few drops of a phage mixture in its mouth.

"They no longer use bacteriophages in this galaxy, but their knowledge of them is very helpful to us," Zoa said.

"Yeah," Peter said. "And Zoa and I will duplicate some of these tools and techniques back home."

I look at Zoa with admiration. "This is exactly the kind of treatment you were hoping to find. So, is it realistic to believe you can reproduce this on Earth?"

"Not exactly, but we can use the principles to guide us and come up with some good targeting phages."

"How do you know what will work with the different bacteria?" asked Allan.

"Yes, good," said Zoa.

"We need your help with AI," her young apprentice said, "to help us find different combinations that work."

"The Ambarans have shown us much in the areas of bioelectricity and magnetism. These forces apply within and between cells, organs, and our entire body," the passionate nurse said. "I have a new understanding of electrotaxis, which is when cells are directed by an applied electric field. It is an area that medical and physics communities on Earth have been slow to research and integrate."

Zoa showed us dynamic, diseased 3D models, which she cured using the new techniques. "It isn't as advanced as the methods used in this universe, but it's a good next step for us. The electrome is an intriguing part of my primary goal."

"Electrome?" I said.

"Yes, have you heard of our bodies' microbiome or microorganism network?"

Allan and I nodded.

"The electrome is the body's electrical and magnetic network. Every cell has a charge that can be measured and modulated. To have a full understanding of ionic channels and how they work with surrounding cells is critical for us to master so that we can heal our people faster and without toxic medicines."

Once again, the lab was proof that we could work together. Zoa was fulfilling her role admirably and saw to it that Peter and Allan were part of the solutions.

After their presentation, as we headed back to Inner 1, Constance breezed past us.

"Hey, what's the rush?" Allan said.

"Sabine recommended something. I'm on my way to check it out." She picked up her pace, and we tried to keep up.

Peter ran in front of her, flipped around, walked backwards, and continued asking questions. "What is it? Has Sabine finished her module?"

"An area to recharge. And you will have to ask her."

"You mean a place to help with your caffeine withdrawal?" Allan shouted from two strides behind.

"Push off." Constance waved her hand over her shoulder as if shooing away an annoying fly.

"Allan, did you do something more to get on her bad side?" I asked.

He rolled his eyes. "I just asked if she would help me at the tables when we get back home."

"You didn't!"

"She's high strung about it 'cuz her brother made her do some sports betting for him. I'll turn her around."

"Just because she's a math savant doesn't mean you can use her for your own gain. It's unethical."

"Maybe for you, but it's just smart in my eyes." Allan smirked.

Peter asked Constance, "But where are we going?"

"We?" She glanced back at her impromptu entourage and sighed. "Fine, we're going to the CRC."

"I've heard about that place, but I didn't want to be the first to try it," Allan said.

Peter's long legs helped him keep up with her. "Isn't that where you get your car—uhh, I mean body supercharged? I like to remember things in terms of cars."

"Really." Constance shook her head at the youngster's memory tricks.

Peter scowled. "But what does CRC stand for? It's not Car Re-charging Center."

Without expression, she said, "Cellular Renewal Center."

"Oh yeah, that's what it stands for. I remember now."

Allan, only one stride behind, said, "From what I've heard, it might be just your thing. Luckily, Sabine has come to your rescue—well, *our* rescue."

On our first day, he'd teased Constance about being on edge without her coffee. She understood it was a psychological addiction; any caffeine in her body was long gone, but that fact didn't seem to make a difference.

Before entering the CRC, she had her biometrics read by a scanner like the one in the health lab. With the all-clear, she rushed into the CRC's many rows of recessed squares.

The British savant stepped into one square, about six inches down.

Allan's eyes floated across the recharging center. "I can't think of a better guinea pig. If she comes out unscathed, I'll try it myself. Even if we won't know what the Ambarans are changing in us until it's too late. When—"

I rolled my eyes at Allan. "Come on. You're putting a conspiracy spin on this too?"

He rubbed his hands together. "Just tryin' to keep it real."

Once Constance was in place, she vanished.

Peter gasped and turned to his idol. "Hey, where did she go?"

Allan shook his head. "Dude, don't you ever use your neural files?"

"Sure." Peter's cheeks turned rosy pink. "But I . . . I like to discover things in person."

I reassured him. "The squares emit light waves beyond our visible spectrum but can camouflage whatever it surrounds. Don't worry; she's still there."

"Thanks, doc."

"Why do you insist on calling me doc?"

"Because you act like one and in a few years, you'll have the paper to prove it," he said.

In fewer than five minutes, Constance exited. I could've been mistaken, but she seemed to have a spring in her step.

"It has renewed every cell in my body. The center uses energy and harmonics to bathe and balance each cell, with an emphasis on the mitochondria and telomeres."

Based on her apparent results, and without questioning the technical details, I decided to recharge, too. "Perhaps I'll give it a go." I tried to shuffle over to the scanners casually, but in my eagerness, I must have resembled someone late for a flight.

"Hey, wait for us," Peter said as he and Allan followed.

We stood on our assigned squares and waited for them to activate. Seeing Peter's trepidation, Allan said in a longing voice, "I'm glad I got to know you. Goodbye, buddy."

They vanished.

Like with Constance, we emerged revitalized in under five minutes.

"I feel good..." Allan tried to sing the line like James Brown. "Sharp and ready to conquer the universe."

The newly rejuvenated savant turned to me. "I'll give him a wide berth. I wonder how long the effects will last on him?"

Peter hopped around like a jumping bean. "I could run a marathon. What about you, doc?"

"I am more awake and sharper, like I just had two cups of Earl Grey. And my muscles"—I stretched and flexed my arms and legs—"they feel stronger."

"Well, Connie, looks like you found yourself a caffeine substitute."

Constance snarled at Allan but stayed in her blissful state. Without warning, she strolled towards the CRC again.

"Is she going through twice?" Allan asked.

Peter mirrored Allan's dismay. "Maybe she's addicted already."

Allan let out a smug laugh. "I think the scanner is turning her away."

She came back to us. "We can go in as often as we like, with the biometric reader's approval. There is a limit, but it varies from person to person."

"And I'm sure you'll find out what that limit is, Connie, won't you?" said Allan.

"Listen, *Al*, I don't know why you think I'm dependent on coffee. I never drank more than three cups a day back on Earth."

He laughed again. "Sure, sure."

She leaned over to me and whispered, "I also had four cups of black tea every day."

Constance did have a sense of humor—subtle, but there. Maybe the CRC wasn't the circadian schedule she wanted, but it could help her cope.

Allan said, "But seriously, this is something we should try to build back home. It has useful regenerative properties."

"I agree, but we can do that after we avert the disaster," I said, expecting him to push back.

"Sure," he said squinting at me.

It seemed my concern over people accepting my role as team leader had proven to be unfounded. It was time to leave my imposter syndrome behind.

CHAPTER 10

LOST SENSES

Outer 2's Terrain Point

The Ambarans kept us at optimal physical health without us lifting a finger. No gyms required. However, in acknowledgment of our need to come together in a lighter way, they created low-gravity courts for ball games, as well as high-gravity tunnels for walks.

My sport of choice was walking in the tunnels. Zoa and I would occasionally walk together and work as a team to clear our path.

Our first visit, however, hadn't been as straightforward as we expected.

We put on less sophisticated adjuncts than what we used in assignments and passed through a door to the tunnels.

There, we stood in the entryway like awestruck teenagers. The tunnel connected to five other translucent appendages; they, in turn, stretched out into the Complex like an octopus with tentacles.

"Wow," I exclaimed.

"Yes, they must be beautiful at night."

We walked at a moderate pace for about five minutes.

"This is nice, but I don't understand why they're called high-gravity tunnels. I don't feel any difference," I said.

Zoa lifted her legs waist high and marched. "Yes, maybe it will get harder as we work our way farther in."

A couple moments later, Zoa held her head and stomach. "Oh no, I don't feel so well."

"Me neither. Every part of me is compressed." I rubbed my abdomen. We were struggling to lift our feet when our headgear came to the rescue. "Lower the settings for a less strenuous walk."

"Did you hear that?" Zoa said in a low, slow tone.

I nodded and selected a reduced setting, much to the delight of my internal organs, which had dropped to my feet.

"That was not good at all." The nurse pushed her stomach and chest back into place.

I closed my eyes for five seconds to get over the nausea.

"Watch out, Victoria!"

A bluish haze five times my size appeared and headed straight for me. A fraction of a second later, I was inside it.

"Waaa huuuhhh aaah gooooo?" I sounded like I had potatoes in my mouth. The haze broke down the sound wave. I couldn't discern a single word I was saying, so Zoa had no chance.

She tried to hold back the giggles.

I sped up but couldn't break free. Surprise turned to panic as my cage followed me, matching my every step.

Speaking directly to the adjunct, I said, or more accurately thought, "How do I exit this blue haze?"

"Bring heart and brain into coherence—once synchronized, the obstacle dissipates."

Back home, we trained research subjects in the same technique to help them lower their stress levels before brain scans.

I focused on my breathing and heartbeat to achieve coherence within seconds. The blue haze vanished.

We finished up in the tunnels and headed for the Re-Hub. The scene was one I thought I'd never see.

"Doc, look!" Peter's face lit as he held up a strange sight. "Earth fruits."

The Ambarans had surprised us with simulated Earth food. There were apples, pears, grapes, bananas, and strawberries.

"These taste so fresh, as if they were just picked." Ana tried one piece after another.

"The food looks the same as Earth's," said Sabine, "but they haven't quite matched the taste."

Mr. d'Orsini smiled at me. "Real food. This is what we need. The Ambarans came through for us."

All agreed that everything tasted "better" than the versions back home. Our hosts had also provided typical Ambaran fruits and vegetables. Every shade of blue seemed to be represented, along with sharp yellow-greens I'd never seen before in foodstuffs.

"What about this one?" Peter held up a purple, tube-shaped item to Allan.

Tomas pointed at his friend. "I can tell you it's not meat. The Ambarans don't kill living things." He gave me a cheeky smile.

"Here goes..." Peter took a bite from one end. A greenish pulp came sliding out the other end but retreated a moment later. He clasped one end and took another bite. The tube bulged, but nothing came out. "They are so slippery—difficult to eat."

Holding it with both hands and concentrating like he was about to perform surgery, he pushed down in the middle, and a lump of pulp appeared. Peter snapped off his first bite.

"Hmmm . . . sweet, but savory once out of the tube." He pulled a strange face before issuing his verdict. "I think this is one of those foods you either love or hate."

Either way, the expanded menu was going a long way to endear the Ambarans to the team.

Being in the Re-Hub with everyone was a rare treat for me. Unlike most members, eight times out of ten I ate in my residence. On Earth, I'd never enjoyed dining out because of the competing food smells, noises, and diners' energies.

I had considered inviting guests to my residence for a meal and chat. After all, with a meal consisting of a vial—no clanging utensils were required. My reluctance came from wanting to protect my personal space. It would be difficult to backtrack if I let someone in and we didn't enjoy it. There was also the issue of privacy with my ever-present monitor, Anthea. If I couldn't have a private conversation, then I wouldn't have a guest.

A few assignments and rests later, I decided to find out more about my roommate, other than her lack of boundaries. Perhaps she could keep secrets, and my hesitation about having guests was unwarranted. I needed the basics first.

"Ohhh, Anthea!" I called out in a melodic fashion.

"Victoria."

"Are you voice-activated, or constantly monitoring?"

"I can be both or neither, depending on your needs."

"Right. So, if I don't require you to monitor, then can I set you to a different mode, like privacy mode?"

"That is correct. I would automatically switch on to direct you to an assignment or meeting." After a pause, she said, "Unusual."

"Is it?"

"As explained previously, all specifications on my modes were transmitted to you on your arrival day and after your neural scan showed missing information. However, once again, they are not in your memory."

"And now should I be worried?"

"Your brain is healthy. I will notify the Ambarans of this anomaly."

"Please let me know what they conclude."

The Ambarans had planted, downloaded, and decoded vast amounts of information. Had they tinkered too much with my brain? They were doing a great deal with humans they weren't familiar with. I was living proof that their techniques weren't infallible.

"I have re-sent the residence monitor specifications and complete Earth Complex schematics to you."

"Thank you. I have one more request. Can the next module or assignment include our whole team? We need to work and learn together."

"Your request has been granted for the next assignment."

Ambaran efficiency was refreshing. "Thanks. Now, please go into privacy mode until I request otherwise."

"Privacy mode activated."

I smiled at my small but significant victory. I had my space, and mind, to myself.

○ ○ ○

When I arrived at Inner 3 for our next module, my friends greeted me with smiles, patted each other on the back, and chatted about their latest experiences. It was exactly what I needed to feel connected to the team.

A hush descended upon the room when the module's AEH entered. "I am the Lost Senses AEH. My name is Rein'li." He had a crew cut, stood five-eleven, and had sparkling, bluish-green eyes.

"At this point in your stay, you have learned the basics and your bodies have settled into a new way of existing. It is time to explore your . . . capabilities."

No one else seemed to notice, but this was the first time I'd heard an AEH pause in search of a word.

The AEH angled his head up as if listening to something. With an intense stare, he looked at Ana.

"What? Did I do something wrong?" she said.

He didn't respond and moved on to Allan, who played it cool and just stared back.

Rein'li made deliberate eye contact with each of us for three seconds, as if sizing us up.

He continued where he had left off. "As humans, you are predominantly composed of water and energy. This combination allows you to detect magnetic shifts in your world."

There was something about his voice, or maybe his manner. Something . . . very familiar. Was he like another AEH we'd met? Or did he remind me of someone on Earth? I struggled to make a match. Every word he spoke played a chord in my inner world. I became queasy and disoriented, like two distinct realities were colliding.

"Breathe and focus," he said in my head. I did as instructed and tried to stay on the surface, like everyone else.

"For instance, on Earth, when there is an impending tsunami, energy builds up between the tectonic plates. This storage of energy creates a change in the magnetic resonance of the ocean, particularly near the epicenter. Any human capable of magnetic tuning would sense the changes many Earth weeks in advance and could take the necessary steps to prevent loss of life. While there are Earth humans who possess this sense, most are restricted or distracted by their daily lives. The result is a diminished or nonexistent sense."

He is reading a page out of my life's book—a closed and guarded book.

In an instant, he had explained one of the most horrific experiences in my life—the holiday with Anne in the Maldives.

For ten months, we'd planned our fortnight in paradise. We took a seaplane for the last leg of a twenty-three-hour trip. As we flew over the water, I became agitated by a strong magnetic pull. Night after night, I was tormented by nightmares of dead bodies being dragged across the beaches and floating in the ocean. Each time, I woke startled and drenched in sweat. The crystal-blue waters repelled me for the entire stay. Not a single toe of mine would bathe in the idyllic ocean.

Four days after our return to England, a 9.1-magnitude earthquake struck west of Sumatra. It created a tsunami with the intensity of forty thousand Hiroshima-sized atomic bombs. Enormous waves engulfed many islands and killed over 230,000 people.

Through the years I had carried the guilt, wondering if I should have sounded the alarm. However, to this day, I believed they would have discounted me as a nutter.

"Can a person develop the sense if they were not born with it?" Zoa asked.

"Developing magnetic tuning is highly dependent on the individual and their environment. Victoria has a high level of proficiency in this ability."

What? I'm in crisis, and he's sharing intimate details about me—how Ambaran! Just like the day we arrived.

Back to my breathing. I glanced at the faces around the room. All eyes were on me, except Ana's. She kept to herself.

Peter gave me a nervous smile. "I knew you were a witch like my mama and grandmama. You know and see too much, doc."

Witch. Really? Again scientifically researched abilities were reduced to fairy tale labels.

Zoa nodded to me reassuringly.

Rein'li continued as if he hadn't exposed me.

"Other examples of lost senses in Earth humans include energy profiling, particle entanglement tracing, and the ability to see into space-time constructs. These are all tools used in daily life in other human civilizations."

My heartbeat knocked louder as a feverish intensity flowed through me. I glanced down at my reddening hands; they mirrored how I felt. He was dismantling my house of cards one card at a time. *Of course, that's it! I do know him, and . . . I need to get out of here.*

"We will take a break now. Victoria, I would like you to stay."

Stay? I was likely to combust if I didn't get away.

As the team shuffled by, they whispered, and their eyes lingered on me like voyeurs yearning to catch what happens next.

With Rein'li and I alone, the trembling worsened until it became full-on shaking. My mind and body were no longer on speaking terms.

He sat down across from me. "You need not speak. I created a neural connection between us earlier because of your distress. With your consent, I will stay connected."

I nodded, thankful that he had asked permission to stay in my head.

"I feel like I'm wedged between two separate, yet connected, dimensions. What's happening?"

"You are safe. The energy is a part of you, but you deny it out of fear. I will activate a neural process to help equalize your response."

I closed my eyes to focus. Without barriers, he connected to my innermost being. He guided me back to my childhood meditation spot, under the oak tree in Aunt Judy's garden. We basked in each other's warmth. Connected to Rein'li, my surroundings, from the tree to the sky, shimmered with energy.

He took me further back in time. I was two years old and looking out a window in the back of the house. I remembered that moment; it was the first time I'd questioned my existence. In the next instant, Rein'li brought me back to when I was an unborn baby. Again, I recalled a memory. It was the energy I had felt in the comfort of my mother's womb, yet I knew it was not her energy.

I needed answers. Using my training, I forced myself back to the surface and opened my eyes. "I recognize you but don't understand how or why."

"I will answer your questions in time. However, we cannot discuss this any further during your stay."

"There's more. As a girl, I spent hours gazing at the vastness of space. The constellations didn't intrigue me, nor did the planets. This may sound rather crazy, but I wondered if I was left behind." A lump formed in my throat as my body tried to keep the secret buried. I looked away from him. "Who or what would give me heightened awareness and ensure I knew there was so much more . . . not on Earth, but elsewhere? It's cruel. Now that I am on Ambar, I cannot explain why, but every part of me feels aligned with you, the real Ambarans, and your universe. It's as if someone erased my memories and dropped me on Earth, but the feelings and innate knowing remained." The words flowed from my mind to his with ease and certainty, like indisputable facts. Yet with each admission I became more scared by what it could mean.

Content with our connection, I mentally entered his space to see his reaction to a confession that bordered on an accusation. I could sense that he wasn't surprised by my words, but rather conflicted.

A couple seconds later, he expelled me from his inner sanctum with a blinding light force. "No, Victoria. You cannot go there. I opened the channel to help you, not for you to delve into me."

Finally, I knew a little bit more. I could connect beyond what he expected. He didn't have total control. Why did an AEH have conflict, and how could I see it?

"Your subconscious has started integrating the information to ease your turmoil. However, you will not gain conscious access to the answers while you are here."

I looked at him with pleading eyes. "Why not? I need answers."

"Your focus must be on saving Earth."

His face revealed nothing, but there was something. No one ever says a thing can't be discussed unless, of course, it's something.

As he said, I was more settled with each passing second, even though he had not answered my questions. And now, I had more.

"There is one more thing, Victoria."

Another clue? I held my breath.

"By now, you have learned that you are uniquely qualified to lead group efforts back on Earth. However, there is one other who possesses an essential ability."

"Someone else has one of my abilities? I want to know who, but please, don't expose me again with more revelations. These people are from Earth, not Ambar. They are not so accepting."

"They need to know your abilities as much as you need to know theirs. You have used all of the abilities I mentioned," he said.

"I thought so. What exactly do you mean by particle entanglement tracing?"

"Remember when you lost your small hairclip when cycling?"

"Yes, it was Aunt Judy's. I fell over, and everything came pouring out of my bike bag. The clip was missing for months. Every so often, I would tune into it and try to see if it was being worn by another. The answer was always "no". Then one day, I went into my garage, and a phrase blasted into my mind . . . false bottom."

Rein'li smiled and said, "Yes, I remember saying that to you."

"That was you?" For the first time, I realized he was also present outside my sessions. "I went to my bike bag and pulled at the bottom. A removable piece popped up and revealed the hairclip. But how is that entanglement?"

"You were tuning into particles from you that were still on the clip."

"That sounds crazy even from you," I said.

"It is well known in our universe. Victoria, you take these abilities for granted, but the team needs to know what you can do."

I rubbed my left temple. *Here we go again—I will be on the outside.* "Can you explain why they are so accepting of my role as group leader?"

"They received the information in closed neural data pockets. They accept the facts without knowing the details."

"I see." I had researched more than a few people on why they did things. Their answers ranged from "I don't know, it just feels right" to "It's just me."

Rein'li called the group back together.

Zoa came in first and positioned herself next to me. "Are you okay? What's going on? Your eyes are a bright green-yellow."

"I'm fine now, thank you," I lied. My eye color revealed the truth.

Zoa touched my shoulder in her caring way. "Good, but let me know if you want to talk."

Ana was a lot less sympathetic. She sneered at me and whispered something to Allan.

Rein'li observed it all and delved into the next ability. "Unique energy profiling allows us to connect to another person's energy. Like a fingerprint, each human has an energy signature that we can tune in to anywhere. Pino has a strong capacity for this."

Pino? I wasn't expecting that.

Peter did a double take. "Papa Pino, you can do this?"

Mr. d'Orsini frowned. He reacted similarly to me, less than enthusiastic at not having a say in what the Ambarans revealed. "Si," he sighed.

"When you know a person's energy profile, you can pick up another's thoughts, emotions, and physical states over vast distances. This comes with training and a developed awareness. Victoria has a well-developed sense of UEP."

No surprise there. I could sense Aunt Judy's state of mind and body without seeing or talking to her.

Allan gave a lopsided smirk. "Look, I can grasp the advanced technology here, but this is sounding spooky and far-fetched."

He was as unaccepting as ever about anything outside his field. I only wished he wasn't so public with his mistrust and pushback.

Rein'li did not respond. "Zoa, you have used this ability to a lesser degree with your father. How did you explain this?"

What? Mr. d'Orsini, Zoa, and I could all do UEP to varying degrees?

Zoa was her usual grounded self. "In my family, we accept strong connections. We thought it was because of our deep love and care for each other."

The reserved Italian seemed unusually agitated as he listened to Zoa. "Can I stop UEP permanently?" he said.

Zoa and I exchanged puzzled looks.

"Pino," Rein'li said, "you cannot unlearn a person's energy print or profile. However, with training, you can control your response."

Why did he want to turn off his ability?

"Right then, could I use UEP to keep track of my fiancé?" Constance's light-hearted comment surprised me.

Allan leaned over to her. "Don't worry if you can't do UEP—technology can keep track of your man. But who knows what he's up to when you're not there for four months."

"Not that it's any of your business, but I wanted to get away to think about things." Constance looked down. "I'm not sure I'm ready for marriage."

Zoa asked, "Can you limit how long you feel another person's state?"

"Yes, Zoputa, through training. During the experiential lab, you will test, develop, and strengthen your UEP skills."

"Do I have to do the lab since I don't have this freaky ability?" Allan said.

"All will participate. Our goal is to ensure you can all tune into each other back on Earth."

Allan grunted and shook his head.

Although I didn't know the exact event that would threaten Earth, I was certain UEP would come in handy regardless of the crisis. I'd already been using it often over the years.

Peter nudged me. "It's funny, yeah? Since the beginning of history, we've wondered if there was life beyond Earth, but *we* are the proof."

"What do you mean?" Ana said.

The young Czech explained. "Those with super abilities are expressing ancient genes. But where did those people come from?" Peter seemed to have a particular focus on finding evidence of life outside Earth. Maybe it was something he debated with his friends.

Zoa added her insight. "It may well be in our genes, but we can't read all that genetic information yet."

Ana had disengaged. Was she accepting their explanations or discounting them?

"I think many people have experiences with abilities they can't explain. Yet there are rational explanations if we widen our perspectives and knowledge." Zoa turned to the astronomer. "But they are frightened and think their families and friends won't accept them."

Rein'li directed us onward. "In this experiential lab, you will practice energy profiling." He brought up a maze of rooms in a 3D image. "You will work in labs within this layout. A group member is needed to communicate concepts and guide others. I have chosen Victoria for this role."

He turned to me. "Do you have questions?"

"Yes, but not about this," I said neurally and gave him my best I-am-not-amused stare.

I wanted to be alone in my residence, where I could figure out some of the many things that didn't make sense. How was I able to delve into Rein'li's mind? I assumed he was autonomous, like Vintar. *Unless* . . . Unless he was an Ambaran occupying the AEH in proxy mode. A shiver ran down my spine at the same time as excitement rippled through me.

Rein'li looked over the team and said, "It is outside our covenants of engagement to reveal details of what you must prevent. However, we can train you in skills that will be most useful to you during and outside of a crisis. This lab will help you develop UEP and provide good experience for Victoria as team leader."

Mr. d'Orsini showed off his skills over two rounds.

"You're a natural. I hope it has helped you in your life," I said.

He reacted like I had just delivered unwelcome news. "Al kontrario, it's the problem, I tell you."

"Sorry?" I understood his Italian, it was close enough to English. It was the meaning I didn't understand.

He turned away and said, "I cannot continue with this lab."

We finished up and returned our adjuncts. As we parted ways, Peter approached me, not with his usual cheeky, boyish smile, but like someone weighed down.

"Doc, how did Papa Pino do?"

"He got 100 percent on the first two experiments but missed most on the last."

"Yeah—and he asked how to disconnect it earlier. Why would he want to do that?"

"I'm not sure."

Peter shifted from one foot to another as if standing on melting asphalt on a sweltering summer's day. "Uhh . . . I could ask him about it, but I don't think he would be comfortable speaking to me. Besides, you understand psychology, doc. You can help him."

"I'm not a psychologist. I don't work with people; I analyze them through data."

Peter blushed and continued his nervous shifting. "Yeah, that's what I mean. You understand people more, and I understand cars."

We walked towards the discs. I said, "We'll see, but no promises."

I had a disc to myself for the ride back to my residence. With new clarity and confidence, I directed its every move. I dipped, turned, slowed down, and sped up. It was the ride of my life. We usually had no control over the transportation, reaching our destinations by defined speeds and routes. *But today, things have changed. I am different. And I'm not alone—I have Rein'li. And I have Mr. d'Orsini and Zoa, who share one of the same abilities as me. There are people who can understand me. Life is good.*

My heart and brain knew Rein'li, disguised as an Augmented Earth Human or not. Yet I remained puzzled—why couldn't we speak of our connection? How could an AEH from Ambar have been with me since the very beginning of my life?

After several rest and research periods, I created a dedicated space where images of Earth's and Ambar's galaxies surrounded me. It helped my perspective. My focus, however, was on two things—Rein'li and our connection. I hoped seeing my two homes in parallel might trigger the next layer of information forwards from my subconscious to my conscious mind, allowing me to see how he could be present in both places.

At the beginning of each meditation, I sought Rein'li. After nine attempts over what was at least five days, I grew frustrated. He never joined me. By following the same protocol used on Earth, I assumed he would be there for me. It should have been easy with us both on Ambar.

That's it! I'll use UEP to tune into him. I can detect his energy and pull him into my meditations.

I searched for his energy and found him with ease on my first attempt. "Rein'li," I called out neurally. "Rein'li."

Suddenly, he appeared. "Victoria, focus on your primary goal." He vanished from my mind.

He'd been with me all my life. What had changed? I needed answers.

I searched again and again, after seventeen attempts, I stopped seeking him out.

But I know one thing to be true, on Ambar, I belong and feel deeply connected. Nothing he could say can change that.

CHAPTER 11

FALLING SHORT

pproximately ten days later, and with no sign of Rein'li, we started a module to test our skills and collaboration abilities.

With one look at Sinethemba's outfit, Mr. d'Orsini reacted.

"Are we going to fight each other?" He pointed at the AEH's head and trailed down to her feet.

"Holy . . . what are we being tested on here?" asked Allan.

She was kitted out in what looked like a graphene suit, but it changed color every ten seconds. At one point, she resembled beach sand speckled with broken shell fragments. Her head garb changed along with her outfit. The only constants were her brown eyes and long, partially visible aquamarine hair.

"Hello Earth team. We are here to test your individual and collaborative abilities. You will be in two teams for a two-part simulation of an incoming asteroid."

"Is that what we will be faced with back on Earth?" I asked.

"I will answer your question after this test."

The team let out a frustrated sigh.

Allan asked, "Can we choose which team we want to be on?"

"The teams are already designated. In a moment, each of you will wear a team jacket. Each team will perform in a designated center and will not be visible to the other team. Should any of you reach an unacceptable stress state, the adjunct will request you to take yourself out of the active area."

"For how long?" asked Allan.

"Until your biometric readings are within an acceptable range. There is one more detail you need to know about. Should you at any time enter a stage where the derivations always yield a negative result, your team's activities will be stopped."

"Yeah, game over," said Peter.

The competitive Sabine asked, "Do we get extra points for continuing for longer than our competitors?"

"This is not about points; it is about survival. Your adjuncts and outfit generator will show you which team you are in . . ." She raised her hand and we stood on our toes in anticipation. "Start."

In a flash, we were all in our team suits and rushed to the assigned areas. Constance, Peter, Marcus, Tomas, Wu Li, and Sylvia were in my team and wore shimmery green jackets. The other team, in shimmery white jackets, included Allan, Pino, Zoa, Ana, Sabine, Ragini, and François.

Pino said, "I could have designed better suits than these."

"And you will, but not until you return to Earth," said Sinethemba.

"Si?" He smiled like he'd won a gold medal.

The scene was already set when we walked into the simulation center. The asteroid was a small oblong shape in the distance.

The sight of Earth brought tears to our eyes. Did others miss their former lives, or were they afraid of losing Earth completely?

Marcus said, "I miss home." He shed no tears, and I didn't hear a sniffle. Still an AEH to me.

First, we agreed that we needed data points on the asteroid. Our math savant started crunching numbers.

The rest of us went through various possibilities to prevent the asteroid from hitting Earth. Nineteen-year-old Tomas came up with the strangest idea—a super large magnet. The idea we agreed upon came from Constance, who had one ear on our progress as she calculated the asteroid's size and trajectory. We would send two kinetic impactors or specially designed spacecraft, to break up the asteroid.

Peter, Wu Li, Marcus, and Sylvia designed the projectiles. During this phase, Wu Li became overly stressed and was taken out of action.

We were all exhausted after hours of envisioning different solutions and scenarios without rest. No breaks were allowed.

Once Constance finished, we needed to confirm her work. I caught sight of her fingers moving at high speed as we entered her numbers into the simulation.

"Stop," I said as I went closer to her.

"Close your eyes for a moment to entrain your brainwaves to mine. We should be able to keep you in a healthy zone, so you don't get knocked out of the process."

Her eyes widened. "We can do that?"

"I hope so." I slowed my brainwaves and tuned into hers. My heartrate slowed as I maintained a consistent steady low-brain-wave state.

When I sensed she had entered the right state, I said, "Okay, you're ready to continue."

She opened her eyes. "I feel much calmer. Maybe you can teach me to do that on my own?"

I nodded and smiled. "Go." She rejoined the team and we confirmed that her calculations were perfect.

Next was a simulation on the feasibility and effectiveness of the craft design. This phase had to be repeated five times before we got it right. We verified it was space-worthy, but beyond that we needed to wait for the full simulation.

That's when a sudden flash of Mr. d'Orsini's face came into my head with a strong emotion—defeat. I hoped it wasn't true.

After an hour of final checks and calculations, we were ready.

"Run the full slow-speed simulation," said the anxious savant.

After some heated discussion between Peter and Constance, we decided to make one craft lighter because it needed to go further.

We launched. With every second my breathing became shallower. Impact of the first craft was followed within moments by the second one hitting. The asteroid broke into two sections. Constance frantically made recalculations on the new formations.

Suddenly, a fragment splinted off the larger half and was flung towards Earth.

"No, no, no," echoed through the team.

I turned away. It was over. Constance and Peter shifted culpability from one to the other.

"Why isn't the simulation ending?" Marcus said.

Three seconds later the fragment burned up in Earth's atmosphere. Success.

With a healthy dose of relief and happiness, I said, "Well done, everyone. We did it."

Later, both teams came together for a well-deserved break. Sinethemba pointed over to a transparent, waist-high wall. "It is time for a nutritional vial."

We dashed over to the dispensers.

Allan asked Peter, "How did your team do?"

"Yeah, that was the scariest thing I've ever done," Peter said. "Do you think they had us do that because an asteroid is on its way to Earth?"

"I don't know, buddy,"—Allan shook his head—"but we didn't save Earth either."

"What!" Peter grabbed his vial. "You didn't save Earth?" He raised his fists in triumph. "We did."

"How?" said a dismayed Allan.

"We busted the asteroid into bits." Peter motioned an explosion with his hands.

The entrepreneur dropped and shook his head. "I knew that was the better solution. The group voted to put a laser out into space and obliterate a small part of the asteroid to change its trajectory. It didn't work."

Peter said, "We split ours, but a small piece cracked off. We thought it was going to do some serious damage, but it burnt up."

Snarling, Allan said, "It wasn't a fair match; you had the math savant." He looked over at Constance. "Next time, I want her on my team. Then I know we'll win."

I stepped closer to Allan and whispered, "You may want to mend some fences since you can't see winning without her." A mischievous smile crossed my face. "Good thing we are all on the same team when we get back home."

He grunted, and we headed back to Sinethemba.

Before we could properly celebrate, the adjunct advised us that the second part of the simulation would begin in moments. We had to manage the aftermath of a seventy-two-mile diameter asteroid impact on Earth. It created a global crisis with long-term environmental damage. With only a few months' notice, people made pseudo-cities underground and contained areas above ground.

The teams remained the same, but this time the other team was slightly more successful than us due to the number of lives saved. Zoa pushed them to success with her experience in emergency care and new knowledge of advanced medical techniques. Both teams made good use of AI for diagnostics and management of people and the environment. Temperatures plummeted and Earth was without sunlight for many years. No circadian rhythms for anyone.

We all wondered how close the exercises were to what would really happen back home. What were the Ambarans preparing us for with these scenarios?

After a rest period, we reconvened. Both teams were dejected by the outcomes.

Sinethemba said, "The consequences experienced by both teams is just the beginning. The stressors of living through the crisis will affect generations to come." Sinethemba had put another nail in the coffin.

"Do we need to avert the disaster completely?" I asked.

"Prevent or mitigate it, because even with your best efforts, there will be unpredictable and unavoidable repercussions. I can tell you one detail without overstepping prescribed boundaries. Asteroids are natural occurrences in space. Your people will create the coming disaster threatening all life on Earth."

"No asteroid," was repeated through the room.

One word suddenly hit me—unpredictable. Through the adjunct I communicated privately with her. "Will I be able to *see or sense* the coming disaster when we are within my window of twenty-one days?"

"Yes, in stages."

Hearing that one piece of information was both freeing and debilitating because it meant we could direct our efforts, but there would be more pressure put on me.

As I digested this new revelation, Zoa asked, "Can you explain how stressors would affect many generations?" The nurse would not be defeated; she wanted to understand the consequences.

"Crisis stressors are influential as early as conception and continue as the baby develops. Sperm cells carry information on the male's stresses, and these instruct genes to turn on or off. Earth scientists have yet to master the manipulation of gene expression or suppression."

With a mischievous smirk, Allan asked, "Would a child born here be healthier because our biochemistry is more balanced?"

Peter gasped. "Oh, no."

Others nervously snickered. I gave in to a slight smile. Despite the somber module, Allan added a speck of levity.

"Yes. However, with the level of modification your bodies have undergone, we do not expect you to have reproduction capability for the duration of your stay."

In an instant, Zoa asked a follow-up question. "Excuse me—if we can't conceive a child here, what about once we are back on Earth?"

"Your sterility is a temporary condition while on Ambar."

Allan said, "Seriously, I think it would be a good experiment for the Ambarans to see an Earth human giving birth."

Ana shook her head and glared at him.

Constance, who seemed engrossed in something with her adjunct, diverted her attention for a moment to give Allan a belittling sneer. "Really!"

"What?" Allan snarled. "An Earth woman having a baby here would add to their database."

"You physically cannot conceive a child here," Sinethemba confirmed.

Whispers filled the room.

Sinethemba had mentioned the level of modification we had undergone here. But they were still learning about us, and their tinkering wasn't 100 percent reliable. They couldn't even get information to stick in my brain.

What if things go wrong and we don't regain normal functioning?

With Sinethemba and Allan's exchange finished, she said, "A warning for all of you."

We planted our eyes on her with that opening line. "When a species' brain does not develop in a healthy way, the next programmed level of evolution will not occur, instead remaining dormant. On Earth, your ultimate potential was thwarted early on and has never been achieved. The next event will either destroy Earth and your species or allow you to make fundamental changes to your world."

She had revealed another layer of our challenge. It wouldn't stop once the event was over. We were expected to change the direction of humanity on Earth.

"How far behind are we compared to humans in your universe?" I asked.

"Eons."

"What do we need to do to evolve like other humans?" Zoa asked.

"People, social structures, values, and environment must all reinforce each other. All these areas must excel to bring about positive developments on Earth."

"Shouldn't we focus on the one disaster we're preparing for instead of trying to fix all of humanity?" I said.

"Your response to the crisis holds the power to determine the path of your planet: either towards a perilous journey leading to its demise or towards a more stable and healthier civilization. By utilizing the skills and knowledge acquired here and working together, you have the potential to prevent the imminent danger and facilitate the evolution of your world."

I was deflated by the enormity of what we needed to accomplish.

Sinethemba communicated neurally to me. "You must use your abilities while directing others to do the same."

"I understand, but I need help and more details."

"Victoria, you are here to receive our help but details are not possible without us crossing unacceptable boundaries."

The AEH addressed the group again. "In analyzing your DNA, we detected a time when your communities had a healthy balance. However, over the millennia, humans on Earth have experienced fear of each other, abuse, injustice, and a lack of safety and love. Thus, they developed away from their potential. What remains are brains shaped by what they *need* to survive. A broken civilization creates broken brains."

Some shrunk their postures with the weight of the world on them; others jostled as they huffed and puffed to show their agitation.

Sinethemba motioned to us with both hands. "Save your world and then save future generations by making foundational changes. Even a small group can be equipped to make great changes."

○ ○ ○

A time construct still eluded us, but what felt like over a month later, a few of us got together to come up with a communications strategy for when we return. We would need to answer questions from families, friends, and strangers on everything from the crisis to where we've been for 121 days.

"Earth's isolation from the intelligence and advancement here is striking and disturbing. It has put us significantly behind in every area." Constance cleared her throat. "I'm not sure I *want* to go back. We are healthier now and with their resources we would be able to do incredible things."

"True," Ana said. "Earth's location not only affects what I see in the sky, but kinda what we believe, and how we live. Here the younger civilizations have mentors from nearby planets who can show them different possibilities. Being remote has kinda limited our perspectives."

Her insight and candidness surprised me. I hadn't seen it during assignments.

Zoa took a deep breath and frowned. "I too am disappointed in how the medical industry has developed. It is slow to recognize some essential areas, such as cellular energy medicine and the electrome. On the other hand, I don't want to live for hundreds or thousands of years, as they do here. On Earth, living longer means seeing more horrific events. I could not handle it."

I nodded. "It has been disheartening to learn how we've developed and how far behind we are. We have to bring back healthier ways of living."

A prolonged silence loomed as we all appeared to drift off into our own thoughts.

"I am scared people won't be interested in hearing our solutions when we cannot share how we have gained our knowledge," said Zoa. "My family thinks I am in a remote village in Nigeria offering medical assistance. A friend lives there and has agreed to send letters from me to my family so they don't worry too much."

"I've been thinking about that. We can say we are part of a small global think tank," I said.

"Yes, my friend, that is a good idea," said Zoa.

Constance added to our list of dilemmas. "The numbers don't add up. First, we need to save the Earth. If we succeed, we must prevent further threats to our existence by making monumental changes that normally take centuries. Yet we'll have to do them within our lifespan."

I said, "Yes, and for some reason our hosts think we *can* do it."

"Have any of you learned how we can teach others back on Earth?" I said.

"I've been looking into ways to spread best-practice medical procedures." Zoa glanced down at her fingers as she pushed each cuticle back one at a time. "There are so few effective options. I hope the Ambarans help us find the best ways to make the biggest impact."

Thinking out loud, I said. "Maybe they will let us use their technology for implanting information in the subconscious."

"God, I hope you aren't serious." Ana's hand sought the spot on her left chest where her cross normally resided.

I grimaced. As I replayed the idea in my mind, it sounded a lot less appealing.

The savant held her hand up. "One more thing—can we find out how long we have been here?"

I shrugged. "I wanted to know that too. Vintar said time passes differently here because of their location in the universe. We experience time phasing where some days feel like weeks, and others pass like long minutes."

Without warning, Ana started sobbing. Not a whimper or a gradual sniffling, but full-on, open-the-floodgates outflow.

"What is it?" Zoa reached out to her with a supportive touch.

Constance stared at Ana. "Did Victoria say something wrong?"

Ana cupped her hands over her eyes. "No, no. It's just"—she blotted her tears away with her sleeve—"so hard questioning the foundations I've kinda built my life on. The culture of my people has existed for thousands of years, and now I want to abandon it. And the future is so dependent on us. Well, I'm not sure I can . . ."

Zoa put her arm around Ana. "Is there something specific troubling you?"

Constance and I looked at each other, bewildered.

She wiped her tears away again. "It's everything. Sometimes, I feel like the ground beneath me is crumbling. What I thought was truth is just one interpretation by a people, country, or group. What's real and what's a storyline to fulfil a past generation's agenda? In modern life, who makes the rules and determines our belief system?"

"We understand." Zoa gave Ana a sympathetic smile. "I think people have done their best with what they know on Earth. Yes, there are harsh injustices and inequalities, but those don't stop us, because we are born to keep going, keep improving." Zoa turned to Constance and me. "When we return to Earth, we will all do our best to apply what we have learned here. Hopefully, along the way, we will change things for the better for humanity."

Zoa's wisdom and calming nature halted Ana's tears but not her whispered prayers.

"Lord, make me an instrument of your peace. Where there is hatred, let me bring love. Where there is offence, let me bring pardon. Where there is discord, let me bring union." She kept her gaze downward and took a deep breath.

I found comfort in her prayer and hoped she would embody it.

"Lord, make me an instrument of your peace. Where . . ."

Constance, Zoa, and I exchanged glances as Ana continued praying on repeat mode.

Zoa reached out to her. Her touch jolted Ana out of automode. The tender nurse whispered something in her ear. Ana smiled. "Yes, St. Francis of Assisi."

Afterwards, Zoa and I headed to the tunnels for a walk. As we entered, she gave me *that* look. "Victoria, this artificial environment is changing us too much. I agree with Constance's conclusions on our quality of life, but we've also become more serious and much more predictable. Some people are acting like twins with a special connection. But they are also losing their unique identities."

"Can you give me an example?" I said.

"Peter and Sylvia finish each other's sentences. Sabine and Constance agree 90 percent of the time, regardless of the topic. Ragini and Li come from different cultures and generations but now understand each other as if they share a past. Those are just a few."

"I see. Interesting, but not necessarily bad. Those closer connections will help us back home." The effort required to walk increased. I had to fight to get every word out. "The Ambarans have balanced our hormones and suppressed anxieties. I hope it lasts long after we've left." I looked at Zoa. "What about you? Are you more connected to someone"—I winked—"other than me?"

She chuckled and patted my back. "Of course, and yes. I have a connection with someone else—Pino."

I smiled and gave Zoa a look to suggest there might be more than a platonic connection with the suave Italian.

"Oh, no, no. We understand each other beyond what we should for the amount of time we have known one another, but—there's no spark."

Although I had known Rein'li for as long as I could remember, our relationship helped me relate to Zoa with Pino. "Does it help you or bring you comfort?"

"Yes, but it isn't natural. I have known some men for over twenty years and there isn't this kind of connection."

"Shared dramatic experiences often have that effect. See, the changes have upsides. We are not only healthier, but we are getting stronger, physically, mentally, and emotionally."

Zoa said, "I agree with those changes, but haven't you noticed? No one shows an interest in developing a relationship here. Even Allan has backed off from Ana."

"Oh, that is serious," I said, half joking.

She fell a few steps behind. "Let's make the walk easier."

We took a few strides before she began again. "Like you, I am a people watcher. When we first arrived, some showed romantic interest in others, but this has lessened or disappeared over time. I think it's very unnatural. We're moving away from our natural selves, or . . ." Zoa glanced to her right and left to ensure no one was within earshot. "Maybe the Ambarans are suppressing our emotions and physical desires *too* much."

I squinted at her. "With so much on our plates, I think people may find it difficult to fit in romance. We may be at our emotional or psychological threshold . . . where we can't handle any more than what we already have."

Zoa stopped walking and held her arm out to stop me. With a long face, she delivered a warning. "I know what I see, and I tell you, this isn't natural or good."

"I know it's difficult, but we just need to keep our heads down and keep going. The Ambarans are taking us to a healthier neutral position to build upon."

"Yes, but how will they know when we're there? They understand other human civilizations, not ours."

"True, but maybe they were acknowledging our progress by providing solid food."

Zoa gave a half nod in agreement.

"What do you suggest we do?" I asked.

She stared at me like she was searching for the right words. "Has no one else spoken to you about this?"

"No, but I can ask around."

"Let's keep this between us for now. I pray we get through this phase and end up in a better one." She turned away as if to reset. "Speaking of changes, have you noticed Ana hasn't been wearing the outfit with a cross on it?"

"Yes. Out of habit, she tried to touch it earlier."

"She removed it several modules ago. I hope she's okay." Zoa held out her hands in prayer position. "Being here is challenging her faith."

"Let's be fair; this experience is challenging many of our ideas," I said matter-of-factly. "It's to be expected, considering we are Earthlings living in a foreign environment."

"Yes, but it is difficult for her; she is a strict Catholic. Religion has provided her with structure and support, as it has for me. Her entire inner world will be unsettled if she doubts her foundation."

"She mentioned 'agendas' earlier, but I thought she meant it generally. She was talking about religion?"

"Maybe both," Zoa said. "If things don't appear to be adding up for her, she will overturn every belief until she reaches a level where things make sense, based on facts and faith."

"I wonder how others are reconciling their religious beliefs with what we're learning here. You're a practicing Christian—how are you doing?" I asked.

"I find safety in my traditions. I pray every day for our group and our home."

After the tunnels, Zoa asked, "Have you struggled in any area?"

"Since being here, I've realized a few things that will change my life back home," I said.

She nodded and gave me a supportive smile, signaling me to continue.

"As Constance and Ana said, our perspectives are so limited because of our insular civilization. How will we adjust after being here? We live nowhere near our true potential because we don't learn to access abilities outside the norm."

She fretted. "I understand and believe it has been more diffi-cult for you than most of us."

"I don't know how I will readjust—or if I can."

CHAPTER 12

SEED

On Ambar, my neuroscience research and projects were beyond anything I had done on Earth. I focused on how much Earth human brains could tolerate and the best means of knowledge acquisition. My experiments with Malcolm on optimal brain usage barely scratched the surface, compared to what I had learned on Ambar.

After five cycles of intensive research chronicling the development of early human brains on three other planets, I went to check in on the team. Were people becoming the same, as Zoa mentioned? Was Ana still struggling with having her foundation challenged? Acting out of impulse and spontaneity, I sent a request to a transport disc.

Take me to see any team members.

My eagerness to see how others were doing waned when I ended up in a deserted area. The internal map confirmed ten people behind a barrier set to privacy mode. Curiosity sparked, I got off the disc and walked around as I waited for the barrier to vanish.

Although I didn't know what I was missing, a small part of me felt left out.

Are they on a special project? I'll contact Zoa. She'll know what's going on.

Through my neural communications, I requested my friend's location. Her location was unavailable. *She could be here, but I can't hang around much longer like Billy-no-mates.*

A moment after I got on the disc, the privacy barrier disappeared. Allan, Ana, Peter, Zoa, and six others were there. I hopped off the disc, eager to find out what the meeting was about. As people eyed me, I picked up on nudges to each other, folded arms, and surprised faces.

Zoa's eyes widened. "Na wa."

"Hi, what's going on?" My voice shook as a wave of uneasiness went through me.

"Okay." Allan turned to the others. "We need to discuss this with Victoria now." He had a neural adjunct on, unlike everyone else, and stood with his chest puffed out like an alpha-male gorilla. The wild-haired AI wiz couldn't quite pull it off.

Zoa said, "If you don't mind, I'd like to start."

I heard a disgruntled exhalation from him as he shook his head.

Zoa stepped up to me. "The Ambarans are supplementing our bodies and brains to a level we no longer feel is necessary." She tilted her head down and spoke in a warning tone. "Sometimes, you must go with what the people want, even when you think it's not the best option for them."

"Let me make the point clearer," Allan said. "We don't need *any* of it. We are all in agreement. The controls need to go." He stood cross-armed, and his voice grew louder with every sentence. "Just because we're here doesn't mean we can be served up on a platter for the Ambarans to do whatever they want. They need to stop messing with us!"

Before I could respond, Peter stepped forwards. "Doc, I feel like a car with a high-performance engine, but someone else is driving me. You understand, don't you?"

Allan was influencing the young Czech. *Why isn't Papa Pino here to steer his youngling?*

"What do you want to do?" I asked.

With a smug look, Ana said, "We want to live without their interventions, starting today." She seemed to relish being the one to deliver the news to me.

I scowled at the idea but didn't get a chance to respond before the astronomer added to their case. "Let's face it, when we are back on Earth, we won't have the Ambarans' technology to keep us in line. And we'll have to save the world. We need to practice what we're learning . . . on our own, not as controlled people."

She had a point. We would be back on Earth without the benefit of the Ambarans' internal and external technology. But now wasn't the time to take away the interventions. To reject their enhancements was signing our own death certificate.

The others stood listening, adding an occasional gesture or sentence to confirm their support. It didn't surprise me to see Zoa there; she had her reasons. However, unlike Allan, she didn't espouse the conspiracy theory of the Ambarans controlling us for their own gain.

Outnumbered, I asked, "What's next, then?"

Allan turned to the group. "We want to meet with the hosts."

There were unanimous nods and verbal affirmations.

"Victoria, will you join us?" said Zoa.

Not pleased with her extending an invite, Allan sneered and mumbled something to Ana.

"Yes, thank you." I didn't want to go, but I needed to see how things evolved. "I'd like to be there."

"It's done!" Allan grinned. "A host will meet us here. Let's get back into our meeting formation." Apparently, he had made a neural request and gotten an answer from the Ambarans at their usual speed.

We entered the meeting area and sat in a U-shape. A Conduit joined us at the front within seconds.

My diaphragm and stomach vibrated like I had swallowed a rattlesnake. Allan's intensity caught me off guard. I feared the outcome when the Ambarans denied the group's request—mutiny. We were making a 180 degree turn at dizzying speed. When had all this happened?

With no time to waste, I sent a private disclaimer to the Conduit. *I am here as an observer and don't agree with their position.*

Allan represented the group and explained their desires with his usual righteous attitude.

The opalescent being offered an answer via our neural comms within seconds. "First, your request is dangerous, considering the state of your planet. However, I will discuss it with the Ambarans. Next, each member must decide for themselves. Last, regardless of your decision, we will continue the basic nutritional supplementation for everyone."

The discontented ringleader wrinkled his forehead. "Fine, notify the three members not here, but we don't want incremental changes."

"What happens if some members want to stay as they are?" I asked.

Allan answered over the Conduit. "They're sad. That's what happens."

I snapped back. "Do you mind? Not everyone wants the same as you." I stood up and faced the team. "Do you all realize what a dangerous game you're playing? This is gambling with Earth's fate."

"You don't know that. And not everyone"—Allan shook his head—"wants to accept everything on Ambar without question like you." The room went quiet as people appeared to hold their breath, waiting to see how the tit-for-tat would end.

"I will notify all team members of the decision on this matter through your residence monitors," said the Conduit.

Everyone shuffled out except me. I remained seated in a daze and closed my eyes. We were living at optimum levels. Why would the team risk so much just so that they could feel like they were in control?

Zoa came back in. "Are you okay?"

"What?" I sneered at her. "How could I be okay with this?"

The supportive nurse reached out to hold my right arm. "Do not think the worst yet. You know I favor removing the controls so we can behave more like our true selves and see where our strengths and weaknesses are."

"But how can we learn at the rate we need to?" I knew the answer—we couldn't. "I feel like this is the end."

"We might surprise you. Everyone understands what's at stake. If the change doesn't work out, the Ambarans will help us make corrections. Give us a chance." The Nigerian's voice did not calm me in the slightest.

I covered my face with my hands. "How can you be sure that this won't be our ruin?"

"I am not certain, but we should try to live more naturally. People must reach their goals without superhuman intervention. We can be Earth human and still learn what we need to." Zoa was so optimistic; she confounded me with her utter belief in people. Whereas I feared the worst.

I imagined Allan freed from the hosts' intervention; his paranoia would increase. Others would be overstressed by the magnitude of our work. What would AEH-Marcus choose, or at least claim to choose? Would he support my side and say he has kept the enhancements, or assume he'd look more human if he opposed the Ambarans?

○ ○ ○

I struggled to understand how an almost certain outcome could be denied by so many.

The verdict didn't come at the usual speedy Ambaran pace. Hours passed before Anthea relayed the decision.

"The Ambarans will allow team members to choose. It is part of self-determination for sentient beings."

"What!" I shot out of my seat. "How can anyone be allowed to put a whole planet in jeopardy?"

Anthea said, "Your logic is flawed. There are no absolutes established by allowing Earth members to determine how they wish to live."

"Well, I'm not the numbers person, but I don't need to be to see that this equation is broken."

"Nine out of fourteen have opted to live without Ambaran enhancements."

"Great—the majority." We were it—Earth's only hope of survival and they were willing to risk everything. Why would the Ambarans allow nine people to thwart our mission? Was I missing something?

After days of reclusive contemplation on doomsday scenarios, I was invited to a group meeting on Outer 5.

Team status: Ceased or diminished—Neurotransmitter and hormone modulation, metabolic process enrichment, and interfaces with the Complex.

The last item caught my attention. Clearly, our hosts did not want uncontrollable Earth humans roaming at will or using all the features in the Complex, so they limited access. At least, regardless of the choice people made, we would all continue the nutritional supplementation.

Would I be entering the Earth Complex Zoo, or would there be no visible difference? One thing I knew for certain, there would be a drastic decline in their performance levels.

I stood at a side entrance watching for a couple minutes, then slowly walked towards them. Most said, "hello" and smiled. Their reactions and interactions seemed quite normal.

I sat with Peter, Constance, Zoa, and Mr. d'Orsini.

"Hey, doc." Peter sheepishly glanced at me.

"Peter."

I looked over to Zoa and Pino. "How are you both?"

"I feel a little different, but I can't put my finger on why," said Mr. d'Orsini.

"Maybe because you stopped the controls?" I scanned his posture and facial expressions, looking for a sign of his nervous tic.

"No, I wanted to see how the others did first." He gave Peter a wry smile.

"Oh, you're one of the five members, including myself, who opted for no change." Mr. d'Orsini hadn't jumped at the opportunity to return to his former self.

"We are in a strange world, and these are serious times. I need all the help I can get to squeeze"—he pretended to squeeze a lemon—"the most out of being here."

Peter struck me as rather quiet compared to his usual exuberant puppy persona.

"And Peter, how are you?"

He looked down. "Me? I don't feel any different . . . but I don't want you to be upset with me."

I couldn't hide how I felt. "Don't take it personally. I just think it's a mistake for us to second guess an advanced civilization when they are trying to help us."

"Zoa, do you feel any different?" I asked.

"I feel very well. We were just talking about how our individual training is going."

"And?" I said knowing the answer regardless of what she replied.

"There are some differences, but I will still achieve my goals," said Zoa.

Pino interjected, "Zoputa, do you think everyone without the controls is the same as you?"

"I can answer that," said Constance. "I know the stakes and may have to work a bit harder. But I know it's real and not something that will leave me once we return home."

"What percentage of your workload can you get through now?" I asked knowing that she tracked everything.

"Eighty-seven percent, with the same level of retention," she answered.

"I'm not putting too fine a point on it, but"—I waved my hand towards her—"you're a savant. What chance do others have?"

"I don't know," she said in an unemotional tone.

Just then Ana and Allan joined us.

Constance asked, "How much work are you two able to clear now?"

"I feel more connected than ever," Allan stated emphatically. "This was the best decision we've made since our arrival."

Ana cleared her throat. "I kinda notice some differences in the time it takes to complete tasks. But I think with practice, it will get better." She glanced at her partner. "I'm glad I stopped the interventions because I feel like this is the real me." She laid her hand on her upper chest.

Maybe people were ready for fewer enhancements, but whether we could still succeed was in doubt.

Marcus was sitting on the other side of the room with François and Wu Li.

As I approached him, I heard Marcus say, "I think you two are crazy. There is no way you can keep up with me on team projects. I'll have to carry both of you."

I smiled at them and asked, "Carry them?"

"They opted out, which means they can't access the same areas for training. They also won't have Ambaran assistance to assimilate the information," said Marcus.

"Have you two,"—I looked to the French cave guide and Li—"noticed changes?"

François said, "Oui, I'm thinking about going back to the controls for a few reasons. But I'll wait a bit longer just to see how I get on."

It hadn't occurred to me that some might want to reverse their decision in favor of intervention. Perhaps more would if I didn't pressure them. It was still a loss because we were wasting valuable time trying out unproductive things. At least the AEH wasn't pretending he had opted out.

○ ○ ○

Two rest periods later, a Conduit appeared remotely in my residence with shocking news.

"In light of recent development with your team, we will be sending AEH-Marcus to Earth with you."

"W-h-a-t?" My world slowed down and everything went silent as I tried to process the startling statement, which wasn't a request. "Are you allowed to send an AEH to Earth?"

"Yes, to help rescue your planet."

Though in a half-stunned state, I could see an upside. "If AEH-Marcus comes with us, does it guarantee Earth's survival?"

"No. It will increase the possibility," said the Conduit.

I was starting to see how the Ambarans came up with the idea. Our chances of success went down with some team members choosing to work without their enhancements. By offering up an AEH to help us, they were increasing our odds.

"What happens to the real, sorry,"—bad time to offend the Ambarans—"Marcus, the Earth human?"

"We will take care of him," the Conduit said with its usual lack of emotion.

"What the hell does that mean?" My hands trembled and I suddenly felt very unsafe. I rose from my chair.

The Conduit said, "He will not be harmed."

I squinted in distrust. "How do I know you're telling me the truth?"

"You have trusted us this far."

That answer didn't calm me. Had I been too trusting? A twenty-pound kettlebell sat in my gut.

"We will use the ingested neuromodulation matter to induce a pre-determined dream. He will have a new purpose in life. No team members will see Earth-human Marcus."

"You can't just extract a person from their life. He has family and—" The penny dropped. My shaky voice gave away my utter disbelief. "You're going to send Marcus to some isolated part of the world so that you can replace him with the AEH."

"Your success is uncertain, but at least with AEH-Marcus the team's chances are greater."

"So why don't you just swap all of us out with AEHs? I don't mind staying here a bit longer, maybe until Earth is safe." I probably shouldn't have offered up the team like that.

"We cannot implant ourselves to that degree within a civilization with intent to steer it."

Only a few minutes ago, the idea of an AEH on Earth sounded horrific, yet now I accepted it. "Please, I need to be alone. This is a lot for me to take in."

"Victoria, this team represents Earth's sole opportunity for survival. Our role is to help you save your planet and its people. We have agreed that sending an AEH would be the most effective assistance once you return. Remember your role. You must establish the highest level of connection possible between the team members."

"Right, connection." I collapsed back into my seat. "I'm sure you already know, but on Earth we have communication devices to stay connected. So at least I don't need to worry about that one."

The Conduit said, "No. Communication technology will cease to operate at critical times."

"Of course it will." I rubbed my forehand. At least the chat with the Conduit gave me another warning. No phones. "How long before we return to Earth?"

"Fifty-one Earth days."

"And, we will have 187 days on Earth before the event, right?"

"Yes."

"Do the others know all this?"

"Yes."

I hadn't heard anyone speaking about timing. Possibly because it was a distant piece of information that they couldn't see or something so familiar they accepted it lock, stock, and barrel. It was scary how we seamlessly integrated information planted by the Ambarans.

"Considering that I haven't been able to control my team or guide them to make the best decisions, do the Ambarans still think I'm the right one for this role?"

"You have a unique brain, which is why you are the leader of SEED."

"Sorry . . . SEED?"

"It is the name we use for the Earth group—Society for Earth's Evolutionary Development."

"SEED, sounds ambitious."

"If you prefer less awareness, we can help you."

"I'm sure you can." I giggled like a person teetering between madness and understanding. "I'll be fine. Don't start messing with my brain more than you've already done."

The host stared at me before vanishing, leaving me mulling in an ethical mess.

We'd be going home with an advanced being posing as one of us.

I sat thinking. Thinking about those without Ambaran interventions. Were they the smart ones? Thinking about Earth Marcus. Thinking until . . . I couldn't carry the burden of truth any longer.

As leader of this group, I could decide what to share and with whom.

O   O   O

I boarded a disc to Zoa. She would be the first of the group to know the truth about Marcus.

If Zoa had still had the original level of intervention and connection, she would have known of my arrival through internal communications. But these weren't normal times. She was no longer as integrated to the Complex.

The disc took me to a place I didn't know existed. It was an arena—of horror. Every ill in existence was displayed before me. From the starving to the suicidal, the insane to the physically wounded, all were in crisis. I caught sight of Zoa tending to a young, emaciated girl who couldn't sit up. She handed the child a vial. After a few minutes, the child walked away.

Next, Zoa moved to a group with recently torn limbs. She used a portable emergency kit, filled with devices, vials, bandages, and medicines. Her ability to de-escalate those in the throes of agony was impressive. A man lay on the ground with his arm freshly blown off. Zoa walked over to him with a container, like a cooler for drinks on a hot day. She pulled out an arm and without using stitches or surgical tools she attached it and wrapped the connection between his stub and the limb with a bandage that melded to him like flesh. Within minutes, he moved the fingers attached to his new arm.

The scenes continued, quicker than my eyes could track. Each new tier brought increased brutality and conditions. She ran in and out of war-torn areas, disaster zones, and hospitals.

Was this part of her training? It was more intense than anything I'd seen before, on Ambar or Earth.

After her stellar responses to all the scenes, she switched to a hospital scene. She was performing diagnostics on an older man. Suddenly, she burst into anger and thrashed her tools onto the floor. A moment later, a gunman entered the room in a fit of laughter.

Zoa locked eyes with him then stabbed herself in the chest with what looked like a warrior's knife. I covered my mouth in horror.

He opened fire, scattering bullets across the scene. Zoa fell to the ground in a pool of blood.

"No!" I instinctively shouted as my body quivered.

In that instant, the simulation stopped. The scenes vanished. Zoa stood in front of me, gushing with rage, frustration, and sadness. I barely recognized her.

"Zoa, I don't understand. Wha—" She had always radiated care, warmth, and kindness. What part of her had created this?

"Na wa, Victoria! How—" She shook her head.

"What's going on here?" I berated her, not with conscious thought, but as a shock reflex.

"I wish you hadn't seen that," she said. She held my right elbow and guided me away. "Please, let's leave this area—I will explain."

I nodded nervously. I wanted to leave and never return to the horrible scene.

As we walked away, Zoa said, "My friend, I am so sorry."

"I'm sorry too." In my eagerness to reveal truths to her, I hadn't considered how I might trespass on her personal space.

Zoa frowned. "I forgot that I wouldn't receive an alert if someone came to see me. But being disconnected allows me to run this kind of simulation."

Still trembling from the horror show, I said, "I didn't know about this place . . . or that violent simulations were possible here in the EC."

She gave me a sympathetic smile. "The simulation area takes memories and weaves them together with my goals. Everyone feels and looks real because of the increased visual saturation. With the Ambaran controls, the intensity was greatly reduced; it was frustrating me."

"But it was horrific. Why would you want to create this?"

"Let me explain. We have fifty-one days left to become better than we ever dreamed we could be. These scenes help me prepare for whatever we'll face, and they also serve as an outlet for my stress. With each simulation, I perform faster and have more success."

"But that last scene didn't feel the same as the others."

"It contains my father. I couldn't do anything to stop the cancer from spreading. I spent five long years battling the disease with him. So many false hopes. In this simulation, every time I get the same verdict, I allow the gunman in. The knife—my father's favorite—was from his collection of old military weapons."

"I'm so sorry. As a nurse, it is in your nature to help save people. I can't imagine the pain you feel." I waited for her to make eye contact with me, then continued. "But you can't change the past, not here or on Earth."

We sat for a while in silence outside the simulation area. I couldn't tell her about AEH-Marcus and give her reasons not to trust the Ambarans.

Back in the safety of my residence, my thoughts were on Zoa. The simulation scene had shaken me with its brutality and extreme demands on my friend. Yet, despite the worst odds, Zoa was still going to fight to save the world.

Could I show the same unwavering commitment to a glimmer of hope? I performed several crisis preparation and response exercises. I took a page out of Allan's book and made contingency plans for my contingency plans. I used my ability to see twenty-one days before an event. In one scenario, we stayed together once back on Earth and travelled to the site of the impending event. Another attempt had us travel to the location from our respective homes. End result—we needed to stay together. Ambaran simulation technology had input everyone's skills and abilities into each exercise. Earthquakes, tsunamis, asteroids, nuclear war, and global pandemics drove each simulation. I lost track of how many attempts I made. No scenario worked. We didn't get close to a partial success. But like Zoa, I owed it to everyone to keep fighting.

○ ○ ○

After a rest, I sought out Rein'li. He was not locatable via Anthea, the disc, or my adjunct. Like a stalker, I searched the EC high and low and asked a few SEED members and Conduits if they'd seen him. No one offered information. He was becoming a figment of my imagination. Weary and dejected, I abandoned further attempts to "bump" into him and sought solace on the Outer 4 platform amongst the cosmos.

On most occasions I was alone up there, but Ana was about to go up this time too. We stood eyeing each other at the end of corridor T-1.53.

"Oh, hello," I greeted her with disappointment.

"Hi, listen, I . . . uhh, just got here. I kinda want to . . ." Was she expecting me to leave but didn't have the guts to ask outright? The platform could hold a hundred people when fully expanded. However, I doubted any size would accommodate us.

"Me too." We stood awkwardly, ogling each other.

Ana straightened her spine, trying to make her five-foot-one body taller. "I'm going up to study their third galactic quadrant, so I will be a while."

"Fine with me," I said. My jaw tightened, and I prepared to stand my ground and go up with her. A game of brinkmanship wasn't the respite I wanted, but I wouldn't yield to her.

She sighed and rolled her eyes, unconcerned about hiding her discontent.

With one final step forwards, we were transported to the platform.

I indicated my readiness via the adjunct and waited for the platform to adjust its size based on the number of occupants. We ended up confined to a twelve-by-twelve-foot square, big enough for ten friendly people. We went to opposite corners and peered out into space.

As we ascended, I felt a strong magnetic pulling, like I had felt previously during the module with Vintar. It was getting stronger. On Earth, when the feeling grew, the event was getting closer in time. Would it be the same here?

I immersed myself in the history of nearby galaxy clusters to take my mind off the pulling sensation. About twenty minutes in, I felt someone behind me. Ana was in my space.

"I kinda need to ask you something." Her voice trembled, and a scowl engulfed her face.

As I attempted to predict her question, I mirrored her frown.

"Are you—" She paused, folded her arms in front of her, and with each hand she grabbed either side of her waist. A classic defense posture with a twist.

"Yes, what is it?" I asked.

She stared down at my feet and took a deep breath. "You're one of them, aren't you?"

How am I to answer such a ridiculous question? Should I bother?

"Just to clarify—was that a statement or a question?" Was she convinced, or was there still a bit of room for truth?

She threw her arms up in the air. "Oh! Just answer the damn question. You're from Ambar but disguised as one of us, aren't you?"

I laughed at the thought of it. "I don't know how you came up with that one, but the answer is no."

"I knew you'd deny it." She turned away for a moment.

"Then why ask?" I spoke with my hands to show my exasperation. "How can I prove it to you?"

"I don't know, but . . . Okay, I'll tell you how I know." She took a step back. "First, you were the only one allowed to see Marcus when we arrived." She held out her right thumb to count. "Next, our assignments have uncovered your abilities like magnetic tuning and energy profiling, something you share with Ambarans." Her pointer finger went up. "And I'm sure there's more you haven't revealed. Third,"—her middle finger shot up—"during the first health lab, Zoa said your blood type wasn't one of the normal ones. You made it look similar enough not to cause too much suspicion. And,"—another finger popped up—"you disappear for long periods of time and aren't close to any of us. Well, maybe you are kinda close to Zoa. But when you are around us, it's only on the surface." She flashed all four fingers up at me.

This could have been why the magnetic pull was increasing. Was our encounter going to end badly?

"Wow. It sounds like you have it all worked out, and no doubt you've shared your revelations with others." Tilting my posture forwards in an assertive stance, I defended myself. "Ana, you've taken bits of information and put them together to form a bizarre and inaccurate picture. And you call yourself a scientist? Shame on you. What happened to the scientific method, where you observe, hypothesize, test, and then conclude? I'm not one of them, but if this is how you treat someone who's different, then I'm not sure I want to be one of you." I was firm in my defense, but had I been in her position, I might have reached the same conclusions. Let's be fair, there weren't many on Earth who knew about my abilities and accepted me.

She squinted and locked eyes with me like she was trying to provoke. "Well then, explain your blood?"

"I have a blood phenomenon where my blood's Rh factor changes—rare, but still from Earth. To date, it has never been grounds to disown me from humankind."

She shook her head and reached over to touch her fabric cross, but it wasn't there. Her eyes froze in fear as she took a step back. It was as if she had realized that the army meant to protect her had left. "Uhh . . . it's just one of many things not normal or right about you."

"You think you're onto something, and maybe you are. But what you've discovered is that we're *all* different and have varying degrees of sensory awareness.

"I hold my breath when I hear someone struggling, knowing that we all need to be our best. That's why I cringe whenever Allan floats one of his conspiracy theories or rallies others to diminish the Ambarans' input." My voice got louder to emphasize our mission-critical state. "Do you feel like that, Ana, or are you just focused on yourself and Allan?" I couldn't stop two people from talking, but the conspiring duo could create real problems.

Like a dog with a bone, she held on to her story. "We all understand the importance of being here, so don't go there. Yes, I kinda show my emotions, but at least everyone knows who I am." She glanced to her left and back at me as if she had switched gears. "What about the time you and Constance were discussing her fiancé? She asked who you were close to. You mentioned your aunt, Malcolm, Anne, and your *cat*." She glared at me with disgust. What did she have against cats? "Then you said, 'I don't collect friends.' Is that because you need to distance people so they don't discover who you really are?"

"When my best friend and I were at university, I'd flippantly said, 'I don't collect friends.' It was a humorous way of saying that I didn't need *many* friends, just a few trusted ones. Everyone has accepted the comment and moved on, except you."

She looked down like she was considering my explanation. Maybe I was getting through to her.

The truth was, being isolated from others was not always easy, but it was more difficult to be a part of them. To fully integrate felt wrong and disingenuous. Here, I wanted to create close friendships, but to hold the Ambaran's secrets required a bit of distance.

Perhaps, if I told her about them, she might leave all the speculation behind.

"I feel fear deep in me, like my mother did when my family was in danger." Her voice trembled. There was a frightened girl behind the bully she presented to me. "I pray you won't hurt me." She crossed herself twice.

"You're afraid of me? What do you think I can or would do to you?" Was she going to strike preemptively to prevent me from hurting her? My body went into readiness mode. "Ana, I can't change what you think about me. I can only tell you the truth, which doesn't seem to matter because you want to believe something else. Have you spoken to any other team members about your theory?"

"Only Allan, and I won't tell anyone else because . . ." She took another step back and folded her arms again. "I don't want you to get angry and hurt me." Like minds attracted, even in another universe.

Odd as it may seem, with my mind and body in defense mode, I felt some sympathy for Ana. She had convinced herself of a tormenting idea. It was time to take action to prevent something bad from happening. "I think we should go back down to Outer 4."

"Yes," she said, before walking back to her corner of the platform, as far away from me as possible.

On our quick descent, I contemplated her accusations. I couldn't categorically deny or confirm them. There would be no winner on this platform. We were both losers because we distrusted each other so much. Perhaps she would trust me more if I confided in her about Marcus and swore her to secrecy. She wouldn't see me as an Ambaran if she knew the decisions they'd made without me. It would release me from the enormous burden—no more carrying it alone.

As we came to a stop, I approached her. Ana glanced at her exit route before turning to her perceived nemesis.

One line is all it takes. "I have one last thing to say."

Marcus isn't Marcus, and unless we hide the real Marcus and return with an AEH, we have a slim chance of survival. She wouldn't be expecting such a revelation, and it would take her focus away from me.

At that moment, I felt a strong resistance. My intent was just to divert her attention. It wasn't a good enough reason to confide in her.

What can I say now?

She stood there, wide-eyed, waiting for my final words.

"As long as you continue to search for reasons to shut me out, how do you expect me to feel like I belong?" *Yes, that's quick thinking.*

She stared blankly at me and opened her mouth to say something—then stopped.

We parted ways. The pulling sensation had nothing to do with Ana, even though it had become stronger than ever.

My next choice for a confidant would be Constance. She was brilliant, steadfast, and would keep a secret. I needed her to calculate our chances and consider every permutation of the news.

CHAPTER 13

SIX

The pain of a hundred thousand volts of electricity passing through my cranium woke me after what felt like a very long rest. All matter morphed into lava-like streams of indistinguishable shapes. This was not my usual smooth transition from a resting state. Just a short time ago, I'd been on the platform with Ana. It was a strenuous interaction, but nothing to bring on high levels of physical pain.

"Victoria, stay in one position. We will subdue the pain," said Anthea.

"We? Who's we? What's happening to me?" Forced into a fetal position, I groaned like a wounded animal.

"I have intercepted your pain receptors."

"I still have these pulsating thuds . . . and everything is blurry." I rubbed my eyes and held my head.

Suddenly, the lava flow stabilized into solid shapes.

"Make your way to Outer 8. Ambaran representatives await your arrival."

"You want me to walk in this pain? What's going on?"

"Make your way to Outer 8. Ambaran representatives await your arrival." I understood Anthea's repeated message, and what she wasn't saying. She didn't have clearance to tell me more.

"Okay, but I need a few moments to get my bearings." Outer 8—I hadn't heard of that one before.

I stumbled to my waiting transport, which secured me and took off. As the disc zipped along, I tried to follow its route, but couldn't focus without feeling queasy.

On arrival, a deep blue opalescent Conduit and an imposing six-foot-seven female AEH greeted me. The AEH, named Tau, had a kind face, soft brown eyes, and slightly upturned lips, but she showed no emotion. I tried to see more details, but I was like a drunk trying to focus by tilting my head left and right and leaning in.

"Victoria, there has been an accident." Her neutral tone gave me no clue as to the seriousness of the event.

The Conduit beside her looked *through* me like it was mentally somewhere else.

"What kind of accident? With whom?" I assumed the incident was responsible for my head pain but didn't yet understand why.

"Come with us," said the opal being.

We walked through a wall, like the entrance to my residence. I recoiled as waves of rolling air tainted with medicinal smells and a metallic taste assaulted my senses.

A dull blue glow emanated from five pods. *Are the pods creating the light, or is it the contents? The occupants might be an alien species who have come to Ambar for treatment.*

Conduits were positioned throughout the area and worked with a sense of urgency—albeit calm and focused. I had come to expect Ambarans to have everything under control; this felt different.

"Why aren't they talking to each other?" I asked.

"They are communicating neurally; it is the most expedient form of communication," Tau said.

"Right, of course. I'm still off-center from the pain." Although my head didn't hurt, I carried another type of pain I couldn't articulate. "Who's in the pods?"

Tau turned to me. "The accident involved five members of your group."

"Five . . ." As I spoke everything went into slow motion. The planet stopped revolving, and my body set like stone. My mind rushed to the nearest pod, but a body of stone wasn't fluid or fast. My steps were lethargic. The first pod encased François. He lay unresponsive in a fluorescent blue-green fluid with specks that lit up, probably healing material. Although enshrouded, he looked like he was resting well.

Next was Ragini; I knew little about the shy woman. She was floating in the same substance as François.

"Are they alive?" My lips quivered at having to ask the question.

"We are doing all we can." Tau looked over to each host.

In an instant, my body and brain went numb. We walked a few slow steps forwards to the next pod. I held my chest for fear of who I would see. I couldn't do it. I closed my eyes before we reached it.

Tau said, "Would you like me to tell you who you have yet to see?"

"Yes."

"Sabine is in the next pod. Peter and II-AEH Marcus are in the last two."

"Nooooo! Nooooo! Say it isn't true." I begged her, as daggers pierced my heart. Stress hormones rampaged through me, releasing a wild, primal assault as the dark crevasses of my brain awakened. My heart palpitated like a metronome set on presto tempo.

In a soft voice, Tau said, "Your body's enhanced matter will ensure that your vitals stay within an acceptable range during this crisis."

Moments later, I stabilized. Whether my body had triggered the tranquilizing response on its own or the hosts had intervened didn't bother me.

I cleared my eyes. Sabine was glaring at me as she convulsed and foamed at the mouth. The disturbing scene lasted for a fraction of a second before a fluorescent-green liquid energy swallowed her up.

"Help her!" I turned to Tau. "Help her—she's alive!"

"We are helping in every way we know."

I fought my body—it wanted to collapse. My mind spun in fits as I dragged myself to Peter and AEH-Marcus. They were not convulsing. I got closer to Peter. His eyes were open. The once bubbly, gregarious nineteen-year-old looked like a specimen floating in formaldehyde. I delved into his mind as I had done with classmates at school.

He was awake.

I grabbed Tau's arm. "Listen to me. Peter"—I pointed to his pod—"is alive. He's still in there, still conscious. We can save him and, perhaps, Sabine too." I squeezed so hard my hand cramped. She didn't react.

Two seconds later, a chain reaction started. The glow went out on Sabine's pod—Peter's too. They darkened, one by one, until not a single pod was lit.

"What's happening?" My eyes rolled across the scene. "Do something!" There was no denying it. I knew what was happening—the worst thing imaginable.

The Conduits' attempts gave way to resignation. My heart sank, and the rest of me followed as a metaphorical black hole sucked me in—void of the slightest trace of life. In that instant, I became a fractured being. Although in Earth time I'd only known them for a couple months, on Ambar, it felt like many years.

Without speaking a word, Tau picked me up and carried me like a baby towards a transparent, domed structure. Inside, an individual of green light was already waiting. Tau sat down with me still cradled in a curled-up, traumatized position.

The being's light reminded me of the lead Reviewer.

"Hello again, Victoria. This is an unfortunate day for us all." It was the same being, but they were no longer just in my head. As it radiated in front of me, I smelt the same after-storm smell.

I stood up with Tau's assistance. "Are all five gone?" The gaping hole in my psyche held the answer.

"Yes, we are sorry. The four members of your team and II-AEH Marcus were in an experiential lab where they shared consciousness with a remote AEH. Including the remote AEH, all six perished after a neural overload. Five died instantly."

"That's not true. I saw that Peter and Sabine were alive."

Tau remained quiet and fixed on the Reviewer.

"By the time you saw them, they were displaying only residual reflex responses. The overload left them with trace energies, which dispel slowly. Before your arrival, we attempted to save them using advanced methods and materials, but they were too weak to accept them."

A raging monster woke inside me. Having completed many sessions of thought control in my residence, I switched to my own neural communications. I transferred my thoughts and emotions faster and in a higher amplification than spoken words.

"Can you sense the rage inside me? Do you know loss of this magnitude? Can anyone on this planet *feel*?"

The Reviewer said, "We understand your emotion but will not engage with you in an adversarial way. Victoria, you are in shock. However, whether it is one of us, an Ambaran, an AEH, or a Conduit, every being on Ambar has the capacity to feel."

I wanted to lash out, to cancel the rest of our stay and get my remaining SEED members back to Earth safely. Yes, they were *my* people.

"How can they be . . ." I couldn't say the words. "What about safety protocols to stop such a thing from happening to anyone, let alone to four Earth humans and two AEHs?"

"It is more complex than that, Victoria."

"Well then, why don't you tell me *exactly* what happened!" I needed the facts to understand the unfathomable.

"The members were in an experiential lab with a remote AEH, as part of a galactic exploration module. They went off to meet researchers near a space seam. At that point—"

"But I completed that assignment with three others plus Peter. We didn't do that lab." Distrust rushed over me.

"These individuals had advanced two levels beyond all others. The accident occurred on Outer 4—"

"Outer 4?" I whispered, and dropped to my knees, smothered in a blanket of guilt and death. *I should have told someone. Could I have prevented this tragedy?*

"Victoria . . . you knew?" said the Reviewer in a private neural message. The tone told me everything. They hadn't known the accident was coming, and they didn't know I knew. My training to keep them out of my mind had worked—unfortunately.

Tau turned to me. Although she was expressionless and hadn't heard the discussion between me and the Reviewer, I—the guilty Earthling—must have given her some signs.

The Reviewer continued on a common neural connection between the three of us. "The accident occurred on Outer 4 when linked to an AEH, whom they had successfully linked to on another occasion."

There was no blame put on me. No questioning. No telling off. Maybe I couldn't have changed the outcome, or it couldn't be discussed in front of Tau. Needing to hear more about the accident, I parked the issue of my complicity.

The lead continued, "The team had been researching our universe's seams and was eager to see them from a closer perspective. Seams are where layers of our universe come together, reacting much like the tectonic plates on Earth. They collide, creating warps in space, spindles, mega-energy bursts, and waves of destructible forces that emanate throughout many of the nearby galaxies. With the team connected to him, the remote AEH traveled to a seam in a distant part of our universe known for its dramatic but calm natural events."

"Calm?"

"The zone is not dangerous. It has been stable for over 513,000 Earth years. Our prediction models are 99.5 percent accurate; the remaining half percent are rare, spontaneous conditions we cannot account for," said the Reviewer. "Normally, such incidents occur on a much smaller scale, causing little to no disruption. They offer unique research and viewing opportunities like your natural wonders on Earth."

Over 513,000 years since the seam had reacted so violently, and it came alive when members of our team were viewing it. What were the chances?

"What happened to the remote AEH?" Rein'li came to my mind. Surely, if it was him, I would've felt it in every cell of my body, and my mind would have splintered and shattered into a quantum of energy. "Who was it?" Like Mr. d'Orsini and his former tic, I massaged my forehead with every question to prepare my brain for the answer.

Tau turned to me and joined the conversation for the first time. "We lost two AEHs—II-AEH Marcus and remote AEH Kasif-EC9. He was an explorer designed to show SEED members our universe during assignments. His lab received an energy input thirty times greater than it could handle. He stopped functioning in under a hundred milliseconds. This seam reaction was one of the strongest ever recorded."

"Where is Kasif-EC9 now?"

"He is here on Ambar." As I watched Tau speak, her eyes changed. They did something peculiar—her iris and pupil merged and displayed images.

"Your eyes . . . are those memories?"

"These are scenes from the lives of Kasif-EC9 and Identity Imprint Augmented Earth Human Marcus," Tau said in a flat tone.

"Although we do not expect another space disturbance like this one in the near future, for the duration of your visit here, we must ban experiences and contact outside Ambar," said the Reviewer.

I understood. In times of crisis, it was best to batten down the hatches, take stock, and prevent further loss.

For a moment, the Reviewer's green light faded. "Victoria, I will explain the restrictions, but it is only for you to know."

My chin fell onto my chest. "I can't keep any more secrets from the team."

The Reviewer did not respond.

After ten seconds, I said, "But I want to hear the truth. So, yes, I agree to keep it confidential."

"This lab has brought up a serious issue for us. As part of our culture, we record any natural or unnatural events that impact our universe or people. However, in this case, we *cannot*."

"You can't register the deaths of our people or your AEHs?"

"Your visit here is not without controversy. There are those who believe your presence puts everyone at risk, both in your universe and ours. We have managed these concerns locally, but it is best if your existence remains unknown outside Ambar's realm."

Now it's making sense. For security reasons, the Earth Complex isn't visible to non-Ambarans. I was naïve; I hadn't appreciated how others in their universe might react to us.

"Some, in the galaxy, consider bringing you here to be playing with Earth's humanity in a way not approved of by our people or culture. The Ambarans, on the other hand, are more accepting of your species and were eager to host you in an effort to save Earth."

And there it was … like in sci-fi movies, a prime directive which stated that one shall not interfere with another's civilization. Hiding us in the planet's core hadn't been about a single questionable species conducting a search. The Ambarans were hiding us from everyone.

"A portion of those aware of your visit are apprehensive about our ability to keep a primitive offshoot like yours from affecting other beings."

My mouth dropped open. "Primitive off—"

"Whatever classification others give to Earth humans, our utmost priority is to protect you while you are here. However, history is not in our favor."

"Sorry, history?"

"There have been other human species, like yours, in adjacent galaxies. They destroyed themselves along with other species."

"They were like us?" I said as I attempted to process two things. One, we weren't the first humans of our kind, and two, the Ambarans had first-hand knowledge of humans like us.

"How did they destroy themselves?"

"Based on many civilizations over vast amounts of time, we have learned that any human species diverting from a narrow developmental path is a danger to themselves and others."

"Have there been any exceptions?"

"No. However, we believe Earth has a chance to become that exception. This is why we are helping to save Earth and humanity."

"Why might we be the exception?"

"Your brain development is different enough from the failed human civilizations that you may not succumb to the same fate. I cannot disclose more information to you at this time."

There was more to their agreement to help us than I knew. And now I felt more vulnerable than ever, knowing we needed such a high level of protection.

The Reviewer continued, "No life form can enter or exit a seam area without being registered by a surveillance network. While outside the Earth Complex, Kasif-EC9's life sign showed as Ambaran, not an AEH, in order to protect your people's identity. After any catastrophe, all planets confirm loss of life. The Ambarans have acknowledged the loss of one."

"Sorry, but the Ambarans lost two AEHs if Marcus is included. Why aren't they acknowledging that?"

"Only Kasif-EC9 was physically at the seam. All others were present through an advanced neural connection, which cannot be accessed by anyone outside Ambar."

"I see." Our discussion was surreal. In my numbed state, I went through the motions. "How will you communicate the accident to my team?"

"We will administer a rest time and transmit a neural message. It will contain all the information they require."

"They will find out as they sleep?"

"All SEED members, other than you, will have their emotions dampened. They must stay focused on their goals."

"But you have calmed me as well, haven't you?"

"When you arrived to receive the news, the hosts managed your neurotransmitters. However, your brain quickly responded and continued without further intervention."

Surprising myself in the situation, I thought of Constance. "Could you tell Constance now? I'd like to be here with her." I wanted to give her more time and space to process the loss of our team members. For her, losing Sabine would be the hardest. They had become the best of friends.

"Constance will experience three minutes of raw emotion before receiving increased and sustained intervention. She is on her way."

"How will you help members cope with this tragedy?" Through dozens of studies on how grief affects the brain's physiology and cognitive abilities, I knew all too well the importance of correctly dealing with grief and its stages. But that was in a different world.

The Reviewer said, "Your team will accept the accident and process it within hours."

I crinkled my forehead. "A few hours to grieve our friends isn't enough or respectful."

"It is vital for everyone to focus on their objectives. Members will perceive that they have had adequate time to process the loss. Perception does not abide by a linear timeline."

As I thought about Peter, Sabine, François, and Ragini, I realized I hadn't asked one critical question.

"All team members, except me, had a dream that compelled them to go to Norway. But why? How did you select these particular people?"

Again, the Reviewer's light flickered slightly. "These individuals were chosen because of you."

My mind flashed back to Marcus. He said he came out of his dormant state because of me. What was I missing?

"Me? I don't understand."

"They all have an innate ability to connect with your brainwaves. During our first discussion, you transmitted the coordinates that awakened others."

During most meditations, I visualized radiating calmness and love in my neighborhood, the city, the country, the continents, and the world. It was a natural thing for me to do, but perhaps there was more to the practice.

"Awakened them for what purpose?"

"To assist you. On this occasion, to prevent the destruction of Earth. Another feature of their brains is that they are highly malleable to further development."

I nodded and bit down on my lower lip. The four members submerged in a preserving fluid were called to action by my brain. "Can I visit the pods again?"

"I will take you to them," said Tau.

We had walked ten steps when she stopped in front of a fuzzy gray wall. Puzzled, I looked to her for an explanation. The partition disappeared, and the pods of death lay before us, immersed in pulsating waves of yellow and blue light.

I watched the currents phasing in and out. "What do the waves do?"

"They preserve the area. You can go in."

Tau stayed at the front, and I walked alone to the first pod. I didn't have the emotional depth to cope with what surrounded me. Yesterday, they had shared, laughed, and played. Now, they lay still and lifeless, without feeling, thought, or hope.

Wait a minute. Were they really without thought? On Earth, breakthroughs in neuroscience and AI had enabled comatose people to awaken after many years. Why couldn't it happen here? I hadn't been thinking in a clinical or professional way, but perhaps . . .

I rushed over to a nearby Conduit and asked for clarification.

"Are you sure the team members don't have the slightest remnant of synaptic activity?"

"Only residual traces of energy remain, which can trigger the appearance of life."

"Get the Reviewer for me," I demanded. Realizing I was the only one who knew them as Reviewers, I clarified. "The individual I just met with."

Within seconds, a live image of the Reviewer appeared.

"You're from an advanced civilization with abilities to do things we, from Earth, cannot begin to think about. Are you telling me that my team members lack any neural activity, and you and I can't do anything to revive them or reverse the damage?"

After seeing how they'd gotten the real Marcus out of his dormant state, with my help, I had a hard time believing we couldn't do anything for at least one team member.

"Victoria, Earth human brains are more fragile than others. Any efforts beyond what we have tried would be inhumane experimentation."

My hopes plummeted, and my anger rose. My primal limbic system was making its debut on Ambar. "I don't believe you!" I shouted and pounded my fists into the Reviewer's image. "I don't believe you! You've been able to manipulate our bodies, behaviors, memories, and emotions since the moment we arrived, yet now you say you can't do anything?" I stared at the pods. "We're supposed to be going home together."

"I assure you, we have done all we can," said the Reviewer before vanishing.

My legs wobbled, and Tau rushed over to support me. Through my tears, I snapped at her and the Conduit. "Leave me alone!" They took a step back. "Leave me alone!" I repeated. Whether startled by my emotions or honoring my request, they left. Bargaining and denial clumped together to give way to anger. I was on an accelerated grieving path.

Four SEED members—or five, if we included the AEH Marcus—lay stunted in time, their eyes permanently shocked open. I turned away from their haunting stares; their final gaze was not for me to match. I was not deserving. Casting my eyes down, I crept by each one before sitting at the foot of Peter's pod and spiraling. *It's over. You were supposed to go home in just over a month. We can't go on without you.* I felt their judging eyes upon me, filled with condemnation. Coming to Ambar had cost them their lives.

As I sat in the desert of death, a mirage appeared in the distance. The pulsating, yellow and blue waves around the pods obscured its form. The apparition was stationary for a few minutes before it split in two and came closer. The vision became clearer, then. It was real—Constance and a Conduit.

I stood up within arm's reach of Constance, paralyzed by the magnitude of what I needed to express. How would she comprehend the hell that lay before her? She stared out at the pods and walked around me. There were no words or actions worthy of her attention. With my back to her, I whispered, "I'm so sorry."

She began her survey of team members, whizzing by all of them before doubling back to look at François. I wondered why she didn't spend more time with Sabine. To give her space and time without me in view, I returned to my sitting position on the floor next to Peter. When Constance walked by, I glanced up at her to make contact, but she didn't reciprocate.

Her face was pastier than usual, but it was her bloodshot eyes stewing in their fiery red sockets that startled me. She was being consumed from the inside. Did she want to take me with her into the brimming smolder of her heart? I took solace in knowing that her pitchforks could not be sharper than those I had willingly impaled myself upon.

I settled on watching her fingers counting in slow motion. It was like waiting for a bomb to go off. You know it's going to happen but don't know when. Each second was a painful stitch in the tapestry of doom.

Then, it happened.

She pierced the desolate scene with her cries, akin to the agonizing sounds of an injured baby impala. She was begging Sabine to wake up. The 180 seconds she was given to experience raw emotion were long.

I covered my ears and waited for it to be over. My perception of time was that an hour went by before the silence took over. Ambaran intervention.

Soon, Constance approached me. "I'm ready to go."

I searched my mind for the right thing to do. Should I coax her to stay and work through her emotions, or was it unnecessary now that the Ambarans had influenced her reactions?

Tau escorted us to the discs.

Despite my preference to retreat and be alone, I knew I shouldn't leave Constance in her current state.

Once on board, I said, "If you'd rather not be on your own, you can stay with me."

Constance stared at her feet and, with a measured cadence, said, "I *want* to be alone. I have so much work to do."

"Okay, but I'm here if you want to talk."

She closed her eyes. "When I was younger, I didn't understand people. My brother, Grant, used me, but I relied on him until he left—then I had no one." She opened her eyes and clasped her hands together as if wanting to stop the counting. "I never had a close friend. Until Sabine. She understood and accepted me unconditionally. And now—now, I've lost her. It will not be in vain. I will make her proud of me." She stared at me with steely determination in her eyes.

"You and Sabine had a special relationship. She will stay in your heart forever."

She nodded and pursed her lips together.

Although she and I had different lives, we were also similar. Like Constance, I counted the number of genuine friends I had on one finger. I, too, had difficulty being around people. Being an island socially felt best to me, but I didn't want to be stranded there. And rightly or wrongly, we both had an unyielding focus on our goals.

We went our separate ways without exchanging another word or glance.

When I entered my place, the ever-attentive Anthea announced, "Residence adjustments have been made to help you through the loss of your team members."

She had dimmed the lights and changed the scene to the stony beach Aunt Judy and I frequented. How I yearned for one of those days, far away from here and now.

I sought refuge in my rest chair to ride the alternating waves of intense grief and numbness.

Before and after rests, I walked around in a trancelike state. I ran from thoughts about how I could have warned the Ambarans about an impending accident. Losing four SEED members on a planet with advanced beings, who I thought could cure all human diseases and ailments, was incomprehensible to me. Perhaps I did need more Ambaran intervention, like the others.

I had felt connected to the Earth Complex and Ambar. Now, I was unplugged. There was no energy or life anywhere. Agonizing seconds passed like long, arduous days. Hunched over with the weight of disillusionment, I dragged myself back to the rest circle. A period of uncertainty had started. We were vulnerable even in the middle of an advanced civilization where everything was understood and supposed to be in exquisite order.

The lower brainwave pattern that had brought me peace in the past was merely another layer of misery. I didn't care if tomorrow came.

The next moment, Rein'li appeared. So much time had passed. I sat broken, not wanting to connect with anyone.

"Victoria, you inflict guilt upon yourself, like a weapon, but it is not yours to wield." His voice sounded different, almost longing.

I didn't know where to start, so I didn't.

"You must continue with your objectives and help your group. Keep searching for answers to your questions—about you."

In my fractured state of mind, I agreed and offered no cross-examination.

"I would like to guide you to a place to ease your pain. Do I have your consent?"

I nodded, although I didn't believe anything could make a difference.

He slowed my mind until I temporarily lost my ability to recall what had happened. The view was of their galaxy. It felt like home.

$$\circ \quad \circ \quad \circ$$

News about the accident had gone out to everyone as they rested. The Ambarans didn't want to risk a panic or an uprising. Whatever measures they took, I hoped it would give them the results they wanted without too many side-effects for our team.

I regularly put myself through a memory check. I had full knowledge of what had transpired, although the old saying "you don't know what you don't know" came to mind. The anguish blaring through me at high volume was something I wished they had abated.

A moment after I opened my eyes from a rest, Anthea had instructions for me. "Victoria, take your nourishment and meet your team at the Delta Center, area 7.3.25."

"How are they?" A lump in my throat muffled my words.

"They have been informed, visited the pods, and are convening to commemorate the team."

"What's been done to help them through this?"

"Endorphins, serotonin, oxytocin, and dopamine levels were increased to counterbalance negative reactions. Prefrontal cortex stress pathways have been inhibited to maintain clearer cognitive abilities. Their enriched neural cells will continue to support the processing of emotions and the body's sympathetic response. All other control settings remain the same."

"Sounds fairly comprehensive."

"It is the least amount required to manage their emotional states and continue acquiring knowledge."

The outfit generator dressed me in black.

Before leaving, I accessed team statistics. What felt like ten days since the accident had actually been just over two Earth days. A flash of anger zipped through me. The grieving period was too short. Our team, minus five—how could we possibly have a chance to save Earth. Sabine would no longer cross paths with the real Marcus in Germany. My former hiking companion could continue living his life without interference. Couldn't he?

Too many questions in my vulnerable state. Less thinking, more doing.

I entered area 7.3.25 and found the remaining SEED members dressed in stark mourning black. Life-sized images of the fallen five provided the only light.

Zoa hugged me. Allan, Ana, and I greeted each other, minus the hugs, even though I was ready to put aside our differences.

"Can I talk to you for a minute?" Allan inserted himself between me and Zoa. "I can't believe the Ambarans couldn't transfer any consciousnesses to AIs or something similar. Did they do everything possible?"

I got a little closer to his left ear. "Our hosts have assured me that they did all they could."

"Sure, of course." He turned to walk away, leaving me wondering if there was something more to his comment. When he was one step away, he turned back. "Why did you and Constance visit them before the rest of us?"

"They needed us to confirm the group's passing."

He tilted his head. "Why you two?" Apparently, his critical thinking centers were intact.

"I didn't make the decision, so I don't know." I wasn't about to be cross-examined.

"Right." He stared at me with squinting eyes before his impressionable astronomer friend pulled on his arm. She had been standing behind him, listening, but was noticeably quiet. He turned to her, mumbled something, and led her away.

"Is everything okay with Allan?" asked Zoa.

"Yes, he's just trying to make sense of things, like we all are."

Constance was missing, and that worried me. I didn't know how autism would play into her coping ability.

I made purposeful eye contact with each person and searched their faces for glimpses of judgment or blame, any inkling ... but nothing. No one, except possibly Allan and Ana, was blaming anyone for losing team members. I was grateful for the Ambarans' methods and results.

"In times like this, we must be there for each other," Zoa said with eyes full of tears. "I only wish Constance was here with us. Should we check in on her?"

"I think she needs time," I said.

Zoa put her hands in prayer position. "I hope she will join us when we revisit the pods."

"She's already said her goodbyes," I reassured Zoa. "Being around everyone may be too much for her."

"Victoria, I don't want to sound like I'm giving up but," her words trembled as she spoke, "tell me, is our fight for Earth over?"

I tried not to look petrified. "I'm hoping the Ambarans will give us more help. They have to."

"Let me know if you want me to speak to them with you," said Zoa.

By anyone's standard, the group was remarkably stoic as we stood mourning. Constance never showed up. After a subdued goodbye, we remembered each departed friend with a story. Essential members of our team were dead. And I was the sole member to know our stay was opposed by others. If that got out, at least one person would think the five team members weren't the victims of a natural disaster but were attacked. What would become of us now? Had we lost not just our friends, but any chance of saving Earth?

During one of my long stretches of gazing out into space, I recalled what I saw and felt when I visited the five team members.

Should I trust what I saw in Peter's eyes, or what the Reviewer and Conduits told me? If it wasn't the truth, what else could they be lying about?

CHAPTER 14

FRIEND OR FOE

Labs and assignments started up again within hours of the fallen five's remembrance. Constance came out of her accommodation but remained focused inward, beelining it to Outer 4's platform at every opportunity. There, she told me, she stared out into space as time slipped through her fingers, uncountable. She asked questions with no good answers. I hoped the exquisite order of space comforted her, and maybe gave her time to identify a pattern or two.

I retreated into the depths of my home to work on the case for increased Ambaran involvement. They needed to save Earth, otherwise SEED would be the last Earth humans in our universe and theirs. My request for a meeting with the Reviewer was accepted, but the time was not specified. I would be contacted.

As I waited, I drowned myself in proposals and permutations of what Ambaran help could look like. It was difficult to make specific recommendations without knowing the nature of the doomsday disaster. The common variable in all solutions was sending AEHs back with us. In my mind, as they were created here, we could have as many as needed. The idea had its limitations. Perhaps the Ambarans wouldn't be allowed to create a rescue team and send them to another universe because it would leave too great an imprint. Surely their position had changed with the loss of team members.

During one of my more delirious moments, I considered blackmailing our hosts. I would threaten to reveal our presence to everyone in their universe, or at least the part I'd have access to, unless they dramatically increased their assistance. Which brought me to another problem. I didn't know how to communicate with anyone outside the EC.

The most feasible solution was for them to send back technologies and maintain contact with us until the event had been overcome.

Another idea—increase the stakes. Let them know we would start to shift Earth's evolutionary path. That's when I remembered they were already thinking that, hence their name for us—Society for Earth's Evolutionary Development.

I shifted my focus to understanding the Ambarans' and Reviewers' perspective on us. How might Earth's civilization evolve?

The evolutionary development of humans in Ambar's galaxy looked very similar to ours, in the beginning. However, with the benefit of moderated environments and social structures, guidance from remote advanced societies, and inherited technology, their paths had deviated sharply from ours. The physical structure of their brains changed to reflect their environment. Could we change Earth's course at our stage of evolution?

Suddenly, the lighting dimmed, and my research materials vanished. Background music, a rhythmic theta/delta piece, started playing.

I should've seen it coming. Exhausted by too many consecutive hours of analysis, and my obsessive-compulsive method of tackling it, I was being brought back into balance by my residence. It was my cue to restore through meditation. Within seconds, I lowered my brainwaves and heartbeat and entered a deep level of consciousness.

Well into my sublime respite, I heard a faint voice. "Victoria?" Anthea never interrupted me during research or meditation.

Uncertain if it came from inside or outside my head, I responded out loud. "Yes."

"Allan is here to see you," Anthea replied.

She's interrupting me for him? During the mourning period, I set my status to "engaged - do not disturb." I hadn't bothered to change it as I was immersed in my studies. It clearly wasn't working.

"When?"

"Now."

"This isn't the best time. I need at least twenty minutes to rise from my current state."

"He has rated the visit as urgent."

I grumbled and gave in. "Okay. You can let him in when my brainwaves enter a more awakened state."

As I worked through levels of consciousness, I heard a thud like he had leapt into my place.

"Victoria?"

Anthea said, "She will see you in forty-five seconds."

I drifted out of my meditation area, still disoriented from the quick ascent.

As soon as he caught sight of me, he said, "We have to talk." His speech pattern seemed faster than usual.

He bounced around my residence. "Your residence is so small." He crunched up his forehead. "Why aren't you using more space?"

"I prefer a cozier home. The EC is big and at times overwhelming." The small talk gave me a couple seconds to become more alert and tune into Allan's state of mind.

He shook his head. "Weird. Anyway, look, we need privacy." His eyes shifted from side to side.

I understood. "Anthea, privacy mode." With a single audible tone to confirm my request, she could no longer hear or see us.

"What's going on?" I stretched and tried to mentally prepare myself.

"Hey, I thought you should know—people are talking about home." Allan stayed fixated on me. Unusual. "We have learned all we need, and we want to leave while we still can."

Allan was letting me know about the disruptive talk of others? Interesting. "What do you mean 'leave while we still can'?"

"People are struggling. It was a good move to remove the controls, but the withdrawal has been hell." Allan walked over to one of the big windows that looked out into space. "We've had to learn to function again on our own."

I appreciated his reflections on the change. "I understand that. Is there anything I can do to help?"

"Yes. We need to go back home now. I would've spoken to the Ambarans, but seeing how they made you team lead—well, here I am."

He hadn't called me that before. "Right. Good to hear that people feel ready to return. We leave in just over a month, once we complete our assignments."

"Sure, sure, but everyone feels overmanipulated, controlled, analyzed,"—he punctuated with his fist in the air—"and treated like guinea pigs in an alien laboratory. We want it to stop now."

"Everyone? Most are without the original controls. And I haven't heard about this being a big problem. If anyone's distressed, they should come to me, as the team lead."

He curled his lip in disgust. "Come to you? What a joke. Even without the controls, we're specimens on a petri dish. They're putting us through trials to find out where our limits are. But they've learned enough, and so have we."

"You're right. They are learning about us, but we're getting the better end of the deal because it's our planet that's in danger of annihilation. That's why we are here."

"Okay, I'll say it. Isn't it enough that they've killed five of us?" He shook his head and clenched his teeth. "What will it take for you to wake up?"

"Look, everyone is grieving, but we need to be careful not to lash out at Ambarans." Although the team wasn't grieving in the usual way, I wanted to leave room for some emotional overflow.

Apoplectic with rage, he snarled and stomped his foot. "I've spoken to everyone, and they all agree with me. We will not go to any more assignments," he said with an air of defiance and absoluteness.

In my half-meditative state, I struggled to understand how we'd gone from working so well together on labs to this hostile conversation. "What? Who's 'we'?"

"You go along with every damn thing the Ambarans want. When they degrade us, you don't push back. Now they've killed team members... probably the latest addition to their specimen collection."

He trembled like an addict needing a fix; a feverish sweat dripped down his forehead. Of course, this wouldn't have been happening had the Ambarans kept their previous level of neurophysio-intervention. The Ambarans' work had been too precise. They had dealt with mourning memories and emotions but left everything else uncontrolled.

"Really? We're still in mourning and under tremendous pressure to perform. If this is your way of . . ."

"Are you in cahoots with them? Or maybe Ana is right. You're one of them." He took a step closer and raised his voice.

I froze, not knowing if or how I should reply.

"Answer me, dammit." His motions were disjointed and erratic, like he was about to jump out of his body. He sprang forwards to within twelve inches of my face.

"This is crazy. You're angry and frustrated. Taking it out on me won't bring them back or save Earth. You are—."

"No! Don't psychoanalyze me. So many times, I've searched for you using our location system, but you disappear without a trace. That's when you meet up with them."

"I'm like you. I—."

"Ana told me your blood isn't like ours; yours changes. No Earth human's blood does that." With a look of betrayal, he squinted at me with his beady brown eyes. In a soft voice, he said, "During Lost Senses, Rein'li told us about your magnetic tuning ability and particle entanglement skills. That alone wouldn't have set off warning bells, but out of the blue he sent us on a break." His eyes got wider. "Wait, you didn't leave, did you? You and Rein'li stayed to discuss keeping your identity secret. When we came back in, your eyes were a bright yellow, not an Earthly human color."

"We didn't . . ."

He raised his pointer finger to my face and edged closer. I stepped back, smacking up against a barrier.

His fiery breath burned my face as he proclaimed, "Get us the hell back home. Everyone agrees, it's time to go."

Like a feral creature, he foamed out the sides of his mouth. To stop him from devouring me, I inserted my hand between our faces and turned my head, gasping for a breath of less toxic air. Hopefully, he wouldn't sense my fear.

"Allan, you need to calm down so we can have a civilized conversation and work this out together."

He leaned forwards. "No, dammit, I won't back down this time. We thought you were one of us—*some* considered you a friend." He spat the words out at me.

"Step away," I demanded.

He took a half step back. "You've made us prisoners in another universe. And we're the lucky ones. Peter, Sabine, François, Marcus, and Ragini probably discovered something they shouldn't have, and now they're *dead*."

"No, you're trying to make sense of a tragedy. But looking to blame isn't the answer. It was an unfortunate accident."

"See!" He tugged at his thick locks of hair. "That's the problem; you believe everything they tell you. For one stinking moment, think for yourself. Unless—you can't."

He sounded like Ana but more aggressive.

Frozen with fright, I was silent, and his imagination filled in blanks and warped events.

He grabbed my shoulders. "Are you one of us—an Earth human?"

"Of course I am. But I'm afraid." I took the leap of faith and hoped making myself vulnerable would get through to him. "Strange things happen at home and here too. I feel close to the AEHs and Reviewers, like I understand them better than our people. But it's because they accept me. Do you realize how scared it makes me to have abilities beyond everyone at home yet . . . " The release of finally telling someone brought tears to my eyes.

"Poor you." He was momentarily expressionless. "But it won't work. You know why you're the team lead when others are more qualified. It has to be you. The Ambarans want one of them in the role." Intent on getting the answer he wanted to hear, he shook me like a rag doll and repeated, "No—more—lies." His hot, sweaty hands moved up to my neck.

My amygdala was doing its job, narrowing my vision to keep my predator at the center of my attention.

"Stop, Allan!" I struck his arms with mine, broke his grip, and dropped to crawl away.

"I'm taking back the control we *should* have, that you so willingly gave away."

My hearing devoted itself to two sounds—his words and his erratic breathing. I had managed to drag myself a few feet away and stand halfway up before he tackled me again. He positioned himself over me like a rabid coyote about to devour a baby deer. I watched in slow motion as his hands approached my head.

"Please—" I gasped. "Stop! This won't solve anything."

He looked away from me. "No. On Ambar, we're experiments. As long as we obey them, they'll show us what we could've been. They plan to change us permanently so we can do *their* work on Earth."

"That's not true," I whispered. "I'll tell you . . ."

He shook his head like something was loose inside. "To hell with that. Do you think I trust anything you say? You're one of them. I'll prove it!"

Giving up all hope that our talk would end well, I called out, "An—"

He clutched my neck. I hit him over and over wherever my arms could reach, but with all his weight upon me, and his viselike grip on my windpipe, I could not call for Anthea to come out of privacy mode.

"Come on, Victoria, use your powers!"

What's he expecting of me? It's not like I have super strength or the ability to throw him off me.

"Show me who you really are!"

Unable to take the slightest of gasps, and fearing for my life, I went deep into my mind and released a wave of energy outward before fading into darkness.

○ ○ ○

"Victoria. Victoria." A voice called out.

I couldn't speak or see. *Did Allan strangle me to death? Am I in a quantum dimension of the multiverse where dead people go?*

"Victoria." I recognized the voice—Anthea.

"Yeee . . ." I couldn't get the word out. *Does that mean I'm dead?*

"You are still alive."

But how can she be reading my thoughts and talking when she's in privacy mode?

"What—what happened?" I closed my eyes, hoping to regain my senses. When I opened them again, I found myself lying in a half-upright position in a curious chair with blue and green energy bands covering me.

"This chair—"

"A rest chair in emergency treatment mode; it can monitor and repair. We have evaluated you for neurological and respiratory damage and tissue injury. The treatments were successful. After a rest, you will make a full recovery."

"What's going on?" I didn't wait for her to answer. "Where's Aa—Al . . ." I went into a coughing fit and felt a burning pain across my neck.

"Allan attempted to take your life. When his biometrics showed him to be in a critical zone, I came out of privacy mode."

"His biometrics? Not mine?" As if things couldn't get more confusing.

"He was unconscious and had sustained electrophysiological injuries. Treatment has been administered to him in his residence."

"He was unconscious too? What injuries?"

"Neurologic and cardiac injuries due to a directed neural-electric overload from you."

"Me?" I tapped my chest over and over. "There must be some mistake. I passed out when he was strangling me. I didn't do anything."

"You fell into a deep rest pattern after a spontaneous depletion of mental and physical energy reserves. Think back, and you will find that you released a targeted burst of energy."

I closed my eyes to help me recall the horrible moments. "Yes, I faintly remember. I wasn't sure if I was dreaming."

"An Ambaran representative will speak to you about the incident and inform you of Allan's status."

Certainly, Ambar had to forbid attempted strangulation. What had they done with Allan?

"I'm ready now to speak to someone about A . . . A . . ."

"An Ambaran representative is outside your residence."

"Rein'li?" I hoped the Ambarans knew to send him.

"No, it is not the AEH Rein'li."

An AEH entered, but I remained in the chair.

"Hello, Victoria. I am K^Lys." It was pronounced "Kee-lews," with the first syllable high-pitched. She had ivory skin, dark brown eyes, and hair resembling layers of green flower petals. "I am here to discuss the status of the Earth Complex."

"Status of the Earth Complex? But this is about Allan."

"Before beginning, we require a witness." In an instant, a dynamic image of a Conduit appeared to my right. K^Lys positioned herself on my left.

"Why do we need a witness for a talk about Allan?"

K^Lys said, "This is an unprecedented incident for the Ambarans and those you call 'Reviewers.' They requested both of us to be present."

Crime hadn't been included in any of our assignments. *How will they respond to attempted murder?*

K^Lys started the official discussion. "You will not be permitted to leave your residence until SEED is brought back into balance."

"Is this because of Allan?" I grimaced at the thought of him. "Are you afraid he's going to hurt me again?"

"Allan is recovering in his residence. Two days before coming to see you, he started a movement against the Ambarans."

I had immersed myself in research with no clue as to what was going on around the Complex. "A movement? He has followers?" The injustice riled me to stand up, but the chair tilted back and increased the intensity of the energy folds securing me.

"The team believes he has valid points."

It seems far-fetched; he thinks I'm Ambaran and started a rebellion. Is my subconscious making this up? I must be dead.

"Victoria, you are alive," Anthea repeated.

"Oh . . . I didn't realize you were still listening in on my thoughts." I had worked hard to train my brain so that no one would hear them. But thanks to Allan, I no longer had control. "Can you stop that?"

"Yes, I have ceased emergency access to your thoughts."

"Does everyone know what he's done to me?"

"Allan cannot recall the details of his visit to you," K^Lys said. "Your energy burst erased his memory. During this period of recovery, SEED members believe you are researching, and Allan is developing a plan to get the team back home early."

"I can understand Ana fueling or being fueled by Allan. But who else believes his rantings?"

"Out of the eight members, the majority are terminating their schedule of activities and want to return to Earth immediately."

I closed my eyes, "Who are they?"

She said, "Zoa has—"

"Zoa? What? Why hasn't she tried to contact me amidst a rebellion?" My stomach twisted into knots.

"Zoa did not want to intrude on your research because of the do-not-disturb status. She agrees with some of Allan's points; however, she does not agree with his approach."

I sighed in relief. Zoa had not joined in the fanaticism. I wished she had tried to contact me and labeled it urgent. I would rather have heard from her than Allan.

"Constance questioned Allan's ideas but concluded that the Complex had reached a tipping point and the outcome was inevitable."

"Okay." My heart sank. Of course Constance, as a former actuary, would have evaluated the data. It would become a simple equation for her if she saw the people turn one by one. Maybe nothing could balance out the loss of Sabine, and she just wanted to return home.

"Pino partially agrees with Allan," K^Lys continued. "However, he is unwilling to deal with issues in the same way."

After the loss of our team members, I didn't think things could have gotten worse. Yet most had turned their backs on our objectives. The seam accident may have caused them to give up any hope of saving Earth. Everything was unraveling. SEED had become a shell of its potential. My mind, heart, and body broke and withered.

"I need to get out there and talk to everyone. It's time for some cold, hard truths." Again, I tried to get out of the chair.

"The chair will not release you until your body metrics are at optimal levels. It is reconstructing damaged areas from near strangulation," Anthea said.

"There is much turmoil in the Complex. SEED members have triggered a cascade of dangerous thinking and behaviors," said K^Lys.

"But if I could go and speak to everyone." As I said the words, it dawned on me that the Ambarans were letting the conflict continue. "Why don't you stop it? You control two members other than myself by modulating hormones, neurotransmitters, nutrition, and response levels. And the other six, you can reactivate their controls. Why allow this conflict to continue?"

"Allan convinced members to revolt against life in the Complex and our methods of assistance. With such behaviors coming naturally to Earth humans, the hosts are observing its progression without further intervention for now."

Earth humans in action—showing off our inherent nature. We were laboratory rats of our own making, or . . . In a flashback to my first meeting with the Reviewers, I remembered how easily they agreed to help Earth when I asked them. Was this what they wanted to see . . . our true selves in order to compare us to previous versions of humans in their history?

"We've become an experiment." I looked up at K^Lys. "What are they hoping to see?"

"The Ambarans want to see if the revolt will be a self-correcting episode. It is an opportunity for them to observe uncontrolled humans in an environment rich with knowledge, experiences, and resources when they have everything to lose. As you know, one experiment is worth a thousand theories."

"So the rebellion continues,—I raised my arms emphatically— "and we waste valuable time, but at least the hosts will get their empirical data."

K^Lys looked at me with soft eyes. "We will not allow the rebellion to go on. You have a decision to make on behalf of SEED."

I swallowed hard. "What decision?"

"We must sedate the group or return them to Earth sooner with their memories wiped from the day they entered the cave in Norway."

Such an option showed they had given up on us. "What would sedation look like?"

"For as long as SEED is in the Earth Complex, we will quiet those areas of the brain and body involved in creating aggression, anger, and fear. Levels of interventions will be greater; thus, members may appear lethargic and unemotional until their brains adapt to the changes. Their biochemistry will be altered with the existing enhanced cellular matter."

With my mouth hanging open and eyes blinking, I must have appeared witless. "Lethargy and apathy . . . are there any other downsides or side effects?" I was familiar with sedation on Earth but not on Ambar.

"Whatever you decide, we must erase their most recent memories of this conflict. They cannot reference thoughts, memories, or emotions that could incite another uprising or affect future decisions."

"Ohhh." Allan's accusation was becoming a reality. He had forced me to be "in cahoots" with the Ambarans to control everyone's behaviors. How foreboding of him! "In both choices, memories will be erased, to a greater or lesser degree." My voice got weaker with the mere mention of it.

"Yes, and neither choice is risk-free. We are reaching our capacity for what we will attempt on Earth human brains. Any process must be as minimalistic as possible."

I felt a sudden shift in my body and knew the chair would release me. Slightly less agile than I was before near-strangulation, I stood up and turned to K^Lys. "What are you saying?"

The AEH glanced at the host. "Members may not tolerate or assimilate the neural modifications."

I gasped at the thought of losing more members. "This isn't a choice. To have any chance of saving Earth, we have to continue here. You can't send the team back without memories of what they've learned." I shook my head in disgust at the suggestion. "What about Zoa and Pino, who didn't join Allan's rebellion—will their memories be erased?"

"Yes—we cannot have some team members with incomplete memories and others with full memories of the conflict. There is little time for delay."

Every second dragged on as I tried to come up with an alternative for the most serious ethical dilemma of my life.

For a momentary reprieve from the pressure, I walked over to a wall that spontaneously morphed into a window overlooking space. *I am part of an infinite multiverse, yet a microscope has zoomed in on me and caught me behaving like a detached scientist experimenting on unwitting subjects. At least in my work on Earth, people knew they were participating in research.*

Taken aback by their ultimatum, I changed direction. "I was hoping to speak to the Reviewer about some solutions." Returning earlier with a mind-wipe would ensure Earth was lost. I couldn't believe they were willing to do that unless they had a back-up plan.

In an instant, the Reviewer appeared before us. Although it was the third time I'd met the Reviewer, I was still taken aback by the beauty and power of its energy, even in an image.

"We must work together to ensure your success here and back on Earth," were the light being's first words.

"Yes, I agree but I don't believe memory-wipes and sending us back early are a good solution."

K^Lys said, "The mind-wipe would not take away all skills and abilities learned here."

"But how can you be so specific about what you remove?"

"We will suppress most recent memories," she said.

"I see. I wish you had clarified that earlier." There was no misinterpreting my impatient tone. Looking to the Reviewer, I said, "Why can't you sedate them, and we finish up here with lighter workloads. When it is time for us to return you . . ." Dare I suggest it? "You send four AEHs back with us to take the place of the four we lost, plus an additional one to replace Marcus's AEH."

Without a second's hesitation, the Reviewer said, "We agree." They continued, "However, all five AEHs must return to Ambar once catastrophe has been averted."

"If we don't succeed, will your AEHs die with us?"

"Yes."

Bewildered by how easily I'd negotiated extended help and how quickly they'd risk the lives of their own, I froze, not knowing if I was missing something or being duped.

K^Lys said, "Your team is currently in a simultaneous rest. They will awaken with no memory of a rebellion and will spend the remainder of their stay under sedation."

"What level of sedation? Will they still be able to experience and learn things?"

"They will be unable to display extreme emotions, but will continue their training," said the AEH.

"With the loss of team members and the rebellion," I said, "can you give me any more specific information on how to best prepare for the disaster?"

The Reviewer said, "We will transport SEED to a suitable strategic location to manage all elements of the impending event. Although these measures are beyond our usual level of involvement in a civilization, this is an exceptional case."

"Thank you. I . . . *we* are grateful for your help. However, I need to ask you for something else." I paused, looked at K^Lys and the Reviewer, and took the psychological leap. "We can't easily recover from the accident and this rebellion. Even with the AEHs, expecting a team of fourteen to save a whole planet seems impossible. Could you transport a colony of Earth humans here?"

"Evacuating Earth people to Ambar would require extensive resources and considerations by other planetary systems in the galaxy. Ultimately, it does not guarantee long-term survival for the species in its current state."

To my ears, it sounded like it was possible but would require more effort by them. "So that's a 'no'? Are you willing to risk losing an entire planet's population?"

"You must learn the nature of the catastrophic event and work together to find a solution that preserves the species. This is Earth's destiny."

It was challenging to fight the case when I wasn't as informed as they were and didn't understand their universe.

The Reviewer left as quickly as they had appeared.

"You can tell your team about the plan after their rest. You need to build trust and confidence with them," K^Lys said.

Amid my internal wrestling match, something Allan had said bubbled back up. *Am I "too agreeable" with the Ambarans? Do I need to push back more?*

From as far back as I could remember, I could look into people's eyes and see their life forces. Yet when I had thought Peter showed signs of consciousness, the Reviewer had told me it was residual and not real life. I believed them over what I had seen. But what if I was right?

"Not now," I whispered. I couldn't start second-guessing the Reviewers and everything on Ambar. This wasn't the time.

But now, Allan had handed them proof that even when given the resources to evolve, we reverted to our narrow and primitive ways of thinking. Perhaps we did need controlling and quarantining from all other species.

"I have one more question. How far back will you need to go to remove the rebellion from their memories?"

K^Lys said, "We will go back to two days after the seam accident. SEED members will accept their muted emotions as the norm for a team in mourning and be determined to continue."

Scowling, I expressed my astonishment. "Al—" I coughed. "Allan won't remember the harm he's done? And I won't have justice as I would on Earth?"

"On Earth, you would be permanently damaged from attempted strangulation and Allan would be dead."

"Dead because of me?" I had not yet dealt with what I had done to him. Perhaps it was too much for me to accept at that moment. I didn't want to be a danger to anyone, not even to the paranoid chap who tried to strangle me.

"Yes."

"But every time I look at him, I will relive the trauma."

"Would you like us to remove those memories from your mind?"

I threw my hands over my face. What was more important—remembering the truth and Allan's criminal potential, or having the ordeal expunged from my psyche?

Trapped, I said, "I'll keep the memory. In defense of SEED, although the rebellion is against our hosts, I feel responsible. I didn't do enough when the people talked about the lack of privacy or timeframes. Allan complained that you were too controlling—deciding when and how we rest, eat, learn, and interact—and I didn't follow up on Zoa's concerns about our unnatural changes." I dropped my head in defeat. "All of this could have been avoided if I had done more."

"Victoria, how you lead your team is something for you to reconcile. However, *you* did not create the rebellion."

"Is there any way a SEED member would find out the role I played in this whole ordeal?"

"No," said K^Lys.

My viewpoint changed; I watched from overhead like I was someone else. My isolation gave me objectivity. Yet a not-insignificant part of me felt terrifically powerful . . . and evil. All my life, *they* had victimized me with the same behaviors on display in the EC. This felt like retribution, no matter how I tried to dress it up.

"I need to be alone." Alone with the good and bad versions of myself.

Within moments of the Conduit and K^Lys leaving, Anthea announced she was going into privacy mode. I thought it odd but figured she was giving me space to heal or dwell on my actions, depending on which side of my guilty conscience I looked from.

An instant later, Rein'li was in front of me.

Frustrated by his sudden appearance, I covered my eyes with my hands, and part of me wished he'd just let me be. "Why do you only connect with me when things aren't going well?"

"I cannot let you struggle with these matters on your own."

"Why not? Everyone else does."

"It has been difficult for you, but erasing the SEED members' memories will help bring them together; it is necessary to succeed. I will ensure your safety and well-being going forwards."

"How can you say that when I don't see you, in person or in meditations?"

"Victoria, on Earth, I am there when you need guidance. Here, on Ambar, I am always with you but not traceable."

"In my mind, I see myself walking on a frozen lake where the ice always breaks from under me. Why can't I predict when people turn against me? I always seemed to be surprised."

Rein'li said, "You are trying to understand their personalities. Tune into their energies instead."

He guided me in a meditation where everything was in balance and right in the universe. Afterward, we surfaced, but I couldn't recall the contents of the meditation. Before I could ask him to stay, he left.

Anthea said, "Victoria, I am in full-monitoring mode."

Considering recent events, I doubted Rein'li could ensure my safety. And why did he need to be untraceable to me?

One thing was clear. Ambar was making me stronger in every way. Had Allan awakened something in me or was it all the training? Who was I if I could no longer control my abilities?

Before going into rest mode, I made a request to Anthea.

"When I wake from every rest state until we leave, please say the following to me: Marcus—Rebellion—Strangulation—Five AEHs to Earth."

If my memories were tampered with, at least I'd know it. I recorded it as an acronym in my private notes "Mrs Five."

CHAPTER 15

SEED UNITY

As a result of losing four members and Marcus's AEH, surviving an assassination attempt, and maneuvering through a rebellion like a grand puppeteer, I was left on shaky ground, both emotionally and mentally. The idea of forging deep and lasting friendships built on sharing, honesty, and integrity was a distant fantasy. Instead, I felt isolated and adrift.

And as if the weight of the world upon my shoulders wasn't enough, I faced a new terror within myself. Could I, in my darkest moments, unleash my inner fury upon the unsuspecting?

Ambar had changed me.

Anthea broke into my thoughts. "Victoria, as requested . . . Marcus—Rebellion—Strangulation—Five AEHs to Earth."

I went through each key word and recalled what I knew. My memories were intact.

"Meet everyone in the Delta Center Inner 1.3. Your next team assignment will begin."

Three Earth days had passed since the enemy from within invaded my space. Two memories had haunted my rests—Peter's eyes and Allan's sweaty hands. Both created visceral memories for me. But everyone else's memories would have started back to two days after the accident.

Would it be like visiting patients in a sanitarium? Could I look into their eyes? I would be living a different reality than everyone else. Compartmentalizing and lying had to become strong competencies.

My thrusting heartbeat propelled me forwards. The aftermath of my decisions would be paraded before me. Without the Ambaran enrichments, I would have sweated bullets and turned gray in the time it took to get to the Center.

Once at Inner 1.3, I scanned everyone's faces for clues of vacant personalities and lost memories. The energetic buzz usually present at the beginning of an assignment had been replaced by a subdued library murmur. However, people still chatted, smiled, and embraced. It was not a sanatorium.

Zoa approached and hugged me. "Hello, my friend. It feels so empty without the others." She spoke in her usual warm way, but something was not quite right. She was not lethargic, but more solemn.

"How are you?" I asked, trying to disguise my anxiety.

"Mourning the loss of our friends but continuing my assignments." She rubbed her hands softly. "My heart is shattered, but I—I don't know . . . *if* I feel. What is the point of continuing?" Zoa spoke as if she had lost more than friends. She had lost herself. She went deeper into a dismal place in her mind with each word spoken.

What have I done? The sedation has resulted in Zoa losing the will to live.

"What can I do to help you?" I asked.

The heaviness of her eyelids drew her gaze downward. "I'm seeing myself from the outside. My body is well, but . . . my mind is slow and heavy." The sound of her voice didn't relax me as it had in the past; it profoundly saddened me. Of all the SEED members, I'd lost the one person who connected with me on more than a superficial level. Why did the hosts have to sedate the kind, wise, and warm Zoa? She would never rise in revolt. They should have calibrated her sedation better.

"I'm sorry you're struggling." *And it's my fault.* "Have you spoken to anyone about this?"

"My monitor made adjustments." She took my arm, and we walked towards the meeting point. I struggled to walk as she used my arm for support and pulled on me with every step. "My vials change with every nourishment. The hosts are caring for me. They do what they can, but they cannot heal what only time can."

"True." I lowered my head with the unbearable weight of regret. The modifications hadn't restricted her empathy, but I'd lost Zoa. It was a heavy price to pay for my decision.

The ever-perceptive woman noticed my reaction. "What troubles you?"

"It's nothing. I'm just a little anxious about the next assignment without our whole team."

Whether or not Zoa believed me, she didn't reveal. "Yes, me too."

"Look," I said, and nodded at Mr. d'Orsini.

The Italian put his arm around me and whispered, "It's good for the team to come together." He kissed me on each cheek. Mr.

d'Orsini behaved within a normal spectrum, although he was more physical with me than before. Perhaps he was grateful for those still alive, or were the neural interventions having odd side effects?

The team assembled at the transport discs. Ana and I acknowledged each other from afar with a nod. I smiled at the sight of Constance and made my way to her.

"Hello," she said.

"How are you coping?" I asked. My mind went into overdrive as I scanned her. Facial movements, typical. Posture, rigid as usual.

"I'm determined to make a difference," she said in her usual controlled fashion. "My trainings have doubled."

Either Constance was buried in the throes of denial, or the Ambarans had done a better job with her than with Zoa. The result was a driven woman, not someone who'd just lost her best friend.

I was about to ask a follow-up question when I noticed one person was missing from the group.

"Where's Allan?" I tried to ask it in a normal tone, but my voice cracked when I said his name.

"Don't you know?" The savant's blank face told me nothing.

I waited for her to elaborate but dreaded what words might come out of her mouth. In an airy voice, I said, "Where is he?"

She scowled, clearly wondering how I hadn't been informed. She motioned with her hands for us to go towards the transport area. "He came out of a rest and didn't recognize anyone . . . retrograde amnesia. He can't remember his name, where he is, or what he did in the past, even yesterday."

Was it the energy surge I gave him or the sedation? Dismayed but not horrified, I wanted to reply, *Oh, is that all?* Regardless of the reason, his amnesia could solve a number of issues for me. Instead, I switched to a clinical mode. "Was he tested for explicit and implicit memory?"

Zoa heard my question. "Allan can't remember where he has lived or what kind of dog he has."

I whispered, "Clear examples of explicit memory loss."

"And he couldn't recite his ABCs," Zoa said.

His implicit memory was affected too.

Constance nodded. "The hosts are treating him."

As we approached a disc, I partially feigned concern, plastering a worried look over my face. "How did this happen?"

Zoa said, "The Ambarans are uncertain. From what we know, he hadn't done anything out of the norm."

The hosts and I had wiped Allan's memory in its entirety, whether intentional or not.

"We are beyond coincidences," said Constance. "Either stress is taking its toll, or the Ambarans are intervening again beyond what we can handle."

My eyes widened at her accurate guess. She and Zoa had a detached acceptance of Allan's memory lapse; the sedatives were working. How would I be acting if I didn't know about the rebellion and strangulation?

As we disembarked from the discs, AEH Noha greeted us. We had arrived at Outer 3's project lab.

Noha said, "First, I want to acknowledge the loss of your team members. It was an unfortunate accident." She closed her eyes for a few seconds before continuing. "Second, you are here to learn and return to Earth to avert a serious threat to the planet. In this module, you will work with AEHs Barton and Jorge to increase connections. Your connection to each other is vital to your success. You must use UEP to sense each other's state. All of you need to understand the strengths and weaknesses of your team members."

AEHs Barton and Jorge entered the lab. They were identical, both male and my height, with silky, brown hair down to their shoulders and cocoa skin.

Noha said, "We will split into two groups initially, then join together at the end. Before you can interface neurally with an AEH, you must be trained. To expedite the process, we have modulated the adjuncts to magnify your brain power."

Tomas bounced at the idea. "Will I have superhuman powers?"

His question reminded me of Peter . . . lovely, bouncy Peter.

"Your actual brainpower will remain the same; however, the adjunct will magnify your thoughts. We will test your abilities and competencies through a series of simulations. You can remain in the lab until your brain reaches a 50 percent fatigue level."

"Allan would be the first one to drop out," Constance teased.

With a caustic spike in her voice, Ana said, "Unbelievable. If the Ambarans are successful in giving him back his memories, I hope he doesn't remember you."

Zoa smiled at Ana and patted her on the back. "Allan would have liked this challenge."

"Your assigned AEH will take you through exercises in preparation," said Noha.

Victoria will be in observation mode to assess your performance.

The outfit generators once again put everyone in team colors, shimmering green or white. My outfit didn't change.

I watched Zoa languish. She stood off to one side with her head drooped as if someone had siphoned out her life force.

A strange sensation interrupted my focus on my friend. The AEHs were discussing someone—me. Logically, I had no reason to think I was the subject, but at the risk of sounding irrational, the air between us seemed heavier. I queried the feeling, as I would have back home when I felt a similar energy.

The result? I troubled them for some reason. Mind reading was not one of my abilities, but their thoughts were so clear it created a detectable marker. My second attempt to probe them came up fruitless; they had slammed the door on my eavesdropping.

○　○　○

After hours of basic training, a pause was scheduled. Noha said, "Nutritional vials await you in the O3 N2. I will notify you when to reconvene here for the experiential AEH lab."

At the checkpoint, I sat within earshot of Ana and Tomas.

"Allan should be here for this project. I'm so worried about him," said the astronomer. "Do you think it's kinda good or bad that we haven't heard anything yet? Maybe we should ask Noha. They should just tell us"—she shook her head—"not leave us hanging, wondering what's going on. They keep too much from us." She nudged Tomas. "Say something. Don't you agree?"

Tomas pouted in sympathy. "Yes, he would've liked to occupy an AEH. I think he'll come out of this okay."

I listened and stayed quiet.

Considering the neural manipulation needed to take everyone back before the rebellion, SEED members were acting within normal parameters—a little less sharp, but acceptable. The Ambarans had done well, except with Zoa.

I carried pervasive guilt for my Nigerian friend. Remorse seeped into every thought, glance, and movement. If people had had all their wits about them, or knew me better, they would have recognized my guilt and preoccupation.

How does an innocent person walk? Without guilt, would I make more eye contact? Should I be more extroverted so they don't suspect something . . . or would that be suspicious?

The team stopped socializing to listen to a neural message.

Young Tomas wore a confused expression. "Noha extended our break." He looked at me. "What's going on?"

"I'm not sure," I answered in a steady tone to avoid fueling any nervousness in the team. I'd considered telling everyone the plan for returning to Earth but thought it best to wait for an update on Allan.

During the break, I went to my quarters.

"Anthea, what's Allan's status?"

"He is undergoing limbic system regeneration and neural re-connection for physical impairments."

"Has he lost his memory because of what I did or from the sedation?"

"Your energy burst was not a directed procedure; it was un-controlled and affected many areas of his brain."

He wasn't my favorite person in the world, but I didn't want to permanently damage him and risk having zero chance of saving the planet. "Will he make a full recovery?"

"Recovery is undetermined."

"Un . . . undetermined?" My voice cracked.

"Yes, undetermined. He may suffer brain damage and loss of physical ability."

"If he doesn't make a full recovery, our chances of saving Earth will be even lower."

I paced through my intentionally small residence carrying world-sized guilt. But it was the only place I could be without a mask to hide my part in Zoa's and Allan's conditions.

"What about Zoa? Without making things worse, can the Ambarans do something?"

"The hosts are recalibrating her."

"What?" I couldn't believe they were tinkering with her mind again. "Why?"

"Your concern for her was detectable to the AEHs."

"My *concern*?" I said, insulted by the minimization. "Four members have lost their lives, and two more members are in questionable condition. Then there's the guilt of manipulating everyone—which has created a high level of cognitive dissonance for me. I'd call that a bit more than concern."

I wished for the life I had had back on Earth. Being a reclusive researcher kept everyone safe and me guilt-free . . . except when it came to whether to intervene and tell someone what I saw.

"Since when does my preoccupation stop a lab?"'

"The AEHs could hear your thoughts and feel your intense emotions. They decided the lab could not continue."

"Ahh, yes, I sensed that, but how is it possible? I didn't mark my thoughts for them, and I shouldn't be able to read their minds."

"That is how it works for all other SEED members. However, one of your communication genes turned on early in your stay. The gene is responsible for direct communication to advanced brains."

I had reached my threshold for information disclosed too late. "This gene expressed itself soon after my arrival?"

Was that why I'd been able to connect so intensely with Rein'li here? Although it didn't explain how we had communicated back on Earth. I would've asked, but I didn't think Rein'li would want it disclosed.

In exasperation, I said, "Great, another thing to differentiate me from my team."

"Victoria, the hosts are working to resolve Zoa's biometrics. The lab will continue when Zoa is within an acceptable range."

"Could she end up worse?"

"The adjustments carry limited risk; they are superficial."

I took the ray of hope. "So, the hosts will bring back the Zoa I knew before the rebellion and sedation?"

"The Ambarans want to remind you of the limitations. The Earth human's brain is unlike any others in our universe. Intricate modifications to your brains will always carry a risk. The affected may never go back to their former selves."

"Right, hopes adjusted."

I went back to an earlier thread in our conversation. A gene to speak to advanced brains. Although I made light of it, the revelation struck me. What if Allan and Ana were right? No, it can't be. It's just the result of years of brain training.

"Anthea, can you explain why my brain can't keep implanted data? And how do you account for the advanced brain communication gene turning on in me? Before you answer, how do you explain what I did to Allan?" I swallowed hard as tears formed in my eyes. Saying all these things out loud felt like I was connecting to something at the core of my existence.

"I cannot explain."

Shaking my head in denial, I said, "But you're of an advanced civilization and understand eons more than me. You must have some theories."

"I know you are the leader of the visiting group who must save Earth."

"Really? You're avoiding the question?" In an irritated tone, I said, "Do you want to know what I think?"

Anthea was quiet. Perhaps she recognized it as a rhetorical question.

"You can't explain because you don't have access to that information. It's above your paygrade, as we say on Earth." Nothing like taunting organic nanoparticle AI.

◯ ◯ ◯

An upside: Days had passed with no sign of unrest or discontent—and therefore, no brewing rebellion. A downside: My accommodation, which I expanded ten-fold to give me more space to breath, was not big enough for the raging battle inside me between ethics and rationalization. I questioned my sanity at times and, as predicted, those times brought on a rest. I took solace in the hosts tracking and maintaining my physical and mental health.

"Victoria, the experiential lab is ready to reconvene," Anthea said.

"Yes!" A moment later, though, my enthusiasm waned. What would Zoa be like?

The Ambarans were taking a long time, and unlike with Marcus, I wasn't getting any updates.

The team gathered to collect adjuncts; they were as calm and orderly as when the assignment had started. However, there was no sign of Zoa. I scanned the faces around me and beyond. There was panic in my surveying, like a person searching for a family member at the end of a war. In my state of mind, I was ripe for hallucinations to spare me any reality where Zoa wasn't there.

Ana also searched, but for someone else.

Four members conversed and when one of them moved forwards, another was revealed—the warm Nigerian nurse. We caught each other's eyes; hers sparkled. Her smile was relaxed yet beaming. Round two.

I was in front of her in the blink of an eye, reaching out with a light touch. "Zoa. It's good to see you."

She smiled and hugged me. "Hello, my friend. Yes, it is good to be with everyone again. I have stayed in my residence and enjoyed long rest periods—one was for six hours."

I studied her face, eyes, and speech pattern. "It has done you well."

She gave me a sideways smirk and laughed. "I'm happy to see you."

"Me, too," I said with a healthy dose of relief, happiness, and hope for the future.

With Zoa found, I turned to Ana. She was still looking for Allan. Her head drooped. There was no sign of him.

Back in the lab, Noha assigned team members to AEHs.

Ana whispered something to Tomas before withdrawing into a conversation with herself. Maybe she was debating whether to ask about Allan.

She turned to the AEH. "Noha, if I can't concentrate enough, will I be able to end the session?"

"Excellent question!" said a voice from behind us.

It was Allan. I stood in a semifrozen state.

"Allan! It's about time." Ana ran over, hugged him and was about to kiss him but stopped short.

He half-smiled without a sign of recognition or friendliness.

Ana's eyes widened with dread. "You know me, don't you?"

Tomas and Sylvia rushed to Allan's side and waited for an answer.

"You . . . um . . . what are you talking about?" Allan said.

Ana dropped her head in disappointment; others reacted with a gasp.

He grabbed Ana's shoulders and stared at her. "Hello, babe. Of course I know who you are."

"You!" She slapped his arm. "I—we've been so worried about you." Ana gazed into his eyes as if her knight in shining armor had trotted in on his white horse.

We clapped at his return.

"I don't know what you were worried about. If you're going to have amnesia, this is the place to be." Allan came across confident as ever. "The hosts' knowledge and skills are awesome. They've been testing my memory and recall ability. I remembered so many details from my childhood, and I can recall a list of up to 225 random things or images."

He was so grateful for the Ambaran care; there was no more suspicion or talk of them doing anything with ulterior motives other than helping us.

As they walked to Ana's group, he dragged his right leg.

Ana scowled. "Is your leg okay?"

"Sure. The Ambarans said it will take a while for my brain and leg"—he touched his head and then his right thigh—"to align, but it will happen. Nothing to worry about."

A wave of relieved smiles swept through our group. I smiled with genuine happiness; we'd lost enough team members. It was time to put all this behind us. With the Ambarans help, they seemed to think we still had a chance to save Earth with the nine of us and five AEHs.

Noha said, "Victoria, you will participate in the lab by tuning into your team members as they enter simulations."

It was exactly what I needed to understand how things would work back home.

Four team members connected to Jorge, not to experience through him but for him to guide them in the simulation. The other four connected to Barton.

We had three pieces of data. One, two countries would exchange nuclear missiles in four hours. Two, any decision or approach needed to have the support of three people. With each decision made, the appropriate technology would be provided. Three, the outcomes of all actions and responses would be viewable quickly via time-lapse.

Suddenly, we were thrust into a chaotic city scene with blaring sirens. Constance and Allan immediately set up a command center. A map appeared and revealed different land masses than on Earth.

One country's missile was closer to its target than the other country's missile.

That's when it happened. I could see Constance's calculations, even though they were in her mind. I knew exactly what she was trying to determine.

A moment later she said, "We can't be in two places at once. The disaster zone of the second missile will be greater than the first."

I said, "I concur. Focus majority efforts on the second and ancillary efforts on the first."

Allan nodded and created workflows with resources instantly. He said, "Ana and Zoa, focus on emergency care and containing the fallout of the second missile."

Ana rose to the challenge. I could see her working on redirecting much of the explosion into space.

"Ana, good idea. Proceed," I said as Zoa also gave her approval.

The AEHs helped Ana and Zoa by providing technologies and methods.

I spoke directly to all three AEHs. "These solutions are beyond what we have on Earth. Are you saying that these types of technologies will be available to us?"

Noha replied, "Yes, although not to this level. The five AEHs going with you will bring greater help than what is available on Earth."

Mr. d'Orsini said, "Li can help negotiate between the countries to stop further attacks."

"How do you know this?" I said.

"UEP helped me sense where Li would have the most impact. There are two groups of people in each country who are getting misinformation. He can get through to them."

"Brilliant," I replied.

As I tuned back into Constance and Allan, I saw they were creating a shield like the barrier we had created previously with the Ambarans. The team completed it in record time.

It was very clear that connected to the AEHs, the teams performed well beyond what would be expected from sedated people.

The simulation stopped just after the missiles were launched.

Noha said, "Your teams have performed well. We have identified areas for improvement and where AEHs can be of the most use."

"Is that a compliment?" Allan asked with a wide grin.

"Yes," she replied. "Yes," both Barton and Jorge echoed.

We finished the lab with a new appreciation for each other's abilities in an emergency and for the guidance of the AEHs.

"It was good for us to work together. We have come a long way since our arrival," I said.

Everyone nodded.

I looked around at the group. "There's something I'd like to discuss."

"Is there anything wrong?" Zoa leaned towards me.

"No, I have much needed good news."

It was time for me to test how well the Ambaran sedation and intervention worked.

"I know all of you have been given intermittent updates on our return home. As of today, we leave in seven Earth days. Our first day back will be critical. We will need to quickly get up to speed on what's happening around the world."

"And we will still have 187 days, right?" asked Tomas.

"Yes, but we should narrow down the potentials within our first couple days back," said Constance. "We will need the rest of the time to coordinate our response."

"Indeed. All domains need to be checked, from environmental and space to health. These are your specialties, so I know you have it covered. And remember, Sinethemba told us it wouldn't be an asteroid."

I looked down and prepared to tell them the most important piece of the briefing. "Due to the loss of five fellow team members, the Ambarans have agreed to give us more help back on Earth."

"Thank God," said Ana.

Constance asked, "Will they help us to avoid the disaster or just mitigate it?"

I answered, "Mitigate it, which is the level of action they have been approved for. But let me explain what this help will look like."

"They're not going to invade Earth, are they?" Allan jested.

His question hit me like a bucket of ice-cold water. Was he serious or joking? I smiled and shook my head. "No, not this time around." If I treated it like a joke, then maybe everyone else would.

"Right, good." Allan accepted my answer.

"They have offered to send five AEHs with us. I'd like to hear what everyone thinks of this kind of help."

Allan let out a nervous chuckle before offering up his opinion. "No invasion, just a small alien SWAT team."

"Are you saying you are uncomfortable with their offer?" I looked him straight in the eyes. "If so, can you give us some alternatives?"

The AI entrepreneur looked nervously around at us. "No, I think it's cool, and from what I just saw, they're an awesome addition."

"It seems to me the Ambarans are truly trying to help us." Zoa spoke confidently and clearly to the group. "I don't think we should turn down their assistance."

One by one each person shared their perspective.

"Where will they live?" asked Mr. d'Orsini. Zoa and I gave him a puzzled look. "Si, si, it sounds like a strange question, but I have homes where they can stay."

"That's lovely, thank you. So, it sounds like we are all in agreement," I said.

Constance put up her hand. "Will they live on Earth for the foreseeable future? They would outlive us."

"No, the Ambarans specified that they must return once they help us through the crisis."

"That makes sense," said the savant.

"Which AEHs are going back with us and can we get them to make things for us?" asked Allan.

"I see where you're going with this, and I don't know is the answer to both questions. But—" I glanced over to Noha. "They will help us save the world."

"I think Ana and I will have to clean up our air and soil," said Sylvia.

I nodded. "Right, so with only a week left, let's focus and get as much knowledge and simulator experience as we can."

They nodded and set off, except one . . . Zoa.

She whispered, "Victoria, please excuse my boldness, but is there something going on that you wish to share? I'm here for you." She leaned in. "Ubuntu. Do you know this word?"

I shook my head. "No, what does it mean?"

"Ubuntu expresses our interconnectedness and the belief in a universal bond of humanity. We and the rest of the team are connected. We will take your lead."

A chill ran down my spine. "Thank you. I needed to hear that."

"You are different. I can handle that, but you need to trust me with the truth." Each word delved deeper into my psyche. "You're a neuroscience researcher—so, by nature, you analyze people and their behaviors. What have you seen that makes you hide your soul from us?"

She cupped her hands. Her thin fingers and small wrists looked so frail. Yet she possessed the strongest energies I had come across in the group.

I tried to suppress what was bubbling up faster than I would have liked. Teary eyed, I said, "Oh, Zoa, you really don't want to know."

She reached out and touched my hand. "Yes, I do. You're not alone, yet you isolate yourself. Why?"

We stared at each other the way Albert and I would do in our stare-offs—except, being a cat, he always won. I teetered on the edge of the proverbial cliff. *When is she going to give up and let me off the hook . . . or is she ready for my revelations? Will the hosts allow me to have a confidant?*

"Zoputa,"—her proper name came from my heart—"I wish I could tell you." If there was anyone, I would share my burdens with, it was her. This was my opportunity, yet I couldn't risk giving her doubts about me. Especially about something that even I wasn't clear on—Who was I?

"Thank you for being a caring friend. It means so much to have you here."

With a bewildered expression, she tilted her head. "But tell me, why did you use my proper first name?"

"It felt like the right thing to do."

"In my family, our birth names are always spoken when hearts and minds connect." Zoa touched my hand. "Zoputa is always here for you."

I could think of no words worthy enough to follow hers.

"Would you mind if I"—she looked down and frowned—"share something with you?"

"Please do." I smiled and nodded.

"I've been having a recurring dream." She looked at me like she expected a reaction.

"Okay," I said. Was that a guarded response? What would I have usually said?

"I dream that members rise up in opposition to the Ambarans—and you." Her eyes widened in fright. "Allan leads them."

She had handed me a ticking bomb. With a lump in my throat, I said, "Allan's suspicions are seeping into your subconscious."

With a flushed face, no doubt visible from two planets away, a varying speech pattern, and an artificially flippant attitude, I had all the signs of someone caught out.

"But the dreams are so clear. You don't think they're premonitions?" she said with a shudder.

I paused and pretended to think about her idea. "It's one thing to talk about Ambaran controls and seek to lessen them, but to rally people into revolting would jeopardize our ability to save our world. He wouldn't do that."

She shook her head as if trying to shake off the thought of a rebellion.

"Perhaps, now that we've spoken about the dream, it won't continue." I hoped that was what an innocent person would say.

She nodded, breathed deeply, and forced a smile. "I don't mean to worry you, but I wanted to share it."

"I understand. If they continue, we can try cognitive behavioral therapy to release it from your mind."

Zoa's face relaxed. "Thank you."

For now, they were only dreams. But was it inevitable that others would dream or remember details of the rebellion eventually too?

CHAPTER 16

UNANSWERED

We completed our independent sessions at the same time, and the hosts directed us to Inner 1.5. It was my first time there. The views were unlike anywhere else in the Delta Center. It looked like thousands of nautilus shells merging, with overlapping iridescent lights streaming in from all sides. Within two minutes, my mind was entranced.

With all nine of us sitting on a bench, it suddenly rose and split into segments, one per person. The newly formed chairs arranged themselves like in a small cinema. A Conduit and AEHs Vintar, Rein'li, and Noha appeared before us.

My heart and mind embraced Rein'li.

Vintar said, "SEED, you have learned and experienced much here. However, it is time for you to return home."

Allan, Ana, Sylvia, and Tomas jumped with joy. Zoa, Pino, and I gasped. Li dropped his head down into his hands. Constance looked like she was in shock, but she was probably doing calculations.

"As agreed, you will have been away for 121 Earth days, including travel time when you return," Vintar continued. "Prepare to depart in five Earth hours."

My eyes locked in on Rein'li. I had known the time would come, but it felt too soon. My heart raced and ached.

With their message delivered, the AEHs left. Rein'li didn't attempt to communicate with me. He had said he would be there for me, and that I didn't need to be alone. Yet I stood alone, more conflicted than when I had arrived.

Zoa stared at me and said something. I couldn't wrestle myself out of the hole of unexpected despair. Group members became foreign objects whirling in a sphere around me. I directed all my efforts towards getting as far away from everyone as possible. I ran off.

Hopping onto the closest disc, I propelled it as fast as I could with my mind.

I reached my residence in a flash and entered in the nick of time to collapse in despair. The day was here. I should've been happy. Instead, I had unresolved questions, concerns, and doubts.

Could I trust the team once we were back on Earth, without Ambaran enhancements? Would Zoa's recurring dream start to feel more like memories to her? If others regained any kind of recollection of the rebellion, I might come face-to-face with a mutiny.

If we saved Earth, would I find fulfillment, or flounder due to my knowledge and connection to Ambar and Rein'li? On Earth, I lived in the pain of rejection. On Ambar, I lived in a world of acceptance where my abilities were part of everyday life and had names. I wasn't a freak here.

"Anthea, I need to speak with the lead Reviewer."

"You must rest first."

"Why?"

"Your metrics are suboptimal for travel."

○ ○ ○

I rose from an intense rest. "Anthea, how many hours before we leave?"

"Two hours."

"Can I meet the Reviewer now?"

"I will advise you when the Reviewer is available. You should continue with your preparations until then."

With a press of the generator's button, my clothes changed. Once again, I wore mourning clothes—a black turtleneck, black jodhpur-like trousers, and black boots. I glanced around my place, then leapt out of it to catch a ride.

The disc transported me across the Complex. I wanted out. I needed a way to leave the Complex. In that instant, Rein'li connected neurally with me.

"Victoria, a protective barrier has been activated on your disc. You can view the surroundings, but no one can see in. Any scan of the disc will show you as an Ambaran. I will stay connected to you and show you more of Ambar."

The disc whizzed across vast spaces, turning every structure into a blur. It rose and, without warning, I glided through the exterior of the Complex. I was outside. A twinge of fear went through me. *Am I a fugitive now?*

"No one knows of this excursion," Rein'li said.

If only he were here with me and not just a neural communication.

"I'm scared," I said.

"The Ambarans agreed to help save Earth. They will."

"We wouldn't have the slightest chance without the AEHs. There's something else, and it's selfish, but I wish I didn't have to leave Ambar and you. Of course, I'll focus on saving Earth, but it won't make up for the state of half-existence that I'll be returning to. It will be more dissatisfying now after being here."

"I understand and will always be with you wherever you are."

The disc floated across entire cities that were nearly invisible as they mimicked the terrain.

Pointing to a mountain range, I said, "Those are the cities the group viewed with Vintar."

Rein'li and I zoomed down for a closer look.

"I can see a thin aura-like energy surrounding the cities. What is that?" I asked.

"It is a bio-synthetic energy field that controls all substances or incoming traffic. We will not be going down there."

I giggled nervously. "Of course, we don't want to draw attention to us."

Between views, I sought answers from Rein'li.

"We leave in less than two hours. Please tell me who you are and how you've been able to communicate with me for as long as I can remember?"

"You must wait for that information. All the answers are within your mind and will come forwards when the time is right."

"Will the time be right when I'm in my last moments of existence? I don't want to die with so many unanswered questions."

Silence.

"Rein'li?"

He said, "I feel you. You exist in my every breath and heart-beat." He was cracking.

"Please stop. I am torn between two worlds and don't know why. Unless you are going to explain, then don't share. It only makes me feel worse."

"Forgive me." His answer struck me as atypical for an AEH.

"If you won't tell me who you are, then answer a different question. Do I still have control of my abilities? I don't want to hurt anyone when I get angry or frustrated with them."

"The energy overload with Allan has made you aware of your potential. When you are in danger, use it to your advantage. Continue your training to control it."

"I'm not sure I have such restraint."

I felt Rein'li guiding me to a lower brainwave pattern. In an instant, my body synchronized with the transport. As I flew across skies of bright pinks, greens, and violets, I also crossed a mental threshold where the disc became like an appendage. It responded to my every breath and thought.

"This is freedom and connection. Thank you, Rein'li."

○ ○ ○

After my Ambaran escapade, we had one hour and fifteen minutes left.

There were places I wanted to etch into my mind forever. At the top of my list was Outer 4's viewing platform.

Zoa joined me for one last gaze. Though her demeanor was calm and consistent, I sensed something else.

She kept her gaze focused on the cosmos. "I have something to tell you."

I looked over at her; she didn't reciprocate. Would it be another blow before we depart?

"I would have told you sooner, but I needed time." No eye contact, coupled with regret for not telling me sooner. I stilled and waited for the bad news.

"Pino has had great difficulties because of his UEP abilities and connection to his twin brother."

I nodded. Pino had confided in me about what had happened.

Zoa continued, "Through his training sessions with Rein'li, he believes he can handle things now. Which is good because we have agreed to continue our relationship back home . . . as a couple." Her eyes lit up as she spoke, and her face settled into the look only genuine happiness brings.

I smiled with relief and hugged her. "I'm so happy for you."

Listening to Zoa, I recalled the horrid simulation of her trying to save her father. Today, a different woman stood next to me. She had a plan to release herself from the family tragedy, and she had found a partner.

"I really am happy for you both."

"Are you telling me you didn't already suspect?"

"I didn't say that." I pulled a coy expression.

Scowling, she said, "Again, I am sorry you witnessed the simulation; I haven't repeated that scene since. When I saw how distressed you were, I realized the event had pained me for too long."

"You don't need to apologize. I felt bad because of what you and your family had gone through."

She nodded. "Thank you."

We descended from the viewing point and found Constance waiting for us.

"I located you through my internal map." She looked up. "I will miss this."

"Me too," I said. "Our experiences on the platforms will be unmatchable back on Earth."

"No, I mean, I'll miss being able to find people so easily," she said. "Even though I liked to count my way everywhere, using an internal navigation system was nice to see where everyone was and to get to unknown places."

"Oh!" I had missed the mark. "Of course, you meant the locator."

Constance turned to me. "Have you read the latest updates in the group database?"

"No, I've been immersed in other things."

"When we arrive, we'll contact our families and tell them that our think-tank was extended for another four months."

I assumed we'd stay together. "Right, sounds like a good plan."

We walked, and Constance explained how she and I should coordinate our first week back.

Allan and Ana joined us.

"Hey guys, how's it going?" Allan said.

Zoa grinned. "My friends, let us spend our last moments on Ambar together."

"Cool. We can hang out at the Re-Hub on Inner 1, where we started," Allan said.

"I'll join you in a bit. I have something to do first," said Constance.

After everything we'd been through, we were connected as a group and best of all, I was part of it.

"Pino is on his way," Zoa said.

"Man, you read my mind!" Allan said.

"I will tell Sylvia, Li, and Tomas to meet us there," Ana said. Suddenly, she cast a suspicious gaze in my direction. "Or maybe you can do that with your mind." She followed the unexpected suggestion with a smile.

In the Re-Hub, we sat in our original seating area from the first day, with vacant seats for Peter, Sabine, François, Ragini, and Marcus. I was still the only one who knew Marcus was alive and well on Earth.

Sylvia said, "I can't believe we'll be leavin' soon. Is everyone ready?"

Zoa's eyes popped open. "We have so much to do back home. I'm not sure we could ever feel completely ready."

"I'm going to miss this place," said Allan.

Ana nodded. "Imagine how dissatisfied Constance will be without her outfit generator."

"Yes, between the infinite wardrobe, time saved on bathing, brushing teeth, and travelling . . ."

Allan said, "And don't forget the CRC."

"True," I said as I pointed to Allan. "She's going to be a nightmare for at least the first few months."

Zoa and Sylvia laughed.

"We'll all go through a period of adjustment," Zoa said.

I glanced away momentarily. "I've just received a message. The AEHs will be joining us at the pods."

"Will they be ones we've already met?" asked Ana.

"I'm not sure." I hadn't considered that Rein'li might be one of those going back with us. I was sure he would have mentioned it.

Constance arrived and took the reins. "Is everyone clear on what to do once we get home?"

Allan grinned. "Sure—we stay together. I'll set up a command center so we can identify hot spots. The AEHs will be able to get through more data faster than us. We'll shortlist the most volatile areas and then wait for confirmation."

The discussion continued a bit longer before I received a communication requesting that I meet a Reviewer. I boarded a disc and ripped through the EC at superspeed, like I was on a critical mission.

I arrived at a wall in the Delta Center and passed through the barrier into a small alcove. Simultaneously, a Reviewer appeared.

"Victoria." I recognized the voice and brilliant green light. "We have news about the team members who visited the seam."

"Oh, I see," I whispered like I'd seen a ghost. The thought of our lost team members instantly brought forwards images of their eyes—the same eyes that had plagued me during many rests since their passing.

"We have taken the life forces of the four Earth members and transferred them to AEHs here in the EC. They will live for the average length of an Earth human."

"But you told me they had no trace of life in them. So I was right?"

"The life you sensed consisted of mere traces. Your presence, while you waited for Constance, increased their consciousness enough for us to transfer a portion of their psyches."

"I suppose it's too much to ask that they be the AEHs that go back with us?"

The Reviewer said, "They cannot. This concludes—"

"No, wait. I want to ask you something."

"I am aware of your desire to return to Ambar."

"Yes, I'd love to spend more time here. I could stay in the EC. This galaxy contains at least a hundred planets that can sustain human life, but on Ambar my identity can be concealed."

"We will maintain the EC as a research center focused on primitive developments from the human blueprint."

"Does that mean I can't return?"

"Your people have seen and learned what they need to bring about changes on Earth. You are an integral part of their efforts."

"Yes, despite the losses and challenges, SEED has learned enough to make changes back on Earth. I only hope it will be enough." I swallowed hard to push down the emotions. "I want to return to help save the planet, but it won't stop me from feeling ripped apart on the inside." I placed my clenched fists over my chest and illustrated being torn apart.

"What do you find painful?" asked the Reviewer.

"Back home, they don't acknowledge or cultivate abilities taken for granted on Ambar. Earth can only ever offer me a state of half-existence. But here, I am complete." I suppressed all thoughts and feelings of Rein'li. He wouldn't want those discussed.

"Back on Earth, you can develop those things you will miss about Ambar."

"I doubt that."

I switched to our internal communications mode in a flash, so my thoughts could stream with intensity to the Reviewer. "Is there something different about my brainwaves that allowed you to use me as the recipient of your warning? How could I spontaneously visit ECHRC2D on my first day here? Also, a communications gene turned on and allows me to speak neurally to the AEHs. And what I did to Allan, that's not Earth human, right?"

The Reviewer didn't stop me or deny my statements.

"My abilities alienate me on Earth because others don't understand them. Now, I've learned they have names—magnetic tuning, energy profiling, timeline viewing, and particle entanglement tracing."

I paused and considered one more reason to return. I didn't want to resort to it, but I had nothing else left in my repertoire. I took the shot, like a Premier League footballer with the ball in overtime. "I need to return to be with Rein'li." As the words came out, a flutter of embarrassment struck me. I wasn't acting like a silly schoolgirl; this was far worse. I had revealed intense feelings for an AEH, Ambaran, or some other type of being. *Goodness—what is he?*

"Focus on SEED and find your answers through it. You have a chance as a unit with the five AEHs."

"Why can't you speak about him? I've been communicating with him since I was a girl." I pulled out all the stops to plead my case, including those that Rein'li refused to discuss with me.

"We know of your interactions with Rein'li. Complete your objectives on Earth."

"Seriously? Things aren't adding up. I need answers."

"You can continue to connect with Rein'li back on Earth. We will see each other again. Prepare for SEED's departure." The Reviewer disappeared, or at least was no longer visible to me.

That one sentence, 'We will see each other again,' echoed in my head and gave me the strength to leave.

○　○　○

I returned to my residence and put my travel suit on. Steeped in mixed emotions, my mind tried to ignore what my body was doing on autopilot.

"Goodbye, Anthea. Thank you for everything."

"Goodbye, Victoria." That's all she, or it, said. I had expected as much, or as little.

With every step I took to the disc, I left part of myself behind. The disc seemed slow, as if reluctant to take me to my departure point. My mind desperately held on to every second.

I was the last to arrive at the pods. Mine was closest to the entrance; I wouldn't have to interact with anyone. There was a distinguishable air of excitement to which I didn't contribute. My peripheral vision captured SEED members saying farewells to each other and entering their travel vessels.

Hoping something would come up to prolong my stay or ensure *my* return, I waited until everyone else was snug in their pods.

No reprieve came. I stepped into my pod, where the gelatinous interior membranes wasted no time connecting to me. Before I was completely encased, a message came forwards. Knowing it would be a housekeeping message, I barely had the energy or inclination to listen.

"Victoria." I recognized Rein'li's voice. *He* wouldn't have systematic instructions for me. My heart sped up. He said, "I will be there. You are not alone."

A moment later, my pod was sealed shut.

The membranes encased me, ensuring I couldn't react except in my mind. As I digested his statement, I wondered if it was a nice gesture, or if it had a deeper meaning?

What would we face once we arrived on Earth? Did he know the details and wanted to reassure me?

As my brainwaves slowed, bringing me closer to a sleep state, another neural communication came through.

"Every instinct in me wants to tell Victoria. We should not be sending her back. You and I know this is not right. An AEH could take her place," Rein'li said.

"It would set a precedent." Another familiar voice, the Reviewer. "We would risk irrevocable damage by not sending her back with SEED."

"All our interactions with other species follow our principles, but this is not the same," Rein'li countered. "We know who she is. How much longer do you intend to keep this from her?"

CHAPTER 17

THE BEGINNING

A pervasive aching shattered my blissful travel state. Transitioning out of suspended consciousness wasn't easy.

A sudden cool rush flowed across my head, and the membrane loosened its grip. Although still unable to see, my hearing returned and let in shrills of agony from all around me. The team was under attack, and we couldn't fight back. Still bound to our pods, we were at our most vulnerable. My heart raced. It helped wake me up. There was a strange presence with us, and it felt inches away from me. Would I be its next victim?

The membrane had freed my body, but I still couldn't move or see. Fear coursed through my veins. I held my breath as a brightness volleyed across my eyelids and created an opening near my left eye. A man . . . just a man. He didn't seem violent as he shone a light on my face.

"It will take a minute," he said and vanished from my view.

Soon, my mouth and nose were freed, but I struggled to breathe as my full lungs reacted to the foreign Earth air. I sat up and spewed the Ambaran life-sustaining substance until the flow reduced to a dribble out the sides of my mouth. Vomiting was the next stage as spasms rippled across my abdomen. In between regurgitations, I wiped my eyes clear to see who was screaming.

Each cocoon's glow lit up the surrounding area. My pod was the only one positioned horizontally. I spotted Zoa and Tomas to my right, their faces half visible. Both cried out in pain.

The man who had helped me went over to Zoa and shone a light across her eyes. The light came out of his hands. What in the world … The penny dropped. He was one of the five Ambaran AEHs.

Fully released, I stepped out of the pod sheathed in its membrane with oozing nodules. However, this time, the encasement disintegrated into a fluorescent puddle, unlike when we arrived on Ambar.

Only the AEHs were walking around. All others, with the exception of me, were still bound and writhing in pain. The horrific sounds reminded me of Constance's cry when she visited Sabine's body after the accident.

"What's happening?" I said to the male AEH tending to Zoa.

"It is the transition. This one is difficult for them."

"But can't you ease it?"

"It is a natural process. She is almost through the worst part."

I leaned in to my nurse friend. "I'm here, Zoa. You'll be out of pain soon."

She and I locked gazes. Two minutes later, the pain subsided, and the membrane released her.

A female AEH released the binding around Pino's eyes. Only low guttural sounds could escape through the wrappings.

"He's having a hard time of it," I said.

"Yes, I am trying to isolate the problem." She held her hands up to his head. "Close your eyes."

"Why? What are you going to do that I can't see?" I asked in a suspicious tone.

"Pino, close your eyes." She glanced over at me.

"Oh, right. Yes." I watched as she placed her hands on his head like a skilled osteopath performing cranial manipulation.

An audible crack came from his skull, yet he reacted as if he'd just received a muscle relaxer.

I smiled with relief at the AEH. "That seems to have worked. What did you do?"

"I realigned his skull plates," she said as she freed his face.

We turned away as his body expelled what was no longer needed.

Her characteristics were much more in line with Earth humans than the other AEHs we'd met on Ambar. Of course, the pod suit made it difficult to see much of her, except her long brown hair, face and five-foot-five body.

"What's your name?" I asked.

"Wyrobe."

"My name—"

"Victoria, we know who everyone is," she said in a neutral tone.

I shook my head. "Right. Of course."

One by one, the team cycled through the stages of detachment. As bad as the process was, we were back home, alive and well.

A quick survey of the cave revealed it to be bigger and craggier than the one we departed from in Norway.

Constance and Sylvia joined me at the far end of the cave.

"Where do you think we are?" I said.

Sylvia pointed up. "Those are stalactite-like lava formations."

"Okay," I said, uncertain why she was pointing out cave features.

The environmental expert and horticulturist said, "We are definitely not in Norway."

Constance nodded. "She's right. Norway has no tectonic plate boundaries, so no volcanoes to produce lava."

As we turned to rejoin the others, Allan approached. "Was Ana with you?"

"No." Constance was as succinct as ever and dashed off.

Sylvia and I shrugged our shoulders. "We haven't seen her," I said.

At that moment, Wyrobe approached me. "Victoria, there is a problem."

"Oh, what's that? Are we trapped in here?"

Before she could answer, Constance, who was standing on a large stone, sounded like a town crier. "There are only thirteen puddles. Thirteen. Not fourteen . . ."

Although I trusted Constance's tabulation abilities, I ran over to the pod remnants. Others spun around right where they stood, holding out their fingers to count.

My eyes darted around the cave. "Maybe her pod transported to another part."

Allan zipped round us and the puddles erratically.

Wyrobe was next to me in a flash. "Ana is missing."

I scowled at her. "Missing?"

"What the hell!" Allan said as he and Tomas stormed over to us. Ana's forlorn partner stepped up within six inches Wyrobe's face. "Where is she?" His expression reminded me of the day he tried to kill me. Although, I doubted he would try such a stunt with an AEH.

"We do not have information on Ana's location," said Wyrobe.

He rushed over to me. "You're in charge here. Do something."

I wanted to reassure him and go through the options together with Wyrobe. However, in that moment, the trauma he had inflicted on me, which he had no memory of, flashed before me. I went into freeze-mode.

"Well?" Allan glared at me. "Are you just going to stand there doing nothing?"

Zoa came to my side. "We'll find her. Don't worry." The nurse rescued me. Perhaps she noticed my fight-flight-freeze reaction.

A tall male AEH with short black hair came forward. "My name is Sone. I have surveyed the cave. There are five passageways. Three are narrow tributary tunnels that lead deeper. The two others are larger and easier to navigate. That one"—he pointed to the one on the right—"is our exit."

Constance said, "We should check inside and outside in case she ended up somewhere else and is dazed."

Allan nodded as he bit his bottom lip and appeared on the verge of breaking down.

I snapped out of my frozen state and moved to the center of the group. "Right, let's split up into four teams and each takes a path, but not the one leading out. Once you've searched a passageway, meet back here. Then, if we haven't found her, we'll look in the last tunnel together as we exit."

"It's quite dark in here," Constance whirled around. "But a reduced pod glows bright enough to be spotted from a distance."

The other team members nodded as they glanced at the puddles.

We dispersed with a sense of urgency. Wyrobe, Zoa, and I took the tightest tributary.

After a couple minutes, I said. "Can we talk through what could've happened to Ana?"

"There are only three possibilities." Wyrobe guided us further into the dark hollowing. Her suit glowed brighter than ours, making it easy to watch how she got through narrow spaces. "She may have been transported elsewhere."

Zoa said, "Does that mean somewhere close or far away?"

"Either." Wyrobe hoisted us up through an opening. "The second option is that she is caught in the quantum spindle."

Zoa gasped and grabbed my arm. "Would she survive?"

Our AEH companion said, "Yes, if she does not remain in there longer than five Earth days."

"What's the last possibility?" I whispered, fearing we'd lost her forever.

"She could have stayed on Ambar."

I stopped in my tracks. "What? They wouldn't allow her to stay on Ambar." My incredulous tone revealed what I thought. Surely, if I couldn't stay, she couldn't either.

Zoa looked at me with bewilderment but refrained from commenting.

We shimmied through a narrow space and Zoa called out for Ana, whilst I waited for Wyrobe to elaborate.

"There may have been circumstances that prevented her from transporting immediately."

"Wouldn't she just arrive late then?" I asked.

"Correct," said Wyrobe. Her answer made me hopeful.

After an arduous search, we reconvened at the designated spot. Ana remained conspicuously absent.

"Now what?" said Allan.

"There's the last tunnel—the exit. She could've transported there or even outside," I said. "Also, Wyrobe can tell you the possible explanations for Ana's absence."

Team members nodded. "We know already."

"We will guide everyone out safely," said the AEH male who had helped me earlier. "The first part is narrow, but then it widens." He and Wyrobe led the way, with Zoa and I right behind.

In the back, Allan, Tomas, and an AEH walked slower as they searched every inch of the way and called out for Ana.

Sylvia caught up with our lead group and nudged me a couple times before I looked over at her. "This is terrible." She glanced ahead as if checking to see if the AEHs were listening. "Do you really think we'll find Ana?"

"I hope so." I continued surveying the ground and the walls for a sign that she'd arrived.

"Who's he?" Sylvia pointed her chin at the male AEH.

The AEH turned and looked at Sylvia. "My name is Auro."

"They 'ave good hearing even on Earth," Sylvia said.

After twenty minutes, we came upon five large beige sacks with a note attached to the first one. "Clothes for those in need." I tore the taped message off the bag to have a closer look. It was signed "Marcus S."

Marcus Steibel? I snapped my head around to see if he was waiting for us. It didn't make sense. The Ambarans wiped his mind of all memories associated with us and them.

As I lost myself in thoughts, the others changed out of their travel suits and into jeans and t-shirts. Not everyone had the right size, but they were relieved to be out of the membranes.

"Oh man, 'bout time," Allan said as he tore off his pod suit. "I don't want to wear this foul thing a minute longer."

"Auro, can I have a word?" I said.

We went off to the side. "Do you know who these are from?"

"According to the note you are holding, they are from Marcus S."

"And who is he?" I said in an impatient voice as I tested how informed he was.

"Marcus was a member of SEED," he said, as if it was common knowledge.

"Indeed." I clenched my teeth and whispered, "But the Ambarans wiped his memories of us and Ambar."

"Yes. However, they used his ingested organic matter to elicit a dream that he felt compelled to follow. It instructed him to bring clothes and shoes for fourteen adults."

"But what if he's still here and the group sees him? They will know him, but he won't recognize them. Wouldn't that be a rather tricky thing to explain?"

"Marcus is back in Germany."

"How can you be certain?" I asked as he handed me a set of clothes.

"Unique energy profiling allows us to locate him."

"So I could use my ability too?"

"Yes, when you are in a lower brainwave pattern."

Auro and I rejoined the group. However, I was stuck on the fact that, once again, the Ambarans had accessed or implanted information without consent. It rattled me more now that we were back on Earth. What were we capable of doing without full knowledge?

"So why can't we use energy profiling to find Ana?" I asked.

"The pod suit limits our ability to trace. It acts as a barrier to prevent unwanted interference during travel."

"Interference?"

"Natural anomalies," he said.

Ten minutes later, my half of the team exited the cave to a wonderfully earthly sight. The sun was rising, and the landscape glistened in the early morning rays.

At that moment, I recalled the Reviewer promising to return us to a strategic location relative to the coming disaster. Where were we?

Zoa and Pino shared heartfelt hugs and wiped away tears. Most likely, they were tears of elation at being back home mixed with worry for Ana and for the task that lay ahead.

After a few minutes, Allan and the remaining team members emerged from the cave. Allan sprinted out, scanning the surrounding area for any signs of Ana.

The team and AEHs gathered, with a mixture of relief and trepidation, to discuss Ana and plan our next steps.

Wyrobe said, "We are in an area known as the Lava Beds National Monument in California."

Allan's eyes widened. "We're in the USA. Awesome. I'm back on home soil."

"Scusa, before we go on." Pino held his hand up. "We all know Wyrobe and Sone but"—he pointed to the other three AEHs—"could you introduce yourselves to everyone?"

The gender-neutral AEH next to Constance said, "My name is Baka."

"Auro," said the AEH we'd followed out.

The second female AEH said, "I am Khepera. There is no need for you to introduce yourselves to us. We know everyone in SEED."

She spoke faster than the others, which made me wonder if it was indicative of her personality.

"Grazie," said our polite Italian.

Wyrobe got us back on track. "We will take you to the predetermined area where you will establish your base."

Allan, in a defiant stance, stepped forward. "You and the other AEHs can leave, but the Earth team is staying right here until Ana returns."

"This is not possible," said Auro.

Allan locked eyes with him, flanked by Tomas and Li. "Look, buddy, don't tell me what's possible."

I felt a shiver go down my spine as I exchanged a quick look with Wyrobe. Despite their outward calm, I sensed something shifting in response to the posturing of SEED members.

"Allan, you know we have to stay focused on saving Earth." I controlled my words and voice, so that I didn't sound aggressive or insensitive. "Otherwise, we will lose Ana and our world."

"Seriously!" He faced me, his finger pointing accusingly. "You're willing to give up on her so quickly?" He got closer and whispered in my ear. "You're such a hypocrite. Sure, we're all supposed to make strong bonds, but as soon as things get tough you abandon us and side with"—he took a step back and grimaced at the AEHs—"them."

My face flushed, and my body felt like it was on fire. Allan had triggered me.

In an instant, the AEHs of Ambar had the seven citizens of Earth surrounded, and at the center of it all, was me.

That was the beginning.

○ ○ ○

Thank you for reading the first book in the QUANTUM SEED series. Brace yourself as Victoria and the team's journey picks up speed in book two. Returning to Earth, they are thrust into an epic challenge to rescue humanity from the brink of destruction. With time running out, they must confront the looming catastrophe head-on and, if victorious, guide Earth towards a more certain destiny. Along the way, bonds are forged, alliances are tested, and Victoria unravels the astounding secrets that define her very existence.

Did you enjoy QUANTUM SEED, Book One? Please leave a review and let others know.

Amazon
Goodreads

Want monthly updates and short stories written from the characters point-of-views?
Sign up for my newsletter: **www.LThorsrud.com**

Find me online:

Facebook: **www.facebook.com/LThorsrud/**
Instagram: **www.instagram.com/LThorsrud/**
Website: **www.LThorsrud.com**

ACKNOWLEDGEMENTS

The best a new writer can hope for during the writing process is supportive family and friends. I have had the best support from both. OR has been a constant for me, JH's input was always spot on, and Chris (Bunty) has given me valuable feedback on more manuscript versions than anyone should be asked to read.

Special thanks to The Ohio State University's Astronomy Department for their time and help creating Ambar's exoplanet system.

ABOUT THE AUTHOR

Trained at age eleven to explore different brainwave states, L. Thorsrud has always been intrigued by the brain's capabilities. For writing QUANTUM SEED, a two-volume series, L. Thorsrud drew inspiration from personal experience and research.

Although Thorsrud spent many years in the corporate world, a fascination and love for neuroscience remained a constant backdrop.

The author has lived in five countries and currently resides in the USA.

If you enjoyed QUANTUM SEED - Book One, please look out for the conclusion of the series, QUANTUM SEED – Book Two.

Website: **www.lthorsrud.com**